3:30 A.M.—DOA

"I want this location cleared before our taxpayers start filling the streets. Crime Scene may have a coupla more hours yet, but the ME's already cleared the bodies for removal. Of course," the uniform captain added with an apparent edge, "it's your call, Savage."

Savage knew why the edge was there. Because he was the ranking detective supervisor at a homicide scene, he called the shots, not Ratcliff. Captains like Ratcliff had to accept that fact, but they didn't have to like it. "Gotcha, boss," Savage soothed. "Well, I guess I better go take a closer look."

Savage felt a chill as he entered the taproom. The feeling attacked all the senses. It went beyond the visual assault of twisted and blood-soaked lifeless bodies. There was always that aroma, that aura, that presence that clouded the air. It was always the same, and thirty years in The Job didn't make it any easier. These scenes never failed to dredge up stark reminders of one's own mortality.

MANHATTAN SOUTH

JOHN MACKIE

AN ONYX BOOK

ONYX
Published by New American Library, a division of
Penguin Putnam Inc., 375 Hudson Street,
New York, New York 10014, U.S.A.
Penguin Books Ltd, 80 Strand,
London WC2R 0RL, England
Penguin Books Australia Ltd, Ringwood,
Victoria, Australia
Penguin Books Canada Ltd, 10 Alcorn Avenue,
Toronto, Ontario, Canada M4V 3B2
Penguin Books (N.Z.) Ltd, 182–190 Wairau Road,
Auckland 10, New Zealand

Penguin Books Ltd, Registered Offices:
Harmondsworth, Middlesex, England

First published by Onyx, an imprint of New American Library,
a division of Penguin Putnam Inc.

First Printing, July 2002
10 9 8 7 6 5 4 3 2 1

PUBLISHER'S NOTE
This is a work of fiction. Names, characters, places, and incidents either
are the product of the author's imagination or are used fictitiously,
and any resemblance to actual persons, living or dead, business
establishments, events, or locales is entirely coincidental.

For Laura Elizabeth Mackie, my mother, who taught me to read books. And for John Gilbert "Eddie" Mackie, my father, who taught me to read people.

ACKNOWLEDGMENTS

Anyone serious about writing fiction for publication needs a guru with a million how-to answers, and a willingness to share them. David Hagberg was mine. My eternal thanks to him for imparting to me the Fiction Writer Facts of Life.

Writing the book is one thing—getting it represented and published is quite another. My thanks, therefore, to John Talbot, of the John Talbot Literary Agency, for his steadfast belief in my work. And to Doug Grad, my skillful editor at NAL.

Thank you also to Sharon Townley, Suzanne Mather, and Emily Cole, my critical readers and good friends, who were so generous with their knowledge and time, encouragement and support.

ONE

Tony DiLeo thought Candace Mayhew every bit the looker in the flesh as she was in the photographs he'd been given. Long and shapely legs supported a sublime torso with dangerous curves in all the right places, and she had that come-hither, breathy voice that reminded him of his first love, Marilyn Monroe. Even her wispy blond hair and bedtime blue eyes fit the mold. She was forty-five.

Seated on one of the two stools at the corner of the bar, she was packed nicely into a sheath-type thing slit way up one side. Sipping at an Absolut Seabreeze in a tall glass, she cooed suggestively as dark-eyed and swarthy Donny Cesare pawed at her partially revealed thigh and whispered naughties into her gold hoop earrings. Cesare's weight lifter's physique was not hidden beneath a black Armani jacket. He was at least ten years her junior.

Three stools away, Tony nursed a headless Miller Lite and eavesdropped while pondering what had brought this Waspy honey and her Little Italy tough guy together. He concluded that it must be Cesare's robust youth that turned Candace Mayhew on; her husband was in his early sixties. For sure it wasn't Donny's good looks or taste in jewelry. The Stallone wanna-be was no movie star, and his nugget watchband and matching pinkie ring were gaudy even for Tony's tastes. Cesare was working on his fourth Beefeater martini but still looked straight as an arrow. Tony remembered when he had that kind of tolerance.

Gilt-speckled mirrors filled the niches of the Romanesque stone arches that backed the bar at La Florentine, and a three-watt bulb barely glowed above the computerized cash register that stood between two banks of top-shelf liquor. It was the brightest light in the room. Tony felt it fit that Jimmy Roselli's "Mala Femina" echoed from the jukebox as the cheating wife put another lip lock on her lover du jour.

DiLeo took a sip of his beer and checked his watch. It was twenty minutes after one, and his sixty-four-year-old bladder screamed for relief. The wait and kitchen staffs had finished their side work and had gone home a couple of hours ago. The piano player had quit at one. The last of the black-vested busboys had also waved good night after running noisy upright Hoovers across the scarlet carpet of the adjoining dining room and setting up for tomorrow's lunch crowd. Tony was always amazed at how easily they folded those cloth napkins into lilylike table adornments. The short, balding bartender, who looked to be about his own age, squinted myopically through slipping horn-rims as he totaled a fistful of guest checks at the register. The only staffer left, he was starting the nightly closeout.

Candace Mayhew and her hot-blooded goombah would soon have to make their move to the Lucky Stiff Inn, or wherever it was they were planning to consummate their horny little tryst. Maybe they'd even do it here, Tony thought, having concluded that the muscular Cesare either owned or managed the joint. The guy might wait till everybody left, then bend her over a desk in his back-room office or screw her brains out right on the bar. Tony's guess was that they'd probably opt for the satin sheets and bubbly whirlpools of some Jersey or Queens cheater's motel.

Now the last soul in the joint besides the loving couple, Tony eased his size 50 portly frame from the tight-fitting stool and flapped his Citibank MasterCard at the bartender. He dropped the card onto the mahogany and made his second trek of the evening to the distant men's room; it was time to take a last leak, then get outside to his nondescript Honda Civic and check on the cameras. He wanted to catch the lovers' exit, then follow them to—wherever.

Tonight's was the first observation he'd made in this case, and he wished he could've hung a wire at the corner of the bar where the couple played kissy-face. The torrid parts of their conversation in the last hour would have given J. Sidney Parker a lot more of what he'd need to show adultery. Parker's client, Harmon Mayhew, could then slip the knot of his tainted ten-year second marriage for a fraction of what it might cost him otherwise. According to Parker, Mayhew was going broke. His business was on the ropes and the big bucks were no longer there. Tony understood. Why should the guy have to turn over half of everything he'd worked his whole life for to some bitch who couldn't keep her panties on when he was out of town? Harmon Mayhew was in Honduras all this week, so mama'd gone out to play in the mud.

Pressed against the urinal, trying not to think about his enlarged prostate, restricted urethra, and slow pee stream that never totally emptied his bladder, DiLeo instead considered the current surveillance. It was the latest in a long string of matrimonials that'd been referred to his one-man PI agency by the law firm of Parker & Schlafly. When those of some means in New York City suspected spousal infidelity they called on attorney Sid Parker, who in turn called Tony. If the spouse was in fact fucking around, then they didn't stand a chance. Tony DiLeo would hover tirelessly— like the Goodyear blimp at a Super Bowl—video cam and Canon AE-1 at the ready. He even had an event recorder mounted behind the grille of his surveillance car. He always delivered. It'd taken many years of late-night tailings, and countless motel-door crashings, to achieve his degree of competence. Tony no longer accepted assignments from other law firms. At his age he figured he'd paid his dues and now worked only for Parker & Schlafly. Since most of their clients were upper-crust, he ate and drank in some of the best restaurants and saloons in New York City, all, of course, on the P&S expense account. He liked La Florentine. Their marinara was excellent.

Finally, unable to wring himself completely dry for what might be a long ride ahead, Tony stepped back from the urinal and zipped up. He turned to the sink, rinsed his hands, and ran them, still wet, through his thinning gray hair. Reaching for a paper towel, he thought he heard a series of muted popping sounds that weren't part of Jerry Vale's "Old Cape Cod" piped into the men's room through ceiling-mounted speakers. There were six of them, and they'd come rhythmically in sets of two—like puny backfires from a one-lung motor scooter. Maybe the jukebox was fucking up, he thought. DiLeo finished drying his hands and tucked in his shirt. The music seemed to be playing fine again as he lumbered back through the darkened dining room.

The god-awful sight that greeted him in the dimly lit bar caused his bladder to drain completely.

They were dead. There was no doubt about it. Candace Mayhew was still seated, her head resting on the bar. Face up, eyes wide open and already glazed in death, Cesare lay in a heap on the scarlet carpet below her, a broadening halo of blood forming at the back of his head. Judging by the guest checks scattered about like a tossed deck of playing cards, the bartender had to be somewhere behind the bar with holes in him. Confused and fearful, he started in three directions simultaneously. He wanted to see if the bartender was still alive. He wanted to get to a phone and dial 911. But most of all, he wanted to bolt through the front door out onto the safety of Third Avenue.

The moment of indecision was costly. Out of the corner of his eye he sensed movement in the faint light. A blur was sweeping toward him. He jerked his head around to see the gotcha end of a silenced pistol supported in an outstretched fist. In that eternal millisecond of disbelief, Tony's subconscious fast-forwarded through the entire Hail Mary. He never heard the weapon's muffled pop, but he felt the mega-explosion inside his head . . . then total darkness.

TWO

When the phone roused him from a dead man's sleep at 3:30 in the morning, NYPD sergeant Thornton Savage didn't know the who, how, or why, but he presumed the what and the where. Someone had been murdered in Manhattan, somewhere between the Battery and Fifty-ninth Street. His bailiwick. The notification from Detective Operations hadn't startled him much. When it was his team's turn to be on call for the Manhattan South Homicide Task Force, he never really expected a full night's sleep. On the first ring he tossed the covers fully back and accepted his fate—three hours' rest was all he was getting tonight. He was it, and he was up for the day. Let the games begin.

According to Operations, there were three DOAs: two males and one female. A fourth victim, Anthony DiLeo, a licensed private investigator, was hanging on at Bellevue with just a shred of a chance. He'd been shot once in the head but was still alive.

Most of the city's normal people were happily practicing REM on cozy Posturepedics or Beautyrests when Savage arrived at La Florentine. In the deep hours before dawn, the sky being scraped by Manhattan glass and steel was jet-black and clear, and Gotham's air rode gently on a mild spring breeze. For once, the city actually smelled good.

He pulled into a warm spot just vacated by a Seventeenth Precinct radio car and parked his unmarked Crown Victoria behind a blue-and-white Crime Scene Unit van. One of two EMS ambulances that sat idling nearby sounded as if it had marbles banging around in the crankcase of its noisy, soot-puffing engine, and a somber dark green medical examiner's meat wagon was double-parked at a hydrant next to a radio car on Third Avenue. Two young uniforms from the Seventeenth were posted as doormen at La Florentine's entrance, checking identification and preventing unauthorized access. Neither slick and pushy paparazzi looking for gore nor the idle curious were getting past the two eager rookies. The men stepped aside without question, though, at Savage's deliberate approach. One look at him, natty in a steel blue pinstripe and Allen-Edmonds wing tips, and they didn't ask to see his tin—he had Homicide boss written all over him.

Savage often felt he had been born to The Job. He was the eldest son of a retired inspector, the brother of a former second-grade detective, and the nephew of the most senior lieutenant in Emergency Service. For generations that was the norm in the predominantly Irish Catholic neighborhoods of the Central and South Bronx where he'd grown up. Unless a son was so academically superior as to win himself a full scholarship to go on to become a doctor, lawyer, or Indian chief, he usually wound up taking the civil service test and becoming a fireman or a cop—or pulling wire for Con Ed. Few went into sanitation. That job was the birthright of other men's sons from Brooklyn and Queens whose last names usually ended in a vowel.

Despite being a football-scholarship graduate of Fordham, where he had majored in legal studies, Thorn Savage still became a cop. He had no regrets— he loved The Job. He often said he'd rather wear the navy blue of the NYPD than any colors of the NFL. He liked blue. The guys in his precinct cracked that he even dreamed in blue.

Inside La Florentine's chandelier- and track-lighted

dining room, Savage scanned the usual medley of police blue and medical white that always colored these events. Morgue attendants and EMS techs were gathered in muted conversation just outside the kitchen's swinging doors. Detectives, gold shields pinned topsy-turvy to wrinkled lapels, scribbled memoranda while conferring with their uniformed counterparts. The random flashing of strobes from the adjoining bar added a surreal quality. It could have been the opening night of a DeMille epic at the old Paramount.

Savage spotted Sergeant Dan Woodruff talking to the ME in the center of the huge dining room. The equine-looking supervisor and his Night Watch team had been the first investigators on the scene; they in turn had made the request for Homicide to respond. Woodruff had also spotted him.

"Okay everybody," Woodruff announced. "We can all go home now. The cavalry is here." No one in the room bothered to look up.

"And not a moment too soon, it would appear," Savage countered, making his way along a row of neatly set, cloth-covered tables. "Just steer me to a coffeepot, Dan. The cavalry's still half asleep for crissakes. Don't you guys have any regard for a gentleman's personal life? Calling him out at this hour of the morning?"

"You got a gentleman's life all right." Woodruff said with a smirk. "We should all have it. No old lady breakin' your balls, no rug rats, no freakin' grass to mow, no bullshit. Where I come from they call that lucky."

"Where I come from they call that *smart*," Savage said, playing the banter game, thinking *lonely* might have been more accurate. He winked and grinned as he shook the man's hand. "Good to see you, Dan. Any of my team here yet?"

Woodruff nodded toward the bar. "Jack Lindstrom's here."

Following Woodruff's nod, Savage looked over at

the tall, slender, and balding Lindstrom standing inside the bar area. He was busy conferring with a photographer from Crime Scene.

"As usual, I see you made good time, Thorn." Dan Woodruff knitted up his brow. "You know, if your creases weren't so goddamned sharp, I'd have to think you sleep with your freakin' clothes on."

"I live down in the Sixth," Savage reminded with a shrug. "At this hour it's only a ten-minute ride."

Woodruff lowered his voice conspiratorially. "Still got that rent-controlled place on Sullivan Street?"

"Better believe it. They're gonna have to carry me outta there."

"Man!" Woodruff muttered in envy. "You got it made."

To cloak his own thoughts on that subject, Savage flashed an agreeable smile. "So, tell me, good sergeant, what've we got here?"

"Three and a half dead. The bartender, the manager, and some foxy mama are all night-night. We think the manager got it first. The guy's built like freakin' Mr. America. Then the woman right next to him. They each got two in the head. Don't think they really knew what hit 'em. The whole thing prob'ly went down in seconds."

"The bartender?"

"Shot once in the left armpit," the ME piped in, lifting his arm in illustration. "I think the man had raised his arm in a defensive movement. Then, as he turned, he was shot a second time in the back. That one went through his heart."

"Prob'ly lookin' to split," Woodruff suggested.

"Robbery?" Savage asked.

"Don't think so." Woodruff took a deep breath while scratching below his right ear with the topside of his pen. "I'm thinking it's lookin' more and more like a professional hit. Lots of cash in the till, money in their pockets, and jewelry never touched. We found another cash box in the manager's office with thirty-six hundred and change in it. It certainly ain't shapin' up like no robbery, but somebody sure decided to make a lotta people dead."

"Who found them and when?" Savage twisted his shoulders and sucked in his back, allowing a morgue attendant carrying an armful of empty body bags to squeeze past.

"Exterminator. Comes every Wednesday morning between two-thirty and three to fumigate the kitchen. Typical restaurant stuff. Guy's got his own key, but when he got here at two fifty-five the place was wide open. He walked right in and found the mess. If he hadn't, this guy DiLeo woulda bled to death."

"He's the *half*, right? How's he doin'? Operations said he was a few quarts low."

"When they took him outta here EMS figured he was circlin' the drain. But they got him in the OR now, and maybe he's got a shot."

"How'd we establish that he's a PI?"

"PI license in his wallet, along with a carry permit."

"Was he packing?"

"Nothing recovered. He wasn't even wearing a holster. His permit was for a .38 Colt, but we're thinkin' that everybody here got it with something a little stronger. Prob'ly a nine."

"We got IDs on the rest of them?"

"Yeah, pretty much. Still tentative till we get notifications out, and get positives from next of kin. According to the woman's New York driver's license, her name is Candace Mayhew. White, forty-five, 333 East Seventy-third, apartment 21-G. We sent a Nineteenth Precinct unit over to her building, The Clarendon, but the doorman said her husband's out of town. Your guys'll have to follow up on that notification. The muscle who ran the joint is Donny Cesare. The sector team from the Seventeenth knew him. He's a positive."

"Donny Cesare? Isn't he a Gambino bit player?" Savage asked.

"One and the same." Woodruff's horse face expanded with a broad toothy grin.

"I didn't know Donny'd become a restaurateur," Savage said, enjoying his own half-awake sarcasm while fishing in his jacket for a fresh roll of Life Savers. "But his presence sure lends credence to your idea of a hit."

Woodruff gave a self-satisfied nod.

Savage peeled away the snug foil wrapping and popped a Wint-O-Green into his mouth as he subconsciously looked for holes in the theory. "Anybody?" he asked, holding out the roll. There were no takers.

"If they were looking to do Donny Cesare, why off everybody else?" Savage asked, talking more to himself than to Woodruff. "That's not usual mob MO, even if the hitter was an amateur. And," he added, taking a long-distance gaze into the barroom-cum-slaughterhouse, "from the looks of things, this guy was nobody's amateur."

Woodruff stretched rusty eyebrows and shrugged. "Well, for one thing, we think the broad may have been his squeeze."

Savage took Woodruff's assessment at face value for the moment. "Tell me about the bartender," he said, deciding to put the question of motive on the back burner for a while.

"Hugh Aloysius Byrne," Woodruff replied, flipping back one page of his notepad. "Sixty-three. Bronx guy. Shit! You gotta know him, Thorn. He's been around for years. Prob'ly tended bar in every mill on the East Side. He shoulda took the night off."

"And this other guy, DiLeo, the PI. What about him? Was he found at the bar, too?"

"Nope. Halfway between the bar and the front door."

"Possible he walked in while this was all goin' down?"

"Nope. We got a half-finished glass of beer and an ashtray full of burnt-out Marlboros on the bar, three stools over from where Cesare and the broad got it."

"Maybe the shooter's?"

"Nope. We found DiLeo's MasterCard card lyin' on top of the till, and he had a near-empty pack of Marlboros in his jacket pocket. We're bettin' that they're his prints on that beer glass. You can have them do a comparison against the prints on his pistol permit app."

Savage turned his attention to the diminutive and bespectacled Dwight Spencer, the translucent-skinned, effeminate medical examiner. Conscious not to squeeze too hard, Savage enveloped the man's small, almost dainty hand with his huge mitt. "Busy night for you, eh, Doc?" Savage said in polite small talk. Towering above him, Thorn looked down on the man's shiny scalp and a couple of moles that showed through sparse gray-blond hair that was combed straight back.

The birdlike ME responded with a dramatic roll of his gentle-looking blue eyes while grunting a terse, "Yeah." Then he turned away and went back to his notes.

"Ah, shit!" Woodruff muttered as he looked across Savage's shoulder.

"What's wrong now?" Savage said without moving his lips, a questioning frown creasing his brow.

"Something scummy this way comes."

Damon Ratcliff, the tart and self-important Division duty captain, had emerged from the men's room. He was in full uniform. Recognized as one of the department's rising stars, Ratcliff had been sent to Harvard at the taxpayers' expense for a master's degree in urban management. Like most rising stars, he had spent his entire short career in patrol, so he didn't understand the detective function and was recognized in the Bureau as a man who didn't like detectives. "Where's the rest of your team, Savage?" he asked. "Time to start earning some of that special money they pay you homicide prima donnas."

"One's already here, boss," Savage assured him dutifully. "The other two should be arriving at any minute. They all responded to their pages."

Looking down his nose, Ratcliff asked, "Isn't a homicide team supposed to consist of one sergeant and *four* detectives?"

"That's correct, sir," Savage acknowledged. "My fourth man retired two weeks ago. The department's yet to backfill the slot."

"You overworked?" Ratcliff asked with a surly smirk.

"No, sir. The three I've got are the best in the job," Savage calmly replied.

"Unh," the uniformed captain grunted. "I want this location cleared before people start filling the streets. Crime Scene may have a coupla more hours yet, but the ME's already cleared the bodies for removal. Of course," he added with an apparent edge, "it's your call, Savage."

Savage knew why the edge was there. The rules stated that, as the ranking detective supervisor at a homicide scene, he called the shots, not Ratcliff. Captains like Ratcliff had to accept that fact, but they didn't have to like it. "Gotcha, boss," Savage soothed, then shot a glance at Danny Woodruff. Nothing had to be said. Their eyes spoke volumes to one another. Ratcliff wasn't some garden-variety asshole. With a Harvard master's, he was a highly educated one.

"Well, I guess I better go take a closer look, eh, Dan? Patrol wants the street back, and we should try to cooperate." Savage turned and began to weave his way through the dining room toward the bar, leaving the tart captain with a scowl on his face.

Following tight on Savage's heels, Woodruff muttered, "Fuckin' hard-on."

Savage felt a chill as he entered the taproom. The feeling attacked all the senses. It went beyond the visual assault of twisted and blood-soaked lifeless bodies. There was always that aroma, that aura, that presence that clouded the air. It was always the same, and thirty years on The Job didn't make it any easier. These scenes never failed to dredge up stark reminders of one's own mortality. He knew from experience that everyone in the room probably felt the same way. Despite the hivelike bustle, they all spoke in moderated tones and moved about quietly, like a family at Aunt Bertha's wake. He stood off to the side as Ollie Beyeler from Crime Scene finished taking one last wide-angle shot.

Stepping up onto the brass rail, Savage leaned across the wide mahogany bar. He took only a cursory glance at Huey Byrne's body sprawled facedown on the floorboards behind it, then moved along the row of spindle-back red-leather-upholstered stools and hunkered down next to Cesare's tangled form. The man's legs were crumpled and his arms were hooked beneath him at unnatural angles.

"He must have been dead before he hit the floor," Jack Lindstrom speculated, squatting next to Savage. "He's collapsed like a marionette."

"Morning, Jack," Savage said with an agreeing nod.

Neatly dressed and soft-spoken, Detective Jack Lindstrom was a man of average looks. A chess player and left-brain thinker, he believed there was a logical solution to every crime. "The Swede," as he was known, was the team's invaluable detail man.

Making no attempt to move Cesare's body, Savage turned the man's head and probed his close-cropped, wiry hair with a swizzle stick to reveal the gaping wounds in the back of his skull.

Above Cesare, her head resting on the bar and her body corralled between the wraparound arms of the stool in which she still sat, was Candace Mayhew. A purple tongue flopped from her twisted mouth, and wispy ends of Clairol-blond hair wicked the coagulated ooze that ringed her head. Her unshining eyes seemed to be staring at a half-finished cocktail in a tall glass. Leaning in for a closer look, Savage aimed a penlight on her left temple area. The circle of muzzle-blast debris that scorched the paling flesh of her high cheekbone told the tale.

"Shooter must have had his piece stuck in her ear when he fired," Lindstrom muttered.

Savage picked up on the unmistakable scent of Giorgio—the favorite of his recently estranged girlfriend, Maureen. "Shell casings?" he asked.

"Nothin' down this end of the bar," Lindstrom explained. "But Crime Scene came up with one nine millimeter Glock near where DiLeo fell. It rolled under the jukebox."

"Great. Sounds like our shooter's a tidy sort—cool enough to hang around and do some housekeeping. It musta really pissed him off when he couldn't find that seventh casing."

"Yeah," Lindstrom agreed. "Ballistics'll be able to fill in some of the blanks about the weapon."

"Unh," Savage grunted. "And if DiLeo survives and doesn't wind up a veggie, maybe he'll have some answers too."

Andric Valentin Karazov learned how to kill people at an early age. At sixteen he crushed his father's skull with a manure shovel and buried the man's bludgeoned remains under a peat mound on the outskirts of their Ukrainian farming village. The senior Karazov never knew what was coming when the lights went out for the last time. He was sleeping his way through a vodka-induced stupor after pummeling Andric's mother for yet another imagined wifely misdemeanor.

Andric was young, but, in his sobbing mother's words, "it was time for him to leave the Steppes." With only a few hundred rubles and a rucksack of meager belongings he fled Russia by way of Bucharest, Belgrade, and Budapest, then settled for a time in Marseilles. In each city he made connections, and in each city he honed his craft.

Now, many years and countless killings later, the man renamed Andrew Karis relaxed on the thirty-fifth floor balcony of his Lower Manhattan apartment that at one time had stood in the shadows of the World Trade Center. Well connected with criminal organizations both in the United States and abroad, he was a freelance contractor doing what he did best, with an excellent reputation for high-quality work at fair prices.

Naked beneath an embroidered silk robe he'd picked up years ago in Tokyo while studying bonsai culture, and shod in velvet-and-rattan thongs he'd bartered for in a Bangkok street market, Karis prepared his tea and waited for the sunrise. Although his ears were noticeably large and long lobed, it was his mole-like eyes that were his most recognizable feature. Deeply recessed beneath a massive forehead and overhanging brow, they were forbidding and cold. Set in above high and square Slavic cheekbones, they gave one pause, like dispiriting entrances to unexplored darkened tunnels. Widely spaced teeth, disproportionately large even for his big head, appeared as yellowing ivories set off against the ebony flats of an aging keyboard. He was not a handsome man.

Scrupulous in thought and deed, Karis demanded precision of himself, but he'd fucked up this morning and he was angry. The contract that had come to him through one of his brokers had been for the Mayhew woman. Taking her out of the picture along with her mobbed-up boyfriend would make it appear to be a gangland hit. Case closed. But he'd had to throw in the bartender—at no extra charge, of course—to erase an eyewitness. Sometimes these extras were unavoidable in his line of work. He wrote it off as a cost of doing business. It was that *other* guy, the one who'd appeared out of nowhere, that had him deeply pissed. Why hadn't he known the guy was there? Inexcusable. Sloppy. Totally out of character. But the more he thought about it, the more it dawned on him that no real harm had actually been done. Dead men tell no tales, he reminded himself, slowly dunking a bag of

Twinings into a mug of steaming water. Any investigations would now become even further confused, he concluded, and took a tentative sip of the strong Darjeeling.

The terrace was always a comfortable place to order his thoughts after a job, especially in the spring. Home to his assortment of five-needle pines and needle junipers, all in the Moyogi style, the terrace projected from the building's northeast facade and provided a grand view of the South Street Seaport, Fulton Fish Market, and the lower East River flowing between the gothic stone towers of the Brooklyn Bridge. Morning inbound traffic was already beginning to build, and the drone of tires whirring against the span's roadway, now constant, was suddenly interrupted by the ringing of his phone.

Cup in hand, he slid back the shoji screen that separated the open-air terrace from the world of miniature warfare that was once a living room. Thongs slapped at bare heels as he moved along the jade green runner that served as a no-man's-land. To his left, Napoleonic cavalry threw themselves in heroic charge against the artillery emplacements and bayonet-wielding regiments of the First Duke of Wellington. To his right, the badly outnumbered Ninety-third Highlanders and Scots Grays of the Heavy Brigade engaged the Russian cavalry at Balaklava. Not one of the silent leaden troops stood taller than fifty-five millimeters. He passed his hussars and cossacks, and the Russian grenadiers of the Pavlowski Regiment. Every surface and shelf in the huge room, save those reserved for his *Juniperus squamata* and *Ficus benjamina,* was an armed camp.

Bypassing his cordless, cradled in its recharger atop a black lacquered console in the hallway, he picked up the hardwired telephone on the kitchen wall. He did not speak.

"Hello, Mr. K. This is a dear friend." It was the correct voice, using the correct coded intro. The same voice that'd called at eleven last night with the *go* and location on his latest assignment.

"Hello, dear friend," he replied. "What can I do for you?"

"There is a problem."

"Oh?" Karis said, setting the cup of tea on the counter and picking up his spray mist bottle.

"There is a news story breaking on the radio. It concerns the downing of four ducks at an East Side watering hole. It occured sometime early this morning, so they are saying."

"Is that a fact?"

"Yes. That is a fact."

"What seems to be the problem?" he asked, casually spritzing the tiny leaves and aged bark of his prized Kingsville dwarf boxwood. The fifty-year-old specimen was only twenty inches tall, and its spread was wider that its height.

"One duck is still aloft. You were told right up front—a loose end in *this* matter cannot be tolerated."

"I understand." He set down the spray bottle. It was jamming again—he would need a new one.

The line went silent. Karis kept the receiver to his ear until he heard a dial tone, then hung it up. He pondered a moment, reached again for his tea, and headed back to the terrace. En route, he turned the radio on to an all-news station, then noticed that his especially rare forty-two-piece grouping of French infantry, cavalry, and artillery was overdue for a good cleaning.

THREE

Savage searched throughout La Florentine's bar and dining room, looking for his Crime Scene pal Ollie Beyeler. He knew Ollie was there—he'd seen him earlier. He checked the men's and ladies' washrooms without any luck, and finally found the expert technician in the restaurant's kitchen, dumping a measured potful of water into a Bunn-O-Matic's reservoir.

"You're a man of many talents, Detective Beyeler," Savage jested, as he walked up on his friend. "Can we add coffeeologist to your already lengthy résumé?"

"You may!" the bug-eyed man responded while flipping the coffeemaker's ON switch. "I'd never make it as a short-order man in some Greek diner, but I know how to make a stand-up cuppa coffee for crissakes."

"I'm sure you do, O great and knowledgeable one," Savage intoned. "But would you be good enough to don your crime-stopper's hat for a few minutes?" Savage leaned forward in a slight bow, hands clasped in supplication.

"O pathetic seeker of knowledge." Beyeler played along, bowing back. "What dost thou require from the knower of all things?"

"But a few moments of your precious time is all that this humble servant seeks, O guru of crime scenes, smut magazines, and drip-grind canteens."

Beyeler's head shake and snorting laugh signaled

that he had no retort. He'd been bested once again. He gave the Bunn-O-Matic one more quick look. Apparently satisfied that the coffee was brewing properly, he accompanied Savage from the restaurant's kitchen out to a dining room booth where Jack Lindstrom was already seated.

Beyeler was a top-notch crime scene tech, who, like Jack Lindstrom, was into minutiae. Savage wanted to tap into their insights and compare some theoretical notes.

"Not much to tell you here, Thorn," Beyeler began. "What you see is what you get. It was one shooter, and he was very efficient, and *very fast*. He put two quick ones in Cesare's head, then two in the blonde's. Then he took the bartender down."

"Okay," Savage said. "But, what are you basing *very fast* on?"

"The groupings," Beyeler said. "The two wounds in the back of Cesare's head are only millimeters apart. Both those rounds were squeezed off almost simultaneously at point-blank."

"I'll buy that," Savage agreed. "Same thing with the woman?"

"Yeah. Basically. Except both of her wounds were in the left side of the head. One in the temple, and one in the left ear."

"That means the shooter came up from behind Cesare and fired straight into the back of his head. Right?" Savage asked.

"Right," Ollie said.

"Then turned to his right to take out the woman."

"You got it."

"Looked to me as though she had her head turned to the extreme left," Lindstrom piped in. "Either already looking at Cesare, or in possible reflex to the sounds of the first shots. That would account for why her entrance wounds are three-quarter frontal, rather than straight in from the side or three-quarter rear."

"On the money, Jack." Beyeler nodded.

"And the PI, DiLeo?" Savage asked.

"Gotta figure he's an afterthought," Lindstrom suggested. "I don't see him at all in the original plan. Completely different MO."

"Okay," Savage drawled. "Now, let's talk out the choreography."

Savage quickly sketched a crude layout of the premises on a cocktail napkin. The drawing indicated the dining room and bar in relation to the rest rooms, kitchen, and office. "Let's assume that this *was* a mob hit and our shooter knows his mark is in the bar. He comes in and whacks Cesare and the woman, and takes out the bartender for good measure. At this point the shooter doesn't even know that DiLeo exists. Maybe DiLeo's in the john. You with me?"

Beyeler and Lindstrom nodded.

"Being the fastidious type," Savage continued, "the hitter scours the floor at the end of the bar and recovers all his empty shell casings. Nice and neatlike."

"Then," Lindstrom interrupted, running his finger along the napkin drawing to show DiLeo's probable path. "this guy DiLeo strolls back into the bar from the men's room, all fat, dumb, and happy, and spooks the shooter. That would certainly explain why he was found on the other side of the room, far from where we believe he'd been sitting."

"Right," Savage said. "The shooter gets surprised by DiLeo's unexpected appearance. He intercepts the poor bastard way over by the jukebox and does him. He then looks for, but cannot find, that shell casing, so he splits."

"Okay, Thorn," Beyeler acknowledged. "I'm still with ya. But . . . ?"

"But! You're thinking," Savage said, "why in hell would DiLeo leave the relative safety of the toilet and go marching back into the bar after hearing at least six shots fired?"

"Right." Ollie shrugged. "Why the hell would he?"

"Maybe DiLeo never heard the shots," Savage of-

fered. "*Maybe* DiLeo is deaf, which is unlikely for a guy making his living as a PI. *Or . . . ?*" Savage let the question hang and waited for someone to cap the theory.

"Or . . ." Lindstrom murmured, ". . . maybe it was a silenced weapon."

"Bingo," Savage said.

"*Yeah!*" Beyeler agreed. "And if we're talking silencer, then we're definitely talkin' hitsville."

"Okay," Savage went on, doodling geometrics on the edges of the cocktail napkin. "If this *was* a hit, would you presume that Cesare was the main target here? Based solely on the fact that he was shot first."

"I'd say that he was the target," Beyeler replied. "Hell, he was more than half a wise guy. What're you thinking?"

"Did you see the size of him?" Savage asked, brow crimped as he leaned toward Ollie. "If I'm the shooter—and *everybody* in the fuckin' room has gotta go—believe me, I do him first."

Beyeler pondered momentarily, then slowly nodded tentative agreement. Lindstrom sat silent, biting at the inside of his cheek.

"So," Savage pressed. "it is conceivable that even though the woman was the second to be shot, she, or the bartender—or even DiLeo, for that matter—may well have been the shooter's main target. Can I get you to buy into that as a possible scenario?"

"Why not?" Ollie shrugged and stood. "The scene's atypical of mob MO in other ways, so I'd have to say it's possible." He began drifting toward the kitchen. "Want some coffee?"

"In a minute," Savage mumbled contemplatively, sliding from the booth. Pocketing the doodle-enhanced sketch, he headed back toward the bar.

Diane DeGennaro, one of only two first-grade detectives assigned to Manhattan South Homicide, and one of only a handful of female first-graders within the entire department, had arrived with Detective Richie

Marcus, Diane's regular partner both on and off the job. That their ongoing relationship of many years was more than professional was an open secret at Manhattan South. Though both were well liked, some within the twenty-one-member unit were often jealous of Richie's seemingly inexplicable, Svengali-like way with women. Diane DeGennaro was a fine-looking lady. And there was more than one guy in the outfit who felt that Richie's well-developed paunch and Harley chopper style should disqualify him from playing house with such a stunner. Apparently, Diane felt Marcus had much in the way of redeeming qualities. Some of the jealous at MSH wondered what those qualities could possibly be. Nonetheless, Marcus seemed to draw women like bees to nectar.

"Well, boss, what's the plan?" Diane asked Savage in her soft, deferential style. "Where do you want us to start?"

"I want you and Richie to follow up on family notifications. Make sure they've all been made. Then touch base with your connections over at Joint Organized Crime Task Force. We need to know everything we can about Cesare. What's he been doing? Was he currently under investigation? And most important, was he, or had he ever been, a government witness against any of 'the boys'?"

Savage settled into his groove and kicked it up a notch now that the crew was complete. Thorn knew each of their strengths, and utilized them accordingly. His team—though one investigator short—generated great output without expending maximum effort. Well schooled, they'd all been here before and done it a thousand times. They knew better than to try to reinvent the wheel.

"You *gotta* figure this is a mob job, Thorn." The typically cocksure statement came from Richie Marcus. Diane's playmate tortured every syllable over the rasp of his whiskey-and-Winston-trained larynx.

Savage didn't bother responding. He looked on in

silence as stern-faced morgue draymen muscled unco-operative limbs and rigid torsos into giant-size zippered bags. Cesare, the Mayhew woman, and Huey the leprechaun had their toe tickets punched and ready. They each had confirmed reservations for private, temperature-controlled accommodations at the Hotel Rigor Mortis, all tips, taxes, and transfers included.

"Freakin' Donny Cesare's been on the fringe of organized crime since I was in Public Morals fifteen years ago." Marcus continued his gravelly discourse. "He operated a few skin flicks and strip joints over on the Deuce, and ran an after-hours club down in the Village. On top of that, he's been known to dabble a bit in loan sharkin' and extortion. I know for a fact that he took a little fall for a bookmaking operation once upon a time."

Cup of steaming coffee in hand, Jack Lindstrom sidled up. "Sounds like Donny-boy covered an awful lot of bases. Did he ever take any of *your* pony action, Marcus?"

"Screw you, Jack," Marcus growled. Cesare's shrouded carcass was flopped heavily onto a wheeled stretcher next to them.

Savage broke from deep thought. "No doubt, Cesare's mob links have got to be our main thrust," he began. *"But . . . ?"* His wiry and wild Celtic eyebrows twisted into a blustery question mark.

"What else you thinking, Sarge?" Lindstrom asked. "Jealous husband? Jealous wife? This looks a little heavy for that, don't you think?"

Savage slid half-glasses from his nose and huffed a cloud of breath onto the right lens. "It may be far-fetched," he acknowledged, wiping the eyepiece clear with a cocktail napkin. "But, you know, we're going to have to rule it out." He repeated the process on the spectacles' left lens. Turning to Diane DeGennaro, he set the glasses back onto the tip of his nose. "Find out Cesare's marital status. As for the Mayhew woman, we need to interview her husband and extended family members. It might be good to hear what was going on in those marriages from someone other than spouses. Whoever pulled the trigger here was a methodical pro and those people don't come cheap. Somebody somewhere's payin' a big tab. We're gonna have to rule out Cesare's wife, if he's got one, and Candace Mayhew's husband."

"Her old man's supposed to be out of town, right?" Diane asked.

"Yeah. Which may or may not be a very convenient alibi," Savage continued. "You may have to track him. Also, I want Forty-ninth Street between Second and Third thoroughly canvassed. It's full of residential brownstones, and I don't have to tell you they're occupied by some of the wealthiest folks in town. That means each household probably has staff. If so, we need to talk to them too."

"Maybe somebody was walking their dog early this morning," Marcus interjected, stating the obvious intent of Savage's directive. "Maybe somebody got home late from a party."

"Right. Somebody might have seen something. You and Diane'll cover that." Savage turned his attention to Jack Lindstrom. "Ballistics, latent prints, autopsy reports, life insurance policies. The usual, Jack."

"Gotcha."

"Oh, one more thing, Richie." Savage turned back to Marcus in afterthought. "I'm worried about midtown parking regs. As soon as they kick in, those sonsabitches from Tow Away'll start hooking up to anything that ain't movin' and dragging it off to the pound. I want Violation Tow notified. I don't want them puttin' a hook on anything within a two-block radius of this place. Not until we give the okay. I want anything that turns into a pumpkin safeguarded until we've determined it has no connection here."

"Read you, boss." Marcus turned on his heels and headed for a phone.

Savage stifled a sudden yawn, carefully unwrapped another Wint-O-Green, and headed in the direction of the restaurant's kitchen and its commandeered Bunn-O-Matic. Despite the pompous uniformed captain's optimistic appraisal of what remained to be done, Savage knew it would be hours before they'd be able to clear this crime scene. And what he needed most right now was a caffeine jolt to get his brain shifted into high. Later, when satisfied that all preliminary bases had been touched, he would make the visit to Bellevue Hospital and follow up on the PI, Anthony DiLeo.

The chunky black woman in an aproned uniform set a silver tray down on the mahogany lowboy, then waddled in dense carpeted silence to the master suite's drapery-covered window. Fleshy arms jiggling like Jell-O, she tugged at the pulley cords, opened the drapes, and allowed Wednesday morning to flood the room like raging white water from a burst dam.

"Senator Maloney, sir," she sang in her high-pitched, Trinidadian lilt. "Time for you to be gettin' up. It is goin' to be one beautiful day, sir."

Gerard Maloney unraveled his rotund self from his scrambled comforter in the canopied bed. He sat up and rubbed the heels of his hands into heavily hooded eye sockets.

"Is it six-thirty already, Twyla?" he muttered, squinting to see the glowing digital numerals of the clock radio on his nightstand.

"My, Senator M, but you lookin' awful tired this mornin', sir," the maid observed. "You feelin' awright today?"

Grumbling something that even he found inaudible, Maloney gawked about the room in a daze and raked his fingers through a thick shock of snow-white hair.

"Seems you just haven't been yourself these past weeks. I swear it's that damn ol' politics what's got you down. You be needin' a good rest for yourself, Senator. You deserve it."

Maloney *was* exhausted. He'd finally gotten home to the brick-and-stone Forest Hills Tudor and dragged his tired carcass into his own bed at one in the morning. Yesterday's quickie through New Hampshire was tiring, but it had been a must-do if he was going to announce his candidacy for the presidency of the United States. Though the real campaigning still lay months down the road, he had to build new party acquaintances and strengthen the old ones within that critical primary state. Anyway, the congressional recess that got him out of Washington for a couple of days would soon be over, and he and Christine could get back to their second home in D.C. Confident that he'd sweep the primaries and lock up the nomination, he still hadn't decided whether he would then relinquish his senate seat. This, he thought, could be his last hurrah.

"Brought you some nice fresh-squeezed orange juice, Senator. I put it in your favorite glass, with three ice cubes, just the way you likes it." With a troubled look on her moonlike round face, she laid out his robe and slippers as she had done for the last twenty years. She set fresh towels and washcloths on the vanity in the adjoining bath, and, with a final heave of her mammoth chest, turned toward him. "There be anythin' else, sir?"

"Yes," he mumbled. "There is." Looking straight into her eyes with his Killarney blues, he sucked her into a mild conspiracy. "Make me one of your special breakfasts today, Twyla. I'm starving. And don't you go telling Mrs. Maloney how much I ate, you hear?"

"You know I won't be sayin' nuthin', sir. But you know how Lady M has that un*canny* way of knowin' everything. She'll find out, you know that. She counts every one of your calories, and don't want me giving you nuthin' full of cholesterol. That lady wants to keep you healthy."

Yeah, she wants to keep me healthy all right, he thought. I'm the key to her whole damn power network. "Mrs. M won't be out of bed till at least nine," Maloney insisted. "How is she going to know?"

"Oh, she out of bed already, sir. She got a phone call a little bit ago."

"Phone call? At this hour?" The expression on his florid face became one of concern. "Hmmm," he uttered, heading for the bathroom as the unhearing maid waddled from the bedroom.

Hunched in the marble-walled shower, enjoying the high-pressure needles of hot water playing against his aching back, Maloney thought about how he'd gotten into the cauldron of high-level politics. Of course, he knew it had been the lure of the almost unbridled power that he'd found much too great to ignore. Truth be known, it had been too great for Christine to ignore, too. She loved playing the political game and thrived on the recognition that it brought. Twice, they'd made the cover of *Time*—once when he was first elected senator from New York back in '86, and again last September when his name began to be circulated as the probable front-runner in the next presidential election.

A one-day growth of stubby gray beard vanished from his ruddy cheeks and deeply cleft chin as he shaved. Standing now before the bathroom mirror, he thought about how important it was to Christine that he win this election and take all the marbles. Dispensing patronage like a benevolent monarch to clamoring and grasping supporters was a thrill of orgasmic proportions of which Christine's political libido never seemed to get enough. In that regard, at least, she was insatiable. To her, politics was a drive, a basic and instinctive need, and she protected her turf like a Doberman. To him, it had meant hobnobbing with the giants of industry, sipping cocktails with Hollywood's elite, and golfing with presidents. Not a bad way to spend one's life.

Playing the political game had always made great demands on the mind, to be sure, but now he was beginning to feel some of its effects on his aging and less than well-maintained body. A modern presidential run would be a struggle for a man twenty-five years younger, but, at sixty-two . . . He spent the next fifteen minutes on the porcelain throne waiting for nature to take its ever-more-deliberate course.

At 7:15 he descended the sweeping staircase and took his place at the head of the table in the Edwardian dining room.

"Where's Mrs. M?" he asked quietly as Twyla presented an oval platter full of bacon-covered Belgian waffles and placed the freshly ironed *New York Times* before him.

"Don't rightly know, sir. But I'll find out," she answered, pouring his coffee.

Right from the outset of this political season, Christine's confidence had been complete. So much so that she'd begun negotiations to sell their four-thousand-square-foot duplex in central Georgetown. During all the years he'd served in the Senate, it had been the perfect place for her to entertain her court. But Christine had her eyes on another house in D.C., a much larger *white* house, and had self-absorbed ambitions of controlling a much larger court.

Polls conducted last year by his staff, and by several nonpartisan organizations, had shown him to be the overwhelming favorite for the party's nomination, especially since Vice President Cavanaugh had stepped on his own prick big-time in a campaign funding screwup, leaving himself damaged beyond repair and highly vulnerable in the primaries. Those same polls showed that the opposition party had no real, formidable candidate on the horizon. He was, at least at this point, looking very much like a virtual shoo-in. With the nation's economy having rebounded nicely, and inflation and interest rates as low as they'd been in decades, Christine felt the time was right for him to formally announce.

Everything about his political fortunes had begun

to fall so nicely into place, he thought, slathering every square of the waffles with whipped butter, and turning to the *Times* editorials. Big Money saw this as their year and Gerard Maloney as their man. The war chest of almighty dollars necessary to gain the coveted nomination was guaranteed. Serendipity, Christine had assured him. It was *his* year and he couldn't lose. She wouldn't allow it. He crammed a forkful of syrup-dripping waffle and a half strip of crisp bacon into his mouth and slowly chewed.

Then, two weeks ago, they'd gotten that letter. The double-spaced, typewritten, catastrophic, poison-pen piece of garbage that had pierced his chest like a fiery spear. It had devastated Christine. He'd never seen her so angry and withdrawn. Everything in their lives had to be put on hold, even the sale of the duplex in Georgetown. Gerard Maloney's past had come back to haunt them.

"Where's my wife?" he inquired softly, as the attentive maid reappeared to top off his coffee. "You told me Mrs. Maloney was already up." Covering his mouth with a napkin, he squelched a nervous belch.

"She gone back to her bedroom, sir. Back to bed for a spell," Twyla said, smiling, gathering up the evidence—platter, butter dish, and syrup boat. "I wouldn't worry about that old phone call, though. Whatever it was, it sure lifted up her spirits."

FOUR

Blinded by the glare that dominated the eastern sky over Queens and Brooklyn, Savage carefully steered the dark green Ford across First Avenue at Thirty-fourth Street. The early morning sun, introducing a clear and cloudless day, dared him to view its retina-melting orange ball straight on. He flipped down the visor, turned right, and, still squinting, jockeyed for one of the few available spots behind Bellevue Emergency.

Stepping from his car, he looked up at the austere and soot-darkened brick structure of Bellevue's original building. Severe in its architecture, almost medieval, it seemed to be peering down at him like a hideous gargoyle. He headed to the adjacent modern wing.

With the sound of sirens wailing somewhere in the distance, he waited outside the emergency entrance as a team of paramedics lifted an old woman in a wheelchair from the rear of an ambulance. Oozing bubbling drool and looking like she was in la-la land, the old woman's head flopped around like a spring-necked doll's. An emaciated beagle mix came into view; the mongrel lifted its scrawny leg and spritzed the side of the building.

Any thoughts he had were swallowed up by the ear-splitting harshness of Con Edison jackhammers. A nearby crew was chopping a crater into the parking area's asphalt. The city was awake.

The waiting area of Bellevue Emergency was its normal zoolike self. The main passageway was choked with wheelchairs and gurneys overflowing with the city's sick and injured, poor and homeless. Mindful not to step too near anyone, Savage contemplated his best route through the gauntlet of misery to the information desk.

He gave a wide berth to a scraggly homeless man in tattered clothes. The wino probably hadn't seen a bath in years and reeked to high heaven. With an imaginary phone pressed to one of his hair-filled cauliflower ears, he seemed to be holding his own in a loud argument with God only knew who. He looked a hundred, but was probably only in his thirties.

A morbidly obese woman didn't seem to hear the screaming baby she held in her lap—she was too busy swearing in gutter Spanish at the five other children huddled around her. A dozen telephones rang continuously like a bell chorus, vying with a bloody-faced black woman for the attention of several nurses and an orderly with a pinched face who busily ignored her at the triage desk. The woman was loud, foul-mouthed, drunk, and obnoxious. Savage had no difficulty understanding why someone had taken the time to tune her up. These were the painful hangovers that the city's municipal hospitals suffered each and every morning. Savage *hated* hospitals.

He got the information he needed on Anthony DiLeo from a staffer at the reception desk and, in his strongest gait, headed for the west-wing elevators and the third-floor physician's lounge.

Still in surgical scrubs when Savage got there, Dr. Greta Dresner was slouched on an overstuffed sofa, her bootie-covered feet propped atop a magazine-strewn coffee table in the cluttered and less-than-sterile area. She put down a dated, dog-eared copy of Frommer's *Belgium, Holland & Luxembourg* and reached up to shake his hand.

"Coffee, Herr Sergeant? Juice?" the bleary-eyed neurosurgeon asked, gesturing halfheartedly toward the kitchenette off the main room. "The coffee is not so good but it is hot." Her words snapped in Teutonic rapid fire.

Savage snatched a glance at the kitchen's scuzz-covered counter, nasty from prehistoric spills, and littered with unwashed coffee cups and crumbs. A quarter-pound stick of yellow ooze sat amid dirty paper plates, half-eaten donuts, and petrified bagel remnants. With a tactful smile, he shook his head.

"No thanks, Doc. Full up."

Reaching down, she pulled the paper booties from her shoes, then stood, stretched, and yawned widely. "It was a busy night here, Sergeant," she said without looking at him.

Dresner had the strident manner of what he imagined a Hapsburg aristocrat would have been like.

"You want to know about Mr. DiLeo, the gunshot victim," she said. Breathing out a tired sigh, she popped the tab of a six-ounce can of grapefruit juice and dumped the contents into a clean paper cup.

"Yes," he started, then hesitated, not willing to compete against the nasal harangue coming over the third-floor intercom.

"Doctor Caliendo, please come to the three-west nurses station. Doctor Caliendo . . ."

"Caliendo?" the woman muttered, and shook her head in disgust, momentarily ignoring Savage. "Now there is a goddamned laugh. That man is on his way to eighteen holes somewhere by now." Hoisting the cup to her lips, she swallowed the juice in three long gulps, then turned a blasé glance back to Savage.

"How is Mr. DiLeo, and what are his chances?" he finally continued.

"DiLeo just might make it. He is a stout man. I'd say it is eighty-twenty in his favor."

"Good news. Glad to hear that."

"He has lost the right eye and there will be a considerable hearing impairment if he does survive. He will also have other problems that will require additional surgeries and prolonged therapy down the road."

"Such as?"

"The bullet shattered his cheekbone, but did not enter the brain. It traveled, instead, along the inside of the skull and lodged in the inner ear, damaging the semicircular canals."

"Isn't that gonna screw up his balance? His equilibrium?" Savage broke in, merely out of curiosity.

"*Yes,* Sergeant," the tired doctor snapped. "That comes under the heading of *other problems.*" Lightning seemed to flash behind her.

"I see," he answered, taken aback. "Were you able to recover the bullet?" he continued, in a decidedly new, more formal tone.

"*Ja!*" she blurted. "Of course I did. It has been put aside for you. My initials are on the envelope. It has been sealed; no one else touched it. You will have to leave a receipt for it downstairs."

"Will do," Savage assured, digging in his pocket and unraveling an emergency Wint-O-Green, wondering why in hell this lady wasn't practicing medicine in Düsseldorf or Buenos Aires.

"What about Mr. DiLeo's memory? Will he be able to recall anything of the shooting? And, if so, will he be physically able to speak?"

The surgeon shrugged her ample shoulders and scratched at her bloated chin. "His long-term memory should be unaffected. As to this immediate incident, it may take him some time to remember any of the details—if at all. Severe trauma, you know. But aside from some maxillary pain," she added, shrugging again, "he should be able to speak without much problem."

"Where's he now, Doctor?" Savage asked, ignoring

the silent vibration of an incoming call on his cell phone.

"Still in Recovery—fourth floor. Just closed him up."

"Then where?"

"Neuro ICU. I know you want to talk to him, but, as I told his wife, he won't be coming around for some time now. He could be under for another eight hours or more."

Only a few intimates could have discerned the subtle expression change that hinted Savage's disappointment. As things stood, Anthony DiLeo was the best hope for any real information about the perp. Eight hours was a long time. By then, Savage thought, the shooter could be in Egypt.

"That's my best guess," she added, with a haughty, almost dismissive about-face.

The interview was over.

Flashing his shield and bumming the use of a quiet niche adjacent to the third-floor nurses' station, Savage began to feel a heady queasiness as he dialed the return number that blinked back at him from his Nokia. The odor from a nearby custodian's antiseptic-charged mop bucket disturbed him. His mind began to play a shell game with an insistent subconscious that wanted to dwell on the *true* significance of the acrid smell.

It finally located the door that enclosed his most deeply suppressed and painful memory, and tore away its reinforced seal. His jaw tightened and his eyes went out of focus as he was drawn back twenty years. Back to the storm-slicked night when Joanne and Jennie slipped forever from his life. He remembered the call that told him of the awful wreck. He remembered racing like a madman to the hospital way the hell out in Smithtown where they used to live. But one thing he would *never* forget was the antiseptic stink of the emergency room that night when he found he was already childless, and soon to be wifeless. Jennie would have been twenty-eight last Thursday. He sucked it in.

"Marcus, Manhattan South Homicide."

The cheese-grater voice mercifully snapped Savage from his funk and brought him back to the now. "Yeah, Rich," he mumbled into the phone, as if rudely roused from a deep sleep. Then, quickly gaining his composure, "I'm still down at Bellevue. Whatcha got?"

"Tons of shit, boss. First off, is that guy DiLeo gonna make it, or what?"

"Looks like he's got a fair shot."

"Good. We just had a '96 Honda Civic towed into the Seventeenth, and you won't believe what we found."

"Try me."

"Just like you said, Tow Away came up with the car. They found it around seven-thirty, parked all by its lonesome on the east side of Third between Forty-eighth and Forty-ninth, just down from the La Florentine. It came back registered to Anthony DiLeo, Ford Street, Brooklyn. I'm pretty sure that's out in Sheepshead Bay. I didn't know if you wanted me to give the car a toss, or what."

"So?"

"*So,*" Marcus replied with a devil-may-care chuckle, "I went ahead and tossed it."

"Anything?"

"Plenty. Surveillance logs and cameras. Cameras everyplace. He had a camcorder and a thirty-five millimeter tucked under the front seat. The thirty-five millimeter showed six exposures."

"Anything else?"

"He had a photograph of Candace Mayhew clipped to the sun visor."

"*Awright!* That gives us a pretty good idea of why *he* was there."

"No question. But not only do we now know the why, we also know the when. According to handwritten notes I found on a clipboard on the front seat, he'd tailed her from her residence on East Seventy-third, to La Florentine. She arrived there, alone, at ten fifty-five last night."

"Hmm."

"But wait!" Marcus stressed. "As they say on TV, 'There's more.' The best is this: DiLeo had a Panasonic event recorder bolted right behind the car's grille for crissakes. He probably used it for highway tails. This thing ain't no piece of shit. Lindstrom says it's got remote telephoto and zoom, and goes for about four grand."

"Jeez, you'd think something that delicate would get all loused up by the weather out there under the hood."

"Totally weatherized—real professional job. But judging by where the car itself was found parked, it appears that DiLeo had that sucker honed in on La Florentine's front door all night. How do you like them fuckin' apples?"

"Love it. But was the damn thing recording? Was it on?"

"*Yessir!*" Marcus said emphatically, sounding like an overstimulated Satchmo. "According to the Swede, *it* was *on*. He said these tapes can go for six hours, so if the tape was fresh and DiLeo started it at ten fifty-five, we should have plenty of time to spare. I don't believe it; we might have this fuck on videotape."

"Where are the cameras, tapes, and film now?"

"Diane ran them all down to Photo for dupes and enhancement."

Karis flipped back and forth between the pages of the Manhattan telephone directory. He selected a number and dialed. His call was answered on the second ring.

"Saint Clare's Hospital."

"Good morning. I'd like to check on the condition of Mr. Anthony DiLeo. He may have been brought in a couple of hours ago."

"I'm sorry, sir, but we don't show a patient by that name."

Karis hung up, selected another number, and dialed again.

"Good morning, New York University Hospital. How may I direct your call?"

"Yes. I'd like to check on the condition of an Anthony DiLeo."

"Just a minute. What was that name again?"

"DiLeo, Anthony DiLeo."

"I'm sorry, sir, but I can't seem to find anybody by—"

He cut the operator off in midsentence, then tried another number.

"Bellevue."

"I'm trying to check on the condition of a dear friend of mine. His name is being broadcast over the television as having been injured this morning, but they didn't say what hospital he'd been taken to. Would you be kind enough to check and see if he was brought into Bellevue? I would appreciate it greatly."

"Name please?"

"DiLeo, Anthony DiLeo."

"Checking . . ." After a short pause, the woman's voice came back on the line. "His condition is listed as critical."

"What room is he in? I'd like to send over some flowers."

"Neurological Intensive Care. Fourth floor."

It was ten minutes to nine when Savage found Constance DiLeo gazing out through the broad, tinted windows of the fourth-floor atrium lounge. Stoop-shouldered, the diminutive woman in her mid-sixties was staring blankly down at the morning traffic that crept along First Avenue. Her anxiety was palpable from across the room.

"Mrs. DiLeo?" he said softly, breaking into her trance. "I'm Sergeant Thornton Savage, NYPD."

The woman turned and faced him, the deep dark of her Mediterranean eyes highlighted by the redness that rimmed them.

"Connie DiLeo," she said. Her hands, sun wrinkled and age spotted, clenched a string of rosary beads.

"I know this is a very difficult time for you, Mrs. DiLeo, but it would be very helpful if you could spare a few moments and answer a few questions for me. I'll be as brief as possible, I promise."

She motioned to the corner of the plant-filled room and walked heavily to where a pair of low-slung club chairs sat facing each other. He followed. As she sat, she kept her gaze fixed on her hands folded in her lap.

"Are you going to catch whoever's responsible for . . . ?" Her voice trailed off into a gasping sob.

"We're gonna try our very best, ma'am."

"He's such a good man." She looked up from her lap and stared into Savage's face. "And those poor other people. *Why?*" she asked. "Why would anybody . . . ?"

Savage offered a sympathetic shrug.

"How can I possibly help you, Sergeant?" she finally asked.

Even though the woman tried to gather herself and put up a strong front, he could tell by the hollowness of her gaze and the emptiness in her voice that she was on the ropes. He would be quick about it.

"This is going to sound like a very odd question, Mrs. DiLeo," he began. "But it could be very important." He undid the button on his suit jacket as he sat in the chair opposite her. "I have to inquire about your husband's hearing."

She raised her head again, a mildly puzzled look forming across her face.

"Trust me on this. It's significant," he assured her.

Connie DiLeo attempted an answer, but her voice cracked. She cleared her throat.

Savage noted that her wiry, gray-black hair was unbrushed, and her kindly face bore no trace of makeup. She'd been called out of bed in the middle of the night and told that her husband had been shot. She'd had no time, or inclination, to doll up.

"Ma'am?"

"Tony's hearing is fine," she finally croaked. "The man can hear the grass grow." A tear traced down the woman's cheek.

"Can I get you something?" he asked. "A glass of water or something?"

"No. No, thank you. I'll be okay," she said softly. "My daughter's gone downstairs to get me some tea. Please go on."

"We know that Tony's a licensed private investigator, and we believe that he was in that location last night working on a case. Our Pistol License Section informs us that he has a thirty-eight caliber Colt registered. Did he have it with him last night? We didn't recover one. If it's unaccounted for we'll need to put an alarm out on it."

"No," came a new voice from over Savage's shoulder. "My father didn't have his gun with him last night."

The voice was pleasing and unfaltering. Savage turned in the club chair to face a slim-hipped, olive-toned knockout. He figured her for early forties.

"Sergeant," Connie DiLeo said. "This is my daughter, Gina. Gina McCormick."

Savage stood and offered his hand. Looking right in her eyes, he allowed his secondary vision to take in the whole picture. *Nice.* "Savage," he said. "Thorn Savage."

"My father keeps his gun at home in a drawer," Gina continued in a weary monotone. "To my knowledge he hasn't carried it with him in years."

Tony DiLeo's daughter stood five-five, five-six. Long, camel-like lashes shaded her dark exotic eyes like roll-out awnings, and sweeping brunette curls fell across a bulky knit sweater of chocolate brown that draped loosely from narrow shoulders. Their eyes held

for another instant, then he watched as her graceful
fingers slowly worked the tight-fitting plastic lid from
a container of hot tea. She wore no rings on her left
hand.

"Would having his gun really have helped him last
night, Sergeant?" Gina asked.

"Don't know," he answered in a rasp, preoccupied
by the woman's demure yet sultry aura. "I guess we
really won't know until we're able to talk to him."

Gina leaned over and carefully handed the container of cauldron-hot liquid to her distraught mother.
"Both hands, Mom," she cautioned.

"Is it possible that either of you know anything
about the case Mr. DiLeo was working on last
night?" His glance shifted back and forth between
mother and daughter. "Who it may have involved?
Whether it was a matrimonial, corporate, or industrial matter?"

"I'm afraid I can't tell you," Connie DiLeo said.
"My husband rarely talks to me about his work anymore. After all these years together he just goes and
does whatever he has to do." She turned with a lidded
glance to her daughter.

"I do all my father's financial record keeping," Gina
said. "All I can tell you is that he's worked exclusively
for Parker & Schlafly for some time now. They're a
law firm on Park Avenue. They might be able to help
you on that question."

"That's very helpful, ma'am. Thank you."

Savage informed them of the whereabouts of the
Honda, and the evidentiary confiscation of Mr.
DiLeo's cameras and film. He thanked them both for
their time, and as he offered his best wishes, Gina
turned toward the wall of windows. She brought a
crumpled tissue to her face, and softly sobbed. Savage empathized.

Gina wasn't beautiful—he didn't go for *beautiful*.
But she was attractive. Damned attractive. And she
had something else; she had that intangible he could

never quite define, even to himself. That rare mystique that always lit him up. He didn't know what the hell *it* was, but he always recognized it when he saw it.

He wished they'd met under different circumstances.

Gerard Maloney looked up from the op-eds and watched as Christine made her grand entry down the staircase. He could tell by the way she carried herself that the maid had been right. His wife's mood *was* improved—very much improved—over what it'd been these past weeks.

Christine never ceased to amaze him. Not one strand of her short flaxen hair was out of place—one would have thought she'd just left a beauty salon. Even at this early hour, in their own home, every step she took seemed to be choreographed. She never put a foot wrong, she was always *on*. Her hairstyle had become one of her trademarks: businesslike, if not androgynous, yet very chic. It suited not only her sharp, well-defined features, but also her dominant persona. Her makeup—he never saw her without it—was complete too. It added to the cold, professional look that she liked.

Christine's arrival at breakfast this morning was accompanied by the half-hour chimes of the antique grandfather clock that stood at the base of the staircase. Clad in her quilted satin robe, she strode through the English oak–paneled great room and took her place opposite him at the dining table. As if on cue, Twyla emerged from the kitchen carrying a small glass of tomato juice and a fruit cocktail.

Christine laid a linen napkin across her lap.

"Good morning, darling," he greeted her.

"Morning, Gerard. How'd they treat you up in the Granite State?"

"Fine, darling. Just fine." Smoothing his hair, he added, "Got a haircut and shave at the Park Avenue Barber Shop in Concord. Cameras were rolling, I was answering questions—great PR. State party leaders told me I'm going to have to put in some time up there before the primaries, but they all like my experience and maturity."

"Uh-huh. What time did you finally get in last night?" she asked coldly, steering a spoonful of diced cantaloupe to her mouth.

"One o'clock," he said. "We didn't touch down at LaGuardia 'til twelve-thirty for God's sake. I was exhausted."

"Quit complaining, Gerard. You're about to run for the highest position in the world. It's going to take a little bit of effort on your part."

"Running for the presidency will take a *lot* of effort, Christine," he responded with not too much of an edge. "But now we have to wonder if all that work's going to be in vain."

"Stop being a defeatist for crissakes." She sipped at her juice, then, scrunching her nose, began sniffing like a bloodhound, searching out suspicious aromas that filled the air all about her.

She was on the scent, he could tell. "I understand you had a phone call very early this morning."

"Yes, that's right. What of it?"

"What was it about?"

Christine Maloney looked sternly across at her husband and said, "None of your business, Gerard. It did not concern you."

"Oh, I think it did concern me. More precisely, I think it concerned *us*. We're a team, you know," he replied, testily.

"What are you so damned worried about?"

"You know very well what I'm worried about," he said, then leaned across the table and spoke in an angry whisper. "She's going to wait, let me announce, and let me kill myself in the primaries to get the goddamned nomination, then let me blow in the breeze 'til just before election day. Then she'll drop that fucking bomb on me. The bitch has got my balls in a sling."

Christine sipped expressionlessly at her juice. "Pass me the financial pages, please."

"We're going to have to pay her. We're going to have to bite the bullet and just pay her whatever she wants."

"And then what? What about a year from now, two, *three*? She'll be able to tap into us anytime she damn well pleases. Once you're settled in as president, what're you going to do when you get *another* letter from her?"

"Then there's only one alternative the way I see it."

"And that is?" Christine snapped, her eyebrows raised as if daring him to say it.

"What I've wanted to do right along. Just finish out my senatorial term and retire. Don't enter the presidential race. Bow out. Give up public life. Hell, I'm tired anyway."

"You asshole," she snarled. "You empty suit. Haven't you got any moxie left at all? Even if you don't announce, don't you think she'd still come looking? She won't go away. She won't just evaporate. Not on her own, at least."

A strange chill suddenly took him. "What does that mean?"

"It means that I intend to live in the White House. And it means that you're going to be the president. And that's all there is to that."

"What's going on, Christine?" Silence. "Christine?" he demanded.

"Nothing. Nothing's going on," she said.

He felt her eyes burn into his with a contempt-filled glare.

"But if you hadn't been off screwing that little bimbo years ago, and allowing her to be privy to your, shall we say, *less*-than-ethical behavior, none of this would have happened. Now go back to your paper, Gerard. And then get on with your goddamned campaign."

Ramrod straight in his chair, Gerard Maloney exhaled loudly in frustration.

Twyla lumbered into the dining room from the kitchen, carrying a cut-crystal pitcher. "More juice, Mrs. Maloney?"

"No," she snarled. "The smell of fried bacon has absolutely ruined my appetite."

FIVE

It was 9:30 that morning when Savage pushed his way through the grimy glass front doors of the Thirteenth Precinct on East Twenty-first Street. Passing the station house desk he gave an abbreviated salute and a knowing nod to Jake Grimes, the veteran desk lieutenant. Grimes was explaining some departmental facts of life to a nervous rookie who stood before him with a hulking prisoner in his custody, holding a sheaf of blank arrest forms. God bless 'em, Savage thought. By dint of the glint of the rookie's shiny handcuffs, it was probably the kid's first collar.

He shunned the snail-slow elevator and took the stairs in a quickstep up to C-Deck. Detective Borough Manhattan was headquartered in the front offices of the third floor, and Manhattan South Homicide was headquartered in the back. The Borough office had a view, but Homicide's windows looked out to the sloppy mortar joints and tattered yellowing shades in the dirty windows of the neighboring art school.

Savage recorded his arrival in the already buzzing office by signing in on the next available line of the command log. Shirtsleeved detectives, more than one with a telephone receiver growing between a cocked head and a hunched-up shoulder, banged away at Swintec 7040s in the eight-desk squad room. The machines were typewriters with screens and memory, not computers. The office had but one computer and it was kept at the wheel desk. Two banks of five-drawer file cabinets stood like palace guards along the far wall, one on either side of the door that led to the unit's war room. A sturdy oak table in the corner supported a small Sanyo refrigerator and a dual-pot coffeemaker. This was home to the sixteen detectives, three sergeants, and one lieutenant who comprised the Manhattan South Homicide Task Force. Operation of the wheel desk—phone answering, communications, and general office clerical duties—fell to Eddie Brodigan, the limited-duty cop who was temporarily—permanently—assigned.

Sergeant Billy Lakis, the Team One boss who had thirty-two years in the game, called out to Savage from inside the CO's office. Lakis was updating the unit's stat board that hung on the beige semigloss wall opposite Lieutenant Pete Pezzano's desk. The CO wasn't in yet this morning.

"Looks like Team Three caught a heavy last night. A triple, hah?" Lakis asked with raised eyebrows.

"A triple that could still stretch into a four-bagger," Savage replied with a half grin, feeling a slight pinch in his right upper lip. The scar was a permanent reminder of a lesson he'd learned in the eleventh grade at Cardinal Hayes High School—never step in front of a Timmy Donovan left cross.

Savage leaned against the doorjamb, watching Lakis adjust the stat board to reflect the closing of a year-old case his Team One had just cleared down in the Seventh. Their arrest yesterday of two fifteen-year-old Spanish kids had closed out another of the office's gang-related homicides. With Pezzano's monthly report to the chief due in two days, the arrests would improve the numbers of the overall clearance rate.

"Attaboy, Billy," Savage congratulated. "Your team did a terrific job on that case." The clearance rate for the twenty-nine homicides committed in Manhattan South last year now stood at seventy-two percent.

"But," Savage continued, "as long as you're up

there screwin' with the numbers, add three to this
year's Undetermined."

"Undetermined?" Lakis asked in mild surprise.
"Heard it was a mob job."

"That may well be how they'll wind up, but for now
I want them carried as Undetermined."

Something was gnawing at Savage big-time about
this case. He didn't know what yet, dammit. Maybe
Cesare'd been caught skimming. Or maybe he'd vio-
lated the sanctity of *omerta*. Or maybe the Mayhew
broad, besides being married, was also some made
guy's main squeeze. These were all very real possibili-
ties, but the caution lights in Savage's mind were
flashing brightly. There was another element here, another dynamic, something that went beyond the easy-
to-draw conclusion that a low-level galooch and his
foxy-looking bimbo had been executed for crimes
against la Cosa Nostra.

"You got it, Thorn. Undetermined they shall be,"
Lakis said. With a palms-out gesture and a shrug, he
turned and went back to his numbers. "We take one
step forward in this fuckin' joint, then three steps
back. Right? We ain't never gonna win this war anyway," he added sarcastically. "You know that, don't
ya?"

"I know one thing," Savage said drolly before leaving the room. "We're all in this alone. And ain't *none*
of us gettin' outta here alive."

Lakis flashed one of his wide Lebanese smiles, nodded in agreement, and downed the dregs of his cold
coffee.

Savage went next door to the sergeants' room. It
was a ten-by-twelve chamber he shared with Billy and
the unit's third sergeant, Jules Unger, who supervised
Team Two. Unger wasn't in today; he'd used some
lost time to take his wife, Becky, for her biweekly
chemo.

The room was tight. Three full-size lockers, three
desks, and a file cabinet sucked up all the usable

space. Two of the four tubes beneath the ceiling fluorescent's egg-crate grille were dark, and the fixture
emitted an annoying low-frequency hum. Savage
shook his head. He'd made three repair requests to
Building Maintenance in the past month.

He draped his suit jacket on an old Brooks Brothers
hanger and hung it next to the two tailored uniforms
in his well-organized locker. He unbuttoned his shirt
cuffs and turned them up twice. As he rolled the
sleeves he perused the top page of the latest Personnel
Orders tacked to the office corkboard. He saw that
Fiona Rice-Jenkins—a department trial commissioner
with a reputation for lopping off heads—had been
named to the recently vacated post of first deputy police commissioner. Without musing the specifics, he
didn't think PC Thomas Johnson III had made a good
choice there—if in fact it had been his choice. There
was something more, something political, something of
the hand of the mayor in the high-level appointment.

The Personnel Orders—published the day before—
also announced that twenty-five sergeants had been
promoted to lieutenant. He was still safely hundreds
of spots away. Probably another few years, he thought,
if they didn't retire the list before then—which they
no doubt would. Savage had never studied terribly
hard for the lieutenant's test. Being promoted would
be a double-edged sword anyway. He'd like the rank,
he certainly could use the money, but he didn't want
to leave Manhattan South Homicide—he was comfortable here. There'd been some recent rumors of Petey
Pezzano considering retirement. Word was the squad
commander was looking at a couple of acres on a
mountaintop outside Asheville, North Carolina. If
Petey retired, that would open up the lieutenant's slot
here, but a long-standing department policy, supposedly designed to prevent "command inbreeding,"
made transfer upon promotion automatic. Savage, no
doubt, would be reassigned somewhere within the Bureau, but he wouldn't be allowed to stay here.

He turned back to his locker and started to reach in, then realized he'd forgotten why. He stood for several long seconds wondering what the hell he'd wanted to get, unable to remember. The harder he tried to recall, the more blocked his thoughts seemed to become. It dawned on him that this sort of thing was happening a lot in the last six weeks. He shook his head and sighed.

Giving up on whatever the thought was that'd brought him back to his locker, Savage turned and dragged his chair out from the kneehole of his desk, sat down, and began picking through the stack of please-call memos that'd accumulated on his two days off. They consisted of the usual:

Dr. Hartman at the ME's Office, Re: Fowler autopsy.
Davy Ramirez at Ballistics, Case of: Brunner.
Assistant DA Hogue, C/O Pugh and Jackson.

The only memo out of the ordinary was to call Joe Ballantine at the *New York Post,* and it had come in only minutes before he'd arrived at the office. He shuffled through the stack once more, looking for a memo that Maureen might have called. There was none.

It was now six weeks since they'd officially broken up again, but it wasn't getting any easier for him. Maureen Gallo, the only woman in his life—almost—for the last six years, was the first thought he awoke to each morning, and the last thought he had at night. But the real problem was she occupied every spare thought in between. He just couldn't shake her. He'd given plenty of deep thought these past weeks to picking up the phone and calling her. In his heart he wanted to. He wanted to reach out, maybe try again. But he knew better. It would be like blowing on fading coals—at best, he might derive some momentary warmth. If there was any hope for reconciliation between them, the call would have to come from her, and that wasn't going to happen. Time to face it. Maureen was gone.

Suddenly bummed, and in no mood to talk to anybody, Thorn decided he'd return his calls in a little while. Right now it was time for a cup of Brodigan's liquid amphetamine—he needed something to get his heart pumping after yet another shitty night's sleep. He stood up, snatched his mug from the upper shelf of his locker—*that's what he'd wanted*—and headed for the coffeepot.

In thirty-some years of toiling within the department's Photo Unit, eventually working his way up to director of photographic services, Chester Dabzitzki had developed more than a million pictures. In the last ten of those years he'd also developed one phenomenal crush on Detective Diane DeGennaro. Chet was hopelessly enchanted by the detective's cool gray-blue eyes, and secretly longed for a peek at the bod he felt worthy of a Hefner centerfold. He thought the sprinkling of freckles around her tiny nose added an adolescent charm to her fair complexion and belied her once-married surname that ended in a vowel. To him, there was nothing *gindaloon* about Diane De-Gennaro. She could easily be the poster girl for the Irish Tourist Board.

Whenever Diane was around, Chester became a pimply faced teenager desperate to impress the prettiest girl in class. He didn't stand a fiddler's prayer, and knew it, but was putty in her hands. When Manhattan South Homicide needed to jump the line and have photos processed chop-chop, Diane DeGennaro could get it done. Dabzitzki, the undisputed head honcho of room A-79 at One Police Plaza, could never do enough for her.

When the object of his infatuation had arrived at his office an hour ago with the video and film taken from Anthony DiLeo's cameras, Chet had gone right to work. Ten minutes later, the six thirty-five-millimeter exposures had been developed into sharp eight-by-tens of Candace Mayhew. Two shots showed her standing next to a doorman beneath a sidewalk canopy that bore the number 333, the number coinciding with her East Seventy-third Street address. A third shot showed her stepping past the same doorman and entering a cab. The last three shots showed her arriving at, and entering, La Florentine.

It took Chester another forty-five minutes of fast-forwarding and rewinding to see all that was significant on DiLeo's videotape. After viewing and re-viewing it in its entirety, Dabzitzki went to work on sharpening those critical images the investigators would need.

"That's got to be our guy," Diane murmured, her sparkling eyes glued to the monitor as Dabzitzki isolated a series of frames. "He's alone, and the time stamp shows him entering La Florentine's front door at oh-one-twenty-three and exiting at oh-one-twenty-five."

"The actual elapsed time that he's in there is ninety-three seconds," Dabzitzki replied.

"Fast," Diane whispered, her voice revealing a begrudging respect. "He's the only person to come and go until we see the exterminator arrive on the set at oh-two-fifty-five."

"Well, we can tell he's a white male," Chester said, adjusting his glasses. "I'd say he's about six-two, six-three, lanky, if not downright skinny, wearing what looks like a very loose-fitting dark windbreaker."

"Yeah. The loose jacket to conceal a gun. Probably keeps it in a shoulder rig. And did you notice his walk?"

"Yeah. Very stiff and fast."

"Head and shoulders back, chest out. Almost military, wouldn't you say?"

"Yeah!" Dabzitzki nodded his head. "Sort of like a quick march."

"Besides the dark windbreaker, he's wearing dark pants and shoes, and a dark hat. Can't we get the face any sharper?" Diane asked, as she leaned over to squint at the frozen frame. "It's pretty hazy, isn't it, Chet?"

"We've got nothing but his backside and his walk as he's going in. And I've isolated the best possible front-view frame we have to work with as he's coming out. But there's a limit to just how much enhancement we can get even with the new technology," Dabzitzki apologized. His eyes were locked on the monitor as he gently tweaked the computer's contrast controls. "I can keep playing with it, Diane, but we're never gonna get super detail. It's too bad it wasn't daylight when these were taken—then we'd see much clearer definition."

"Can't you enlarge it?"

"I can enlarge it, but the final print will only get hazier."

"Do me a favor. Back it up a few frames. Back to where we saw the side of this guy's head."

"Can do." The darkly dressed image on the screen began moving backward. As the figure turned its head to the right, Chester locked in on the profile view.

"Look at them ears, would ya," Diane said, clucking her tongue. "We might not have great definition, but we can sure tell that them suckas are big."

"So's his head for crissakes," Chester added. "Look at the size of his brow under that cap."

"All right," Diane said, mild frustration evident in her voice. "We got us a big-headed, skinny, middle-aged white guy who prefers basic black when he's dressed to kill. I'd say he goes six-three and probably weighs in somewhere around one-sixty. He's got ears like an elephant and he moves like a freakin' drill sergeant. Anything else?"

"He ain't no damn movie star."

"Could you make me up a dozen prints, Chet? Meanwhile, I'm gonna use the phone in your office to call my boss. Gotta let the team know what I got."

As Diane headed back toward his office, Chester allowed himself a quick sideways glance. *God,* he thought, what a beautiful ass.

*   *   *

Lesson number one had always been: *Never* kill a dying man—or one about to commit suicide—Karis reminded himself as he hung up the phone. But, according to Bellevue's patient information line, DiLeo wasn't about to do either. Sometime within the last two hours his condition had been upgraded from critical to serious yet stable. That guy should've died on his own considering the hole in his head, Karis brooded, as he ran the water at the kitchen sink. But since DiLeo hadn't decided to cooperate, something needed to be done very quickly. If not, Karis figured, his rep as a faultless and efficient technician would be irretrievably lost. He would have to exercise patience though. He would have to wait. The watchfulness of Intensive Care did not allow for the instant of privacy he would require.

In six ranks of seven men each, the miniature squadron stood abreast in close-order formation atop the kitchen counter. They'd failed this morning's inspection, so it was time for uniform maintenance. Karis tested the water, and judging it still too hot, turned up the cold; he continued to ponder the unfinished business that lay in the hospital bed uptown. He couldn't believe he'd only put one in him. What was he thinking? *Always use a minimum of two!* Mistakes like that always seemed to happen when he broke his own rules. He shook his head in self-loathing.

The warmth of the water tumbling from the faucet now just right, he eased its flow and filled a shot glass, to which he added three drops of baby shampoo. He dunked a Q-tip in the sudsy solution, then pinched the cotton between forefinger and thumb, squeezing out the excess drippings. The mixture was soapy and slick, but delicate enough to bathe his silent and fragile troopers.

He lifted the first soldier to eye level and gave it a close examination. In collector parlance, the figure was considered *mint*. It, and the other pieces of this set, were still in the same condition as when they were

first issued in Germany, sometime in the late 1870s.
There was absolutely no wear on any of them, and
every bit of their original paint remained. How lucky
he'd been, he thought, to have acquired the grouping
at auction fifteen years ago. Starting at the top, he
made several tentative strokes on the soldier's helmet
with the dampened Q-tip. He continued across its
shoulders, then down to the upper part of its base
where the dust collection was most visible. Flipping to
the dry swab on the other end of the Q-tip, he quickly
retraced those same steps, absorbing the soapy mois-
ture and the particles of dust collected within.

One down—forty-one more to go.

Savage was impressed by the sketchy, but valuable,
description of the solo hitter that Diane had called in
from Photo. She'd described the guy shown in the
videotape as fiftyish, white, skinny, with Dumbo ears
mounted on a big head. Now, for crissakes, at least
they had something to go on. Thank you, Tony DiLeo.
Diane's call had come in just after he'd made an afternoon appointment with the law firm of Parker &
Schlafly. That was going to be the place to get more
information on Candace Mayhew, and a line on the
whereabouts of her conveniently out-of-town husband.
Ready now to start returning calls, Savage went back
to the stack of messages on his desk and picked out
the most recent one.

*0915: Call Joe Ballantine—City Desk—New York
Post.*

Joe was a one-time drinking partner, who'd pretty
much sautéed his liver in Bushmills Irish, and barely
managed to crawl up the twelve steps. Savage hadn't
heard from him in a couple of years.

"Ballantine, City Desk." The man's voice was weak
and lacked its former timbre. Savage couldn't remember him sounding so puny, so . . . tubercular. He wondered what the man looked like now.

"Joe, this is Thorn Savage. How are you?"

"Thorn Savage." Ballantine suddenly sounded elated. "How's the world treatin' ya?"

"Good. Real good. And you?"

"Super. Hell, I ain't havin' no damn fun, but I sure do feel good. Tell me, why is it that we can't have fun *and* feel good?" Joe sure didn't *sound* good, Thorn thought.

"I've often wondered that myself, Joe. Some heartless quirk of nature I guess," Savage said with a laugh.

"Ever get married?" Ballantine asked. "You were always pretty hot and heavy with that looker Maureen."

"Nah. Still the Lone Ranger."

"Still jumping out of planes? Parachuting? Skydiving? Whatever it's called?"

"Oh, yeah," Savage admitted, knowing Joe was always fascinated by his favorite pastime. "I still manage a few jumps now and then—when the weather's good."

"That's amazing," Ballantine said through a faint laugh, then quickly became serious. "Listen, Thorn. About that shoot-'em-up this morning inside the La Florentine Restaurant . . ."

"Yeah. What about it?"

"I found out you're handling that case."

"Whoa," Savage said. "You're in the wrong calling. You shoulda been a detective."

"Oh, yeah!" Ballantine drawled. "Then I would've really drank myself to death. Listen, Thorn, our information identifies the dead woman as a Candace Mayhew, of 333 East Seventy-third. Have we got that right?"

"Where the hell did you get that, Joe?" Savage asked sharply. "That ID's still tentative. Pending a family notification, we can't release her name."

"We at the *Post* have our ways. Trust me though. It didn't come from one of your boys. Besides, we'd never go to print with a homicide victim's name until we've gotten the green light from the PD. You know that."

"All right," Savage conceded, figuring that Ballantine probably had a contact in the ME's office. "That is the same information we have at this point. But you know we need an ID from a next of kin in order to carve it in stone. As far as I'm aware, a next of kin has yet to be notified. The woman's husband is supposedly out of town."

"Hmmm."

"Something's on your mind, Joe. Whaddaya wanna know?"

"If it's really Candace Mayhew, I dated her once."

"No shit?"

"Well, actually more than dated her. At one point we were talking marriage, but that was a long time ago. She was Candace Miller in those days. I think your victim may be her. My interest here isn't official, Thorn." The man's voice, though dismal, rang with a sincere reassurance. "It's purely personal."

Thorn took another sip of his third cup of Brodigan's coffee and leaned back in his chair. "I'll tell you whatever I know, Joey."

"We were both living out in Rego Park in those days. I was with the *Daily News* then, and she was working as a secretary for some bigwig politician—who shall remain nameless—who was tied in with the Queens Political Club. She was his, ahem, personal assistant."

"And?"

"And, Candace was impressed by money and power. I had neither—this guy had both. Long story short, I found out she was boffin' the son of a bitch, and we broke up. Never got over her though. I'm sure it was that disaster that made me much dearer friends with Johnny Barleycorn."

"I know what you're sayin', man," Savage sympathized.

"Well, anyway. We lost track of one another. Then, about ten years ago, I'd heard that Candace'd gotten married to some older guy, a businessman, and moved to the East Seventies. I'd just like to know for sure if . . . ?"

"I understand, Joe. Would you be up to viewing the body at the morgue this morning?"

"Yeah," Joe replied. His voice was not at all sure.

"I'll make the arrangements, Joey."

It was a good thing this kind of detailed cleaning was only required every couple of years, Karis thought, realizing he'd been at it for over an hour now. As he brought the forty-second and last soldier to eye level, his heart suddenly dropped and his mouth fell full agape when the figurine slid from his soap-slickened fingers. In total panic he tried to recover his grip, his wildly grasping hands clutching nothing but air. The red-and-blue-uniformed trooper was in full free fall, and there was nothing he could do but watch.

"Shit! Goddamned son of a fucking bitch!"

Karis stood shaking in wide-eyed disbelief. Pipelines of blue bulged along the length of his long neck and at the side of his face forward of his temples, his clearly discernible pulse verging on hemorrhage. The prized Heyde lay in pieces on the unforgiving tiles of the kitchen floor. Even though the French infantryman's thin neck had been snapped, the eyes in the separated head still glared with heroic determination from the finely painted face. Fortunately, and surprisingly, the delicate bayonet had remained in the scabbard, neither breaking nor bending.

Attempting to regain some degree of self-control, Karis reminded himself that the Soldier Shop up on Madison Avenue could do an expert repair. But the repainting that would be required on the reconnected neck would downgrade the figure's cachet. The best it would ever be considered now was *very good*. He exhaled loudly in angry resignation and disgust, tore off a sheet of paper toweling, and wiped his hands.

Long-nailed fingers, their bony knuckles protruding like segments on a stick of bamboo, carefully gathered the fractured figurine from the gleaming white ceramic floor. With a quilted pot holder as a cushion, he laid the wounded soldier back on the countertop near its comrades and, from the cabinet below, retrieved a wad of bubble wrap. He gently removed the tiny and irreplaceable bayonet from the trooper's scabbard, and set it safely out of the way behind his Mame bonsai in their fluorescent-lit counter display. Using the bubble wrap, he formed a protective cocoon around the figure's body and taped it in place. He repeated the process with the tiny mustachioed head. From his liquor cabinet, he stripped the purple flannel pouch from a bottle of Crown Royal, placed both padded bundles into it, and pulled tightly on the braided drawstring.

He set his jaw, musing about the uptown trip he would probably have to make to Bellevue. He would combine that trip with a visit to the Soldier Shop.

He grinned contentedly. He'd kill two birds with one stone.

Manhattan's midtown traffic had already reached its early-afternoon peak of congested madness when Savage made a right off Twenty-third and aimed his Crown Victoria north on Park. His cell phone rang as he waited for the light at Twenty-sixth Street. He half expected the call to be from Joe Ballantine.

"Thorn. Just left the Medical Examiner's Office." Savage heard a loud exhaled sigh. "Thought I'd better get back with you right away."

"And? How did it go, Joe?" Thorn asked, even though he could tell.

"It's her. It's Candy."

"Ah, shit. I'm sorry. Is there anything I can do for ya, buddy?" Savage said, while steering around a double-parked UPS van.

"No, not really. What can I say?" Ballantine's voice was low and troubled. "I just want you to know I appreciate your helping me out on this one."

"Anytime, Joey," Savage assured him. "You gonna be okay?"

After a second long, deep sigh, Ballantine said, "Yeah. I'll be all right. Do you need me for anything? A statement or whatever?"

"No, I don't think we'll need a statement," Savage said. "What we are needing, though, is information on some relative of hers that we can notify. Any way you can help us?"

"She's got a sister, Meredith, out on Long Island. I may have a number kicking around at home. If I can find it I'll get back to you. Meanwhile, let me give you my cell phone number. You can reach me there anytime, day or night."

"Terrific," Savage said, scratching numerals onto a pad with one hand while steering with the other. *Easy numbers,* he thought, using his own brand of association. Aside from New York's 917 cell phone prefix, they were merely a repetition of Orel Hershiser's and Don Drysdale's Dodger uniform numbers: 555-3555.

"Listen, if you call my office with the sister's number," Savage added, "and I'm not there, leave the information to the attention of Detective DeGennaro."

As he tossed the phone on the passenger seat, Thorn felt great empathy for his friend, who, minutes ago, had stared at the shattered body of the woman who'd probably been the love of his life. Though still not *officially* the remains of Candace Mayhew, they were, at least, certainly the remains of Candace Miller.

Savage knew precisely where Joe had been coming from when he spoke earlier of a relationship whose wheels came off somewhere en route to the altar. As the Ford navigated the elevated Park Avenue viaduct that wraps around Grand Central, he tortured himself with reflections of his on-again, off-again, sometimes wonderful, sometimes turbulent six-year relationship with Maureen. Distracted, he almost plowed the unmarked into the ass end of a taxi that'd stopped short to pick up a fare; he swerved around it just in time.

Fuckin' cabbies, he thought, popping a Wint-O-Green.

He sped to beat the changing light at Fifty-seventh, and his thoughts switched to the dark and lovely Gina McCormick. DiLeo's sexy Italian daughter had surely turned his head. Was he *that* shallow? Could he be interested in another woman, look appreciatively at her as he'd done this morning, while still being emotionally bound to Maureen? Which he knew he was.

"Shit!"

He hated the frustration he felt when having to deal with questions about himself he was unable to answer.

At 670 Park Avenue, he pulled the Crown Victoria to the curb and tossed the NYPD ID plate on the dash. He was five minutes early for his two o'clock appointment with the Parker half of Parker & Schlafly.

<u>SIX</u>

Savage thought J. Sidney Parker was a huckster. Fact was, Thorn's antenna always raised when he was around assholes and phonies whose first names were initials. He had a thing about that, and for women with hyphenated dual surnames. He hated pretention. Whenever introduced to an F. Lee this, or an F. You that, he immediately conjured up recollections of J. Fred Muggs, the roller-skating chimp from the early days of television.

But there was no questioning Parker's acute instinct for self-promotion, which, no doubt, was how he built his artsy client list. When not handling matrimonials for mere mortals of the likes of Harmon Mayhew, J. Sidney Parker was also New York's divorce lawyer to the stars. He was once the divorce guru for Hollywood heavies who'd had the forethought to make their primary residence New York when they tied the knot. That change of venue would spare them from California's community property nightmare when the time came for the inevitable divorce. Nowadays it didn't make that much difference—they were screwed either way.

To call Parker flamboyant was like calling Babe Ruth a guy who played baseball. With a rakish Barrymore profile—compliments of a terrific rhinoplasty and an overdone chin implant—and a sparkling smile of perfectly aligned porcelain, he even looked showbiz. On the wrong side of sixty, he was a Savile Row dresser who spent lots of time in a tanning booth and somehow got away with shoulder-length hair dyed an absurd carrot orange. The man reeked of money, right down to his diamond-and-ruby-encrusted eighteen-karat Rolex Super President. Savage guessed it retailed somewhere in the neighborhood of fifty big ones. Yes, J. Sidney Parker did all right. His opulent-beyond-belief rosewood-paneled offices looked down on the richest stretch of one of the richest avenues in the world.

"Can't believe Tony DiLeo's been shot," Parker began, settling into his high-backed swivel chair of cream-colored leather. The wall behind him was a gallery of framed certificates and photographs. Parker and Larry King; Parker and some other guy standing with then New York governor Mario Cuomo; Parker behind the wheel of a vintage Bentley convertible; Parker at the helm of a Cigarette speedboat; Parker accepting a plaque at some bullshit awards dinner. On the side wall, hidden from casual view, were framed diplomas from college and law school, bearing the name Jerome S. Pincus. Savage nodded. It all made sense now.

Hell, the guy'd modified everything else.

The diminutive lawyer was almost lost behind the massive burlwood and gilt eighteenth-century French bombé desk. "We'd only found out about it shortly before you called," Pincus/Parker continued, glancing at Savage's NYPD business card. "We heard the story on WINS." He shook his head and frowned. "What happened, Savage?"

Another thing Savage had a problem with, since he'd been a kid, was being addressed by his last name. He and J. Sidney were not going to get on well. "Frankly, *Sid,* I was hoping *you* could shed some light on that very question," Savage answered, watching for the man's response to his intentionally probing, almost insinuating opener.

Parker showed his fangs. "What the hell are you inferring?"

Not a completely inappropriate reaction, Savage thought. "First of all, *I* imply—*you* infer. I'm not implying anything."

"I only know what the radio's saying," the lawyer declared. "Tony and three other people were shot in a bar sometime this morning. Two men and an unidentified woman—those three are all dead."

"Tell me about your relationship with Mr. DiLeo, if you don't mind."

"Tell you what?" Parker's arrogant tone matched his I-really-got-better-things-to-be-doing-than-talking-to-you-right-now glare.

"Whatever you know about him. And what might have prompted him to be in La Florentine's bar at one-thirty this morning."

Parker cocked his head condescendingly and gave Savage a sideways glance. "For starters, I consider Tony DiLeo a friend, an old friend, but I'm not his keeper. So I have no idea why he was in that bar last night. Maybe he was thirsty."

"DiLeo works for you, doesn't he?"

"That's true. Tony's done much of our surveillance work for years. He's got to be the best goddamned tail man in the world. The guy is phenomenal," Parker admitted. "I've been having my secretary call the hospital every hour for an update on his condition. They're no longer carrying him as critical. Is that right?"

Choosing not to hear the lawyer's question, Savage pressed on. "How many cases would you say he's currently working for you?"

"Right now? I'd guess at least five, six maybe. What about my quest—?"

"We've got reason to believe that Mr. DiLeo might have been working one of those cases last night."

"That's entirely possible." The lawyer's glance shifted about the room while he measured his words.

"We give Tony assignments, and when he's got something he gets back to us. He works on his own schedule, and when he's finished he turns in a complete report. But we neither ask for, nor do we get, a blow-by-blow."

"No pun intended, right, Counselor?"

The lawyer snickered lightly through a wry smile. "Surely you're not thinking that there's any connection between Tony's work and these murders?"

"We've tentatively identified the dead woman as Candace Mayhew. Does that name mean anything to you?"

Appropriately startled by the revelation, Parker's jaw went slack.

"Can I take that as a yes?" Savage asked.

J. Sidney nodded and pressed the button on his intercom. "Jean, bring me the *Mayhew* v. *Mayhew* folder." He turned back to Savage. "Harmon Mayhew is our client. Candace Mayhew is his wife's name."

"And can you also confirm that DiLeo was hired by your office to follow Candace Mayhew?"

Replying with a careful and reflective yes, Parker fell silent when his secretary entered. She handed him a case folder, nodded courteously to Savage, then turned and left the room.

"Why were you having Mrs. Mayhew followed?" Savage asked. He knew damn well why, he just needed to hear it for the record.

J. Sidney's suddenly jacked-up brow revealed ashen eyelids. Tanning-salon eye protectors had left him looking like a well-to-do urban racoon. "I think there may be a question of attorney-client privilege involved here, Sergeant," he said.

"Possibly," Savage responded. "But I'm sure you've been retained to represent Mr. Mayhew in a matrimonial matter. What I'm investigating here, Counselor, is a triple homicide."

"Harmon Mayhew suspected his wife was running around."

"Did he know with whom?"

"He had a name, yes."

"Just one guy?"

"Just one guy."

"I need that name, Counselor."

Pincus referred to his case folder. "A man named Cesare. Donald Cesare."

"What does Mr. Mayhew do?" Savage asked.

"*Do?*"

"For a living."

"Harmon Mayhew's in the rag trade. Has been all his adult life. He owns Mayhew Fashions, a women's sportswear manufacturing company down in the garment district. Their offices are on Thirty-sixth, off Seventh."

"Does he do well?"

"Well, let's just say he used to do a lot better. But . . ." the lawyer seemed to catch himself. "He makes a living."

"Is his business in financial trouble, Counselor? Is Mayhew in heavy debt?"

"I don't know that."

"Mmm-hmm. When did Mr. Mayhew first retain you in this matter?"

"Several months ago. Mid, late February."

"Did you put DiLeo on the case right away?"

"No."

"Why not?"

"Tony was busy working on other matters."

"All right then. When did you first assign DiLeo to go out on this case?"

"A few days ago."

This was like pulling teeth, Savage thought. "Why a few days ago?"

"Mayhew was going to be out of town. We figured it would be a good time to put a tail on her. If she was screwin' around, what better time to do it than when her husband was away? If Tony could get some pictures and other evidence, the case would be a wrap and we could move on to a quick settlement and disposition."

"Do you know of Harmon Mayhew's whereabouts at this time?"

Parker didn't immediately respond. He busied himself flipping through pages in the case folder, apparently buying thinking time. Then, standing, as if to dismiss Savage with a nonanswer, "He's out of town."

The fuse to Savage's sometimes powder-keg temper was already shortened by his crappy state of mind. He didn't have time for bullshit. Savage's face tightened; his eyes squinted into narrow slits.

"Counselor, I *really* get bent outta shape when I know I'm being jerked off. You're just not my type—so why don't you just let go of my joint." He stood, looming over the lawyer, and set his jaw for some additional cage-rattling. "We already *know* Mayhew's out of town. *Where* out of town is he? And *when* is he due back? That's what I need to know from you."

Parker cleared his throat. "Is my client a suspect?"

"Not yet, but he's gonna have to answer some questions."

J. Sidney caved. "Honduras," he said. "He's been on business down in Tegucigalpa all week."

"Tega-say-*who?*" Savage was certain he'd never heard that word before.

"Tay-goo-say-gal-puh," Parker enunciated slowly, with rediscovered condescension. "It's the capital city. He's got textile connections down there."

"Do you know when he'll be back? Or how he can be reached? At the very least, we need to make the notification of his wife's death."

Having also recovered his temporarily misplaced arrogance, Parker looked across the garish desk at Savage. "I understand your position, Sergeant. Understand mine. Go ahead and make your notification to Mr. Mayhew, and satisfy with him any peripheral or routine questions you may need answered. But, I'm putting you on notice, should it ever come to pass that

Harmon Mayhew begins to look even remotely like a suspect, you're to cease any questioning and notify me immediately. Do we understand one another?''

"You got it." Savage turned to leave, then in afterthought asked, "By the way, where's the Schlafly half of this outfit?"

"R. Hyman Schlafly died about two years ago."

Back in the department Ford, Savage cell-phoned the office. He had Eddie Brodigan put him through to Diane DeGennaro.

"I need you and Richie to get out to Newark Airport right away," he started. "American Airlines. Flight sixty-six. Arriving at four-twenty."

"American, flight sixty-six," she repeated slowly, presumably writing. "Four-twenty arrival, Newark."

Savage took a quick look at his watch. "If you saddle up right now, you'll make it in time to catch Harmon Mayhew coming through the arrivals gate, and you can give him the bad *or* good news about wifey-poo."

"We're on our way," she assured. "Oh, one other thing, boss. Got a call a little while ago from that friend of yours, Joe Ballantine, the reporter. Nice guy."

"Did he have a phone number for you?"

"Yes, he did. Gave me a name and number of a sister out on Long Island, a Meredith Conway. She's coming in to make an ID. Foregone conclusion though. Her sister Candace was married to Harmon Mayhew, and lived at 333 East Seventy-third."

"That's that, then," Savage observed with finality, then asked, "Did Joe go into his life's story with you?"

"Oh, yeah. He didn't leave out a thing. Told me how you and him go way back. Told me about his booze problem. And gave me his whole tale of woe about losing Candace Mayhew. Guy seemed pretty broken up, angry almost."

"Yeah," Savage said. "Hope the poor bastard doesn't fall off the wagon."

"Said he makes an AA meeting three times a week at some church on the East Side. Tuesday night, Thursday night, and Sunday afternoon. That ought to keep him dry. Don't you think?"

Savage grunted a verbal question mark in response, then asked Diane to put Jack Lindstrom on the line.

"What's doin', Jack?"

"Coupla things, boss. First off, I just got back from Parkchester. I did an initial background on the bartender."

"Hugh Aloysius Byrne?"

"Yeah. Looks pretty much like what we expected there, Thorn. The guy was your typical Bronx Irish Catholic. Quiet bachelor, never married, lived in a two-bedroom apartment with his eighty-five-year-old biddy mother; kept to himself. Small insurance policy, just enough to bury him. When he wasn't on the delivery side of a bar, he was usually on the receiving end, making merry with other BICs. Blah-blah-blah."

"I read ya. What else ya got?"

"This guy, Tony DiLeo, he must have a connection at Lourdes. His doctor, Greta Whatever, you know, the neurosurgeon you were telling me about. She called a little while ago, said he was gaining consciousness and that we could come over and try to talk to him. She also said she was so pleased with his condition that she was getting ready to have him moved out of ICU into a private room."

"Terrific. Listen, Jack, I'll swing by Bellevue and take care of the DiLeo interview myself. Right now I want you to start chasing down any insurance policies that Harmon Mayhew might hold on his wife. Also, find out anything you can about Mayhew Fashions, his clothing manufacturing company over on Thirty-sixth Street. I think this guy may be in deep financial shit."

Christine Maloney was hovering somewhere between damp afterglow and deep thought, the sweaty nape of her neck cradled comfortably by a thick down-filled pillow. Her right ankle and foot were somehow tangled amid the rumpled sheets but she made no move to free herself; she was still catching her breath.

Nothing could possibly compare to the ecstasy of being with another woman, Christine thought, as she turned her head slightly and stared at the sleeping figure of Nikki Rosen lying beside her. Nikki, of course, wasn't just any woman. She was special—the kind of woman who brought more than mere physical intimacy, the kind Christine knew she'd always wanted. Nikki had strength—mental, emotional, and supportive strength. An implacable I'm-gonna-get-what-I-want-out-of-this-world-no-matter-what strength that Christine easily identified with and admired. Nikki had brought all those wonderful qualities with her when she'd walked into Christine's outwardly enviable, yet inwardly empty, life five months ago. But, at the same time, Nikki Rosen was a woman of mystery.

Two weeks ago, as Nikki showered after they'd made love, Christine had slipped from the bed and gone to the kitchen for a drink. Searching the cabinets for a glass, she'd discovered another of her lover's purses. Thinking it an odd place to store a handbag, and struck suddenly with an overwhelming curiosity, she rifled through it at once. Inside a wallet, she uncovered Nikki Rosen's other life. The driver's license, with Nikki's photo, bore the name Nikita Relska, not Nikki Rosen, and showed an address on Ocean Avenue in Brooklyn, not Kew Gardens, Queens. Also, there were several photos of a man. A good-looking, silver-haired man. In one photo Nikki had her arms draped lovingly about him. Christine remembered her first impulse that day had been to confront Nikki, but she'd fought off the urge, thinking it wiser to wait for the right moment. She'd replaced the purse exactly as she found it, returned to the bedroom, and slipped back beneath the sheets as if nothing had happened.

Why Nikki had chosen to use an alias, or act as

though the Queens apartment they always met at was her real living quarters—the same nonperishable foods always in the same place in the fridge, no tampons in the medicine cabinet, no tchotchkes, come on!—probably had a great deal to do with the man in the pictures in Nikki's wallet. He was strong looking, and ruggedly handsome. Despite the disparaging things Nikki sometimes said about men in general, and the fact that she never once mentioned him, Nikki, Christine concluded, was obviously in love with the guy. At least their photos together suggested as much. Maybe he was her husband, or lover. If so, she was probably deceiving him. Maybe he was dead. Who knew? At that moment it made little difference, Christine thought. She would continue to suppress her jealousy. Nikki was there with *her*.

Throughout her adult life Christine had merely endured men. She had no real use for them. Men were scum. Other than riding Gerard's coattails to share in his political power and prominence, she had no use even for him—especially him. He was a hopeless womanizer. The world didn't know that, but she did. The world didn't know that she was the real power, and that without her to steer the course and keep his dumb ass out of trouble, Gerard's serial cheating would have sunk him twenty years ago.

She'd stopped sleeping with Gerard entirely sometime in the mid-nineties. Fact was, they never did much screwing from the beginning. She wasn't interested at all, and he was too interested elsewhere, fucking anything that walked. Although never suited sexually, they were a natural matchup of political ambition and will. With Gerard's Irish good looks and unerring charm, and her rabid determination and brains, it had always been a case of the whole exceeding the sum of the individual parts. No bimbo was *ever* going to break that up. She'd always tolerated the many brief dalliances he seemed to crave—after all, she was doing her own thing, too, albeit with somewhat greater discretion. But lengthy affairs, like the one he'd just had with the brunette from State, were an embarrassing no-no. The brazen bitch was now posted in the American consulate in Brazil. Christine broke into a sly smile, wishing she could've been a fly on the wall when the hook-nosed slut received her notice of transfer. If Gerard couldn't control his tom-cat prowling, then, as usual, she'd have to do it for him.

Although they'd always maintained, to a great degree, separate lives, nobody knew it. On the surface she was the devoted wife of Senator Gerard Maloney, and he was the hand-holding, older, adoring husband who escorted her to St. Patrick's on Easter Sundays. They were, as far as the press and public knew—despite some old, unsubstantiated rumors of her lesbian tendencies attributed to a former chauffeur—the classic, successful American couple. No one knew what went on in their lives just below the surface. No one—with the exception of Twyla—knew about the countless lipstick stains on his shirt collars down through the years, and on his BVDs. No one knew about his treatments for genital warts, herpes, and, at one point, gonorrhea. Gerard was a bastard, but if they played their cards right from this point on, together they would realize success beyond their wildest dreams. She'd been patient, she'd paid her dues, and she was going to be First Lady of the land. Who said there's no justice?

Nikki, on the other hand, was fascinating and deep, more competent than any man in *every* way. With Nikki, Christine Maloney shared not only her body, but her deepest and darkest secrets. Nikki had just seen her through this latest crisis. Nikki had fixed the unfixable, and Christine wasn't about to start asking questions about the man in the photo, or the other name and address. Not just yet. It might upset this very nice arrangement she'd finally found. Christine put her thoughts away, rolled over, and draped her arm around Nikki Rosen's thick shoulders and back.

As Nikki stirred at the gentle touch, Christine murmured into her ear, "I'm spent. Thank you."

Without turning her head, Nikki reached back and rested her hand on the smoothness of Christine's naked hip and thigh. Then, like raisins in raisin bread, kernels of Slavic overtones bled through her English as she asked, "Where does he think you are this afternoon?"

"I told him I was going to a NOW luncheon."

"Did he believe that?"

"Fuck him. Who cares?"

"Oh, I *love* when you talk dirty," Nikki joked, then rolled over to face her lover. "Do you not think he's finally caught on to us?"

"Of course. What's the difference? It doesn't change anything. He still needs me shilling for him, the asshole."

"I understand, but how does he deal with it?" Nikki pressed.

"Gerard had an abusive alcoholic mother and a philandering drunk of a father who couldn't have cared less. He learned as a child the value of lies and obfuscation—even to himself."

"Is he in denial?"

Christine rolled that one around for a minute, then shook her head. "No, it's not denial. Gerard just lacks any sense of shame. The man is insensible to disgrace."

"How much longer are you going to be able to stand him?"

"I've endured his male ego, and his whoring, for the last thirty years. I've played the supportive wife of the respected politician, now on the verge of running for the presidency of the United States. I gave up a thriving law practice to team up with him to get this far. Can I hang on until he becomes President Maloney? You bet your ass I can!" Christine looked deeply into Nikki's eyes, and added, "Thank you. Thank you for taking care of that stone in my shoe."

Nikki nodded.

Needing additional reassurance, Christine whispered fretfully, "You're sure it's all taken care of?"

"I told you, it is done. Stop worrying; the bitch will never bother you again."

"No more letters?"

"No more letters!"

Christine laid her head back into the cradle of the pillow, feeling more secure. Her worst nightmare was over, and she had only Nikki to thank for running off the boogeyman. "How can I ever repay you?" she whispered.

"Oh, I think I shall find a way." Nikki's words seemed to have an ominous ring.

Christine sat up again and stared into Nikki's suddenly stern eyes, eyes that seemed to be adding another element to her words. She felt an uneasy tightening in her stomach. Was it merely emphasis that Nikki was adding with her glare? Or . . . was she delivering a thinly veiled threat?

It was twenty minutes after three when Savage arrived back at Bellevue's west wing and became part of an elevator-cramming contest. Trying to stay skinny, but feeling like the twenty-fifth penny in a roll of fifty, he contended for personal space with fruit-basket-toting, flower-bearing visitors who must all have been cattle in a previous life—they just kept pushing in. Determined to keep his cool, his expression turned deadpan as a cluster of Get Well balloons bobbed lazily in his face. When the doors to the overloaded car finally closed to allow the painfully slow ascent, Savage knew he should have taken the goddamned stairs.

Serviced by eight elevators, Bellevue's U-shaped west wing also had an equal number of emergency stairways. As per fire and building codes, the stairwells were strategically located to allow for optimum evacuation of the floors between ground level and roof. Karis selected one at random. Between the second- and third-floor landings he intentionally tapped his ring against the utilitarian pipe handrail; he listened as the sound it made resonated throughout the stairway shaft like a sonar ping. This, he realized, was an eight-story echo chamber. Setting down the makeshift IV basket he carried, he slipped the chunk of fourteen karat from his left index finger. He dropped the ring into his pants pocket, and reached down to the basket for a pair of surgical gloves. He calmly blew into them one at a time and pulled them on, then wiped the basket's handle with his handkerchief. It was a good thing he'd decided to wear the SAS shoes with the soft soles. If it ever came down to it, he'd be able to keep his footfalls silent.

When the doors of the elevator finally opened onto Four-West, Savage wriggled free. Once in the hallway, he allowed himself to breathe again. Somebody in the corralled herd he'd just escaped had stunk like boiled cabbage, or worse. Annoyed, Thorn checked his suit for wrinkles, then set out to find Tony DiLeo's surgeon.

Dr. Greta Dresner was studying X rays inside a glass-partitioned space adjacent to the nurses' station. Stethoscope draped about her broad shoulders, tuning-fork prongs protruding from her jacket pocket, she nodded as Savage let himself in.

"I was just about to go and get Mr. DiLeo's family," the neurosurgeon said casually, her gaze again fixed on the one frontal and two profile skull shots backlit on the wide illuminated panel.

"Where are they?"

"In his room. Down the hall."

"Is he awake, alert?"

"He's been in and out the past two hours. But during one of the ins, he recognized his wife and daughter. He also realized he's been injured and that he's in a hospital. Most encouraging."

"That's great news. I'm very glad to hear it," Savage said, then schmoozed, "a tribute to the expertise of his fine surgeon, no doubt."

Dresner turned away from the fluorescent screen and faced him, a weak smile breaking through pursed lips. "Flattery will get you every-*vhere,* Sergeant."

"Think it'll get me into DiLeo's room, so I could ask a few questions?" Savage parried, a boyish grin on his face.

Her rare smile morphed into an amused grin. The doctor snapped up DiLeo's chart from the table beside her and moved for the door. "Come, we'll see. If he's awake, I'll let you in. If not, you can come back here with his wife and daughter while I explain these X rays to them. Then you will all better understand what's happened to this man. One picture is worth a thousand words. Isn't that right, Herr Sergeant?"

Four-West was a much different place than it had been earlier that morning. Visitors freely roamed the halls, and there were far more doctors, nurses, and orderlies about. Greta Dresner yielded to no one as she moved like a bulldozer down the center of the bustling corridor.

"Sure is busy," Savage said, smoothly sidestepping a linen cart piled high with soiled sheets and God knew what else. "You guys givin' something away up here?" he asked while timing his steps for the next obstacle, a white-haired volunteer making the rounds with a magazine cart just ahead on his right.

"You got here in the middle of shift change. That's why it's so crazy right now. Too damned many people."

Just after passing the magazine lady they stopped outside room 460. Anthony DiLeo's name had been Magic-Markered onto a cardboard ID sign taped to the wall next to the door. Dresner's name was also listed as the attending physician.

"I don't like the idea of that sign, Doc."

"Floor policy, Sergeant." Dresner shrugged.

"Not police policy." Savage stripped the sign from the wall, folded it, and put it in his pocket. "Some things it just don't pay to advertise."

"Wait out here, Sergeant." The annoyed surgeon pushed on the wide door. "I'll only be a few minutes."

Clasping his hands behind his back, Savage leaned his shoulders against the coolness of the masonry wall. He was determined to stay out of the hallway traffic, but enjoyed watching it as it passed. Directly opposite from where he stood, a hot-looking brunette nurse dashed out of room 459, carrying a bedpan—empty, he hoped. From what he could see, the photograph on her yellow-bordered ID tag didn't do Caroline Durante, RN, any justice at all. The scrubs beneath her bright red cardigan looked like they'd been custom-tailored the way they showed off her dynamite shape. *Whew!* Though she looked weary from the rigors of a long shift, the foxy mama zipped down the hall toward the nurses' station. She was probably finishing up last-minute stuff so she could finally go home. *Tough way to make a living.*

He returned the friendly smile of a young black nursing assistant carrying a stack of neatly folded fresh linens. No more than twenty-one, she was tall, lean, and rested looking; she must have just come on duty. She made a left at the end of the corridor and disappeared.

Savage ran his hands through his hair and squared the knot of his dark blue, pin-dotted tie. One way or the other, in a few moments he would once again be in the company of Gina McCormick. He hoped that her Irish surname was from a former, not current, marriage. She hadn't been wearing a ring, but, he thought, you never know. He ran the back of his hand along his chin, feeling for beard stubble. None. Good. He was ready.

He eased back into surreptitious people watching.

*   *   *

The name tag he'd pinned to his starched and neatly ironed white lab jacket identified him as F. METZGER, LABORATORY; Karis figured he could pass as a Metzger. Besides an additional pair of surgical gloves, the IV basket he carried rattled with Vacutainers filled with ersatz blood samples. He'd created them at home by mixing ketchup and water. To further enhance the prop's appearance of realism, he'd taken the time to stir in small amounts of A.1. Sauce to create varying shades of red in some of the capped vials. Hidden among the Vacutainers, cotton balls, and bandages was a 20cc syringe fully loaded with tea-colored doom juice.

The loose-fitting lab coat was ideal for concealing his shoulder-holstered Glock. And the Crown Royal pouch containing the fractured lead soldier was secure in one of its roomy patch pockets. This job was going to be a piece of cake, and when he finished here he'd head over to the Soldier Shop on Madison Avenue and take care of his other business.

His eyes clicked back and forth as he slipped from the stairwell into the Three-West corridor and mentally photographed the floor's layout. He needed to get some bearings and familiarize himself with the wing's room-numbering system. He turned to his left and walked the short distance to an intersecting hall. There, to his left, he found a comfortably decorated lounge occupied to capacity by pajama-clad patients and their chatty visitors. To his right began a long corridor of patient rooms, bisected at the midway point by the Three-West nurses' station. All the even-numbered rooms were on his right. He didn't have to walk very far. Three doors down he came upon room 360. With an abrupt about-face, he turned and marched directly back to the emergency stairwell.

Confidence-charged, infused with the controlled excitement he always felt when entering the danger zone, he boldly whistled Tchaikovsky's "Russian Dance" as he took the bare concrete stairs one level up to the fourth floor. Finding room 460 would now be a cinch.

SEVEN

Daydreaming about how life would be, living in the White House, and how she planned to redecorate it at taxpayer expense to suit her more modern tastes, Christine Maloney fastened the front hook of her lacy black bra, then reached for the styling brush on Nikki Rosen's dark walnut triple dresser.

"Do you want me to drive you back to Target to get your car?" Nikki asked. "Or, as usual, had you planned on taking a cab?"

"I'll grab a cab at the corner," Christine replied. "Please try to understand. It's just better if we're seen together as little as possible."

Resting atop the twisted snarl of pearl satin sheets, Nikki was propped comfortably against the tufted king headboard, her unabashed nakedness revealing her as merely a bottle blonde. Also revealed was her profound need for breast-reduction surgery, as well as a thick middle and Rubensesque, if not thunderous, thighs. With a concentrated exhale of the first deep drag on a Virginia Slim, she extinguished the match, then casually flipped the smoldering stick into a milk-glass ashtray on the nightstand beside her.

"I really hate to get down to the crass subject of money, *but* . . ." Nikki began, watching as Christine slipped into a pair of black silk panties. "I am going to need the balance, the other twenty-five. The agreement, you will recall, was half up front, the other half immediately upon completion."

"You're absolutely sure it's completed, and that there will be no further problems?"

"Yes," Nikki barked. "How many times must I tell you? She has been dealt with exactly as you directed, and now she is going to leave you alone. You will not have any further problems. Okay?"

"When do you need the money?"

"By tomorrow evening. When you have it, call me. And do not forget, Christine. Just like the last time, it must all be in cash."

"Cash?"

"Yes! Cash!" Nikki scolded, raising her brows and rolling her eyes. "What do you think, these people take American Express or Visa, or a personal fucking check?" In the semidarkened room, the cigarette's tip glowed bright orange neon as she sucked in another heavy hit of nicotine.

"All right," Christine said calmly, almost apologetically, wondering where Nikki's sudden hostile attitude had come from. Checking her slender profile in one of the two tall mirrors that hung above the triple dresser, she added, "It's not really a problem, I'll just cash in some more bonds. I'll have it for you tomorrow afternoon."

"Cash in some bonds! What are you, crazy?"

"No, I'm *not* crazy!" Christine allowed her tone to become indignant. "Where do you think I got the up-front money?"

"Where and how you came up with the up-front twenty-five does not matter. It is not relevant. It would be impossible for anyone to correlate *when* the deal was *made*. But, they certainly could correlate *when* it was *carried out*."

Christine did not respond. She stood in frowning silence, gnawing at a ragged thumbnail.

"Sweetheart," Nikki said soothingly, as she reached over to the nightstand and picked up the ashtray. "If you go cashing in stocks, or bonds, or tapping a savings or IRA account, you are leaving a paper trail. *If* for some reason an investigation ever came close to you—

and I assure you that one never will—a twenty-five thousand dollar withdrawal made by you immediately *after* the fact might be a little difficult to explain."

Pausing, as if to allow those sobering thoughts to sink in, Nikki slowly rolled the accumulated ash from the cigarette, then suggested, "Surely you have that much cash sitting around in a safe-deposit box."

Christine finished sculpting her tousled, short blond hair back into its boyishly waved style. As usual, Nikki was on the ball.

"You're right, of course," Christine said. "I'll get it from one of the safe-deposit boxes."

Karis slipped from the stairwell onto the fourth floor of the west wing and hung an immediate left. As he'd predicted, the layout was more or less a duplicate of the third floor that he'd just reconnoitered. Up ahead to his left, just like on the floor below, was a lounge where patients and visitors made quiet small talk. The moment of highest risk would be when he made the right at the upcoming blind corner. All things being equal, 460 should then be the third room in on the right.

With bold confidence seeping from every pore he made the turn and committed himself to the familiar-feeling long corridor, which again, like on the floor below, was bisected at the distant midpoint by a nurses' station. The hallway itself was an obstacle course of custodial carts, gurneys, portable X-ray machines, and scurrying humanity. With all this activity going on he would blend nicely. He set a direct course for the third patient room on the right.

Problem!

The square jaw in the steel blue single-breasted standing outside the room was no doctor. Karis swallowed a curse that corresponded with the momentary stall in his step. It was as if someone had shoved a steel bar into the front spokes of a wound-up Harley. He idled a moment to regain his poise, and switched the IV basket to his left hand in case he needed the nine.

The obstruction at the door to 460 was at least six-two. He was well turned out, and had an impressive, if not daunting, presence. His slightly receding straight brown hair was beginning to gray somewhat at the temples, and the lines that creased his intelligent-looking face bore the signature of world-class life experience.

Karis felt the man's probing glance. This, he thought, was a definite wave off. After only seconds of hesitation, he decided to continue down the hall as nonchalantly as possible. He had to get past the man and think this through. Nostrils flaring in frustration, and badly misaligned yellow molars grinding in anger beneath his hollow cheeks, he almost bowled over an old woman carrying an armful of magazines as he swept past room 460. He didn't look back. He didn't have to. He didn't need rearview mirrors to know that eyes were following him down the hall. He still felt them.

The man had exuded an animal magnetism with subtle undertones of controlled violence that women would probably love, but that only another graduate of hell could recognize. His athletic body had seemed relaxed, in an almost parade-rest position, but his head was on a swivel that had moved from left to right and back again, as thirsty gray eyes drank in everything that was going on around him. Man, that guy gave off intense vibrations, Karis thought. There's no way a son of a bitch with that kind of bearing could be anything other than a cop.

"Shit!"

He boarded an open elevator opposite the midway nurses' station and rode it to the third floor. If the police had put a full-time guard on that guy's room, he reasoned, the guard would have been in uniform—not in tailored pinstripes.

He would regroup, wait, and be back.

*   *   *

Savage saw that Dresner was not a happy camper when she emerged from DiLeo's room with the wife and daughter. Unexpectedly, the PI had drifted back into ga-ga land, and there was no way anyone could communicate with him, not then at least. If Savage had read the doctor correctly, she was uncertain whether DiLeo's sudden slump was due to lingering anesthesia withdrawal, or something more ominous. DiLeo had been in and out the last two hours, but now he was out. Very out. He could come to again at any minute, or, as Dresner had said, it could be hours.

Determined to question the man as soon as possible after he awakened, Savage decided to stick around. It wouldn't hurt to learn more about DiLeo's injuries, and maybe more about the spicy Italian dish who was his daughter. He followed the women back to the glassed-in X ray viewing room.

Gina smelled delicious. He couldn't identify the scent, but it suited her—sultry and provocative. Standing alongside her mother, she stared intently at the eerie radiographs of her father's skull that were clipped against the lighted screen, clearly absorbing every word of Dresner's forthright diagnosis and her less-than-happy prognosis.

When the neurosurgeon finally stopped her monologue long enough to take a breath, Gina broke in. "What kind of problems can we expect in the long term?"

"At the very least, your father will be left with the complications of Ménière's syndrome," Dresner responded.

"And they are?" Gina asked. Her mother remained silent beside her.

"They can be many and varied," the doctor began gently.

Savage watched the skillful way Dresner was handling DiLeo's worried family. He was impressed. Absent was the authoritarian delivery, replaced by an interesting mix of hard information blended with soothing empathy. He was beginning to like Brunhild. He wouldn't ask her out on a date, but she was growing on him as a person.

"Ménière's is a disorder of the labyrinth of the inner ear," the doctor continued. "Usual symptoms are tinnitus, heightened sensitivity to loud sounds, headache, vertigo . . ."

"Dizziness?" Gina queried.

"Yes, extreme dizziness." Dresner was emphatic about that.

Connie DiLeo broke her silence. "Can anything be done surgically?" she asked, her soft voice a plea.

Dresner replied, "At this point, we believe that everything that can be done has been done." Aiming the tip of her ballpoint at a tiny, clearly delineated white speck visible in the right profile shot, she continued. "To prevent the accumulation of inner-ear fluid in the endolymphatic sac, I've installed this shunt. Beyond that, sedatives may be required to help Mr. DiLeo sleep and rest. If the ringing in his ears becomes too disturbing at night, it may have to be masked."

"Masked?" Connie DiLeo whispered, her thick black-and-gray eyebrows scrunched together in question.

"Earphones," Dresner replied, putting on a smile as she glanced back and forth at both women. "Gentle music piped in through earphones can make sleeping easier for those with this disorder."

Nice try, Doc. It was very clear to Savage that Gina and company weren't biting on the doctor's attempt to inject some small degree of happy enthusiasm into them. He watched as mother and daughter turned and faced each other, their expressions those of quiet resignation. He knew that whether they liked it or not, or whether they were prepared for it or not, their lives had just turned a page, and they were in a whole new chapter. Things would never be the same for clan DiLeo.

A rap at the glass door broke the uneasy silence,

and Dresner nodded to a Korean in hospital whites who poked his head into the room and spoke.

"We're ready whenever you are, Doctor." The yellow-bordered photo ID tag clipped to the man's breast pocket identified him as Henry Park, neuroradiologist. The Korean was accompanied by a bulldog of an assistant who wheeled an empty gurney with MRI UNIT stenciled in bold, red letters across its gray aluminum frame.

"He's the only one in 460," Dresner told the man. "Wait for me; I'm coming with you." She turned toward the DiLeos. "We're taking him down for another MRI. He should be back in his room in about an hour." When the well-what-should-we-do-now? look appeared on the women's faces, Dresner was ready with a pat suggestion. Looking over her shoulder while holding the door, she added, "Why don't you go down to the cafeteria? Have some coffee, or a snack. Or let the sergeant here treat you ladies to a late lunch or an early dinner. I know you haven't eaten all day." She winked coyly at Savage, as if she'd read his mind. Then she barged down the hall toward room 460.

I'm likin' you more and more, Doc. As sleazy as it seemed, this might be his only chance to be around Gina in a more casual, slightly less stressful atmosphere. Of course, he would have much preferred to have met her under better circumstances, say, at a time and place where she was less preoccupied with grief, more receptive to friendly persuasion, *and* when her mommy wasn't around to run pass interference.

The timing certainly wasn't good, but he'd been on this planet long enough to know that opportunities to meet someone he found attractive were few and far between, especially for a discriminating and selective bastard like himself. This had all the earmarks of being one of those rare and fortuitous opportunities— he had to seize it. He heard his sometimes impure inner voice whispering *carpe bimbem*. It wasn't at all clear yet whether it was Gina's heart, or her petite-size panties—if she wore any—that his inner voice was telling him, no, screaming at him, to go after. Either way, Gina McCormick was no bimbo, but she was most certainly centered in his amorous crosshairs, and he wanted at least a chance to fire a salvo or two across her bow to see if there was any hope for future maneuvers. Damn, she was good lookin'.

As Gina and her equally petite mother stared blankly at the eerie pictures of Tony's skull, and rehashed the doctor's diagnostic tour de force, Savage allowed his gaze to follow Dresner, the Korean, and the bulldog as they made the long trek down the busy hallway. Half watching from the glassed-in enclosure as the trio committed to room 460, he saw something that registered a solid 2.5 on his what's-wrong-with-this-picture? seismograph. It wasn't totally earthshaking, but it was strong enough to bring about *bimbem interruptus.*

He'd heard this alarm go off in his head many times before, and he'd learned all too well to pay strict attention whenever and wherever it sounded. It was a street-cop thing, a hunch. Hunches were worthless as courtroom evidence, they didn't count as reasonable suspicion—but they sure counted on the street. Anyway, this was more than a bullshit hunch; it was the coming together of acute powers of observation and a well-honed survival instinct developed after decades of being a contestant in the sidewalk and back alley version of *You Bet Your Life.*

Savage's subconscious had signaled that important information was currently being processed, and for the rest of him to be on standby. He narrowed his thoughts to the scene he'd been watching when the hairs on the back of his neck had begun to rise. His cerebral VCR quickly ran replays and formed overlays for comparison.

Suddenly, there it was.

It was the same stutter step, performed by the same tubercular-lookin' guy, at exactly the same place—just outside room 460. And it wasn't the hesitation in the man's step alone that had caught Savage's attention. It was the "ah-shit!" quality of the hesitation, defined by the stifled frustration he'd read on the man's austere, if not spooky, countenance. The gawk with the IV basket had approached from the corridor's opposite end, and had just been about to enter 460 when he was cut off by the bulldog pushing the MRI gurney. The man had jammed on his brakes, reprised his unconscious stutter step, and looked *very* pissed off. For whatever reason the man had for wanting into 460, he'd been thwarted—*again*. This, Savage concluded, was a man with a plan.

The scenario Savage allowed himself to imagine seemed far-fetched, given his original belief that DiLeo had been nothing more than an innocent victim in the wrong place at the wrong time. But the guy seemed to have a narrow and specific interest in Tony DiLeo's room, and, Jesus, it wasn't terribly much of a stretch to say that he could fit Diane's description of this morning's shooter—tall, skinny, needs at least a size ten hat, ears like fuckin' Dumbo!

He brusquely brushed aside Gina McCormick's friendly invitation to join her and her mother for a bite. "Stay here," he snapped, and quickly slipped from the glass-walled room. He headed down the hall, his eyes fixed with tunnel vision on his enigmatic target.

"Never spook an unwary suspect" was a street cop's golden rule. Be standing firmly on his insteps and have him by the ears before he even realizes you're there. Otherwise, he thought, all sorts of shit could happen. Like foot chases, or drawn weapons, or hostage taking, or even worse. He did not want to let this guy see him prematurely. In fact he didn't want the man to see him at all until he was within arm's reach. Savage moved furtively among the flow of visitors and orderlies and nurses, drafting like a race car behind anyone who could shield him until the right moment. Ninety feet to go. If the guy *was* bad, and if the guy *did* make him, the proverbial contents of the bedpan could really fly around in this crowded setting. Another seventy-five feet.

He was still a good sixty feet away from where he needed to be when he lost his cover. The orderly he'd been in lockstep behind suddenly turned into a room, leaving Savage naked. It was too late—eye contact had been exchanged. The man's tiny little eyeballs had clicked with his in mutual recognition. *I know who you be—you know who I be.* Damn it all. The guy with the IV basket and the cheesy ID tag that didn't look quite like anybody else's—no yellow border— was alerted. He did a one-eighty, and fast-walked to the far end of the corridor where he made a left and disappeared. Savage broke into a run.

With almost the same agility he'd known as a Fordham halfback determined to reach touchdown city, Savage dodged and sidestepped his way past the unknowing and uncaring, who just seemed intent on getting in his way. *Fuckin' cattle.* He turned left at the blind corner just before the lounge, and scoped the full length of the eastbound corridor. The lab tech was gone, but the red door to the emergency stairwell beneath the EXIT sign, about thirty-five feet ahead on his right, had just clicked closed into its metal jamb. He had to go with it. He pulled the .38 Smith & Wesson Chief from his belly holster and made his move.

With no sound to guide him—like the patter of little feet he always liked to hear when chasing possible killers in stairwells that had blind turns at each landing—he went with the odds and cautiously headed down, measuring each step to silence his own leather soles. Any doubt that he'd opted incorrectly vanished when he came across the jettisoned IV basket just below the third-floor landing. Holding his breath, he stopped and listened.

Nothing.

With the .38 at high port in both hands he continued

down the winding stairway, stopping and peeping around each turn, very much aware of his complete vulnerability when on the stairs between landings. When he reached the end of the stairwell, the attenuator-controlled door at the bottom that opened to the hospital's lobby was still slowly closing.

Aware of the panic he could create by bursting into the hospital lobby with a gun in his hand, he held the two-inch-barreled revolver in his right-side jacket pocket, and stepped out into the open.

The lobby was packed, bustling with the energy of people moving with a purpose, but the man he was looking for was nowhere in view. Savage cast a quick eye into the gift shop, the cafeteria areas. Nothing. He looked toward the building's main entrance and saw the exodus of day-shift hospital employees heading out. *Shit, I hate foot chases. Especially in my best suit. This shit's for rookies.* Bolting across the wide lobby, he pushed his way to the front of a line and through one of the sluggish revolving doors.

The five wide lanes of one-way traffic speeding along First Avenue were already swelling with the late-afternoon uptown rush. It looked and sounded like an urban grand prix. But he saw his man bobbing and weaving in the middle of the avenue, adroitly dodging the hurtling taxis that would gladly whack him if he gave them half a chance. Savage offered a silent prayer, but it went unanswered—the rangy bastard made it across. Once on the opposite sidewalk, he continued running uptown, moving in the same direction as the traffic flow. Savage turned on the speed.

Dodging the same unstoppable and unforgiving onslaught of Hindu, Afghan, and Russian cabbies piloting their yellow dreadnoughts, as well as the added peril of homeward-bound suburbanites in their Lexuses, Saabs, and luxury four-wheel-drive SUVs, Savage barely made it to the avenue's other side without getting pancaked. It was now a pure footrace, and whether it was because of his superior speed or greater endurance, Savage saw that he was quickly closing. He had narrowed the gap to less than half a block and was gaining rapidly.

At the next corner, Big Ears darted back into the roadway and jerked open the driver's door of a red Ford Escort that had just pulled out of the hospital employees' parking garage. The car and its lone woman occupant had pulled to a stop, first in line, waiting for the red light to change. A silencer-lengthened pistol was now visible in the man's right hand as he reached into the Escort with his left. He pulled the car's shift lever up into park, then yanked the horrified driver out onto the pavement by her hair.

Thorn watched helplessly as it all went down. He knew that trying to squeeze one off from this distance was pointless. He was still too far away. He might have tried it on some country lane—but no way on First Avenue.

Startled and screaming, the frightened woman clutched tenaciously at the man's clothing as he pushed her to her knees. For some reason—probably shock—she just wouldn't let go. Then came the sickening spit sound as the man pointed the muffled weapon and fired two quick shots directly into her face. Her head rotated in a violent disconnected twist as if her neck were a Slinky. Slumping backward, the woman collapsed motionless at his feet.

Moving not with the long strides of a miler but with the shorter, faster strides of a sprinter, Savage was bearing down. The man glared up at him, hesitated, then aborted a reaching move to grab at something near the woman's feet. He hastily pointed his pistol in Savage's direction and fired two more shots, one of which Thorn heard slam into an aluminum stanchion that supported the corner lamppost he'd just passed. Savage held his fire—too many people—as the man slid behind the wheel of the Escort, stomped the gas pedal, and slammed the car into gear. The car sped away. At Thirty-fourth, it turned against a steady red and disappeared.

Savage stopped beside the limp body in the street.

The neat bullet hole in the woman's lower forehead, right between her eyes, looked like the bull's-eye on a dartboard. It was evenly ringed with first the black, then the blue, then the purplish bruising caused by the horrific trauma of the high-velocity round as it had crashed into her bone-backed soft tissue. There was another entrance wound at her right nostril. She was an attractive brunette in her thirties, and beneath her red wool sweater she wore green surgical scrubs. Savage quickly recognized her as Caroline Durante, the nurse he'd seen rushing around the fourth floor trying to close out her day and get home—maybe to her kids.

She was never going to make it home again.

As the inevitable crowd of onlookers began to accumulate, he pushed his .38 back into his holster and knelt beside her lifeless form; he looked into the wide-open green eyes that still mirrored terror. Clenched tightly in her right hand was a square of white cloth with torn stitching running along three of its sides. He didn't know if it was cotton or polyester, or maybe a cotton-poly blend. But he did know it was a patch pocket, torn from a lab coat. Then he noticed the purple pouch with the golden drawstrings that lay at her feet.

In the distance he heard approaching sirens. Radio cars? Ambulances? Fire trucks? Who the fuck knew? Who cared? It was too late anyhow. Too late for Caroline Durante, to be sure. The guilts were closing in. If only he'd acted, if only he'd been faster. If only . . . if only.

He reached down and gently closed Caroline Durante's eyes.

He felt like shit.

EIGHT

Harmon Mayhew never got off American flight 66 at Newark—never came through customs. No baggage. Nothing. Turned out there was good reason. He never got on the plane in the first place.

An American Airlines ticketing supervisor confirmed for Detectives DeGennaro and Marcus that Mayhew had made the originating flight out of Newark, through Miami, and on into Tegucigalpa seven days ago. Her computer also indicated that Mayhew hadn't checked any baggage for, boarded, or rescheduled today's return leg of his first-class, round-trip ticket. He was MIA.

Resting pudgy hands atop the chest-high ticket counter, Richie leaned forward and squinted at the thirty-fivish supervisor's name tag pinned above a pair of pneumatic 38DDs. "Ms. *Trotter*?" he asked genially. "Could you tell us the date those flights were booked?"

Diane caught the airline broad's lightning-quick scan of Richie's jewelry-free fingers.

Ms. Trotter, a saucy brunette in American's red, white, and blue uniform, smiled warmly at Marcus and tapped one button on the keyboard before her. "On the fourteenth, which would have been two weeks ago," she said breathily.

Diane bit at her lip to keep from puking. "Any record of who booked it?" she asked flatly.

"Well, let's see." Perfectly manicured acrylic fingernails clicked in a fuchsia blur across the terminal's keyboard, punching in codes for the information she sought. She hit the ENTER key and responded, "Five-Star Travel, 307 East Eighty-sixth Street, New York City."

A few minutes later she'd provided a complete printout of everything related to Mayhew's flight itinerary, including her own phone number. "Call me anytime. If you have any other questions, Detective Marcus," she purred.

What a thoughtful bimbo, Diane thought. Marcus and DeGennaro headed back to the parking garage in uncomfortable silence.

"Well, at least we know everything American knows," Richie said, his outstretched hand waiting for the fourteen dollars' change of the twenty he'd given the clerk at short-term parking. "We're gonna have to go through Communications Division to contact Honduran police, and maybe initiate a missing persons down there. Then we can contact U.S. Customs direct for any passport info they may have beyond Mayhew's arrival in Honduras last week. Who you wanna contact first?"

"Five-Star Travel," Diane replied without hesitation. "If they booked his flight, they probably also booked his hotel. Then, at least, we can tell Honduran authorities where Mayhew could, should, or would be."

"Coulda, shoulda, woulda," Marcus uttered, singsong, while pocketing his change and the airport parking receipt. After a self-conscious snort and clearing of his throat: "How come I didn't think of that?"

"Because I'm the brains of this outfit, Marcus, and I don't miss very much," Diane answered frostily. Then, switching to a partially teasing tone, she added, "And don't you ever forget it."

It was almost five o'clock. They were still in Jersey, and the late afternoon traffic going back through the tunnels into Manhattan was going to be horrific. She flipped open her cell phone and dialed the office. She'd have someone there look up Five-Star Travel and contact them before they closed.

"By the way," Diane said casually, while waiting for someone at the office to pick up. "I'm thinking of getting my nails done. Just like *Mizz* Trotter with the phony fuel-injected boobs."

Looking straight ahead at the highway, Richie snorted.

An around-the-clock uniformed-police presence had to be put in place at Tony DiLeo's hospital room—he'd have no more unwanted visitors. Nurse Caroline Durante's red Ford Escort had been found abandoned in front of Shu-Yu, a Szechwan joint on Third Avenue just above Twenty-third Street. Though Crime Scene was still going over the car with a fine-tooth comb, Savage knew that they'd never recover any of the shooter's prints—the guy had been wearing surgical gloves.

The syringe recovered from the IV basket abandoned in the hospital's emergency stairwell was found to be loaded with a mixture of pentobarbital sodium and phenytoin sodium—one to cause a deep anesthesia stage, the other to stop electrical activity in the heart. DiLeo was to have been silently and bloodlessly euthanized, the shit injected right through the port in his IV drip line. Brilliant. By the time his death could've been construed as unnatural, and the chemically induced cause established at autopsy, days might have passed, giving the big-eared fuck enough time to get to Zanzibar.

Diane DeGennaro and Richie Marcus had returned empty-handed from Newark, and Jack Lindstrom was still down at the lab where techs were trying to raise fingerprints from small wads of bubble wrap and pieces of a broken toy soldier. And, the worst, now there was yet another homicide to be listed on Manhattan South's grim scoreboard. It hadn't been a good day.

Adding to the mix was some unusual and heavy-handed pressure from downtown. Newly appointed First Deputy Commissioner Fiona Rice-Jenkins had twice called Assistant Chief Patrick Feeney—the Manhattan South borough commander—who was heading up the shooting investigation. An innocent civilian had been killed, and Savage, she had determined, had been involved in two prior shooting incidents—one in '75, another in '83. Feeney assured her that Savage's actions today were completely justified and well within department guidelines. He had convinced her, but word was she wasn't happy.

During the three-and-a-half-hour debriefing in the chief's office, Savage told and retold the story of the afternoon's events exactly as they'd happened. At 8:15 they finally let him go. It was 8:30 when he got home to 184 Sullivan Street.

The three-story brownstone was divided into three apartments—one on each floor. His was in the middle, one flight up. It was a one bedroom. When Savage let himself into the building he checked his mailbox in the vestibule. Nothing. Right on cue, in response to his unlocking of the inner door and the subsequent creak of its hinges, the shrill bark of Tor Johanssen's idiot Dalmatian erupted from the two-bedroom ground-floor unit. The maddening noise would probably go on for the next ten minutes. Talk about contract killings, he thought. He'd put a contract on that fuckin' dog in a minute, but he knew that Johanssen would go right out and get another one—one probably even more stupid and inbred than the one he currently owned.

"Fuckin' dog," he muttered bitterly, as he trudged up the wooden staircase to the second floor. "Fuckin' *Johanssen*," he muttered wrathfully, as he keyed the lower lock in the deep maroon door of apartment 2.

Inside, he reset the lock and slammed home the dead bolt, sealing out the world behind him. Physically and mentally drained by the events of the last eighteen hours, he'd had more than enough reality for one day. He'd spend whatever was left of it with a few cold ones. No, lots of cold ones. En route to the kitchen, he glanced for a split second at the PhoneMate. It sat beside the lamp on the oval end table next to his denim blue sofa. No messages.

Ray was half dozing in the meatloaf position atop the noisy Kelvinator as Thorn reached into it for his first brew. The cat's love affair with the old refrigerator went way back. He must have liked the way it vibrated, and been lulled by its steady hum. The scruffy tom blinked his huge amber eyes twice with his where-the-fuck-have-you-been? look, whipped his tail one time, and resumed his nap.

"Screw you," Savage muttered to the imperturbable cat, while staring into the cold whiteness of the open refrigerator. "Why don't you do something to earn your keep? Do something about that noisemaking shit machine downstairs." Ray didn't answer. After a moment of foggy deliberation, Savage decided against the sirloin he'd taken out of the freezer that morning to thaw; he was too hungry to wait an hour for a potato to bake in the oven, and he hated them done in a microwave. He dialed Angelo's on Eighth Street and ordered a pie. Half mushroom, half pepperoni. He liked them both, but Ray only went for pepperoni.

Twenty minutes after it was delivered, the mushroom half of the pizza, one of the pepperoni slices, and two Bud Lights were history.

Stripped to dark plaid JCPenney boxers, fresh ankle-length white socks, and a faded, well-worn New York Yankees tee, Thorn passed—fresh Bud in hand—from the dinette area into his overly large living room. He shuffled lazily along polished planks of old-fashioned, random-width hardwood flooring to the oak media center that broke up an otherwise long wall of exposed brick. Maureen had always liked how the gold-toned oak played off the timeworn, darkened brick—she said it was "country and warm." What the hell did he know? She was the one with great taste. At least she'd always said she was the one with great taste. He'd believed her, trusted her; he thought they were going somewhere.

It was Maureen who'd introduced the gleaming brass wall sconces and gilt-framed hunt scenes to the brick wall. It was Maureen who'd turned his stark bachelor digs into the warm, tasteful refuge it was now. Damn, how he missed her. God, how he needed her tonight.

He knelt before the media center, opened the lower cabinet doors, and perused his library of movie videos. There, filed between *The Day of the Jackal* and *The Godfather,* right where it belonged, was *Field of Dreams*. He set the dust cover into the space alongside the television and pushed the tape into the VCR. After taking a long pull on the frosty beer, he flopped heavily into the corner of his overstuffed chesterfield, whose lumpy cushions were beginning to fray at the piping. Ray claimed the sofa's other corner, his belly now full of pepperoni and Bud. The grizzled old tom stayed awake just long enough to paw the final remnants of mozzarella and suds from his battle-scarred face and whiskers, then curled up and drifted into his own field of dreams.

Field was Thorn's favorite film, and he sometimes reached for it—and possibly a beer—on days when his emotional circuit breakers verged on overload. The movie could transport him from the intensity of the city that he both loved and hated, and the sometimes psyche-crushing stresses of The Job. The story could take him off to the innocence of baseball, the soothing serenity of Iowan cornfields, and the enviable fantasy of a good man wholly backed by his woman, no matter the seeming foolishness of his endeavor. Despite the heavy scene where the lead character gets to play catch with his long dead, but briefly reincarnated, father, Savage found the movie compelling and uplifting. He was a half hour into it when the phone rang.

"Thorn?"

Stunned, yet lifted, by the familiar lilt of Maureen's gentle voice, he cleared his throat and uttered a simple, welcoming, "Hi."

"You busy?"

"No. Not at all," he said calmly, while rooting beneath the sofa's cushions, searching for the damned remote.

"How've you been?" she asked.

"Okay," he lied. "And you?" He found the remote on the sofa's graying armrest where he'd put it; he pointed it and the TV screen went black.

"All right," she answered, her voice strong and self-assured, but not gloating. After several long seconds of empty air, she added, "Thorn, I'm only a few blocks away. I was wondering, would it be okay if I stopped over for a few minutes?"

"Sure." *His* voice now strong and self-assured, but not gloating.

He went immediately into the bathroom and splashed cold water onto his face and brushed his teeth. There was no time to shave. He ran a deodorant stick under his arms and spritzed Polo on each side of his neck. He carefully brushed his hair, then put on the navy robe she'd bought for him back when things were good.

Karis rode the IRT number 2 train from Fulton Street, Manhattan, to Atlantic Avenue in Brooklyn. There, he changed to the Q train on the IND line. It was a slow local. The express didn't run after nine p.m.; it was now nine thirty-nine. His brooding anger hadn't diminished in the hours that'd passed since being forced to abandon one of his prized troopers in the middle of First Avenue. Although his facial expression and body language concealed it, inside, he seethed. Nobody'd ever seen his face before—not when he was doing a job—and lived to tell about it. Now there was one who had.

Seated, posture perfect, in the last seat at the rear of the car, Karis stared out at the sprawling lights of densely populated south Brooklyn as the train came to a jerking halt in the elevated station at Avenue U. His eyes shifted to watch three passengers, an old man with a cane and two younger women, rise from their seats and wait on the platform side until the car doors slid open. They got off. Nobody came on. The doors closed. He went back to his brooding.

Three more stops, four minutes per stop, and he'd be at the Brighton Beach station. He estimated a three-to-four-minute walk from there to the restaurant on Brighton Avenue. He'd have five minutes to spare to be on time for the ten o'clock meeting to which he'd been summoned. The train lurched forward. Next stop, Neck Road.

At four minutes to ten, Andy Karis let himself into the Little Odessa. Despite the hour, there were still a dozen patrons—some men, some couples—seated at cloth-covered, candlelit tables, dining on herring or Chicken Kiev, drinking Russian vodka, and speaking Russian. He nodded to Olga, the oxlike hostess-slash-cashier, whose coarse blond hair was twisted into a half-assed bun at the top of her pumpkin-shaped head. Her puffy, veinless right hand fondled the large nuggets of an amber necklace that fell across her massive chest, and she sat, legs crossed and ugly, on a stool behind the cashier's counter. The huge mole on her right cheek made her look, he thought, like Khrushchev in drag. Ugly Olga nodded back to him, then reached beneath the counter and pressed a button that would signal approval for his entry downstairs. He turned into a hallway at the rear of the dining room, walked beyond the rest rooms, and stood before a heavy metal door marked EMPLOYEES ONLY. He knew he was on camera. When the electronic latch mechanism released from the inside, he pushed the door open and stepped down onto a landing at the top of a steel stairway; it led down to a dimly lit basement. Without hesitation he descended the diamond-plate steps as the heavy door closed behind him and self-locked.

Much-needed light and loud balalaika music suddenly poured into the grottolike atmosphere of the darkened cellar as yet another steel-reinforced door swung wide. There, silver-haired Georgei Strelnikov greeted him with the lusty hug of a Russian bear.

"Andric Valentin. Tovarish! Come in, my friend, come in," Strelnikov said with great enthusiasm, Eastern European accents tingeing his English words. When the man relaxed his crushing embrace, he led Karis into the sanctum sanctorum of New York City's Russian mob.

Though considerably taller than his greeter, Karis knew that Strelnikov was easily twice as strong. Even at sixty, the man was a classic example of a Russian hard body. He'd never lifted a barbell in his life, but the short, hairy arms that bulged from his sleeves were like articulated iron bars, and his shoulders lumped from overdeveloped deltoids formed as a young man working the docks of Murmansk. Lifting heavy things came easy to Georgei. So did breaking people in half. He was Relska's primary bodyguard, undisputed underboss, and—despite a notoriously wandering eye—her longtime live-in lover.

"Gotti and the spaghetti-eaters had the Ravenite. But we, my friend, have the Little Odessa." Strelnikov leaned close to Karis and confided, "The only difference being that nobody will ever get a wire into these walls."

The melancholy strains of a three-stringed Russian lute emanated from the colorful Wurlitzer that lit the far corner of the thirty-by-forty fully carpeted space. There were, probably, twenty men in the cellar room, no women. Those not talking or drinking at the well-stocked bar, or shooting pool or watching, sat in small groups playing cards at one of the half dozen tables spaced throughout. The unfinished ceiling above, with its wild profusion of water pipes, heat ducts, and electrical conduit, looked like an Armenian road map.

Karis didn't speak. He followed Strelnikov through the comfortably decorated, albeit somewhat damp, cavern to a smaller back room with a desk, a sofa, and two upholstered chairs. Strelnikov closed the door. They were alone.

"Your exploits of early this morning and late this afternoon have been dominating the news," Strelnikov said. He sat in one of the upholstered chairs and motioned Karis to get comfortable in the other. His contagious smile now gone, he added sternly, "Needless to say, Relska is concerned about fallout that could come as result of second incident. It *was* somewhat messy. Do you not agree?"

Karis didn't respond, but struggled to control his anger at the insult.

"Do we have cause for concern, Andric?"

"No."

"How can you be so certain?" Strelnikov's ample eyebrows twisted into a doubting frown.

"Because I am certain," Karis snapped. "That is why." He did not appreciate having been summoned like a puppy for discipline.

"What of the man who lies in hospital?"

"He should have been left alone," Karis snapped again. "Relska's insistence that I finish him was not prudent, Georgei. He never would have been a problem, even if he . . ."

"But, Andric. If he is alive, then he can talk—no?"

"That man never saw my face. Of that I am sure. I would never have followed up on him except that Relska directed me to. He was as important as fly shit to this whole matter."

"I believe you are right." Strelnikov nodded contemplatively. "So much for that man. However, there remains the matter of the policeman who was chasing you when all that unpleasantness occurred outside Bellevue Hospital this afternoon. *He* saw your face. Did he not?"

"Perhaps," Karis hedged.

"And he could pick you out of lineup, no?"

"Is possible," Karis conceded.

"And he could give firsthand eyewitness testimony against you, no?"

Karis sat, stony and mute. He stared, unblinking, back into Strelnikov's probing eyes, reading the man.

"In short, Andric, Relska considers that to be a very strong possibility. That which could affect or compromise you, could have far-reaching complications for us all."

"I understand the concerns, Georgei."

"Good. I am glad you appreciate our delicate position."

Karis maintained tight eye contact with Strelnikov.

"News reports have described this policeman—Savage—as one of the highest-decorated cops in the city." Strelnikov's eyebrows lifted. "But he should pose no problem for you, Andric."

Karis barely nodded.

"Surely you see, if policeman is out of picture, critical eyewitness link is removed from chain that might eventually lead to us."

"Yes," Karis replied, still unblinking.

"If they lose their leverage on you, then we all sleep better at night. Is that not so, Andric?"

"Yes," Karis said evenly, wishing Strelnikov would get to the point.

"Therefore, Relska wants this matter attended to, but wants no further direct involvement on your part."

"What are you saying?" Karis asked, his face scrunched into a disbelieving question mark.

"Relska wishes you to take care of problem, but

you are to sub it out. You will not participate in its execution." Strelnikov paused, then added, "Make sure it appears as though he interrupted some crime, a street mugging perhaps."

"If you require me to sub it out, then it will not at all be in my hands," Karis responded in emotionless monotone. "And therefore, it will not succeed."

"That is defeatist attitude."

"I have observed this man, Georgei. He is like us. A survivor. His elimination cannot be placed in the hands of lackeys."

"There will be no further discussion on that point. Do as you are told, Andric."

"I will make the necessary arrangements, but I cannot understand Relska's rationale."

"Simple. If there are any witnesses to the policeman's demise, no one will be able to place you there. It will look like totally unrelated happenstance. Then the trail that leads to us will be gone and forgotten."

Karis nodded coldly.

"Wonderful," Strelnikov bellowed, as he rose from his deep chair and poured hundred-proof Stoli into two iceless glasses. "So, to other matters. We slipped you into Honduras last week, Andric. We trust that trip was successful?"

"Totally," Karis announced, quickly downing the vodka. The meeting was over, and Strelnikov's message had been clear. The policeman's link would be removed from the chain—or Andrew Karis would be.

When Thorn opened his door, they stood in awkward silence, staring expressionlessly at one another. Maureen was gorgeous, no doubt about it, and it was all he could do to resist the urge to squeeze her in a crushing embrace, but he pumped the brakes. Her soft, babylike red hair was brushed to the side in that sultry style that he liked, and she was wearing the large gold hoops he'd given her on Valentine's Day two years ago. Dressed in snug, attribute-defining jeans, and a gauzy linen Liz Big Shirt that draped loosely over a matching tan knitted shell, she finally asked, "May I come in?"

"Of course," he replied, snapped from his gazing spell. "Come in. Yes." He stood aside holding the door as she took several tentative steps past him into the apartment. He couldn't help but be reminded as she slipped by that he was definitely a leg-and-ass man. If ever there were to be an Olympic event for such talents, Maureen would surely take the gold.

"You know," he said, puzzled, "I never heard you come in downstairs. How come that friggin' Dalmatian don't bark when you come in?"

"You know she only ever barks at you, Thorn. You ought to be honored. She must think you're some-one special."

Well, at least some female does, he thought. "Can I get you something? A drink?" he asked.

"No, nothing thanks."

Savage could tell by the flatness of her response and the impassive look on her carefully made-up face that she was here on a mission—a mission he was probably not going to like. Making small talk, he went on about Johanssen's spotted pain in the ass. "Why bother hav-ing a watchdog that only barks at the cop who lives upstairs? It just don't make sense."

"Gee, Thorn. Give the guy a break for crying out loud," Maureen chided sharply. "It's common knowl-edge that he's got an apartment full of museum-quality art down there. He's gotta have security."

"Security," he grunted facetiously. "His apartment's got some kind of heavy-duty metal front door—with solid steel jambs—that you'd need a damn bulldozer to knock down. He's got every one of his windows barred like Fort Knox. God forbid he ever had a fire. He'd never get out of there for crissakes."

"Knowing Johanssen, he probably wouldn't want to," Maureen countered. "His collection is all he lives for. He's got a Picasso and a Goya, and God knows what else. Some of those paintings are worth a fortune."

"Yeah, right," Thorn reluctantly conceded. He hoped she'd change the subject.

"I see you're eating well," she remarked dryly, checking out the oil-stained pizza carton still atop the dinette table, and the cluster of crushed Bud cans that crowned the kitchen trash basket. "Pepperoni and mushroom?" she asked knowingly.

"Half and half," he acknowledged, through a strained smile that a condemned man acting bravely might wear.

"Ray get his share?" she asked with a broadening smile, perhaps to lighten the heavy mood.

He opened his palms and gave her an are-you-kidding? look. Then he saw the keys she was clutching. Now he knew the purpose of her mission. He recognized them as she laid them on the table next to the dinner debris. One of the keys was for the downstairs entrance door, the others opened the locks to his apartment.

"I didn't want you to think I'd forgotten to return your keys." Her voice, still self-assured and not at all gloating, was matter-of-fact. He'd returned her keys the night they'd broken up six weeks ago.

Thorn nodded, tongue-tied. His mind surged with emotions. He couldn't think of anything to say.

She moved to the couch, leaned over, and stroked the top of Ray's head. The unconscious cat never moved. Maureen turned and looked at Thorn, and he gazed back into her beautiful blue green gray, deep-set, always mysterious eyes. The eyes he'd stared into countless times, in countless moments of incredible passion. Passion like he'd never known before. Passion, he was sure, he'd never know again.

"Are you seeing someone else?" he asked, not really wanting to know.

"No," she exclaimed casually, avoiding his glance. He'd never known her to lie, but this time he was sure that her no should have been a yes. Maureen never did anything without a plan. But the lie was probably meant to spare him.

"Would you consider trying again?" he blurted out. "I miss you terribly." It was his heart talking. His head was on a Bud break.

"You don't want me back, Thorn. I'm not the same person I was. There's just been too much water under the bridge, as they say."

"You're not the same person you were?" he said, incredulous.

"That's right."

"Who are you now?" he shot back. "Person number three?"

"What do you mean by that?"

"Let me tell you a little story. Six years ago, I met someone. She pursued me and pursued me. She was thoughtful and caring, and never put what was good for *her* first—she put what was good for *us* first. It took me awhile to feel secure, and believe that she was for real. But I eventually did, and fell totally in love with that person. I thought I was going to spend the rest of my life with her. There was nothing I wouldn't do for her. There was nothing I wouldn't try to get for her. But, it seemed, once I'd fallen and committed, that person started to become someone else. Somehow her agenda changed. She became negative, judgmental, faultfinding, and hyper-opinionated about almost everybody and everything. And she developed an incredibly short memory."

"What is it you want, a woman who doesn't have opinions?"

"No. I want a woman who doesn't have them all."

"The lady in your story never changed, Thorn."

"Yes, she did!" he shot back. "Maybe she didn't realize it, but she did. She gave less thought to what was good for us and our relationship, and began considering only what she considered good for her, and her wants. She reverted to being a singular thinker.

Singular thinking by either partner dooms any relationship. The sad part is that she's intelligent enough
to know that. So I have no choice but to conclude
that she knowingly and consciously destroyed us."

"That's not true."

He made a yeah-right face and charged on. "She
wasted a lot of my emotions, a lot of my effort, and
a lot of my money; but most important, she wasted
my most precious commodity—*my fucking time*. Six
years of my fucking time." His frustration and pent-
up disappointment kept fueling his anger. He had to
vent. "Why didn't she just show me who she really
was right from the get-go? We could have spared each
other all this bullshit. Jesus." Thorn exhaled hard.
"God knows who the hell person number three is
gonna be."

"Why did you stick around, then?" she snapped.
"And what's all this crap about wanting to try again?"
Now Maureen's voice had an edge.

"I stuck around hoping that the changes were an
aberration. I kept hoping the person I fell in love with
would miraculously reappear. What an asshole I was.
But now you tell me she's become person number
three. You're right, Maureen—I don't want number
three back, or number two. I've only ever been interested in lady number one."

"Well," she whispered nervously but positively.
"I've gotta be going. I've got lots to do at home."

He stared into Maureen's eyes, studying them, hoping to see a shred of the love that was once there. He
didn't see it. "I understand," he said softly, passively,
his anger muted now, his heart imploding. He walked
with her to the door, placed his right hand on the
back of her head, stroked her soft hair twice, and
whispered, "Good night, Maureen," knowing he was
saying good-bye.

He watched her descend the long, narrow staircase.
He heard the telltale squeak of the front-door hinge
as she let herself out without looking back. He waited

a minute, then quietly closed his door and set the dead bolt.

He collapsed, almost invertebrate, into the same corner of the couch he'd left only minutes ago. An hour ticked by as his mind swirled with anger and doubt, pain and relief, resignation and regret. There was no way he could make things right with Maureen. Only she could do that. There was no way he could make her love him again. Love had to happen naturally if it was ever to work. There was no way to reincarnate what had once been. He had to face it. He had to be strong. He had to let go.

He still loved her.

With a sigh that originated from the marrow of his soul, he aimed and clicked the remote. He tried to drift back into *Field of Dreams,* tried picking up the story right where it'd left off. When the Ray Kinsella character was given a second chance to make things right with his briefly reincarnated father—by playing the game of catch he'd selfishly declined to do as a boy—the sadness and sentimentality of the scene seemed far more poignant and throat-lumping than it ever had before.

The whipsawed lacerations to his psyche began to hemorrhage. He clicked off the remote and heard only the loud hum of the old Kelvinator coming from the kitchen. With the heels of burly palms, Thorn squeezed away the dampness brimming in his eyes.

NINE

"NURSE DIES IN POLICE GUN BATTLE"
Savage gazed at the forty-eight point headline of the morning *Post* that lay folded on his desk. Ringed with coffee stains, a photograph of the scene in front of Bellevue—with his picture and Caroline Durante's in separate insets—took up half the front page. The multicolumned article that ran with it correctly tied the incident to the La Florentine bloodbath from the morning before, and, for the first time, published all the names of those four victims. Based on the phone number called in to Detective DeGennaro by Joe Ballantine, and her subsequent locating of the Mayhew woman's older sister, Meredith, a positive ID had been made. A next of kin having been notified, Candace Mayhew's name had been released to the press.

After defeating the annoying childproof cap, Savage shook three tablets from a Bayer bottle and popped them into his mouth. He washed them down with a gulp of his third coffee and slipped the aspirin back into his desk drawer. The Budweisers hadn't provided the desired anesthetic effect, so around midnight he'd boosted the octane with a monster Rusty Nail, a mix of one-third Drambuie and two-thirds Glenfiddich over ice in a really big snifter. It must have been a triple. He was paying for it now—the "Anvil Chorus" was playing in his head with lots of reverb. He wondered if he looked as bad as he felt.

"Boy, you don't look so hot this morning, boss," Richie Marcus declared, sticking his head into the sergeants' room. "Tough night?"

"Yeah, you might say that." So much for trying to mask his appearance.

"Hey, listen!" Marcus insisted. "You had a tough day."

"So, anything to report, Rich?"

"Well, the Hotel Honduras Maya tells us that Harmon Mayhew checked in on the twenty-first and was booked there until yesterday morning, the twenty-eighth. They claim that nobody's seen him, however, since the afternoon of the twenty-third."

"He didn't check out yesterday?"

"Nope. They said all his shit's still in the room."

"How can they be so certain that he hasn't been seen since the twenty-third?"

"That's the last time he used room service, and the last time housekeeping had to make his bed."

"Is the hotel not concerned about that? You know, like a guy checks in, and then takes a powder—leaving the meter running. Who's gonna pay the bill?"

"I asked them that. They say those things happen. Tourists go off on side trips and wind up overstaying their bookings. They've got Mayhew's American Express number on file—the additional time'll be charged accordingly. They don't give a fuck."

"What about Customs?"

"Just got off the phone with them. They got no record of Harmon Mayhew reentering the States. According to the travel agency he was due back yesterday. That jibes with what his lawyer told you."

Savage gently rubbed his temples. It hurt too much to talk.

"Diane forwarded a request, through Correspondence, to the Honduran police down in Tega-whatever-the-fuck, asking them to follow up on a possible missing persons."

"Anything back?"

"Not yet, but it's probably only about seven in the

mornin' down there. We're gonna start looking for something back from them by midafternoon."

"Ten-four," Savage said, popping an emergency Wint-O-Green to help kill the cottony, morning-after taste in his mouth.

As Marcus turned to leave, Eddie Brodigan poked his head in the office. "Pick up line six, boss."

"This is Savage."

"Sergeant. This is Gina McCormick."

"Hello, Ms. McCormick. How's your father doing today?"

"Thanks to you, Sergeant, he's doing just fine."

Savage didn't respond.

"My mother and I, and my dad, all wish to convey our sincere gratitude for your actions yesterday. If you hadn't been there, and been so much on the ball, my dad would probably be . . ." Her sentence trailed off. "We don't know how we'll ever find a way to adequately thank you."

"No thank-yous are necessary, Ms. McCormick. I was only doing my job." God, how his head hurt.

"I didn't know what to think when you burst out of the room on us yesterday. How did you know that man was after my father?"

"I didn't know. Not for sure, anyway."

"But you made your move. And it saved my dad's life."

"Well, I guess it did. We were able to save one life, but . . ." Savage paused, lost momentarily in a recurring vision of Caroline Durante's life-drained face. "I'm afraid we lost another."

"I know," Gina sympathized. "We've been praying for her and her poor family. You can't blame yourself for that terrible turn of events. You had no control over that man's actions."

"I know what you're saying, ma'am," he agreed, with hesitant conviction.

"When you acted to save my father's life, you had no idea that you wouldn't lose your own. I'll bet that you never even gave that possibility a thought. You're a very brave man. And again, our family is eternally indebted to you."

"Thank you, ma'am." Funny, he thought, as he hung up the phone, how yesterday he'd have given anything to have Gina McCormick somehow in his debt. Today it had little significance. In addition to the hangover from the booze, the guilt about Caroline Durante was eating him up. This was going to be a very long day. He had to find an excuse to get himself out of the office. He wanted to be alone. If the team needed him for anything, they could reach him on his cell phone.

Looking but not seeing, listening but not hearing, Christine Maloney sat in stunned silence as her husband ranted and raved.

"Jeezus, Mary, and goddamned blessed Joseph. There it is in black and white, you power-crazy bitch!" Gerard Maloney snarled the words, saliva flying, as he repeatedly stabbed his middle finger at the pages of the morning newspaper that lay strewn across the dining room table.

"Who do you think you're talking to?" Christine demanded. She'd never seen Gerard become this unglued.

"Candace Mayhew is dead—murdered," he continued angrily. "She was shot down like a dog. So was her goddamned boyfriend, that Cesare character."

Christine snatched up the front pages and quickly scanned the multiple-murder story that police had tied to yesterday's shooting of a nurse. It was an error, she thought—it *had* to be wrong. Nikki wouldn't do this to her. Christine's heart thumped in her chest as the enormity of it all, and the realization of her possible complicity—no matter how indirect—hammered home.

Gerard pressed on. " 'Don't worry about it,' she says. 'I've seen to it,' she says. 'Just get on with your goddamned campaign,' she says. What she *didn't* say

was, 'I've entered into a conspiracy to commit *god-damned* murder—multiple goddamned murder.'"
Frustrated, he grasped at his white mane with both hands and blurted, *"What the fuck have you done, Christine?!"* Then he buried his face in his hands.

Christine could see that Gerard was overwhelmed. Stunned and groping, lost in a state of surreal disbelief, he was riddled with galloping fear. He might even go off the deep end, she thought. He never used the F word.

"I had no idea this was going to happen," Christine said smoothly, her voice barely hinting at contrition. "You must believe me, Gerard." She studied him, watching for his reaction.

He raised his head from his hands and snarled, "Don't tell me that."

"It wasn't supposed to be this way," she snapped.

"Oh, yeah. How was it supposed to be?"

"They were only supposed to be threatened. They were only supposed to believe that if they continued to blackmail us, that we could see them and raise them one. We were putting the fear of the mob into them."

"Fear of the *mob* into them? *Shit,* it wasn't mob fear that was put into them—*it was fucking mob bullets, dammit!*"

"Yes. But I didn't know. I thought that they were only to be intimidated, roughed up even, if necessary. Gerard, I didn't mean for *this* to happen. Why won't you believe me?"

"Believe you?" Gerard whined. "How in hell can I believe you? You've always had your own god-damned agenda."

"Please try." Christine reached across the dining table and placed her hand on her husband's wrist. "I may be a lot of things, but I'm not a murderer."

He pulled his hand away. "Tell me everything, right down to the last goddamned detail. Don't leave anything out, Christine. If there's any way that we can defend against this, I've got to know all of it."

Christine took a deep breath, bit her lip, and exhaled a long, slow sigh. "Do you remember the party at the Plaza, back in early December, the one that was organized to test the waters on support for your candidacy?"

"Yes. I remember."

"I met someone there."

"Oh, really?" Maloney snarled. "Someone you wound up sleeping with?"

"Gerard!"

"Who is he?" Maloney demanded. "Or *was* it a he? After all, I'm not totally unfamiliar with your bedroom proclivities."

"Her name is Nikki Rosen."

"*Uh-huh.* Figures!" Maloney uttered, nostrils flaring. "Is this *Nikki Rosen* involved with the party organization?"

"No. As a matter of fact, she cares little about politics."

"What did she have, a nice ass?"

"Where's Twyla?" Christine calmly changed the subject. "I could use some coffee."

"Under the circumstances, I had to give her the goddamned day off. You didn't ans—"

"Coffee would help clear my head."

"Make it yourself for crissakes!" Maloney barked. "Tell me more about this Nikki Rosen woman."

"We've been . . . staying in touch for about five months. She's very interesting, and *very persuasive*. By the way, do you know any other expletive besides *goddamned*?"

"How long did it take for her to talk you out of your panties? Or was it you who talked her out of hers?"

Again ignoring that line of questioning, Christine continued on her own track. "I was assured she could take care of this problem, Gerard. I trusted her. She said there was absolutely no risk."

"Was she that top-heavy bleached blonde you introduced me to? She didn't look like a dyke."

"That's no way to talk, Gerard."

"Jesus, Christine. That goddamned broad was built like a linebacker. She was a sow. What the hell was the attraction? What the hell *is* the attraction?"

"I think we should line up some legal representation," Christine mused aloud.

"This Nikki Rosen. She's behind the whole damn thing?"

"Well, yes. She's extremely perceptive, Gerard. When we first got that letter two weeks ago, she was immediately aware that I was depressed about something."

"And?"

"I wound up confiding to her about us being blackmailed."

"*Really?* That's just great, Christine," Maloney fumed. "Did you tell her about the land-condemnation deals in Flushing, and the parking-meter scandals that caused Ronny Mankiewitz to kill himself, and all the other shit that Candace was using against me?"

She could see by the purple coloring infusing Gerard's face that his blood pressure was rocketing.

"No. I never told her why you were being blackmailed, and believe it or not, she never asked. In fact, she didn't even want to know."

"She never asked?" Maloney seemed to ponder that for a moment before continuing. "Then what happened?"

"She said she could take care of it. She said it was no problem. She said she had connections who could scare the shit out of those bastards, and make them leave us alone."

"What was in it for her?"

"Nothing. She was doing it as a friend."

"A friend, my ass." Maloney shook his head, and spit out the next sentence. "Nobody—and I mean nobody, Christine—does *sumpthin' for nuthin'*. You, of all people, should know that."

"Please, Gerard."

"You mean she was going to do all this out of the goodness of her heart?"

"Yes, she was."

"Ain't love grand?" Maloney said with a scowl.

Ignoring the sarcastic dig, Christine continued, "But it did cost money."

"How much money?"

"Fifty thousand. Of which we still owe twenty-five."

"We?"

"Yes! *We,* dammit."

"You mean to tell me she had all these people murdered for a lousy fifty thousand dollars?"

"Yes! I mean . . . I guess. I don't know." Christine braced herself for composure. "As far as I knew, the money was only to be used to pay someone to scare that Candace bitch off. Not kill her."

"This thing has snowballed, Christine. It would be bad enough if it just involved Candace and her greasy boy toy. But now there's a dead bartender, a dead nurse, and some other poor bastard who's been critically injured. And every nerve in my body is telling me that you've been led down the garden path by someone with diabolical motives. How the hell did you allow yourself to be suckered in this way?"

She didn't know how she'd been suckered in, but she was going to deal with it. She looked at Gerard, surprised to see his patrician poise on the ropes. She had never seen him so afraid.

"I can't believe this is happening, Christine."

"Well, you better start believing it. It's been done, and there's not a damn thing we can do about it. Stop sniveling."

"When was the last time you saw Nikki Rosen?"

"Yesterday. But I'm meeting her tonight with the balance due. I'm going to pull the cash out of one of our safe-deposit boxes this afternoon."

"The hell you are!" Gerard leaned back in his chair and crossed his arms contemplatively in front of his barrel chest. "Forget that. Under no circumstances are you to meet with her, or go bringing her a goddamned bag full of money. All ties with her must be completely severed. *All ties*. From this point on, it's as if she never existed." He tightened his stare into Christine's eyes. "Do you understand me?"

"All right," Christine said with a smirk. "But that's a mistake, Gerard. A big mistake."

"God," he muttered, "I don't know how we're gonna get through this one."

"Forget God. God hasn't got a blessed thing to do with it. We'll do what we've always done, Gerard. We'll throw the wagons in a circle, and clam up. If we're ever to be implicated, then let's not give anyone *any* ammunition to use against us. *We know nothing!* Okay? And, if you're determined to fear something or somebody, don't let it be the police, or the press, or public opinion. The one we need to be concerned about is Nikki Rosen."

"Yeah, okay. But one more thing. I'm not going to enter this goddamned race. I'll call a press conference for Saturday morning to make the announcement that I've decided not to run."

Christine gaped in stark disbelief. "You're going to back out after all this? When you've got a lock on the election? Gerard, you can't be serious. Why?"

"Why? Jesus, Christine. If you go to a restaurant and the appetizer is shit, and then the soup is shit, and then the entrée is shit—there's no reason not to expect that the dessert is going to be anything other than shit. No more shit. I'm full!"

"Gerard, I agree. You are full of shit."

Diane DeGennaro acknowledged Brodigan's three-fingered wave from the wheel desk and picked up line 3. "This is Detective DeGennaro. How can I help you?"

"Detective. This is Armando Orespé. I am commandanté and senior investigator of the Honduran Police Barracks in Tegucigalpa, Honduras. I am responding to your agency's inquiry regarding a Señor Harmon Mayhew, a U.S. citizen."

"Yes sir, Commandanté," Diane replied, surprised at the man's impeccable English. "I must admit, I didn't expect that you'd telephone us direct. Whenever long distances are involved, we're required to go through our department's Correspondence Unit. It's good of you to get right back to us."

"If we should get cut off, Detective, be assured that a complete report is being forwarded to your agency by our Investigations Detachment."

"What does the report say, Commandanté?"

"Señor Mayhew is dead. His body was found in a ditch in one of our outlying rural areas on the twenty-sixth. Though the area is somewhat outside Teguci-galpa, all criminal investigations still fall under our authority, ours being an agency of the state, not of the city, you understand."

"How have you determined that the body is, in fact, that of Harmon Mayhew? Did he have identification on him?"

"No. There was no identification on the body. But by using the information contained in your inquiry, we contacted the Hotel Honduras Maya and had positive identification made by a chambermaid and a desk clerk. A search of his room at the hotel then turned up his United States passport with his photograph. This is your man, Detective."

"How was he killed, sir?"

"Garrote. His head was nearly severed. We're sure the weapon was a piano wire discovered not far from the scene. Señor Mayhew had been dead about three days when he was found. His body was moved to the holding morgue in the city, where he was carried as an unidentified Caucasian until your inquiry helped us make the connection."

"Do you have any leads in the case, Commandanté? Was there any additional evidence recovered at the scene?"

"None, Detective. But I must tell you, this is surely the first case of murder by garrote that I can remember."

"What do you think all this suggests about the killer, Commandanté?" Diane had already formulated her conclusion, she just wanted to hear Orespé second it.

"A professional, Detective. Someone very skilled in the art of taking life. And surely not someone from here."

A homemade security buzzer sounded throughout the cluttered store when Savage let himself into the Fox Hole on Christopher Street, just off Hudson. The irritating shrillness of the half-assed alarm continued until the sluggish door closed completely behind him.

The shop was loaded with wartime memorabilia—army surplus, uniforms, sabers, flags of all nations, photographs, canteens, insignias, helmets, the whole nine yards. It was one of the five businesses he'd found in the Manhattan phone directory under the listing: Toys—Soldiers. He'd already visited Duncan's down on Leroy Street, but their resident toy-soldier guru was off on vacation and wouldn't be back until Monday next. New York City never ceased to amaze Savage—there probably weren't five such specialized listings in any other phone book in the world.

An angular man in his early fifties, with a large, neurotically waxed and groomed salt-and-pepper handlebar mustache and dark, piercing, battle-balmy eyes, emerged from the shop's back room. The name DAWSON was stenciled on his sleeveless camo shirt, and the green beret on his shaved head was pulled down smartly to the right side of his face. Combat pants were bloused into spit-shined jump boots, and three large hoops of gold dangled from his pierced right earlobe. Savage whistled silently beneath his breath while taking in the vision of this New Age G.I. Joe.

"If you're into *mil-i-tary,* you've come to the right

place," the man sung out boldly, giving himself away immediately as G.I. Josephine.

This guy was a Green Beret like I was a fucking astronaut, Savage thought. Maybe in the Oscar Wilde detachment of the Key West Brigade, but not in the Green Berets he knew. But then again, he reminded himself, this *was* Greenwich Village. Even the sign above the custom closet-design shop he'd just parked in front of next door had read, THE CLOSET QUEEN.

"I somehow got the feelin' you're right about that," Savage replied facetiously as his gaze swept in a rapid one-eighty, trying to take in as much as possible of the paraphernalia that lined the walls and hung haphazardly from the shop's embossed tin ceiling. The place was overwhelming. He pulled his shield case from his pocket and flapped it open. "I'm Sergeant Thornton Savage, Manhattan South Homicide."

"Oh my Goddd!" The man slapped the fingers of his left hand to his cheek and held them there. "Are we talking *murder*? Someone's *dead*?"

" 'Fraid so."

"Oh my God!" he repeated, horrified, as his right hand went to his other cheek.

Savage smothered the smile that wanted to cross his face. "Do you have anybody here, or do you know of anybody who can tell me about toy soldiers?"

"Are you *kidding*?" The man dropped his left fist to his hip in mock disappointment, and cocked his head jauntily. "*I'm* the expert. Just call me Dawson. Why don't we just march over to the toy-soldier department, *shall we*?"

Savage followed as Trooper Dawson led him past a rack of well-preserved U.S. Marine Corps uniforms. "Boy, these dress blues are in great shape," Thorn commented offhandedly.

"Aren't they though? Don't you just *love* the choker collar?"

"Unhh," Savage muttered, wondering how the Village People had missed signing this wacko.

Dawson weaved smartly past a rack of well-worn bomber jackets, a table full of swastikaed helmets and belt buckles, and a fruity-looking, limp-wrist-posed male mannequin dressed only in ass-hugging U.S. Navy bell-bottoms. He came to three large showcases on the other side of the shop, one of which, the middle one, doubled as a sales counter. The glass cases were each eight feet long and filled with hundreds of tiny soldiers and miniature garrison setups. Dawson smiled proudly through his wild mustache as he pointed out the different groupings. "Are we talking Russian, Prussian, German, French, British, Napoleonic? What, pray tell, would you like to know, Officer?"

"Could you tell me about this one?" Savage said, handing Dawson a clear plastic bag that bore a Property Clerk's evidence number on its sealed flap. The two pieces of the broken soldier were clearly visible inside.

"Oh my God," Dawson chimed in delight. "It's a Heyde." He pronounced it "Hi-dee."

"A who?"

"A Heyde. Made in Germany probably in the late 1800s. *Most* desirable among collectors. And, I might add, this one's in unbelievably *wonderful* condition. I know men who would absolutely kill for a complete set of these. Ooh, excuse me. Perhaps *kill* was the wrong word choice."

"Its head is broken off," Savage pointed out.

"Doesn't mat-ter! It's a Heyde!" Dawson sang, holding the bag up to the light to study the pieces more closely. "The head can always be fixed. Heydes are worth much more in the aggregate though, than singly."

"Meaning . . . ?"

"Complete sets fetch far more on the market than the same amount of pieces if bought separately."

"I see." Thorn nodded his understanding. "I gotta

tell you, Dawson. I studied that piece and I couldn't find any sort of marking. Would you mind explaining to me how you know it's a Heyde?"

"They have a *charming* general lack of symmetry. Look here," he said, as he held the package up to eye level and pointed with delicate fingers. "Arms of unequal length, stumpy legs. But, you know, when seen in groups, they capture and please the eye." Dawson again held the packaged figure up to the light. "This little fellow here is French infantry. If we were to put the head back on the shoulders, I'd be willing to bet that the figure would stand at fifty-two millimeters. That, of course, was Heyde's most common size."

"Of course," Savage agreed. "Everyone knows that."

"Most Heydes had their right foot forward, like this one. They had wonderfully carved mustaches—which you can tell I would know about—and oddly thin necks. Which is why it probably broke there. Also, as you can see, the bayonet leaves the scabbard."

"There is no bayonet."

"Oh, there's a bayonet all right. And if you had it, it would fit right into that scabbard. And unless I miss my guess, I would say that this piece is part of a complete set."

"Why do you think that?"

"The paint. It's original and perfect. This is a true collector's piece."

"Don't stop now. Do you know any collectors who might have a complete set of these?"

"Oh, *God*. I wish I did. You'd arrest me on a morals charge if I told you the things I'd do just to get a peek at a complete set of Heydes." Dawson batted his strange eyes for emphasis.

"This guy look familiar?" Savage asked, unfolding a police artist's sketch of the shooter based on his description from last night's debriefing.

"Ugly brute, isn't he?" Dawson remarked, staring

at the rendering. "I never forget a face, but in this guy's case I'd be willing to try. Is he the killer, or the killee?"

"He's the killer."

"Officer, you just wouldn't believe some of the weirdos we get in this place," Dawson confided, shaking his head and rolling his eyes. "Most of them just want to play dress-up. You know, go to Military Night at some of the local dance clubs, looking like Audie Murphy, or Heinrich Himmler."

"I know what you're sayin'." Savage played along, consciously nodding his head. "But what about the picture, Dawson?"

"I think I've seen this guy. I think he's been in here. But I haven't seen him in a while."

"How long?"

"Six months. Maybe a year."

"Has he been here more than once?"

Dawson squinted in concentration. "Yes, definitely. Maybe a couple of times."

"Ever sell him anything?"

"Don't know, I'm not sure. Even if I did"—Dawson lowered his voice to a confidential whisper—"we here at the Fox Hole don't keep much in the way of receipts or records. I certainly don't know his name."

"Okay, Dawson. Where do I go from here?"

"For what?"

"To find the owner of this Heyde. We think it's the guy in that sketch."

"The killer?"

"Yeah."

The annoying door buzzer sounded as two lean young men with military-style crew cuts entered the store.

"With you in a minute, Rod," Dawson trilled suggestively to the taller of the two, obviously well acquainted with him. Turning back, Dawson studied the sketch of the killer and cupped his chin contemplatively in his right hand, "Let me ask around."

"Here's my card, Dawson. Keep the sketch. If this guy pays another visit, or you come up with anything, give me a call at that number."

As Savage left the store, Rod was on his knees, giggling, measuring his companion's inseam for a pair of those ass-hugging Navy bell-bottoms.

TEN

As soon as word came that Harmon Mayhew was laid out—practically sans head—in some morgue in downtown Tegucigalpa, one course of the investigation had to be shifted. On Savage's orders, Jack Lindstrom set aside the inquiries he'd already started into whether Mayhew had carried life insurance on his equally dead wife. According to the Honduran police, Harmon Mayhew was already on his fourth day of harp lessons before his wife got to pluck her first note. Whether he had his old lady heavily insured, or vice versa, was now far less important to the investigation, if not totally moot. The information would still be traced, but for now it was back-burner stuff. Lindstrom switched the slides in his investigative microscope from Personal/Marital to ones marked Business Dealings.

Mayhew Fashions occupied half the sixteenth floor at 180 West Thirty-sixth Street. The building was right off the corner of Seventh Avenue, in the heart of New York's garment center. If Lindstrom didn't know better, he would've thought that he'd entered a sweatshop in downtown Shanghai from the looks of the women working in concentrated silence at rows of chattering sewing machines. All were Asian. The few men who circulated about—stock boys, cutters—all looked like Mexicans. INS could have a field day here. Fact was, they could have a field day at almost any shop in the district.

Standing just inside the shop's entrance, Lindstrom surveyed the large factory room that had the same no-frills atmosphere as every rag trade shop he'd ever been in. Ample, but bare-bulb, fluorescent light fixtures were suspended among air ducts, plumbing, and electrical conduits from the floor above. There was never a finished ceiling in any of these places. Racks of women's sport clothes were everywhere—purples and grays looked to be this fall's main colors. That's good, he thought, momentarily fondling the almost purple tie he'd worn today with his Macy's charcoal gray suit.

Though only a few of the busy pieceworkers even bothered to look in his direction, there was no question that they all knew he was there. Soon enough, he was approached by a stocky man in his mid-sixties, whose paisley necktie was pulled loose at the open collar of a mustard-colored shirt. A pair of black suspenders were buttoned to gray slacks that could have used a pressing. Black horn-rimmed glasses hung from a gold chain around his thick neck.

"You look like a cop. Am I right?" the man asked, a friendly, yet odd, questioning look on his face.

"Right you are," Lindstrom replied, flashing his gold tin. "Jack Lindstrom from Manhattan South." He opted to omit the word *homicide* just now.

"I knew it, I knew it," the man repeated with a toothy smile that widened in self-satisfaction. "The minute you walked in, I said to José, This guy's a cop. See, José," he said as he turned with a what'd-I-tell-you look to a gold-toothed Mexican who was pattern-slicing fifty sleeves at once from a three-inch stack of purple satin. "I was right. I could always spot these guys from a mile away."

José offered an underling's diplomatic grin, and turned back to his work.

"How'd you know I was a cop?" Lindstrom said, coyly indulging the man. "That *is* amazing."

"Since before I was even bar mitzvahed, I could always spot a cop." He snickered, confidently, running off at the mouth. "I used to amaze my friends. I don't know, I just have this *uncanny insight,* you might say."

"You must be an extremely observant fella," Lindstrom continued.

"I'm no *alter kocker*."

"Pardon?" Jack Lindstrom said, narrowing his inquisitive hazels. "This goy don't do too bad with Yiddish, but that's a new one on me."

"Means 'old fart.' I don't miss nothing!"

"That a fact?" Lindstrom replied, lifting his brow. "I didn't get your name, sir."

"Sussman. Murray Sussman." The man held out his hand. He either liked cops, or he was putting on a good show.

"I would guess that you're in charge here, Mr. Sussman. That right?"

"You're an observant fellow yourself, aren't you?" Sussman came close and nudged Lindstrom's arm. "But, then again, you're a cop, you're supposed to be observant. Isn't that so?" Murray had pastrami breath.

"That is so, Mr. Sussman. When you're right, you're right." Lindstrom forced a smile and took a step back. He'd indulged the windy rag merchant long enough. "Take me someplace where we can talk, Murray."

"This way." Sussman gestured toward a glass-enclosed area. "We'll use Mr. Mayhew's office."

"Where is Mr. Mayhew?" Lindstrom fired for effect.

"Mr. Mayhew's out of town on business," Sussman promptly, and seemingly innocently, replied. "But we expect him back any minute now." Sussman turned and led him past two long rows of well-lit cutting tables.

Mayhew's office was small and cluttered. Cartons awaiting shipment were stacked everywhere, and Sussman rolled aside a rack of samples to uncover a chair for the detective to sit in; for the moment, Lindstrom declined. Sussman closed the glass door, shutting out most of the shop's noise but not its view. "I guess you could tell how nervous you made everybody out there. The appearance of the law in a shop full of aliens does that. But every one of our people is legit, Officer. They all have their green cards. I can provide you with all the necessary documents . . .'' Sussman moved aside a dress form and pulled at the top drawer of a filing cabinet.

"I'm sure you can, Mr. Sussman. But I'm not here to discuss immigration and naturalization."

Sussman dropped the folder he'd found back into the file drawer and turned to face Lindstrom. With an innocent-enough shrug he asked, "What then could you possibly want from us? You guys still selling tickets to the policeman's ball? Ha-ha!''

"I'd like to ask you a few questions."

"Questions? Me? Questions about what?"

"Questions about Harmon Mayhew."

Sussman reared back defensively. Gone was the friendly ha-ha grin. Lindstrom could see the first courses of a stone wall beginning to form around the once gregarious man.

"You can ask Mr. Mayhew himself, Detective. He's expected at any minute."

"I want to ask you, Murray."

"Why me?"

"Let's call it precorroboration. We need to see if your answers will jibe with what we find out from Mr. Mayhew," Lindstrom said, knowingly deceiving the man. "Now, we can do that here, or we can do it down at my office. It's your call, Murray."

"Precorroboration? About what? Mr. Mayhew? Mayhew Fashions?"

"All of the above."

"I can't leave here," Murray protested, gesturing with a sweep of his left arm toward the glass door. "I've got a busy shop to run."

"José'll run it in your absence," Lindstrom said authoritatively, glancing at his watch. "You're just about to close for the day anyhow—it's going on five."

Sussman's eyes shifted nervously back and forth as he stood frozen in place. He looked to Lindstrom like a frightened deer framed in the headlights of an oncoming semi. Sussman may have always been able to spot a cop, but Lindstrom could always spot a guy who possessed answers.

"I know nothing about Mr. Mayhew's private life, and very little about his business life."

"Now, now, Murray. Two minutes ago you told me you were a maven. You 'don't miss nothing.'"

"You're just gonna have to wait until Harmon gets here, Officer. Talk to him; I don't know anything." The final courses of Murray's stone wall were now in place. Lindstrom decided it was time to make it all come tumbling down.

"Harmon Mayhew is dead."

"Gevalt!" The man's eyes bugged out, and his jaw hung slack; he began mumbling to no one in particular. *"Oy vay iz mir!* He was due in at seven this morning. I should have known. Harmon was never late in thirty-five years." The man settled unsteadily in the chair he'd offered to Lindstrom. "What happened, Officer? Heart attack?"

"No, Murray. Nothing so tranquil. Mr. Mayhew was murdered. His body was found in a ditch in Honduras. He was only identified several hours ago, although it's believed that he'd been dead for days."

"He was due back from Honduras last night. I expected to see him here first thing this morning. This is terrible. Is it possible that there's been some sort of mistake?" Sussman asked, pleading with his eyes.

"No. He was positively identified by his passport." Lindstrom noted Nixonian dew forming across the man's upper lip.

Continuing to shake his head in frightened disbelief, Sussman asked, "Has his wife been informed?"

"I'm afraid that would be quite impossible. Have you not read this morning's newspaper, Murray?" Lindstrom asked.

Sussman replied that he always read the paper in the evening. Lindstrom brought him up to date.

"Officer?" the man whined. "What makes you think that I might know anything about Mr. Mayhew's life and business?"

"Since I was a kid for crissakes," Lindstrom mimicked, as he clicked his ballpoint, opened his notebook, and took a seat, "I could always spot a guy who knew a lot more than he was saying. I used to amaze my friends. I don't know what it is, Murray. I've always had this *uncanny insight*, you might say."

Savage arrived back at Manhattan South at twenty after six, just as the first drops of a late April shower had begun to dot the sidewalks. The self-assigned mission he was returning from had accomplished two things. First, and most important, it'd gotten him away from the busy office for most of the day. He couldn't stand anyone seeing him when he was severely bummed. When he was in this kind of pain, he had no poker face at all. Second, having started from Duncan's downtown and worked his way uptown, he'd managed to visit every toy-soldier location listed in the Yellow Pages. Those bases were now covered.

After the bizarre, yet very informative, visit with Dawson down in the Village, he'd gone on to FAO Schwartz on Fifth, then Burlington's and the Soldier Shop, both on Madison. Like Dawson at the Fox Hole, the others all confirmed the broken figurine as a fine example of a German-made Heyde, but couldn't offer much more. Unlike Dawson, however, none thought the man in the sketch familiar.

When Savage entered the office and signed in at the wheel, he saw that the war room was already occupied by Sergeant Lakis and Team One. They were doing their second evening tour and were reviewing what they knew about the cabdriver found shot to death on a pier in the Tenth Precinct last night. Needing to huddle with his team, Savage called them away from their desks into the tight-fitting sergeants' room.

"Time to put our heads together, ladies and gentlemen, and recap this entire case," Thorn began. "I'm sure we all see the quickly broadening scope of this goddamned thing. We haven't had anything quite like this in a while." His opening statement was met with simultaneous nods of agreement and concerned expressions on the faces of the three detectives.

"Think we'll be here awhile?" Lindstrom asked, looking at his watch. "If so, I'll put up another pot of caffeine."

Savage checked his own watch. "We've got a lot to talk about, and Team One's already got the war room."

"And we went off the clock an hour and thirty minutes ago," Marcus growled.

"Any suggestions?" Thorn asked, knowing that someone would pick up on this.

"The Watney Lounge?" Diane offered, with a persuading shrug, using the location's code name.

Diane could always read his mind, Savage thought. Well, he hoped not *always*.

At 1835 hours the meeting adjourned to P.J. Clarke's. They were all ready for a cold one.

Now in his seventy-first year of life, Frank McBride had bid farewell to his cancer-gobbled larynx at Sloan-Kettering ten years ago. It didn't slow him down. Never one to be fazed by hardship or misfortune, he just kept going and going. Frank, the senior mixologist at P.J. Clarke's with thirty-eight years of service, and two other bartenders, each half his age, would start dispensing stupid-juice at six and keep pouring until closing, sometimes till 3 a.m. Frank worked six nights a week.

Waddling like an emperor penguin in clunky, thick-soled orthopedic shoes that supported his floorboard-worn flat feet, Frank easily ran circles around the "youngsters," as he called them. Under a thinning crown of fine-spun wavy silver, Frank had the moist, drooping eyes and long ears of a mopey basset, and the loose, fleshy, heavily sagging jowls of a shar-pei pup. Despite the robot-sounding, esophageal voice that burped from the hole in his trachea behind his omnipresent black bow tie, he possessed a sarcastic and rapier Irish wit.

Savage thought Frank McBride was a prince, and knew the feeling to be mutual. They'd been friends for a long time.

The after-work onslaught of suits that had drained from the neighboring East Side corporate bastions had already seized every available stool at P.J.'s long bar. Packed in behind those fortunate enough to be seated, additional numbers formed a three-deep phalanx of noisy, thirsty, well-dressed barbarians. To complete the upscale occupation of the premises, and fill every square foot of floor space with an upwardly mobile type, more reinforcements were on the way. Another average evening at P.J. Clarke's.

Clarke's was a class act, but it hadn't always been so. Once upon a time it was just another Third Avenue gin mill. Featured in the Oscar-winning flick *The Lost Weekend,* starring Ray Milland, back in 1945, it just happened to outlast the Third Avenue El to become one of the few remaining old New York bars. It was authentic, and not a re-creation. It had rich mahogany walls, ornate, finely etched mirrors backing the bar, bentwood and cane chairs, and an old-fashioned mosaic tile floor.

The landmark-status place at Fifty-fifth and Third was Thorn's main haunt, had been for the last twenty years. He liked the saloon atmosphere almost as much as the Watney's Red Barrel they kept on tap. When the team of detectives eased their way through the front door and squirmed a path through the noisy crowd, Frankie McBride automatically drew four Watney draughts. Without being asked, he got them their favorite round table in the back corner by telling a couple of Citigroup junior execs to move. With not a second of hesitation, the men complied. To not play musical chairs in Clarke's when Frank called the tune could mean eventually dying of thirst. Nobody screwed with Frank.

"Busy night," Thorn observed, as Frank transferred bowls of bar mix and the complimentary first round from his tray to their commandeered table.

Frank shrugged and made a face that said, "So what else is new?" He didn't attempt to speak when he didn't have to, and the team was fluent in every one of his facial messages. Frank winked coyly at Diane and, motioning to Marcus, finally spoke.

"If I was twenty years younger, this guy wouldn't stand a freakin' chance."

All, including Marcus, were amused. They all knew that Frank thought Diane the loveliest colleen he'd ever seen, and it was no secret that, as a younger man, he'd had the rep of being a first-rate swordsman.

"I gotta get back to the bar," Frank announced in his eerie voice. "The assholes are three deep. Signal me if you need anything. I'll see that your glasses don't run dry." He winked at Diane again and patted Thorn's shoulder as he waddled off into the crowd.

After they all toasted Frank and savored the first sips of the rich English ale, Marcus opened his mouth to speak but was inadvertently cut off by Jack Lindstrom.

"I spent about an hour and a half at Mayhew Fashions, boss," Lindstrom said. "I found it most enlightening." The meeting had officially begun.

"Hey. Not for nuthin', Jack," Richie Marcus blurted, "but I was talkin'." Seated opposite Lindstrom, Marcus moved his fist in a short jerking motion. "Enlighten this."

"You know, Marcus, you're a typical classless Brooklyn asshole," Lindstrom shot back. "You think you can be rude, or deliver *any* kind of insult, to anybody, so long as you preface it with *Not for nuthin', but*. What the fuck does *Not for nuthin', but* mean anyway? First of all, it's grammatically incorrect."

"I'll give you your grammar right here," Marcus taunted with a wry smile, his index finger pointing to his crotch. "Apologies, Diane."

Thorn looked directly across the table, aiming a mildly amused glance at the woman detective. She rolled her eyes with a here-we-go-again grin. Savage broke the stalemate by turning to Lindstrom. "You were saying, Jack?"

Lindstrom took a pregnant second to shoot a look of vindication at the overruled Marcus and continued. "Looks like there was some very unkosher shit going on over at Mayhew Fashions."

Marcus snorted loudly, momentarily interrupting Lindstrom, then nervously cleared his raspy throat. It was obvious he was pissed. Marcus bruised easy, but Savage knew he healed quick. The perceived slight would be forgotten in minutes.

"First of all," Lindstrom continued, "Harmon Mayhew comes from an old-line New York garment-center family. Back in the late eighties he lived on Long Island, wore too much jewelry, and had a JAPy wife and two daughters. Supposedly he wigged out, gave all that up, and moved to Manhattan, where he met Candace. Eventually married her. Got stung big-time for alimony and child support from his first wife though. That's when he began to feel a cash crunch and started borrowing."

"Who gave you that?" Thorn asked.

"Got it from his cousin, Murray Sussman. The cousin runs the shop, but claims to have no ownership interest in the firm. But, after thirty-five years, there's not much that he doesn't know about the operation of Mayhew Fashions."

"The business in good shape?" Thorn asked.

"On the surface it would appear to be. Lots of staff in the workroom, orders to fill, et cetera."

"When do we get to the unkosher?" Diane asked.

"Right now," Lindstrom said, leaning forward to speak confidentially. "About a year and a half ago, Mayhew Fashions was on its ass. Mayhew had gone for his lungs on winter and spring lines that didn't work. The company ran about a mil and a half in debt, the creditors were closing in, and, according to his cousin, Mayhew was on the verge of taking a full gainer off the Empire State."

"Then?" Richie Marcus, his edge already softening, asked politely.

"Then Mayhew found a new source of revenue out in Brighton Beach and everything got better. Suddenly he was out of debt and back in business," Lindstrom said.

"Perhaps he got some *exotic* financing?" Thorn mused.

"Some exotic *Russian* financing," Lindstrom added, while raising his eyebrows emphatically.

"Some exotic Russian *mob* financing," Diane said, completing the thought.

Marcus squirmed in his chair, snorted, and swallowed the results.

"Most assuredly." Lindstrom nodded. "The cousin tried to dazzle me with bullshit, but when he found out that Mayhew was coming back from Honduras in a box, he caved. He told me that Mayhew had reached out to some sons of Vladivostok who came up with all the funding necessary to bail Mayhew Fashions out. But not only was Mayhew responsible to pay back the entire debt, with interest, he also had to turn over fifty percent of the business to an outfit called Majestic Funding."

"What kind of deal is that?" Marcus demanded, with a disbelieving smirk. "Shit, even the shies in Vegas don't scalp you that freakin' bad."

"The cousin says that Mayhew figured half a loaf was better than none."

"Whaddaya make of the cousin?" Savage asked.

"He ain't nobody's mensch."

"Any line on Majestic Funding? They listed anywhere? They chartered?" Thorn asked, raising the pint glass to his lips.

"They're a registered corporation. I've already re-quested a list of their officers from the state. Should have it tomorrow. I'm willing to bet that this outfit only offers loans to very special clients." Lindstrom looked slowly around the table. "Not that it will come as any surprise to anybody here. Except maybe you, Marcus."

"What else did the cousin give up?" Marcus asked with a smirk, talking through a mouthful of pretzels.

"He said that Mayhew'd been unable to make any payments on the debt for about a year, and the Bol-sheviks were really tightening the screws. On top of that he got no relief from Candace, who was a notori-ous spender. Mayhew had become big-time depressed and confided to his cousin that he was probably gonna lose everything, if not his life. Apparently, things had gotten pretty bleak over there."

"Then what?" Savage asked.

"The cousin doesn't know. Suddenly, one day, ev-erything was cool—the heat was off. Mayhew's depres-sion evaporated and everything was coming up roses again."

"Did Mayhew catch up on his payments?" Diane asked.

"Nope. Cousin said that wasn't it."

"When did this happen?" Savage followed up.

"Last December, January maybe. Right around New Year's."

"And this cousin don't know why the heat came off?" Marcus asked.

"Nope. And I believe him. For some reason Majes-tic Funding took the squeeze off Harmon Mayhew. Something happened to account for that, but Murray Sussman never found out what. Mayhew wouldn't tell him."

"Okay, Jack," Thorn broke in. "I guess we better give Majestic Funding a real close look. Let's see where that goes. What bothers me here is that the muscle took the heat off Mayhew in December, but he winds up DOA anyhow in April. Also, if the Russian mob wanted Mayhew hit, they could have done him in his living room for crissakes. They wouldn't have to chase him to some jungle road in Honduras."

"Unless they wanted it to look as though he had some bad business debts down there," Marcus conjectured.

"But," Lindstrom chimed in, "if Majestic Funding *is* behind this, and is, in fact, Russian mob, why kill Mayhew? Now that they were partners, who was gonna run the garment company? The mob's got no time for that shit."

"Maybe somebody wanted to put their brother-in-law in business," Marcus offered.

"And why kill Mayhew's wife?" Diane spoke up. "She have anything to do with the garment business?"

"Nothing," Lindstrom replied. "According to the cousin, she was a shiksa ditz and something of a trophy wife. When it came to matters involving the business, Mayhew'd always treated her like a mushroom—fed her bullshit and kept her in the dark."

"The cousin know anything about Mrs. Mayhew's *extracurricular* activities?" Diane asked.

"He knew there was trouble in paradise, and he knew that Mayhew'd decided on getting a divorce. I don't believe he knew any of the details, though."

Thorn pondered the next investigative steps as he played with his near-empty beer glass—a fraction to the left, a bit to the right, a little forward, a little back—until it stood precisely in the center of the Heineken coaster. "I want you to get downtown first thing in the morning, Jack," he finally said. "Get a subpoena for all the business records of Mayhew Fashions—ledgers, tax returns, phone bills, accounts payable and receivable. Also, find out who Mayhew banked with. We need to get a look at his business *and* personal-account statements for the last thirty-six months."

"Complete round-robin?" Lindstrom asked, as he scribbled notes.

"Right." Savage nodded. "Although I doubt that one actually exists, I'd also like to get a look at that loan agreement. Failing that, let's see if we can't get a look at the partnership agreement where Mayhew supposedly gave up fifty percent of the business. Let's see who has rights of survivorship. If Mayhew has a Rolodex in his office, let's get that too." Savage turned his attention from Lindstrom, looked across the table, and asked, "What've you got, Diane?"

"Donny Cesare was divorced," she began, "and lived alone in a one bedroom over in Bay Ridge. I located his ex-wife, Carlene. She's living out on Staten Island. Says they've been divorced for six years, they had no kids, and she's happily remarried. She had no ax to grind against Donny and doesn't know anybody who did. The guy was a petty criminal, but apparently, according to her, a very likable one. I think it's safe to say we've got a dead end there."

Savage nodded.

"Two more things," Diane continued. "Just before we left the office I got a call from Dr. Dresner at Bellevue. She said Tony DiLeo's pulled out of his funk, is fully conscious, and can talk. However, she can't vouch for his short-term memory. I told her somebody'd be by first thing in the morning to take a statement from him. She said that'd be okay. Also, I got a call from Davy Ramirez at Ballistics. Comparison of the one spent shell casing recovered at La Florentine with those recovered at the Caroline Durante homicide is conclusive. They were all fired from the same Glock nine."

"All right," Savage said, looking at Diane. "First thing in the morning, go spend some time with Tony DiLeo. See what he's got to say. He probably won't be much help. If he even remembers being there it'll be a miracle. The best we can hope for is that he overheard some conversation."

"Right, boss." Finished, Diane looked to Richie Marcus. It was his cue to finally speak.

"This better be good, Marcus," Lindstrom said, reaching for a peanut.

Marcus quickly told how he'd begun canvassing the residents of East Forty-ninth Street, with negative results, and beyond that, had nothing to report.

Looking amazed, Lindstrom snickered at the brevity of it all, and said, "*Not for nuthin',* Marcus, but is that what you were so goddamned anxious to share with us?"

"Up yours, Lindstrom," Marcus grunted, with a blasé sneer and a quick middle finger. The ongoing Richie-and-Jack rivalry, and never-ending game of one-upmanship, was interrupted by the arrival of another round of Watney's. True to his word, Frankie McBride wasn't letting their glasses run dry.

Savage got right back to business. "Richie, we'll need a search warrant for the Mayhew residence. We're gonna have to toss that place. Pick one up in the morning. While you're downtown, also get a subpoena for their residence telephone records. Let's see who they'd been talking to."

Saving the best for last, and figuring they'd all consumed about the right amount of ale to truly appreciate it, Savage recounted his interesting midday adventure at the Fox Hole. Bursts of laughter erupted from their corner table as he punctuated the story at just the right places for maximum effect. He'd timed it right—the Watney's *had* kicked in. Marcus wondered aloud how Lindstrom might look with a couple of hoop earrings and a shaved head. Not to be outdone, Lindstrom reminded the paunchy ex-marine that dress blues didn't come in size forty-eight-toddler.

When things settled down, Savage told them of Dawson's recognition of the subject in the sketch, and the flaky shop owner's promise to do some unofficial scouting. Since Dawson seemed able to put the subject inside his store several times within the past few years, they all agreed the hired gun may be a local, and not an import, as feared. "All the more reason," Savage declared, "to press this one to the limits. I'm gonna speak to Lieutenant Pezzano in the morning and get the overtime cap removed. We may have to do some crazy hours."

"As long as it's not tomorrow night," Diane said, concerned. "I'm giving a baby shower for my daughter, Sandy. I've got about twenty women coming to my place."

"Friday's no good for me either," Lindstrom spoke up, apologetically. "We've already accepted an invite to Joan's boss's place. I'd beg off if I could."

"Ain't no problem for me, boss," Marcus piped in, smiling through a beer belch. "I'da hadda make myself scarce anyway, the baby shower and everything."

Once the business of the meeting was concluded, Jack Lindstrom didn't stick around. He finished the beer he'd been nursing and headed home to Bayside, Queens, late, he said, for an anniversary dinner with his accountant wife. Richie Marcus and Diane called it a night at nine, saying they, too, were headed home. Savage knew better on both counts.

Clarke's had no pinball machines or any video games for Marcus to play. Clarke's didn't even permit a jukebox for crissakes. No, Beauty and the Beast had gone off to Ga-Ga's in Astoria, or some other slop chute where Richie could hustle some unsuspecting fool at pinball, darts, or billiards. Marcus probably earned as much being a pinball wizard on the side as he did being a cop. Too bad those winnings were usually nullified by his shitty track record with the ponies. Lindstrom, on the other hand, was heading out in hopes of saving his troubled marriage.

Now alone, Savage left the corner table and made his way through the still-jumping crowd. He claimed an empty stool at Frank's end of the bar.

"You okay, Thornton?" Frank asked, with a knowing gaze, drying damp hands on his linen apron.

"Sure, Frankie," Thorn replied. Frank's insight was always good. But jeez, was *he* that transparent?

"I read about you in this morning's *Daily News*,"

Frank squawked. "Front page. Looked like a nasty one."

"Unhh," Thorn grumbled, not anxious to talk about it.

"And," Frank pressed, his bushy eyebrows now arched in concern, "what's goin' on with Maureen?"

Thorn grimaced and frowned.

"She's been obvious by her absence of late, ya know. You guys used to be joined at the hip."

"Yeah," Thorn said. He drained the last of his Watney's and pushed the empty glass across the bar's worn varnish. "Make me a Rusty, Frankie."

Ignoring an obnoxious, half-loaded suit on the next stool waving his empty mug for a refill, Frank stared at Thorn. "Everything happens for the best," he assured.

Thorn swallowed a sigh and made brief eye contact with his paternal friend. Frank's clichéd words had come in their usual cold monotone. It was through his life-weary eyes that he was able to convey emotional nuance. They were now expressing the empathy and concern that his one-dimensional voice could not.

"I always liked Maureen," Frankie said.

"So did I," Thorn muttered.

Two Nails later, Savage paid his sixteen-dollar tab, which would easily have been fifty anywhere other than Clarke's, and also left a crisp twenty on the bar for Frankie. Frank always treated Thorn good. Most friendly saloons in New York will buy back their regulars after every third one. In Thorn's case, however, Frankie McBride would only *charge* after every third one. But then, what were friends for?

After his laryngectomy, it'd taken Frank a full year to master esophageal speech. During that unemployed period, Thorn had helped him stay off the financial rocks. Again, what were friends for?

After a quick head call, Savage left the bar and trotted the half-block through a soaking downpour to where he'd parked his department Crown Victoria. Wipers at max barely kept up with the wind-driven rain as he headed downtown. With only storm-skewed and patternless images in his rearview, and preoccupied with thoughts of Maureen, Caroline Durante, and the vicious fuck with the 9mm, he didn't pick up on the gray Oldsmobile with the rental plates that followed him the entire way.

Thorn found a spot on Sullivan Street just off the corner of Houston. He tossed the department ID plate onto the dash, and did a fifty-yard sprint to his building. After enduring the Dalmatian ritual, and having a brief conversation with Ray, he popped a valerian root and was zonked in his bed by eleven.

She didn't know what the response would be, or how it would come about. To Christine Maloney it was a matter of certainty—it would come. Nikki Rosen would not tolerate being stood up last night, or being fucked out of twenty-five thousand in cash. She would hear from Nikki Rosen, no question. It was only a matter of when. At Gerard's insistence—so that no messages could be left—she had turned off the answering machine on her private line.

Christine had spent the entire day agonizing over her stupidity and pondering her criminal liability. Four people were dead, and it was *her* bare ass hanging out on a splintered, and quickly weakening, legal limb. After considering every possible ramification of her situation, she'd had no choice but to vote herself "most likely to get screwed" out of this whole godawful mess. She'd worn herself out searching her mind for a plausible defense should the murderous trail ever lead police to her door. She'd wondered if Nikki had what it took to stand up and take the weight—after all, Christine reasoned, this was all Nikki's damn doing. Anyway, when it came right down to it, it would be Nikki's word against hers. Nikki would have to take the fall.

Christine had thrashed about under the comforter for hours, desperate to reach the peaceful oasis of sleep. Unable, she'd taken thirty miligrams of Restoril and buried her head beneath the pillow.

The 2 a.m. call could not have been more startling if the Marine Corps band had struck up a Sousa march at the foot of her bed. Christine had jackknifed to a sitting position on the first ring. She'd stared, blinking at the phone as it rang twelve nerve-twisting times, but didn't answer it. She could count on one hand the people who had this number. Nikki Rosen had it. Mildly hyperventilating, she'd called Gerard to her room, and for the first time in many years allowed him to lay beside her. At precisely three, the private line came to life again, jarring their fatigued senses once more. The rings had an insistence; they seemed to warn against ignoring their demanding summons. On the tenth ring of the 3 a.m. assault, Gerard flipped the phone's ringer switch to OFF. Christine gulped another Restoril. Two hours of restless tossing later, they finally fell into a fitful half-sleep.

ELEVEN

Intrusive and ominous, the front-door chimes snapped the Maloneys from their tortured slumber, back to groggy, apprehensive reality. It was exactly 6 a.m.

"We *cannot* ignore this anymore, Gerard," Christine muttered, propping herself up on one elbow, deep, dark circles framing her eyes.

"Don't you dare answer it," he snarled.

"What about tomorrow?" she protested. "And the next day? And the day after that?" Her head ached from lack of sleep and too many sedatives.

"We'll cross those bridges when we get to them dammit. But for now, we're not inviting any problems in. We ignore it, it goes away."

Her husband could be such a schmuck. "*If* this was simply a legal process, we could ignore it, as we often have. But," she said as she stared at him, "this is *not* a legal process. This game has no rules that we can bend and ignore."

"We don't even know for certain that it's her. Maybe it's the damned paperboy, or a goddamned telegram."

Christine looked at Gerard in disbelief. "The paperboy? At six in the morning? Get with it," she scolded. "That's Nikki Rosen, downstairs. And that is one bell we better answer."

"We need more time to think this through," Gerard

argued, grimacing while mashing puffy palms into his reddened eyes. "If we don't answer it, what the hell's she going to do? She'll just have to go away."

"No way, Gerard!" Christine blurted, then snorted a half-laugh of disbelief. "That approach will not work. Nikki is not the type of woman you just simply ignore. And if we do force her to go away, where might she go? The police?"

The door chimes sounded again, and then again.

Slipping easily in unison from beneath satin sheets, they reached for their respective robes and slippers. Light-headed and mildly dizzy, Christine staggered from the bedroom and moved along the open hallway that looked down over a railing into the great room below. Coordination still affected by the sleeping pills, she held tightly to the rail as she descended the winding staircase. Peering down the hallway, through the side lights of beveled, leaded glass that bordered the intricately paneled front door, she was able to discern the outline of a figure standing there—an indistinct blur backlit by the new dawn light.

Her shoulders gave a sudden involuntary jerk when the chimes rang again, the metronomic cadence somehow becoming more insistent.

Christine turned and looked back up the staircase to Gerard. His aging face was tired, the shock of white at the top of his head askew. In his right hand he clutched a small revolver that he had retrieved from his bedroom. She knew they had to get this over with. "I'm answering it, Gerard," she said, not waiting for a response, "and put that damned thing away." Squaring her shoulders in resigned determination, she walked to the front entry.

"Who is it?" she asked, pressing her ear to the door.

There was no verbal response, only another ring of chimes. She turned and again looked at Gerard, who had followed her into the foyer; he nodded in quiet acceptance, and dropped the gun into his robe pocket. She released the dead bolt and pulled on the wide, mahogany slab. A silver-haired stranger stood there. He was expensively dressed, looked strong, and made no attempt to speak. He was sizing her up. His appreciative gaze had taken but an instant, but in that instant she felt herself disrobed by the stranger's deep brown, almost coal black, eyes.

Gathering her robe at the neckline, she asked, "Who are *you*?" unable to conceal the surprise and trepidation in her voice.

"I am Georgei Strelnikov," the ruggedly handsome man replied. "Nikki sent me."

Gerard stepped forward from the shadows of the hallway. "What's your business here?" he barked nervously, swollen hands wringing the life out of his robe's velvet belt.

"I suggest you let me in, Senator. We have much to discuss."

"I swear, I'll have the goddamned cops here in two minutes if you don't get lost," Gerard threatened. "This place is alarmed directly to the station house." His normally florid face was now a deep and angry scarlet. He placed his right hand into his pocket and regripped the gun.

"That would not be in your best interests, Senator," Strelnikov calmly stated, revealing a video cartridge he held in his right hand. "Or yours, for that matter, Mrs. Maloney. I think it would be very wise for you both to view tape, before police get a chance to. I must warn you, however, is rated triple X and contains some *very* incriminating dialogue." The man's dark eyes were piercing, his demeanor ice cold and steely confident.

Christine had seen him somewhere before. Her bowels churned. Fighting for composure and strength, but finding herself totally disarmed, Christine stepped aside and allowed the stranger to enter.

"You should have answered phone last night," Strelnikov said, stepping into the wide, richly paneled hallway. "This could have all been handled so much more easily." Striding aggressively past them as if they were insignificant, the man entered the designer-decorated great room and asked, matter-of-factly, "Where is VCR?"

"It's in the . . . uh, media room," Gerard mumbled, confusion apparent in his stressed-out face. Christine shot him a subzero glare when he pointed in the direction of the wide Gothic arch opening that led into the slate-floored den beyond.

"We do *not* want to watch that tape," Christine blurted, persistently dogging the cocky stranger, two steps behind, as he strode into the media room. Now she recognized him. He was the face in the loving pictures in Nikki's wallet. Realization of what the tape he carried might contain was beginning to dawn. How could she have been so fucking stupid?

"I can understand that," Strelnikov said, nodding. He stopped in his tracks and turned to face them both. "You need not watch it now. But, before I leave, I give you quick synopsis of what you can expect to find on it." The man dropped heavily onto the brocaded arm of a John Hutton–designed sofa. It was part of a pit grouping that sat on a sculpted, floral area rug in the middle of the room. Unconcerned that the custom-made camelback beneath him had cost twenty grand, he flipped the tape onto the sofa's down-filled cushion, and carelessly lit a smoke. Gerard quickly found him an ashtray as Christine stood rigid, arms crossed and pulled tightly into her chest.

Facing Gerard, the man began. "In opening scene, you will see very sexy, and"—he tightened his already narrow gaze for emphasis—"very naked wife, munching happily on her lady friend's . . . how you say? . . . *poosey?* Mrs. Maloney was having herself wonderful time. I am sure, when you get around to watching, you will agree that we have provided lots of excellent footage there." Looking to Christine, he added, "I personally found scene quite stimulating."

Gerard turned to Christine. She saw his frosty, disgusted look and turned away.

"Oh. Have I shocked you, Senator?" The man's expression was one of feigned concern. "Surely you know of your wife's inclination toward her own sex. Well, I'm quite sure that you do," Strelnikov said. "After all, is something that has been widely rumored for years, is not? But, I digress. Do allow me to go on. In later scenes you will see loving couple lying together in bed. There, you will see and hear them discussing the late Candace Mayhew, and the late Donald Cesare. Or do you do remember her as Candace Miller, Senator?"

Jaw tight, Maloney did not respond.

Offhandedly motioning his filtered Camel toward Christine, Strelnikov continued. "It seems that wife is heard telling her friend, Nikki, that those two *had to go.*' And then is heard agreeing to pay fifty thousand dollars to make happen. Tsk, tsk, tsk. Oh, my!"

Christine shouted, "I *never* said that." Then, her whole being filled with burning rage, she sank unsteadily into a Hutton-designed wingback. "Even if I did actually *say* those words, they were meant in a different context. I never intended for—"

"Now, Senator," Strelnikov said, steamrolling over Christine's stumbling attempt at an explanation. "We all know terrible consequences of your wife's determination to handle the Candace Mayhew problem, don't we?"

"How did you get that tape?" Gerard broke in. "I cannot believe my wife would've let herself fall into such a trap."

"There is apartment in Kew Gardens. Mrs. Maloney knows where it is. In fact she has her own key." Strelnikov turned and again faced Christine. "Don't you, Mrs. Maloney?"

Christine bit at her narrow lip.

"She can tell you about bedroom, and how it was laid out. Foot of bed faced triple dresser. Is that correct, Mrs. Maloney? And, above triple dresser were pair of large mirrors. I am right, so far?"

Manicured fingers kneading both arms of the chair, Christine sat in zoned-out silence.

"Behind wall on which mirrors hung was small linen closet kept locked at all times. We set up voice-actuated camera in there, and aimed lens through a hole in wall behind one of special mirrors. Easy, really." He took another long drag on his smoke. "As for sound, we just miked entire apartment."

"Just what the hell is it that you want, mister?" Gerard asked, his voice weary and defeated.

"The twenty-five thousand you owe us, for starters."

"And beyond that?"

"Nothing."

"Nothing?" Gerard echoed.

"Nothing but your friendship, Senator," Strelnikov said.

"Pardon?" Gerard replied, incredulous. Christine took her hand from her brow and looked up in puzzled astonishment.

"Nothing but your friendship, *Mr. President,*" the man corrected.

"I've decided not to enter the race, mister. And I've already leaked that decision to the media. I've notified my top campaign people and called a press conference for Saturday to make it all official. I am not going to run for president."

"Oh, but you *are* going to run," Strelnikov replied, his voice filled with certainty. "You are going to run very hard, and you damn well better win. When you do, you will remember favor of silence about this whole nasty affair."

"Of course." Gerard's reply dripped sarcasm. "Then there will be endless favors expected from me in return. Right?"

"Not endless," Strelnikov responded. "But from time to time."

"You will expect me to exert presidential influences that will be beneficial to you and yours, whoever the hell you and yours may be. Isn't that right, *sir*?"

"How very real politik of you," Strelnikov acknowledged, blowing a perfect smoke ring and allowing a precarious accumulated ash from his Camel to decorate the thick Karastan at his feet.

"I've made up my mind. I'm not running, *goddammit!*" Maloney declared. Turning to Christine, he added, "All that's happened is that we've traded off one set of blackmailers for another. Don't you see? If I don't run, there'll be no reason to blackmail me anymore."

Christine did not respond.

"Candace Mayhew knew all information about your crimes and corruptions that fattened your pockets years ago, Senator Maloney," Strelnikov reminded. "Back in days when you were screwing her pretty little brains out. Do you not remember the condemnation of some junkyard property near Shea Stadium? The kickbacks from that deal alone made you millions."

Christine again felt, and saw, her husband's angry glare.

"I thought you told me everything," Gerard snarled at her, past gnashing teeth. "You told me Nikki Rosen didn't know *what* Candace was using to blackmail me. You said that she never asked, and that you never told her."

"I didn't," Christine said, amazed and confused by the revelation.

"Do not worry, Senator. That shit was petty. The most it could have accomplished, had we ever aired it, would have been to destroy your upcoming campaign," Strelnikov pointed out. "However, we now possess power to destroy your entire life. *Both* of your lives. Conspiracy to commit murder in first degree. Tsk, tsk, tsk. Lots of jail time, Senator. Can you really spare the years?"

"Fuck you. I can do it," Maloney shot back.

"Can your wife?" Strelnikov asked pointedly.

"What about this bitch, Nikki Rosen," Gerard sneered. "Is she not afraid of long jail time? If we go down, she goes down with us. That, my friend, is a goddamned certainty."

"There is no Nikki Rosen," Strelnikov replied coolly. "Let us just say there never was, and leave it at that. The apartment in Kew Gardens was rented under assumed name, and is now completely vacant and swept clean." He turned to Christine. "You may want to go there and check for yourselves. You have key. Only thing left behind is peekaboo hole in bedroom wall where mirror once hung." Strelnikov took one last puff on the Camel, then, with ocher-stained fingers, squashed what was left into the onyx ashtray. Standing, he asked, "Do we understand one another?"

Christine stared at Gerard. There seemed to be nothing to say. They followed Strelnikov to the front door.

"By the way," Strelnikov said, letting himself out. "I come back tonight for the twenty-five thousand. You make certain that it is here."

"There won't be anyone here," Gerard snarled. "I'm scheduled to be in Washington this afternoon." Then, escalating his defiant tone, "And besides, even if I were here, I wouldn't give you the right goddamned time of—"

"I'll be here," Christine broke in, nodding assuredly to Strelnikov. "So will the money."

Closing the front door, she watched through the side-light panes as Strelnikov walked down the slated path to a big Lincoln. Turning to Gerard, she silently led her fuming husband to his favorite club chair in the center of the great room. Standing now behind his slumped form, she began to softly stroke his temples and snowy mane. Long minutes passed in silence. When she sensed that his redlining blood pressure had returned to numbers less life threatening, she made her move.

"Gerard. Honey. Twyla's due any minute. As soon as she gets here I'm going to have her make you a wonderful breakfast. Then, later on, we have to talk." She bent over and kissed him on the neck behind the ear. She could tell that he was responding. She knew he would. He always did.

Thursday morning's sunlight had sneaked past the curled edges of Savage's tired bedroom-window shade, awakening him at seven-thirty, beating the noisy Westclox to the punch by a full fifteen minutes. He always awoke before the alarm went off, but, by habit, always wound and set it the night before anyway.

Maureen used to chide him about being such a damned Scotsman because he wouldn't spring for a modern clock radio and wake to music like the rest of the civilized world. The wind-up on his nightstand was a relic, true enough, but unlike electric-powered versions or clock radios, its timekeeping was unaffected by power outages that might occur in the middle of the night. Savage came from the department's old school—there was never *any* excuse for being late for duty.

He was surprised to see the sun. Yesterday afternoon's shower had become a steady rain by nightfall, and by the time he'd left Clarke's it was hosing the scuzz from the city's armpits in a driving torrent. Despite the Watneys and Rusties, he didn't feel too bad—certainly a lot better than he'd felt the morning before.

He remembered that Johanssen's mutt had greeted him with the usual five-minute serenade when he'd arrived home last night. When he'd let himself into the apartment he'd found a brief message from Maureen on the PhoneMate. She'd read about the incident the day before and had called to make sure he was all right, say how proud of him she was, but all spoken in a self-satisfied, I'm-just-fine voice meant to discourage a return call. He knew it was only the close timing between the shooting and their last meeting that had prompted Maureen to make the courtesy contact. He was sure he'd never hear from her again.

It took him his usual half hour to shower, shave,

and dress. Wearing his Botany 500 glen plaid with an oxford button-down, a mottled tie of bright reds against soft blues, and his cordovan wing tips, he filled Ray's water dish, topped-off his food bowl with the last of a box of Meow Mix, and put a leftover slice of cold pepperoni pizza on a paper plate beside that. He washed down two ginkgo biloba capsules and 750 milligrams of ginseng with a big glass of OJ, and, by eight o'clock, had bid his usual four-letter, staircase good-bye to Johanssen's brain-dead Dalmatian. He drove to Curley's kiosk to pick up a *Post,* dropped his blue pinstripe at the dry cleaner's, and was sipping coffee and reading the sports pages at his cramped desk by 8:30, a half hour early.

Houston had launched a few moon shots from Shea last night as the Astros beat up on the struggling Mets, whose highly touted pitching so far this season had been awful. The Yanks had pummeled the crap outta Detroit, beating them 16–2 behind one-hit pitching. The Dow was up, a four-alarmer in a Bed-Stuy tenement had killed a dozen people, mostly kids, and baggage handlers at LaGuardia and Newark were threatening a midnight walkout. And unidentified but highly placed sources close to the Gerard Maloney camp were speculating that the senator was about to announce that he would not seek his party's nomination for president. Possible questions of health were being circulated. Savage wondered who else would wind up with that nomination. Struggling briefly with thirty-eight down, he knocked out the crossword in ten minutes. *Socmanry?*

Richie Marcus strolled into the office just before nine with *The Racing Form* tucked under his arm, carrying his usual six-course breakfast in a waxed bag marked DUNKIN' DONUTS. His choice of reading material this morning was a tip-off that he must have hustled himself a few bucks last night and was getting ready to lose it all back, and then some.

"Morning, boss," he said, poking his chowder head

into the sergeants' room. "Picked up them search warrants for Mayhew's apartment. Soon as Diane gets back from the DiLeo interview, me and her are goin' over there and tossin' the place."

"Good," Savage said, carefully refolding the *Post*. "Jack and I are gonna visit Mayhew Fashions later today." Then, for no particular reason other than the sake of idle conversation, he decided to check Marcus's political acumen. "See where Maloney might scratch himself from the race?"

"*Scratched?* Who's scratched? What race?" Marcus asked, reaching under his arm for *The Form*.

Savage shook his head, unbelievingly. "I'm talkin' about Gerard Maloney. You know, the senator who everybody's been saying was such a sure bet to run for president, and even a surer bet to win. Paper says he might not run after all."

"Oh, yeah?" If not for the momentary hint of puzzlement that flashed through his eyes, Marcus's expression would've remained a complete blank.

"Let me ask you a question, Rich," Savage said in all seriousness. "Do you vote?"

"Of course I vote," Marcus answered, mildly offended.

"How do you ever know who to vote for?"

"For what?"

"For *president* for crissakes."

"Easy," Marcus replied, not missing a beat. "I find out who Barbra Streisand's voting for, and I go with the other guy." He immediately segued to, "How'd you make out on the overtime cap? Pezzano go for it?"

"He's not in yet," Savage replied, shaking his head, amazed as always at the interesting shortcuts Marcus had for dealing with life's little obligations.

"There shouldn't be no problem, right?"

"Nah. He'll okay it," Savage assured. Then he stuck in the needle. "What's the matter, you short for dough, Rich?"

"Who, me? Never!" Marcus declared, slipping obliquely into the office. "Listen, Thorn. Diane and I are gonna have a little get-together over at her place on Sunday. New York strips, plenty of beer, the usual. Yankee-Boston game is on the tube. Diane's gonna make a batch of those stuffed mushrooms you like so much, extra garlic. Doin' anything?"

"I got no plans. What should I bring?"

"I'd tell you to bring Maureen, but uh,"— *snort*— "my outstanding and finely honed powers of perception are tellin' me that ain't gonna happen, right?" *Snort.*

"Right."

"Finished?" Marcus asked, with a sympathetic shrug.

"Yeah. This time I suppose it is, Rich."

"You oughtta let me introduce you to my ex-sister-in-law. She's about your age—little younger. No cats, no brats, and a tush that's an outstanding achievement."

"No *cats*?" Savage frowned in mock anger.

"Oops! Oh, yeah." Marcus laughed, then issued yet another of his self-conscious nasal explosions. "Forgot about that. How's my man Ray doin', by the way?"

"Good. I'll be sure to tell him that Richie sends his warmest regards."

"Yeah, do that." *Snort, snort.* "So, uh, you comin' Sunday?"

"Diane doing the cooking?"

"Yeah."

"I'll be there."

Marcus nodded, took two steps out of the office, stopped and turned. "Besides," he protested to Thorn with a palms-out shrug. "if God had wanted us to vote, he would have given us some fuckin' candidates. Right?" Then he turned away and headed into the squad room.

Tough to argue with that, Savage had to agree, as he watched Marcus walk to his desk, then, cup in hand, make directly for the coffeepot. At 9:05 Savage's phone rang.

"Sergeant Savage, *sir!*" The voice, striving to be macho, came instead in a quiffy staccato. "This is Trooper Dawson, *sir!* Down at the Fox Hole, *sir!* Request permission to speak, *sir!*"

Savage rolled his eyes, took a breath, and played his role. "Hey! Dawson, how are you?"

"Everything is co-pa-cet-ic, *sir,*" Dawson replied, still in the strident singsong of a military subordinate addressing an inspecting superior.

Savage humored him. "At ease, Trooper. What do you hear from the front?"

It worked. Dawson's style modulated down to normal conversational level. "May I speak freely, sir?"

"Please do," Savage urged.

"I went to this perfectly marvelous cocktail party last night, Sergeant, and did some recon."

"Great," Savage replied, struggling to put enthusiasm into his voice. "What've you got to report, Trooper?"

"Nothing, sir. I didn't find out a blessed thing, sir."

Savage rolled his eyes. Dawson was beginning to sound like some psycho cop buff who'd forever pester the shit out of him while playing Miss Marple. "Okay then, Dawson. Just what was the point of this call?"

"I met this absolutely *stunning* orthodontist there. Name was Morton Goldfarb."

"Yeah?" Savage said, shrugging to no one.

"Well, for one thing, he was playing Rommel—in this absolutely *fabulous* Afrika Corps regalia—which I thought was quite odd, owing to the fact that he was more Jewish than Levy's Rye."

"Unhhh?" Savage muttered with another shrug, wondering where the hell this was all going. He felt as ill-equipped having to feign any understanding of homo dress-up in his conversation with Dawson as he might if having to discuss quantum mechanics with fucking Einstein. But he kept trying.

"And what did the field marshal have to say for himself, Dawson?"

"After he drove me home in what he called his *staff* car—a gorgeous new SL Mercedes with, oh my God, the *creamiest* leather seats—he invited me to attend a Piece Conference tonight at some ritzy loft down in SoHo."

"You don't say. A peace conference."

"Oh, yeah. Piece Conference, *P-I-E-C-E*. It's a big deal. It's a gathering of a bunch of military freaks all trying to outdo one another in uniform dress. I'm going to wear my combat fatigues. I'm no jerk, it'll all wind up as a Crisco party anyhow."

"Look, Dawson. What's all this got to do with my investigation?"

"Maybe nothing. Maybe something. As it turns out, the queen that's hosting the bash happens to be a major collector of miniatures. I've never met him myself, mind you, but I've heard about him. Millionaire magazine publisher. I thought I'd accept the invite and go along. Besides free drinks and getting laid, maybe I can get to pick this guy's brain about the Heyde. Maybe he knows others with major collections. You follow me?"

"Yeah, I follow, Dawson. Good work. What's this millionaire publisher's name? Just in case you go MIA on me."

"Fleming. Hubert Armstrong Fleming. You know, Fleming Publishing?"

"Gotcha. Didn't know he was a . . . uh . . . uh . . . miniature collector."

Dawson guffawed. "I'll get back to you if I find out anything, okay, Sarge?"

"Great. Oh, and listen, Dawson. I really appreciate your time and interest."

"No problem."

"Dawson? One more thing." Savage had to ask, just before hanging up. "Enlighten me. What the hell is a Crisco party?"

"It's like a Wesson party, only neater. *Ciao!*"

Savage dropped the receiver back into its cradle,

trying to shake the images of Dawson's unconventional social life out of his head. He popped a Wint-O-Green, and picked up his coffee. The mug was empty. He headed into the squad room for a refill.

TWELVE

Andrew Karis knew war history. He'd studied every general of note since Alexander the Great of Macedonia and Hannibal of Carthage, through Lee and Grant in the American Civil War, to Montgomery, Patton, and Rommel from World War II. He'd studied the dynamics of how victorious generals won, and the fuckups made by those who went down in defeat. If nothing else, he'd learned that the tide of battle could turn in an instant. He knew that today's odds-on victor could easily become the vanquished and dead of tomorrow. He'd always been fascinated by the role Russian partisans played in Marshal Zhukov's defense of Moscow.

"Hitler's objective in Operation Barbarossa is to crush our beloved Soviet Russia in a swift campaign," Karis bellowed excitedly, addressing his assembled troops. "Ignoring his army high command who strongly argued that Moscow be the main target of their invasion effort, Hitler has decided to swing his forces north and south, short of Moscow, after penetrating our lines. As a result, our forces have gained time to develop new defensive positions and prepare for fierce counterthrusts. In addition, the onset of our ungodly winter has crippled German troop mobility and favored our valiant partisan defenders."

Karis knew that the partisan war had served as much to exacerbate Russia's WWII agony as to hasten the day of the Nazi's departure. History had shown that German reprisals against his people were heavy-handed and ruthless, with whole villages obliterated. As German atrocities were always one of the most compelling sources of partisan recruitment this created a vicious circle that only added fuel to the madness. The cry of Russian Nationalism was: "The Mother-land Calls."

It was not until Zhukov's Moscow Counteroffensive in late 1941 that there had been any indication that the Soviet Union had a chance of survival, let alone victory. And the Moscow battle saw the first real signs that partisans and regular Red Army forces could work together.

The miniature battle for Moscow had been raging now into its third week. The defenders, Zhukov's ragged partisans, with their motley assortment of captured and indigenous weapons, fighting alongside regular Red Army forces, were inferior in manpower, equipment, artillery, and armor. Karis knew, however, that they were far superior in morale, willingness to die, and the ability to cope with the flesh-petrifying cold that had already claimed thousands of the invading Wehrmacht. It had taken him these weeks to exemplify Germany's Second, Third, and Fourth Armies, and their accompanying panzer groups, into the impenetrable line they'd formed along Moscow's western borders.

"It is time for the giant hand of God himself to intervene," Karis declared. "It is time for the daring counterattack that will not only save our beloved Moscow, but forever turn the tide of Hitler's war in Russia." Naked, Karis scooted across the floor and began his troop movements. The Moscow counteroffensive to Hitler's Operation Barbarossa was beginning.

Kneeling on hands and knees, Karis began to carefully shift the Red Army and partisan positions. He separated and re-formed new Russian artillery emplacements to allow for concentrated fire on the weakest points along the German lines. It was their saturation shelling that would ultimately create the narrow corridors through which Russian soldiers could advance and re-form behind the weather-stymied enemy.

Crawling within the twelve-by-fourteen expanse of what once had been a third bedroom, Karis was careful not to tear the sheeting, or disrupt the white Styrofoam that he'd shredded to simulate deep and drifting snow. As he created the confused mayhem of a German armored column and a detachment of Waffen-SS being destroyed by Russian artillery and aircraft, an unconscious smile appeared, warming his face.

Then, as he saw the tide of the Battle of Moscow slowly turn in the diorama beneath him, the look on his face became more severe as he pondered his own circumstances. The best defense always, he reminded himself, was a good offense.

How to deal with his enemy? How to overcome superior strength and numbers? How to emerge victorious from one's darkest hour? These concerns had troubled him since his last meeting with Strelnikov. Killing off a decorated New York City cop was not guaranteed to relieve his dilemma. It could, if not handled properly, intensify those problems. Marshal Zhukov had known that a full frontal assault against the German lines poised against Moscow in 1941 would have been sheer suicide. As Zhukov's partisans and regulars working together did, he too must penetrate a formidable opponent's lines and have his partisans attack from the rear. It was inspired.

He stood and, as if tiptoeing through a minefield, left the bedroom Battle of Moscow frozen in time. He padded naked down the hallway that led to the kitchen. It was time for a hot cup of tea and some deep thought. He had a battle plan to work on.

He looked in his personal phone book for the coded number of one of his partisans, and reached for the phone.

*   *   *

Postponing their lunch, Savage and Lindstrom arrived at Mayhew Fashions shortly after noon. Armed with a search warrant whose ink wasn't quite dry, and freshly issued court orders to seize business and personal records, they found the quintessential rag shop in full preseason tilt.

"What'd I tell you?" Lindstrom said in an aside, raising his voice over the din. "Just like yesterday. The same get-the-product-out, go-go pace."

Wearing his stony game face, Savage panned, expressionless, around the large room, unconsciously clicking off a roll of mental stills as the busy factory scene played before him. He stepped aside, unblocking the aisle, allowing two black behemoths pushing hand trucks stacked with steel-banded cartons to exit. Thorn then nodded his head toward the frazzled nebbish in the center of the maelstrom. "That Sussman?" he asked.

"Good eye, boss," Jack said, deadpan. "In a room full of Leroys, Hectors, and displaced Madame Butterflys, he's the only person who looks remotely Murray-ish."

"*Hectors? Leroys?* Jeez, Jack, you're not sounding very politically correct," Savage said. "Could it be that you're in need of some sensitivity training?"

"Yeah," Lindstrom said sarcastically, under his breath, as he and Savage moved into the vortex of activity to buttonhole Sussman. "Like I could possibly be fucking *politically correct* after twenty-four years in this job."

Having traded in his Gulden's shirt and track-weary paisley tie for a cranberry placket, but still looking like an unmade bed in the pilled, gray polyesters, Sussman seemed frazzled. He appeared to be losing it, trying to coordinate an incoming hundred-bolt delivery of very expensive purple satin while overseeing the outgoing shipments of finished goods to Bergdorf and Lord & Taylor. The underarm wetness on his shirt was fast approaching an earlier set high-water salt mark. One thing about the garment industry, Thorn thought, when things were rolling, these people worked like a son of a bitch.

"Boy!" Lindstrom observed with a devious grin. "He needs us right now like a hole in the head. He's already got one eye on shit coming in, and the other on shit going out."

"Uh huh. And now he'll have to keep the eye in the back of his head on us."

After a quick confab with the harried and preoccupied Sussman, Savage and Lindstrom got situated in Mayhew's office. Seated at a makeshift table composed of two ironing boards lowered to table height and placed side by side, Jack Lindstrom methodically began to do his thing. He would pick through the heavy stuff—Mayhew Fashion's ledgers, tax returns, accounts payable and receivable. Savage, meanwhile, snooped through Harmon Mayhew's desk, file cabinets, and office periphery, down to the wastepaper basket in the corner.

Although Lindstrom had the court order drawn broadly enough to allow for the use of dollies and a crew of strong backs to remove everything and anything, storage-space limitations at Manhattan South made that sort of bucket-scoop evidence gathering an unrealistic consideration. Savage knew that sort of shit only happened on TV or if the feds were involved. God almighty, he thought, how the feds loved to take in property, loved to while away the hours carefully enumerating endless items of shit, whose evidence value was dubious at best if not totally useless. But they loved to generate paper and they seemingly had unlimited storage space. He and Lindstrom would have to decide what, if anything, might be relevant and should actually be taken into custody as evidence or for further examination. They would leave here with no more than a full cardboard box. He'd see to that.

They'd eventually complete their business and get the hell out of here, if Sussman would just leave them alone. He'd been instructed by Lindstrom to remain outside in the shop while the office search was conducted, but once the fabric deliveries had been completed and the Bergdorf order shipped, the noodge hovered, pacing back and forth in the noisy outer room, peering curiously through the glass door. Twice already he'd stuck his head in with annoying questions.

"Looks like our boy Murray just doesn't want to miss anything," Lindstrom said casually, turning the February pages of the ledger.

"Yeah," Savage muttered, preoccupied, as he took a quick tour through the *M*s of Mayhew's Rolodex. "He's like a mother hen out there. If I didn't think we'd be tipping our hand to a possible suspect, I'd ask him if he knew the whereabouts of the loan and partnership agreements. Whaddaya figure his stake is in all this?" he said as he turned his attention to the desk drawers.

"From what he tells me, nada. With both Mayhew and his wife dead, he figures he's gonna wind up out on his ass as soon as the estate's settled."

The contents of Mayhew's desk were not unlike most Savage had seen. Besides a silver-plated letter opener, the center drawer above the kneehole contained the usual assortment of used rubber bands, paper clips, and dried-out complimentary ballpoint pens. There were permanent-ink markers in virtually every color, coin wrappers for pennies through quarters, a rusty nail clipper, and several rings of keys.

He found an age-yellowed menu from Ben's—the big garment district deli up on Thirty-eighth Street—and quickly scanned the sandwich selections. Pavlov was right.

Stacked in the corner of the wide drawer, between a dental-floss dispenser and a few packets of Chinese mustard and soy sauce that had probably been there since the Ming dynasty, Thorn found an inch-thick collection of business cards. Leaning forward in the chair, he dealt them, one at a time, onto the desktop blotter.

A combination business/appointment card implied that Mayhew had been undergoing periodontal treatment at Dr. Nathan Friedlander's on East Thirty-ninth Street. His next appointment was in two weeks. The information on the appointment card also jibed with a handwritten notation, *DDS NF 1:45,* penciled onto the Hirsh Textile wall calendar hanging behind Mayhew's desk. Another dentist's card, that of Dr. Ronald Cairns, showed he'd had an appointment for last February 17th at 2 p.m. Pulling the pin on the calendar and flipping back through March to February, Thorn found that information as well, penciled neatly into the February 17th box as *DDS RC 2:00.* The remainder of the cards bore no notations, and except for the ones from J. Sidney Parker, Attorney-at-Law; Faye Fields, CPA; and the Little Odessa Restaurant in Brooklyn, they were exclusively garment-business-related. The most recent entry on the calendar was a red-circled *FF* on April 14th. It figured—the business card of Faye Fields, the accountant, suddenly fit the puzzle.

Lindstrom set his reading glasses down and rubbed the corner of his right eye with the back of his hand. "Must be needing a new prescription." He yawned. "So far, I'm not finding any mention of Majestic Funding anyplace."

"Ditto," Savage replied. "He doesn't even have a card for them in the *M*s in his Rolodex."

Thorn opened the top side drawer of the desk. It held a broken stapler, an old pair of pinking shears, stationery, thread-spool samples, and a collection of expired Hirsh Textile wall calendars that dated back to 1996. Jerking open the stuck middle drawer that scraped on broken rollers, he found only shoe-shine brushes, a tin each of Kiwi cordovan and black shoe polish, and some used buffing rags. The bottom drawer revealed a collection of *Penthouse* and *Screw* magazines, under which Thorn found a fully loaded Colt Python and a fifty-round box of Winchester .357 hollow points. He flipped open the revolver's cylinder, ejected the six rounds, and, using the reflection of his thumbnail, light-checked the weapon's bore. The stainless-steel gun looked factory-new and showed no evidence of ever having been fired.

"Looks like old Harmon might have been expecting a little trouble," Savage mused. Digging further into the drawer, he found the weapon's original purchase invoice. Dated September 19th, last, it was made out to Harmon Mayhew from Max's Gun World of Miami, Florida. Thorn carried the weapon and its receipt to the "go" box. "Let's remind ourselves to run Mayhew's name with Pistol License and BCI."

"The date on that receipt fits with the timetable that Murray gave me," Lindstrom reminded him. "Remember, he said that Mayhew was really under a lot of pressure last fall."

"Yeah, that was back when he figured he had the life expectancy of a donut in a radio car," Savage said and sat back down. "Well, that takes care of the desk." Swiveling the chair around to face the four-drawer file cabinet behind him to his left, he took a quick look in the second drawer from the top, the one marked *M-Z*. Finding nothing under the *M*s for Majestic Funding, he slid it closed and opened the top drawer marked *A-L*. He would start at the beginning—Aaron Knits.

"Here he comes again," Lindstrom warned with an amused smile from behind his ironing boards while turning another ledger page. "This guy don't believe in giving up."

"Gentlemen," Sussman said, nervily poking his head in the office for the third time. "It's after lunch and I'm sending out for bagels mit a schmear—you interested?"

"No thank you, Mr. Sussman," Thorn replied, trying to sound grateful. Lindstrom shook his head without looking up from the books.

"If only you'd tell me what it is you're looking for, there's a good chance maybe I could help you find it. Don't be schmucks. I know where everything is in this joint."

"No thanks, Mr. Sussman." The tone of Thorn's reply was still pleasant and overappreciative. He always tried using salve first. "It's just better if we do this on our own. You understand. When we're done, if we have any questions, we'll ask. We're going to show you everything we decide to take with us, and issue you an itemized receipt, okay?"

"Yeah, but," Sussman began to protest. "If I was you, I—"

"Murray," Savage interrupted, his tone suddenly abrupt. "If we promise we won't go into the shop and tell you how to sew darts into a ladies blouse, will you promise not to tell us how to do what we gotta do?"

Words obviously failing him, Murray winced and closed the door. Savage winked at Lindstrom. The gonif was stung. He wouldn't be back for a while, with or without bagels.

"Strike three?" Lindstrom asked.

"Strike three, you're out!"

Savage turned his attention back to the files. Ten minutes later he came up with a sealed, legal-size envelope marked *Candace* that was twice folded over and tucked in behind the last hanging *C* file. Carefully working it open with the letter opener, he found it to contain one page of handwritten notations:

80-84.	Land condemn—FM/near Shea 1-2 M.
RM suicide-85.	P/Meters. M dirty. See other indictments at QPC. M slid. C can verify. Saw cash exchanges.

T T Licenses: 10K per to M. (dozens)

Q Blvd recon: 150K to M '82/84 (JCD-concrete
                       contractor) Extended to Al-
                       bany—C can verify

As per M to C.   "CM goes both ways—likes big
                       ladies."

Lots more

Neatly printed in a different ink at the bottom of
the page was the notation "To GS 1116."

"Hel-lo!" Savage peeled the foil back from a fresh
roll of Wint-O-Greens. "Got something interesting
here, brother Jack."

As Lindstrom leaned across the desk and pondered
the coded page, Savage dug back into the desk's upper
side drawer and pulled out the stack of expired calendars. The box for November 16th, last, contained the
handwritten entry *GS-LOR 7:30*.

"Whaddaya make of this?" Lindstrom asked, puzzled, still scanning the coded page up and down.

"Not sure," Savage mumbled, savoring the flavor of
the Life Saver. "It might not mean anything. But I'll
bet GS or LOR could tell us what it means."

"Think our boy Murray might know who they are?"

"He may. We'll ask him before we go." Savage
tossed the collection of expired wall calendars and
Mayhew's desk Rolodex into the "go" box. He also
reached for the stack of business cards. He took the
current Hirsh Textile calendar that had been hanging
on the wall and added that to the growing pile. He
knew there were answers buried somewhere in
Mayhew's abbreviated and cryptic notations.

"I figure it'll be after two when we get outta here,"
Lindstrom said, checking his watch. "Whaddaya
wanna do for lunch?"

"How about Ben's Deli? I'm having this romantic

fantasy about a ton of corned beef on thick slices of
fresh Jewish rye."

"How does that jibe with all those damn health
herbs you take?"

"One cancels out the other," Savage shrugged.
"Figure I break even."

If documentation spelling out the terms of any loan
or partnership agreements Harmon Mayhew had entered into with Majestic Funding existed, those papers
weren't in Mayhew's office. And if Murray Sussman
had any understanding of the code *GS-LOR 7:30,* he
denied it. Savage and Lindstrom went to lunch.

The swaggering, red-faced harp under the military-
style brimmed cap appeared to be in his late fifties,
and his overstated uniform of royal blue with bright
gold piping and fringed epaulets gave him the look of
a generalissimo in some banana-republic regime. He
stood in the street, patent-leather shoes shined to a
fare-thee-well, whistle trapped in a mouth that had
too many teeth, attempting to hail a cab for the couple
that waited beneath the Clarendon's royal blue
canopy.

"That's the same doorman who appears in three
photographs with Candace Mayhew," Diane quietly
observed, as Richie Marcus steered their unmarked
Malibu past the apartment house at 333 East Seventy-
third Street. "The ones taken by DiLeo on the night
she was killed."

"You sure that's him?" Marcus asked, finally eyeing
a vacant parking spot near the corner of Second
Avenue.

"Yeah, I'm sure. He was the one holding the door
of the cab, remember? We were going to have to talk
to him anyhow. Now we can do the apartment search
and get him outta the way at the same time."

"Jeez, how convenient," Marcus mumbled in his
usual, blasé drawl, then asked, "Speaking of DiLeo,
how'd that interview go at the hospital this morning?"

"Savage was right." Diane shrugged. "The guy barely remembers even being there."

"Did he remember being shot?"

"He remembered seeing a bunch of dead people, then a gun barrel being poked in his face. Claims he never got so much as a look at the shooter."

"Jeez!" Pulling beside an empty stretch Lincoln with DPL plates, Marcus slipped the sedan into reverse and began backing into the open spot behind it.

"Notice how edgy Jack Lindstrom was last night?" Diane asked. "How he couldn't wait for the meeting to end so he could leave P.J.'s?"

"Yeah," Marcus said, "I picked up on that."

"Heard he's got some big problems at home. Remember he said he had to leave because he was late for an anniversary dinner with his wife."

"Unh," Richie grunted, pulling forward again to make another approach.

Diane grimaced and shook her head. "He's putting up a good front. There was no anniversary dinner. Jack and his wife split a few weeks ago. Word is she's got herself a boyfriend."

"No shit?"

"Jack's hurtin' real bad."

"You feelin' sorry for him?" Richie said. "Hell, if I was his old lady, I would've left him a long time ago."

"Jack's a nice guy," Diane insisted. "I like him a lot. I do feel sorry for him. Can't imagine why a woman would leave a guy like that."

"This job's got a high divorce rate." Richie shrugged. "What can I tell you?"

"Always wondered what Jack was doing on The Job anyhow," Diane mused. "Always figured him as the engineer or architect type." Marcus snorted.

Parallel parking had never been one of Richie's strong points. In fact, when it came to driving, Jack Lindstrom had always said Marcus had *no* strong points. Thorn Savage refused to ride with Marcus behind the wheel, period.

After numerous back-and-forths, Richie finally managed to get the car somewhat in proximity to the curb. It was then that Diane broke the bad news.

"You're on a hydrant, Rich," she informed her partner.

"What hydrant?"

"The hydrant that I can now see right next to that block-long Lincoln's ass end."

"Ah, shit," Marcus snapped, unduly angry. He continually bopped the limo's rear bumper while jerking the Malibu out of the spot he'd just struggled to get into. "How come only fucking diplomats get to squat on hydrants?"

As Richie fumed on, Diane contained herself from laughing out loud.

Twice more they circled the block searching for a legal place to park. Finally, saying, "Screw it, I'll leave the pass on the dash," Marcus pulled into the Loading Zone right in front of the Clarendon. The doorman, his name, Roger, embroidered in golden lettering on his uniform coat, strutted officiously out of the building to greet them.

Diane turned to Richie and whispered, "Judging by the look on Roger's alky-bloated face, and his arrogant strut, my guess is he's got a BFA."

"You gonna be there long?" the doorman demanded in no uncertain terms. Any doubt Diane may have had about her shoot-from-the-hip opinion of Roger was quickly erased; Roger *did* have a Big Fucking Attitude.

"Lot of that depends on you," Diane replied, stepping from the passenger side of the unmarked Chevy.

"What's that supposed to mean?" Roger snarled, with a hit-me edge to his harsh voice. "I need to have that area left open for my tenants."

"It means exactly what it means, Roger," Diane said, flashing her gold tin. "We'd like to talk to *you*." She noted the spidery veins that crisscrossed Roger's cruller of a nose, and caught a good whiff of last night's Seagram's slipping through his Binaca-shrouded breath.

"Oh!" the doorman said snottily, raising bushy eyebrows to reveal lots more reddened veins muted within mildly jaundiced eyeballs. "S'pose I'm supposed to be impressed, eh?"

"*Hey!* Mr. Charming!" Marcus snarled, communicating in his own brand of nasty as he stepped up onto the sidewalk. "You don't have to be nuthin'. You understand? Just don't be a fuckin' hard-on, *awright*?" Keeping steady, intense, fuck-you eye contact with the man, he added, "Then we can all get along real nice, like. Know what I mean?"

The redheaded doorman seemed to sense his match. Without a word he turned on cushioned soles and led the detectives beneath the sidewalk canopy, then into the white brick, twenty-five-story building. The phone in his microscopic office off the Italian-marbled lobby was ringing. He excused himself and raced to answer it.

"Yes, Mrs. Hardaway," Roger said in patronizing, cloying tones. Then, momentarily cupping the mouthpiece, he whispered sotto voce to the detectives, "Althea Hardaway, 6-A. Real pain in the ass." Turning back to his conversation, he continued, "Right away, Mrs. Hardaway. Certainly, Mrs. Hardaway. I'll see to it." He hung up the phone and immediately dialed out. The detectives listened as he made arrangements with a private car service to pick up Mrs. Hardaway at precisely three o'clock that afternoon and deliver her and her Pekingese to LaGuardia Airport. When Roger hung up, they waited patiently as he carefully logged the outgoing call he'd just made into a composition book.

"Boy, you must work for a real cheap outfit," Marcus said. "What, are they afraid you're gonna gab with your girlfriend when it's slow? You gotta record all your phone calls?"

"Cheap ain't the word," Roger muttered wrathfully,

as he checked his watch to enter the time. "If any of us fail to enter any calls made during our shift, it could mean our jobs. Ya believe it? The bastards actually check." Leaving his BIC pen as a page mark, Roger slid the telephone record back into the top drawer of his desk.

"No wonder you're in such a great mood," Marcus said, one of his disarming, impish grins crossing his rugged face. Diane chuckled to herself, amazed at Richie's incredible ability to deal with jerks and assholes.

"All right," Roger finally said through a resigned sigh. "Whaddaya want?"

"You can start by giving us your full name, address, and home phone number. Then, we need the pass keys to apartment Twenty-one-G. We have a court order for access and a search warrant for those premises," Diane replied, waving both documents.

With a shadow of concern tracing through red, yellow, and pale blue shifting eyes, Roger W. Hogan— "The dubya's for Walter, after my ol' man"—gave the detectives his Bronx home address and phone number. "Twenty-one-G?" he asked, frowning. "That's the Mayhew place. Terrible, that whole thing."

The man turned and pushed a key into the lock of a metal cabinet behind his desk. Inside the cabinet, hooked on panels that turned like the pages of a book, were hundreds of sets of keys. After cross-referencing the coded labels above each hook, Roger removed a set and dropped them into Diane DeGennaro's outstretched hand. "That's them."

"What can you tell us about the Mayhews, Mr. Hogan?" Diane asked.

"Not much, really," he replied casually, relocking the cabinet door.

Marcus half sat on the edge of the desk. "Do you know how they got along?" he drawled huskily.

"No."

"Anybody ever hear them fighting?" Marcus followed up.

"Don't know."

"They have any friends in the building?" Diane queried, handing him a receipt for the keys.

"Really don't think so. They're known for keeping to themselves."

"Did they get many visitors?" Marcus asked, reaching into his case folder for a copy of the shooter's sketch.

"Nah. Like I said, they weren't very social." The doorman's Technicolor eyes shifted back and forth between the two detectives.

Diane piped in, "When Mr. Mayhew would go out of town, did Mrs. Mayhew ever receive any male visitors?"

Roger shook his head.

"This guy look familiar?" Marcus handed over the police sketch.

Without hesitation, the doorman again shook his head.

"When was the last time you saw the Mayhews?" Diane asked.

"Don't rightly remember." Roger seemed to stumble, then added, "Seems I helped Mr. Mayhew into his cab last week. He had a couple of pieces of luggage. Told me he was going to Guatemala."

"You mean Honduras," Richie corrected.

"Yeah, that's it. Honduras," Roger agreed. "Think he said he was gonna be gone for 'bout a week. Surprised he ain't home yet."

"He ain't comin' home," Marcus said. "Mr. Mayhew was found murdered in Honduras several days ago."

Roger's eyes widened in disbelief. The man seemed genuinely stunned.

"You okay, Roger?" Diane asked.

"I'll be okay," the man stammered. "It's just hard to believe they're both dead. He was a decent guy. A good Christmastime tipper."

"When was the last time you laid eyes on Mrs. Mayhew, Roger?" Diane followed right up.

Biting at his lip as if concentrating, he said, "I don't

really remember." Roger shrugged. "Maybe a week or so back."

"Did you see her the night she got killed?" Marcus asked.

"No."

"You're awful sure of that, aren't you?" Diane quizzed.

"I'm positive. I'd have remembered that."

"Were you working that night?" she probed.

"What night?"

"The night Mrs. Mayhew was killed," Marcus pressed.

"I was filling in on four-to-twelves last Tuesday. Papers said she got killed in a bar with a bunch of other people sometime after midnight, which would make it Wednesday. Ain't that right?"

"That's right." Marcus nodded. "So you were working that night, right?"

"Well, technically, I guess."

"Screw technically, Roger. You *were* working, and you *were* here when she left to go downtown. Isn't that right?" Diane bullied.

"Well, I mighta been here, but that don't mean nothin'," Roger shot back, defensive. "She mighta left from someplace else. I really don't remember her leavin'."

"What are you so worried about, Roger?" Marcus kept the man triangulated, then, as if picking at a scab, pressed him harder. "Methinks you doth protest too much." He looked at Diane. She grinned at the incongruity of Richie's use of Shakespeare.

With his voice in upper register, almost falsetto, Roger replied "I ain't worried about nothin'." Then, with another exaggerated shrug of his golden epaulets, he continued, "I ain't got no reason to be worried. I sure didn't kill her."

Diane decided they were done talking to Roger for now, and signaled as much to Richie with a slight pinch of her face and a squint. The strange tenor of the doorman's replies had begun to screech like chalk on her internal blackboard. He was full of shit. She opted not to mention the photographs they had of him helping Candace Mayhew into a cab the night she was killed. It was time to go upstairs and do the apartment search.

"What do you think?" she asked Marcus, as the pair rode the mahogany-paneled, plushly carpeted elevator to the twenty-first floor.

"I think this freakin' elevator car is decorated nicer than our apartment."

"What do you think about Roger?"

"Roger 'Dubya'?"

"Yeah, Roger 'Dubya'."

"He's lyin'."

"Yep."

THIRTEEN

Savage and Lindstrom drove back to Manhattan South, forty-four bucks lighter in their combined pockets, and at least one notch wider in their belts after downing bet-you-can't sandwiches and a slice each of artery-clogging killer cheesecake at Ben's.

"Twenty-two bucks for lunch. *Jesus!*" Lindstrom complained, pulling the unmarked into one of the diagonal parking spots in front of the Thirteenth. "It's gonna be tube steaks for me from now till payday."

Riding the station-house elevator to C-Deck, Lindstrom cradled the box of evidence in his arms as Savage swallowed a corned-beef-with-lots-of-mustard belch, and wondered if there were any Tums or Rolaids in his locker.

They entered the office and found Diane DeGennaro and Richie Marcus already back at their desks. Marcus was knocking out a DD-5 form detailing their search of the Mayhew digs, while Diane studied the black-and-white blowup of Candace Mayhew about to take her last taxicab ride.

"How'd we do up at the apartment?" Savage asked.

"Aside from an oddly defensive drunk of a doorman, who we both agree was lying, we don't have much to report," Diane answered with a shrug of sexy narrow shoulders beneath a curve-clutching, light gray cardigan. It was a good sweater day—for the boys in the office.

"Lying?" Savage asked, cupping hand to mouth, stifling yet another corned beef repeat.

"He denied seeing the Mayhew broad on the night she was killed," Marcus said through a strange grin, leaning his stocky frame way back in his typing chair.

"Possible he just forgot?" Savage asked, knowing better, but playing devil's advocate. "The guy must see hundreds of people come and go from that building every day. I'm sure he can't remember each and every one."

"He remembered," Diane stated seriously.

The look on her face was enough to convince Savage.

Spreading the six glossy prints across her desk, Diane added, "Of course, he's not aware that we have these photographs. Two of which show him yakking it up and smiling with her under the apartment-house canopy, and a third which shows him helping her into a cab just a few hours before she gets herself blown away."

"Those eight-by-tens oughta help refresh his memory," Jack Lindstrom observed. He dropped the box of stuff taken from Mayhew Fashions onto his desk, then stepped around to Diane's desk, which was directly opposite. He began to study the photos.

"I'm not gonna show these to Roger Hogan till we do a little more background," Diane said.

"Like talk to the cabdriver, right?" Lindstrom supposed, as if reading her mind. Diane nodded and smiled.

Richie Marcus snorted.

"I'd really like to talk to the cabbie first. But . . ." She pointed down to the photo of Candace Mayhew climbing into the backseat of the taxi in front of her residence on East Seventy-third. "Here we see Hogan holding the door of the cab for her. If you look closely, you can see that *two* is the first digit of the cab's rear-plate number. The rest of it's obscured by a blur."

"The blur," Lindstrom opined, as Richie Marcus rolled his eyes and smirked, "is obviously caused by a box truck that was driving between DiLeo and the cab at the precise moment that he took this shot."

Savage heard Marcus mumble, "No shit, Dick Tracy."

"What about the other pictures?" Lindstrom asked, as he quickly shuffled through the five remaining photos. "The cab in any of them?"

"Only one other," Diane said. "DiLeo was working with a telephoto lens, and when he took the later shot of her exiting the cab at La Florentine his focus was tight on her; all you can see is a small portion of the cab's open rear door, which is no help. There's no other shots of the cab. I also checked DiLeo's handwritten memoranda. He never noted its license plate."

"Usually," Lindstrom offered with a shrug, "each yellow cab's license plate jibes with its medallion or hack number."

"Hey," Marcus growled, his voice a blunt instrument. "Like we don't know all that." Chuckling out the words, he added, "Our boy wonder is now an expert in freakin' taxicabs."

"What is your problem, Rich?" Lindstrom asked calmly.

"What's your problem?" Marcus mimicked, sitting forward in his chair. "Everybody thinks you're so fuckin' smart. So damn analytical. Too smart to have been a cop. Shoulda been an architect, shoulda been an engineer. Know what I think? I think you woulda made it big-time as a bag boy at Gristede's. Failing that, you'da probably excelled as a shepherd."

Diane shot Marcus a freeze-dried stare. He snorted twice, sucked an incisor, and leaned back smugly.

"What about the OFF-DUTY light on the taxi's roof?" Savage asked, breaking the tension. He peered down more closely at the Seventy-third Street photo. "Seen from the rear the hack number should be lit up."

It, too, was cut in half by the blur of the passing

truck. With the aid of a cheap magnifying glass, borrowed from Eddie Brodigan's desk, Lindstrom decided that the medallion number on the cab's roof light began with the number *2*, followed by the letter *G*.

"Taxi medallions are sequenced starting with a single-digit number, followed by a single letter, then followed by two more numbers," Savage said, sparing Lindstrom from voicing the fact, which might reignite Richie's fuse.

"That's a Ford trunk and taillight," Marcus pitched in curtly.

"You sure?" Savage asked.

"He's sure," Lindstrom said. "He's probably run into the back of enough of them to know by now."

"You pickin' on my driving again?" Marcus asked coolly.

"Talk about being well suited for a career," Lindstrom said. "Your empty head and lousy driving are the things great crash-test dummies are made of."

"We gotta find us a friggin' Ford taxicab whose license plate begins with two, and whose partial medallion number is 2 G. You can do that, Diane," Marcus said, and returned to typing his five.

"Put in a call to Taxi and Limousine," Savage said without hesitation. "Have them provide us with a list of every active medallion that starts with 2 G. Since the last two digits will be numerals, the list can't be more than a hundred. Tell them we also need to know the type vehicle each medallion is assigned to—Ford, Chevy, Dodge, whatever. That'll cut the numbers down even more when we rule out non-Fords. Tell them we also need to know the identity of the independent owners or fleets that own those medallions."

"Then," Diane, nodding enthusiastically, said, continuing her boss's train of thought, "we have the fleets check the trip sheets of their 2 G Fords for that night."

"When we find the one that picked up a fare at the

Clarendon at ten forty-five, and dropped off at Forty-ninth and Third, then we'll have our chauffeur," Savage affirmed. Giving Diane an encouraging thumbs-up, he turned to Richie Marcus. "Tell me about the apartment."

"Tell you one thing," Marcus began, looking up from his typewriter. "The place sure was ritzy. I coulda moved in and gotten comfortable *real* quick."

Savage sensed something strange about Marcus's mood. He'd always thought Marcus had a glass head, and that he could look right inside and read the man like a book. Something was up.

Marcus and DeGennaro both went on to say that they'd found nothing in the apartment that might help explain the violent deaths of the sixty-one-year-old man and his younger wife. The opulent, twenty-five-hundred-square-foot living space they'd searched was neat and clean. It was classically decorated with heirloom-quality furnishings, and bedroom bureau tops were covered with smiling photographs of the two together, albeit probably in happier days. A leather-bound checkbook they'd found on the kitchen counter showed a very healthy eight-thousand-dollar joint checking balance, and Diane reported that Candace Mayhew had an extensive collection of valuable jewelry. On the way out, they'd taped a Property Clerk's seal across the apartment's doorjamb. Now no gold-digging relative could squirm their way into the place and make love to the bounty—not without written authorization from a probate judge.

Jack Lindstrom wound a Property Clerk's voucher into his typewriter and began itemizing the boxful of maybe evidence they'd brought in from Mayhew Fashions.

Back in the sergeants' room, Savage flipped with one hand through the memos and communications that had accumulated on his desk in the few hours he'd been away. With the other hand he probed tenaciously at a caraway seed the size of a football hope-

lessly wedged between two lower molars. He was on
his third toothpick. He'd never learn—it happened
every time he ate at Ben's. Their rye bread was great,
but the *friggin'* seeds . . .

Dammit all! The thought suddenly drifted through
his head. Knowing he was going to a deli for lunch,
why hadn't he picked up some dental floss? Lately
he'd found himself forgetting words, or why he'd
walked into a room. The curse of Alzheimer's had
brought down both of his parents, sucking away each
of their lives, years before either mercifully died. His
father hadn't lasted long, but his strong-hearted
mother had lived, existing like a mindless plant that
got fed and watered, for ten years after she'd been
diagnosed. Thank God for his younger sister, Emily,
and, at the very end, the volunteers at hospice. He
wondered if he should boost his daily dosage of ginkgo
biloba and double up on the vitamin E. He'd stop at
the health-food store on the way home.

Finally dislodging the annoying distraction with a
salvaged section of a third snapped toothpick, he was
able to turn his attention back to the memos. This
time he actually read them.

Call Dawson. *??? Okay!*

A fax from the New York Department of State had
arrived. It contained information Lindstrom requested
about the corporate officers of Majestic Funding.
Good!

Lieutenant Pezzano had drafted a one-paragraph
memo authorizing the overtime Savage had requested
for his team. *Very good!* Richie Marcus'll be glad to
hear that, he thought, then quickly realized that the
man already knew. The overtime approval explained
the shit-eating grin that Marcus couldn't hide.

A handwritten memo from Brodigan said that Gina
McCormick had called: *"Father much improved."*
She'd left a number where she could be reached until
3:30. *Great!* The clock on the wall said 3:25. He picked
up his phone and quickly dialed.

The woman who answered announced, "Kearney and Dunton."

Put on hold, he endured a full minute of canned Mantovani and his somnambulant strings until Gina's formal, yet pleasing, voice came on the line.

"Ms. McCormick, this is Thorn Savage. I'm returning your call."

"Oh, yes, Sergeant." Her voice dropped its business-like tone and became purely pleasing.

"Who's Kearney and Dunton?" Thorn asked casually.

"They're licensed public adjusters."

"Public adjusters?"

"Professional loss consultants. We represent the policy holder in property-damage claims. Fire, smoke, wind, water—that sort of thing. I have a degree in accounting. I head up the appraisal department."

"Gee, that's funny, you don't look like an accountant."

"What do female accountants look like?"

"Do you remember the name Yogi Berra?"

Gina chuckled.

"How's your father doing?" Savage queried.

"Fine. Doctor Dresner says he's a bull, and that he's out of danger now."

"Great. I'm glad to hear it. How's your mom?"

"She's fine too. She sends her regards."

"That's nice. Send her mine."

After a moment of dead air, Gina broke the silence.

"Sergeant. I hope you don't think this too terribly forward of me."

This was beginning to sound very promising. "Call me Thorn, please." He strained at the earpiece—he didn't want to miss anything the lovely Gina might be about to say.

"Thorn," she repeated cheerily, and after another millisecond of self-conscious dead air, added, "I wonder if you'd be interested in having dinner with me tomorrow night. That is if you don't have a wife, a girlfriend, or other plans."

"That's one yes and three noes, in that order, Ms. McCormick," he promptly answered. He couldn't believe his ears.

"Call me Gina. Please."

"Gina," he repeated. "I have no other plans. I'd really like to have dinner with you. Where and when?"

"You like Italian?"

"Who doesn't?"

"Palermo's on Hester? At eight?"

"Palermo's at eight it is." He said good-bye and hung up the phone, leaned back in his chair, and grinned like a sweepstakes winner. Things were looking up.

Savage reached back into the stack of memos. He picked up and read the faxed message from New York State.

FROM: Sarah Morehouse, State of New York—
          Department of State. Division of Investigations.
TO: Detective John Lindstrom, Manhattan
          South Homicide Task Force, NYPD
SUBJ: Information Requested, Re: Majestic
          Funding. A Corporation.

As per your official request, our records indicate that the following named persons are the corporate officers of record for Majestic Funding, 355 Brighton Ave, suite 2-A, Brooklyn, New York. This corporation was formed on August 16, 1997.

President: Nikita Relska
Vice President: Georgei Strelnikov
Secretary: Dmitri Nakovics
Treasurer: Peter Kozyukova

"Hey, Jack," Savage hollered out to the squad room. "Bring in Mayhew's Rolodex, calendars, and that cryptically coded note from that box of stuff." It was an outside shot, to be sure, but maybe some of the Majestic Funding names would correlate with Mayhew's penchant for initials.

After laying the requested items on Thorn's desk, Lindstrom picked up and read the Department of State fax. *"Holy Shit!"* he murmured. "These definitely *are* the sons of Vladivostok, aren't they?"

"Either that or the Russian bobsled team," Savage said, quickly spinning through the yellowed and dog-eared pages of Mayhew's Rolodex. Nothing fit. Then, flipping the pages backward in time, he compared the names of the four corporate officers against all the initials jotted on Mayhew's calendar pages.

"Look at this, Jack," he said, stabbing his finger to the November 16th box. "We may have us a match." He cross-referenced over to Mayhew's cryptic notes and smiled. Although none of the four corporate names appeared anywhere in Mayhew's records, it wasn't much of a stretch to consider that the GS in Mayhew's November 16th calendar notation, *and* in *GS LOR 7:00 1116,* at the bottom of the coded page, could refer to Majestic Funding's vice president, Georgei Strelnikov.

Savage looked up at Lindstrom. "Let's run all these names through BCI right away, for prints and priors. Also, check 'em for warrants."

"Then?" Lindstrom asked.

"Then, we gotta begin taking a serious look at Majestic Funding. I want an eyeball put on that place, ASAP. Right now. Today!"

"You know, I got serious plans for tonight, boss," Lindstrom said with a grimace.

"Oh, yeah," Savage groaned, recalling Lindstrom's personal problems without letting on. "And Diane's got her daughter's baby shower tonight." Suddenly, a sly grin formed across his face. *"Oh, Richie!"* he called out to Marcus in the squad room. "I need you to head out to Brooklyn right now and do a surveillance." After a well-timed, teasing pause, he threw in the hook. "It'll no doubt wind up into overtime. Think you're up to it?"

Marcus beamed back his answer through the glass partition of the sergeants' room, still wearing that same shit-eating grin. Enough said.

The question of who would do the surveillance at Majestic Funding now settled, Jack Lindstrom went back to his desk to call the Bureau of Criminal Investigation and run the four names. Savage went to the last memo in the stack and dialed the number of the Fox Hole. Dawson picked up on the first ring.

"How'd your *piece conference* go?" Savage asked, without identifying himself.

"I've been to better," Dawson responded coyly, apparently recognizing Savage's voice. "But not many. I'd say it was a nine."

"Really?"

"Umh," Dawson purred dreamily. "A good *solid* nine."

"Yes, well," Savage muttered, "got something for me, Dawson?"

"Maybe."

"Lay it on me, Trooper."

"It's like this, Sarge. According to the big guy—and, *oh Gawd,* I do mean the *big* guy—Fleming, the publisher, there was this lifetime collection of marvelous stuff auctioned off at Sotheby's back in May of '84. Fleming was absolutely sure of the month and year. He'd have been there to buy, but he was touring China at the time."

"Was it a collection of Heydes?"

"Everything came from the estate of Desmond Clarence Alt, some zillionaire prosthetics-device manufacturer. He was a noted collector of militaria, and when he died the family auctioned off the whole goddamned shooting match. Can you believe it? *Assholes.*"

"Jeez, that's a bitch," Savage said, working off the cap from a nearly empty container of Tums he'd found in the back of his top desk drawer. The antacids were two years past the expiration date stamped on the back label. He popped two of the tablets into his mouth anyway and chewed. "What about the Heydes?"

"According to Fleming, they auctioned away complete sets of Garibaldis from Italy, Dorsets from England, and Soldats from Spain. Those are basically newer manufacturers that dealt in Euro armies from the late 1800s up to around 1940."

"Slow down, Dawson," Thorn protested. "I'm writing as you talk. What about the Heydes?"

"They also sold off hundreds of William Britains. That guy made beautiful stuff that represented every modern army of the last nine decades."

"But what about the Heydes?" Savage asked, patience dwindling.

"I'm *getting* to that," Dawson snapped, verging on a snit.

Trooper Dawson, it seemed, was not about to be interrupted. He'd risked life and limb—well, maybe not limb, but certainly other vital body parts—to acquire this information and, by God, he was going to tell it all.

"Fleming said they even had a few hundred Courtenays. Today we're talking one to three hundred dollars each for the foot soldiers, and two to five hundred each for the mounted ones. *My Gawd*, can you imagine?" Dawson's tongue clucked in disbelief. "Fleming and I agreed that the auction was a collector's wet dream."

"What-a-bout-the-fuck-ing-Hey-des?" Savage intoned, smoothly articulating every syllable to break into the wacko's tightly focused stream of consciousness.

"I was saving the best for last," Dawson said stubbornly.

"Don't keep me in suspense, okay?" Savage urged, having lost his patience, but struggling to keep Dawson placated with a soothing tone.

"They sold a world-class set of Napoleonic Heydes," Dawson finally announced sharply.

"That what we're looking for? Napoleonic?"

"That's what we're looking for."

"What else can you tell me?" Savage asked, scribbling across a memo pad.

"It was a very rare forty-two-piece set. French infantry, cavalry, and artillery. Fleming didn't remember how much it sold for, but he was sure it brought a chunk of change."

"Could our piece have come from that particular set?"

"Could have," Dawson chimed. "Same period."

"Dynamite. You've done a real good job, Dawson." Savage gave him a verbal pat on the back.

"Can't tell you much more," Dawson said regretfully. "Except that if the piece did come from that set, surely Sotheby's would still have a record of who bought it. By the way, they're at Seventy-second and York."

"They sure should have a record. Thanks, Dawson."

"If I hear anything more, Sarge, I'll get back to you."

"Ten-four. Thanks again." Savage hung up the phone and reached for his jacket all in one motion. "Hold the fort," he announced to his paperwork-buried crew as he signed out of the office. The entry he scribbled in the command log read:

1630 hrs: Sergeant Savage to Sotheby's Auction
             House, 72 and York, in auto # 7146.

                    *   *   *

The conversation was going about as badly as he'd predicted it would. Attempting to soothe the pain of a murderous migraine, Gerard Maloney cradled his forehead in his right hand and gently massaged his temples between his thick thumb and middle finger. His ruddy face turned a deep scarlet as he shouted into the bedroom telephone of his Forest Hills estate. "Don't tell me that shit, Harold. I never told you I was *definitely* not going to run."

"That's the understanding I had, Gerard. What was I, hallucinating? You told me you wanted that leaked to the media. That's what I've had done."

"Well then," Maloney bellowed. "Un-goddamn-leak it! I'm coming back to Washington this afternoon and I want this bullshit behind me."

"I'm not quite sure how I'm supposed to do that, Senator," Harold DeWitt said dolefully, "without leaving some people, friends, with considerable egg on their faces."

"Is there anybody in the media who can place that leak directly back to you or me?"

"No. But there will be plenty of speculation."

"Screw speculation. This whole thing'll be like a free advertisement for us for crissakes."

"That's not how the game is played, Senator. You know that. We may have to go back to some of these same people again someday."

"We'll cross those bridges when we get to them. These people won't abandon us. Are you forgetting?" Maloney exhorted. "I'm going to be the next god-damned president of the United States. These sons of bitches would be wise to cut me a bit of slack." He glanced across the room to his cunning wife, who'd cajoled and convinced him to change his mind. She sat there listening to his side of the conversation and nodding her approval.

"All right," DeWitt said, his words breathy, wrapped in a resigned sigh. "I'll do what I can on my end."

"I'm scheduled to speak at a breakfast with the Council of American Business Leaders tomorrow morning at the Watergate," Maloney said. "That's when I'll deny ever saying it."

"Be convincing," DeWitt admonished.

"I promise I'll use my most serious, concerned, hemorrhoidal look. You watch, this is all going to work to our advantage."

"I can't see how this possibly can help us," DeWitt

said with a frustrated tone. "It reeks of indecision. Voters do not want indecisive presidents."

"But they do want sympathetic ones. Clinton proved that. We'll blame the whole damn thing on jealous opposition. I'm telling you, Harold, it'll work for us."

"Whatever you say, Senator. I'm only going to be your campaign manager, what the hell do I know?"

"Just do it." Maloney hung up the phone and turned to his wife. "Okay?" he asked.

"Okay." She nodded. "Just keep listening to me, and everything will work out just fine. This is all just a cost of doing business, as they say."

The staffer who greeted Savage inside Sotheby's Italian-tiled lobby was a feisty lady who, though well preserved, had to be in her late sixties. She was well dressed, well coiffed, and seemed to take great interest in the broken figurine he carried in the plastic evidence bag. She also seemed to take an immediate shine to him. Most older women did. Savage always figured if he made it to eighty he'd be scoring like a rock star.

Twenty-eight years ago Joy Nickerson had been a recently widowed forty-year-old, with a daughter about to start college, when the lease on her Madison Avenue antiques boutique came up for renewal. Determined not to be shaken down by a greedy landlord who'd decided to become her partner by virtue of doubling her already outrageous store rent, Joy told him to stuff it. Actually, she told him to go and fuck himself.

Needing to quickly liquidate the entire inventory of the shop that she and her dead husband had labored for ten years to put into the black, Joy consigned everything to Sotheby's Auction House a few doors down on Madison and wound up taking a temporary job there. Now Sotheby's was on York Avenue and Joy Nickerson was still with them, their senior staffer.

Through the years Joy had dealt on a one-to-one basis with the likes of the shah of Iran, the sultan of Brunei, and most of the Kennedy women. She'd handled the sale of Jackie's jewelry and most of Andy Warhol's eclectic estate. She'd also dealt with plenty of slick hustlers, many bent on passing off fakes and repros as the real thing. But Joy Nickerson was a master judge in the authenticity of seventeenth to twentieth century artifacts and fine art—she loved the impressionists. She was also an excellent judge of human nature and had never gotten stiffed in any of those departments.

"Come with me, Sergeant," Joy said, winking coyly and doing an agile about-face. "Since you've got the year and month, maybe we can find something in the computer." Striding with the fluidity of a woman half her age, she led Savage down the auction house's central passageway past a gallery of gilt-framed oils.

"Those are all on exhibit," she explained, pointing out a collection of colorful still lifes interspersed with a grouping of verdant landscapes. Massive portraits of foppish eighteenth-century English nobility hung along the opposite wall. Everywhere there was an abundance of fresh, funnel-shaped white flowers that overflowed from dozens of ancient-looking oriental vases, urns, and ginger jars that were also "on exhibit." Two doors beyond the larger of the two auction rooms, she turned into her private office, lavishly appointed mostly in Louis XVI. Like the rest of the auction house, her space was richly decorated with the faint-smelling white flowers.

"Casablanca lilies," she said, before he had a chance to ask. "Sotheby's has a full-time, in-house florist. The flavor changes every week."

"Just like our station house," Thorn cracked, flashing his good-natured grin.

"Tell me again, when did you say we sold these items?" Joy asked, spinning her chair to face the IBM monitor and keyboard that rested on a separate counter next to her carved mahogany desk.

"We believe it may have been May 1984," Thorn replied, dropping into a burgundy velvet wingback and turning it to face the monitor. "Were you guys computerized then?"

"You betcha," Joy said, waiting for the screen to come to life. "We handle so much inventory it would be impossible to keep up without computers anymore. Our company originated in Great Britain in 1766, and the records of every transaction we've ever handled are all archived somewhere. The modern stuff, since the late seventies, has all been downloaded into our database."

"Great."

Her age-spotted, delicate hand gently cupped the mouse. "What was that client's name again, Sergeant?" she asked, steering the cursor and selecting an icon.

"Alt. Desmond Clarence Alt."

"Oh, yes, Alt. A-L-T." She spoke each letter while typing in the name.

"It *was* 1984, Sergeant," she confirmed, as a block of information blipped onto the blue screen. "Alt, Desmond, estate of. Says here that on May 14, 1984, we auctioned off a total of sixty-two thousand, nine-hundred and fifty dollars' worth of collectible figurines, military memorabilia, and miscellaneous."

Savage leaned forward in his chair and studied the information on the screen.

"Will those records identify the figurines by manufacturer or brand name?" he asked hopefully.

"They may. But of course, we need to find the right lot." Joy Nickerson began scrolling through page after page of itemization. "Here they are," she finally said, "Heyde, H-E-Y-D-E. Your information was very accurate, Sergeant. It *was* a forty-two-piece set—auctioned off as lot number nineteen. It fetched seven thousand dollars." She spun in her seat wearing a long face.

"What's wrong?" Savage asked.

"Purchaser, *anonymous!*" she replied.

"Buyers can do that?"

"Been known to happen, provided that payment is immediately made in full, in cash."

"Happen often?"

"When people pay staggering sums for highly collectible or precious items, they feel that anonymity helps reduce the possibility of later theft. If nobody knows who bought it, then nobody knows where to go to steal it." Joy Nickerson shrugged and turned her attention back to the computer screen. She scrolled it up and down. "Every other lot from that sale shows a purchaser's name. See here," she said, as Savage stared across the top of her shoulder. "Lot numbers fifteen through eighteen, described as four separate sets of Courtenay toy soldiers. All purchaser's names are listed. Lots numbered twenty through twenty-five, Garibaldi toy soldiers—all purchasers shown."

"Would you be good enough to give me a copy of everything you've got pertaining to that entire auction? Maybe we can locate and talk to some of those other buyers."

"Glad to." In seconds, a whiny ink-jet printer began spitting out pages.

"Ms. Nickerson. Can you in any way recall that particular auction?" Savage asked.

The woman tightened her face, and shook her head. "We hold, on average, two auctions a day. Which means we've probably held in the neighborhood of some ten thousand auctions since May of '84. I might have been there, assisting, but it was so many years ago, I just can't recall it."

"Is there someone who might recall? Perhaps the person who was in charge of that sale? I'm hoping that someone has a recollection of what this buyer looked like."

She turned her glance back to the screen. "The records show that the Alt estate sale was under the direction of our Martin Van Hogue."

"Where's he?"

Again she spun in her seat, looking gloomy. "Dead," she said flatly. "Five years ago. Sorry."

Savage telephoned Manhattan South from Sotheby's at 1710 hours to check in. The wheelman told him Marcus was set up on his surveillance out in Brooklyn, but that everything else was quiet. It was ten minutes beyond the end of his tour of duty and Savage took an excusal from the field. Having had a heavy lunch he decided on sushi for dinner—it was light and he was due for a wasabi fix—before heading over to P.J.'s for a visit with Frankie and a Friday-evening cocktail. He never drank on an empty stomach.

FOURTEEN

The work was right up Harry Moon's alley, and he'd been handsomely paid, in full, in advance. The job couldn't have come at a better time. He needed the money bad. Besides the ex-wife breaking his nuts for thousands in back alimony and child support, his aging Sedan deVille was in the shop getting a new transmission. With a new torque converter, the bill was twenty-two hundred dollars, thank you, and only a fucking six-month guarantee. There was also the matter of the hundred-a-day heroin jones he'd been developing. *Ahh,* life's a bitch, he thought.

Carefully measuring his speed, and concentrating on keeping a safe distance from the cars around him, Moon drove the van south along the Brooklyn-Queens Expressway as defensively as he knew how in the stop-and-go traffic. Even a minor fender bender now could be disastrous, and probably fuck up the whole damn job. One could hardly stop to exchange license and registration when one was driving a stolen vehicle. And if one tried to leave the scene, where could one run in this constipated rush-hour snarl on an elevated highway? Nowhere.

Preoccupied with those concerns, and more, Moon ignored his two helpers who argued viciously beside him, as the new GMC swung off the BQE and rumbled across the Williamsburg Bridge. George, the big-mouth with the ponytail who was riding shotgun and, by virtue of his oafish size, could be a linebacker on anybody's ball club, wanted mega-loud heavy metal blaring from the van's speakers so he could continue to play his moronic air guitar. Finnegan, the intense psychotic in the middle, had apparently heard enough of the grating noise and quieted the radio by crashing a hammerhead through the dial face. George was spitting out angry threats of retaliation, but it was clear that the half-pint Finnegan had an established upper hand there. On the Manhattan side of the bridge, Moon headed the hot vehicle west on Delancey. At the Bowery he turned right, then made a left onto Houston.

The innocuous-looking white van, with magnetic plastic signs affixed to the front doors reading Crenshaw Painting Contractors, pulled to the curb in front of the three-story brownstone on Sullivan Street. Still daydreaming about how he'd spend the windfall of bucks that filled his hip pocket, Moon checked the address scribbled across the mark's photo that'd been clipped from the front page of yesterday's *Post*. This was it—184 Sullivan. He pushed a screwdriver blade into the mangled ignition switch and turned off the van's engine.

Still bickering and exchanging threats, Mutt and Jeff emerged from the van's passenger side. Opening the vehicle's sliding side door, they busied themselves off-loading stepladders, paint containers, and large bundles of drop cloths. Moon, meanwhile, climbed the concrete stoop and let himself into the building's foyer. He pushed the bell button atop the mailbox to apartment 1. A dog inside the apartment went crazy, barking.

"Oh, fuck," Moon mumbled under his breath. "Nobody said nothin' about no damn dogs." He felt a sudden twinge in his butt as he recalled the eighty-eight stitches that had been required to reattach his right ass cheek—compliments of a junkyard German shepherd—back in '89.

After a long display of unfriendly, chesty canine yelping, the frightening racket inside the building finally subsided, and Moon sensed someone looking him over through the peephole in the foyer's inner door.

"Yes?" he heard a man's voice ask.

"Crenshaw Painting," Harry Moon announced in his best bored monotone. "We're here to do the baseboards in the hallways, and"—looking down at his clipboard—"handrailings and trim on the staircases."

"Awfully late in the day to start a painting job, isn't it?" the voice queried.

"Just want to drop our stuff off and do the priming. We'll be back in the morning to do the finish work."

"Who requested your services?" the voice asked suspiciously.

Again looking at his clipboard, Moon replied, "Says here if there's any question, we're to ask for a Mr. Savage. He knows we're expected."

"Why don't you ring his bell?"

"Did," Moon lied. "Didn't get no response."

After a pause of many seconds, the agitated voice behind the door said, "All right, hold on."

As the dead bolt released and the door slowly opened on squeaking hinges, the baying dog again made its presence known from somewhere within the building. The man who'd answered the door was small in stature, gentle in demeanor, and very gay.

Harry Moon pushed the silencer-lengthened barrel of his gun against the smaller man's ribs. He marched him down the narrow hall that ran alongside the open staircase, and back into apartment 1. Inside, Jo-Jo the Dalmatian darted and leaped, continuing her wild, violent barking. A silenced bullet spit from Moon's automatic, then another, punctuated by a throttled yelp. The dog's piercing bark trailed off to a brief piteous whine, then nothing. Seconds later, there were two more spits in rapid succession.

The two younger men entered the building, each

carrying bundled drop cloths and a five-gallon paint container. Once inside Johanssen's apartment, they unwrapped the bundles to reveal a pair of silenced MAC-10 machine pistols. Opening their paint containers, they each removed razor knives, scissors, rolls of cord, and duct tape. Efficient, they went through the entire apartment. Removing every framed painting from every wall, they protectively wrapped and concealed the works of art in sections of the heavy cloth. Harry Moon, meanwhile, sat down in the small man's still-warm chair. He casually replaced the four spent shells in the clip of his silenced SIG Sauer, then thumbed through a *New York* magazine that lay open to an article on museum-quality art. Harry would get comfortable. Though the mark got off from his job at five o'clock, it *was* a Friday night. They could be there for a while.

A bus, more than half filled with Friday-evening fares, came to a stop in the traffic lane on Brighton Beach Avenue, completely blocking Richie Marcus's line of sight. The blue-and-white diesel-powered behemoth idled behind a line of cars waiting for the light to change.

Marcus dropped the field glasses into his lap, and quickly closed his partially opened driver-side window the rest of the way. On the green, the municipal monster roared to life, belching sooty exhaust all over the new Toyota. "Damn!" Marcus shook his head. "Just washed this fuckin' thing yesterday."

Richie hated the Toyota's dazzling green color; he thought it a bit *cunty*. He'd wanted Diane to get the navy blue, but she'd fronted the five-grand down payment, and also traded in her '93 Chevy. So, fuck it, he had to go along. If they were married he might have pressed it. But just living together made things a mite tenuous. He wasn't exactly dealing from a position of strength. Neither emerald nor turquoise, but something in between, the new Corolla was an eyecatcher. In direct sunlight, it was downright blinding. They shoulda got the navy blue. *Ahh!* Marcus sighed, the sacrifices he made to keep his honey happy.

It was five after seven, and there was still daylight. He'd been parked under the el since 3:45, but the OT clock hadn't actually started running until 5:00. He had two hours OT in the bag already—$76.56. He shook another Winston from the pack and lit it. His sight lines again clear, he brought the binoculars up to his eyes.

A silver-haired guy in a charcoal gray suit seated, Marcus presumed, behind an unseen desk, was still clearly visible through the large, steel-dust-coated window of the second-story office. Richie traded the binoculars for the Minolta with the telephoto. He quickly focused on the man, snapped two shots, and placed the camera back on the seat. By virtue of his moving lips and facial gestures the guy was bullshitting with someone else present there. Awful late hours for a loan company, Marcus thought, as another noisy Q train rumbled along the tracks above. He focused the field glasses around what little of the office he could make out. Save for an old-fashioned black-and-white industrial-type electric wall clock, whose kinked wire ran down to a power outlet, the rest of the bland beige-painted walls were bare. No paintings, no pictures, no calendars, no plants. No nothin'. Above the guy's head, a ceiling fixture gave off weak light. There was a chunk missing from the corner of its frosted lens. You didn't have to be fuckin' Charlie Chan to see that the place had all the earmarks of a classic front.

At 7:30, the puny glow of the ceiling fixture flicked off entirely. Moments later, the hard, silver-haired guy and a big-knobbed middle-aged bottle blonde exited the two-story building at the sidewalk-level entrance. The woman lit a cigarette while the man produced a ring of keys and turned the lock on the glass door. The peeling vinyl lettering on the door read: MA ESTIC

FUNDI G. The shutter of the Minolta rapidly clicked six times.

The man and woman exchanged a light kiss and parted ways. Big Tits went west toward Brighton Third, while the guy quickly crossed Brighton Fourth moving east. With daylight rapidly fading, Marcus slid the camera beneath the seat; it would be of no further use tonight. He slipped the Toyota into gear and began moving east. How male-chauvinistic of me, he thought, snickering snidely to himself, automatically deciding to follow the man. The bitch could be just as bad, if not ten times worse.

Marcus could see that the guy was built like a fire hydrant—short and cast-iron strong. He seemed to give off the same vibes and quiet challenge of a pit bull defiantly patrolling personal turf. He turned into Brighton Seventh and walked to a new silver gray Town Car parked off the corner.

As the man got behind the Lincoln's wheel to drive away, Marcus picked up the Motorola portable beside him on the seat and radioed the plate number to Central. In seconds it came back registered to Georgei Strelnikov, DOB 11/11/39 of 1620 Ocean Avenue, Brooklyn.

Eu-fucking-reka!

Marcus followed as the big sedan moved easily through the numbered side streets of Brighton Beach, turned onto Neptune, and continued out through Sheepshead Bay, to the end of Emmons Avenue, where it emptied onto the eastbound lanes of the Belt Parkway. They were headed to Queens.

As a detective third grade, his overtime rate was $38.28 an hour, plus mileage for using his own car— well, Diane's car. Who lived better than him? Too bad Diane had her daughter's baby shower tonight. First-graders made lieutenant's money; her OT rate was fifty-six bucks an hour. Jesus, he thought, they could be raking in a combined cool hundred bucks per if she were here. He pushed one of Diane's tapes into the cassette player, and cranked up the volume at the downbeat of the Temptations' "Ain't Too Proud to Beg." Thumb tapping the steering wheel, he sang along as the parkway wound through Canarsie and past Starrett City, where his ex-wife and two daughters still lived. Without seeing the road sign, he knew by the fetid aroma filling the car that they were nearing the Sanitation Department's landfill at Fountain Avenue. The wind must have been out of the south, off Jamaica Bay.

At Cross Bay Boulevard, the Lincoln exited the Belt and headed north until it turned into Woodhaven. Marcus moved discreetly within the light traffic flow behind it, not too close, not too far. Driving at moderate speeds and observing all the rules of the road, the Lincoln passed through the Queens communities of Ozone Park and Woodhaven. It crossed Jamaica Avenue, then Metropolitan, and, after passing St. John's Cemetery on the left, turned right onto Yellowstone Boulevard.

Marcus allowed his glance to momentarily fall on the ornate, black wrought- and gilded-iron gates of the Roman Catholic graveyard. His mother was buried there—*bitch*. The mother who'd dumped him and his older brother into an orphanage, a Catholic orphanage, as if that made a difference, when they were just kids. She'd had a friggin' party life to pursue. They never saw her again. He'd never even been to her grave. Since the day he escaped the orphanage by joining the marines, he'd never again set a foot inside a Catholic church. He yanked his attention back to the pit bull in the silver Lincoln and reached again for his cigarettes.

The Town Car made a right on Exeter, went four blocks, and crossed Continental Avenue. They were entering the Forest Hills Gardens: Money Land USA. At Greenway North the Lincoln turned left. It wound its way along the high-dollar, Belgian-block-paved private side streets. Parking here was by permit only. In this ritzy, quiet, lightly-traveled section of million-dollar haciendas, Marcus knew that his tail could more easily be made; he loosened it up—just a bit. Up ahead, the Lincoln slowed its pace to a crawl, turned into Underwood, and pulled to the curb beneath the glow of an old-fashioned streetlight. The ornately cast and multiglobed fixtures that barely lit the Forest Hills Gardens' sidewalks were a far cry from the schlock aluminum jobs that lit Bay Ridge at night, or, Marcus thought, most other parts of the city he was familiar with.

The man's silver hair gleamed yellow in the lamplight as he got out of the car and walked briskly up a winding path leading to a stone-and-stucco Tudor mansion. He didn't even have to knock; someone was there—a broad, blond, waiting to let him right in. Marcus noted the Tudor's street address as he drove by, then quickly circled the tree-lined block.

Just off Burns Street he pulled the bright green Corolla to the curb. As dashboard speakers punched out "Great Balls of Fire," he focused the glasses on the empty Lincoln nicely framed by a convenient gap in the hedgerow he'd parked beside. Reclining the back-rest of the driver's seat three notches, Marcus flicked what was left of his Winston out the window, immediately fired up another, and got comfortable. Sometimes these things took all night, he thought. At thirty-eight bucks an hour, he prayed it would.

It was the first really warm Friday evening of the new spring, and no one in Manhattan was sitting home wasting it. The city was alive with activity. Even P.J. Clarke's had been busier than usual, if that was possible. By eight o'clock, the payday horde of middle-class urban fun seekers had reached the four-deep mark at the long mahogany bar, but their added numbers in no way affected Frankie McBride's ability to keep Savage supplied with double Rusties. His glass never went below the quarter-full line; neither did the Dubonnet that swirled amid the rocks in the glass of the light-skinned cocoa delight who'd wound up on the stool next to him.

Jasmine, a mid-forties fox from Yakima, Washington, in town to attend a weeklong series of cosmetic seminars, had the lithe body of a dancer and a voice that seduced and lulled like the eerie music of a snake charmer. If she'd been a car, she'd have been a sleek Ferrari—well engineered and sophisticated, but built strictly for high-performance. Their conversation—despite the noisy background din—had taken right off, and had been heading directly to the king-sized bed in her room at the Hilton. Along with the cosmetic-industry knowledge she'd gained while in the Apple, she, apparently, also wanted to take home some lusty memories.

Savage could have "gone native"—Lindstrom's un-PC expression—tonight if he'd so wished, but he'd listened to the shoulder-mounted head and opted for an early break. Even Frankie couldn't talk him into having another drink.

Jasmine purred as she handed Thorn her business card. "If you're ever in Yakima . . ."

The million-and-a-half-to-one odds of him *ever* being in Yakima, Washington, just dropped to even money. Reciprocating, he gave Jasmine his card. Maybe she'd call him next time she was in town. As he chewed on the last ice cube from his drink, and motioned "no more" to Frankie, he looked around the busy bar. He knew that some guy in or on his way to P.J.'s, although certainly not aware of it yet, was going to get very lucky tonight.

Walking away from an evening with the captivating Jasmine wasn't the easiest decision he'd ever made, but Savage decided to save his strength, and his liver, for the following night and his dinner date with Gina McCormick. He didn't want to show up at Palermo's with hemorrhaging eyeballs. He sprung for Jasmine's next Dubonnet-with-a-twist, bid the lovely lady and Frankie a good night, and left for home at 9:30.

*   *   *

Cloaked by the blackness of the unlit study, Christine Maloney gazed trancelike through the narrow, cranked-out opening of the stained-glass-paneled casement window. She had an unobstructed view of the well-tended grounds, brick driveways, and slate footpaths leading down to the tree-lined, cobbled roadway that ran past the twelve-room manor. Staring, mind lost in a dozen intricate webs of thought, she appeared as if in a state of suspended animation. It was the rude glare of approaching brights moving up Greenway North that snapped her to. As they turned into Underwood, the big sedan, the same one that'd been there that morning, slowed, its driver seemingly unsure, as if searching in the darkness for recognition of the right house and the right address. Then the car pulled to the curb and its headlights went black. She knew who it was.

Taking a half turn on its crank, Christine closed the window. She moved smoothly from the dark study, out through the dining room, and stopped before the gilt-framed mirror that hung above the matching console in the softly lit main hall.

Her hair was perfect. Nipples, hard and erect, pressed like pencil erasers from the inside of her flowing satin robe. She adjusted and preened for maximum effect, then waited at the front door, peering through the side lights. She was ready.

The same sturdy-looking man, his silver hair reflecting the muted incandescence of the street lamp behind and the treetop-scrimmed rays of the bright moon above, was starting up the long winding path. As he neared the house she opened the door and, without a word, stepped aside, allowing him to enter. Her head much clearer since their last meeting, Christine was back in form. Swinging the heavy door closed behind him, she felt his eyes sizing up her barely concealed flesh. He emitted the intensity of a predatorial carnivore. Cordially, she reached out her hand.

"Forgive me for not formally introducing myself this morning," she said in her most breathy voice. "I'm Christine."

Guarded caution revealed in probing ice-blue eyes, the man offered his hand in return. The paw was indelibly callused from many years of serious labor. "I am Georgei. Georgei Strelnikov."

"Come with me, Georgei," she said gently, leading him through the wide hallway. "Come sit with me. Would you care for a drink? Vodka perhaps? Name it, I have all the best brands."

"Stolichnaya, neat."

Like a courtesan welcoming a nobleman to her parlor, she led the man into the great room, to the same sofa whose arm he'd occupied that morning. Excusing herself, she breezed to the bar in the far corner of the room and cracked a fresh bottle of Stoli. She poured him a tall one, with enough hundred-proof to anesthetize a full-grown Tibetan yak, then fluted a chilled split of champagne for herself.

"Do you have the money, Mrs. Maloney?" he asked directly from across the room, seemingly unimpressed by her warm, suggestive greeting.

"I have the money," she assured. "But first, let's talk." Leaning down, allowing her loose-fitting robe to hang open at her chest, she handed Strelnikov his drink, then sat in the wingback directly opposite. There was a long, silent pause as they exchanged deep, questioning glances. Knowing she had his full attention, she slowly crossed her long, shapely, freshly shaven legs, revealing for a teasing instant an appetizer of her unpantied charms.

"Are you trying to seduce me, Mrs. Maloney?" he asked, his glance shifting back to her eyes. He took a long, measured gulp of the warm liquor.

"Yes," she answered, unashamed and straightforward. "I intend to fuck your eyes out."

He did not respond. He took another sip, and appeared to be looking straight through her.

This was an icy-cold man, she thought. She was intrigued.

"Why would you want to do that?" he asked finally, Russkie overtones trebling the effect of his deliberative monotone.

Christine stood and crossed to the sofa. Sitting beside him, she took a sip of her bubbling champagne, and gently placed a hand on his knee. The man's limb was hard, strong, like a steel beam. "Apparently, I have no secrets from your eyes, Georgei. And you told me this morning that you found me most . . . 'stimulating.' I think that was the word you used."

Strelnikov said nothing, but it was clear to Christine that he was in the mood to hear more. Much more. She would not disappoint. She loosened the belt on her satin robe and moved closer. He took another pull on the warm vodka.

"You need me, Georgei. Believe me when I tell you that Gerard is capable of going either way on this thing. He's notorious for digging in his heels when painted into a corner."

"Which way do you think he will go?"

"Any way I want him to," she gloated with a faint laugh. "Right now I have him seeing things your way, but you'll always need me to control him. You know, of course, once he officially announces his candidacy this place will be swarming with Secret Service agents. There'd be no way you could reach out to him directly. Forget making visits like this. You wouldn't even be able to get a message through to him by phone."

"What are you suggesting?"

"I can be your liaison with him during the election process," she bore in. "Then, once elected, within the White House itself. I can bring about things with Gerard that you and your people would be unable to force no matter what you threaten." She gently stroked the ex-longshoreman's rugged face. "But in return, *my* relationship with you and your people will have to be a two-way street. And, from this point forward, I will deal only with you. No one else.''

"I am not ultimate power. I am merely an aide, a functionary. I do not have final say in all policy. This, you must understand. But,'' he continued, "I do like what I hear.''

"Oh, I understand,'' Christine assured, then patronized. "I think you and I have a lot in common, Georgei. Though each of us may be officially only second in command, I think we both know that we are the true brains of our respective situations. Neither of which could function in our absence.''

Shrugging impassively, Strelnikov drained the last of the vodka, and set the empty glass on the coffee table before him. She could see the persuasive impact that her words, and erect nipples, were having. Men were so fucking easy. She reached for the bottle of Stoli and refilled his glass.

"If, in fact, you can speak for Senator—and we know you can—and, if you can assure us of his full cooperation in future ventures, then I am to tell you that as gesture of good faith and goodwill we are prepared to forego twenty-five thousand you still owe us.''

Christine nodded appreciatively, and swallowed the rest of the bubbly. Its rapid numbing effect would help get her through the coming seduction scene.

"I can, and do, make those assurances,'' Christine whispered, probing the tip of her tongue into Strelnikov's ear.

"One more thing we must know,'' Strelnikov said. "Is there anybody else who could possibly know of Senator's connection to Candace Mayhew? If so, we will need to know who they are.''

"I'll give that question some thought,'' Christine moaned, momentarily ceasing her lobe-licking, while sliding her hand up Strelnikov's rock-hard thigh. He turned and faced her; they kissed. In a flash, the kisses became wet, wanton, and intense. In seconds, his clothes and her robe were strewn across the Karastan and draped crazily across the back of the sofa.

Arching her back in pleasure, and undulating her tight torso to counter each strong thrust he made into her, Christine exploded into a series of incredible orgasms. Peaking simultaneously, Strelnikov unloaded and collapsed, spent, in her arms. Locked together, they lay there and dozed.

"I've never been so well *humped* on a camelback," she teased, finally breaking the silence. "You were amazing, Georgei. I'd forgotten just how good it could be with a man."

"You are fascinating woman, Christine Maloney," Strelnikov uttered, still regaining his breath. His flattery seemed sincere.

"Georgei," Christine said seriously, "now that I think about it, there was a newspaperman named Joe Ballantine engaged to Candace back when Gerard was screwing her. As I recall, when Ballantine found out what was going on, he made an incredible stink and broke the engagement. I've always suspected that he knew a great deal, and was nothing more than a time bomb waiting to go off."

"I will have to look into that."

"Yes. Of course you must," Christine said. "He is a link that someday could break. He's just the sort who could wind up being a big liability to us down the road. Especially in view of the fact that he's an investigative reporter."

Naked, except for one calf-length black sock, Strelnikov eased himself from the fleshy tangle. Sitting up at the far end of the sofa, he reached into his suit jacket draped across the arm. He dug out the pack of filtered Camels, lit one, and sucked in a heavy first drag.

"I want you to take the twenty-five thousand," Christine announced, cradling her bare feet in his naked lap. "I want you to keep it for yourself, and I want you to consider it my gesture of good faith and goodwill with you."

He turned and faced her, but said nothing.

Sensing his reservations, Christine sat up and assured him, "No one on your side could ever know that I've given it to you."

"They would know," he said, his tone uncertain but weakening.

"All you need to say is that the Maloneys have agreed to fully cooperate. That being the case, if what you've told me is true, your people neither want nor expect to see the money. Tell them I intended to put it back in a safe-deposit box. As far as Gerard is concerned, the money's already gone."

She watched Strelnikov blow a long, slow, contemplative stream of smoke as he visibly pondered her offer.

"I like you, Georgei," she said, stroking his neck and shoulders with delicate fingers. "You are a real man. You are somebody I can do business with and feel confident."

"Would you like to take another ride on camelback?" he propositioned, turning to embrace her.

"Do you and I have a deal?" she asked.

"Yes," he replied decisively. "We have done deal. And how about brunch on Sunday?"

"I'd love to," she said, allowing his strong arms to ease her back down.

After watching Strelnikov's Lincoln pull away, Christine returned to the great room. Reaching beneath the mossy grass at the base of the silk ficus in the planter that faced the sofa, she dug out the mini tape recorder.

Rewinding the tape, she played it back in its entirety. The recording was clear as a bell. "Nobody gets the better of Christine Maloney," she muttered with vengeance.

Nobody, she thought. Not even you, Nikki Rosen—

or goddammed Nikki Relska, or Nikki whatever your name is—fucks with me. You may have fucked with my world, but now I'm going to fuck with yours. "Payback's a bitch. *Bitch!*"

FIFTEEN

Sullivan was a one-way street that began at Broome down in Soho. It crossed into the Village at Houston and continued northbound until it dead-ended at Washington Square South. Savage lived between Houston and Bleecker, just on the Village side. His block contained the Sullivan Street Playhouse, two small bistros, and a commercial parking lot interspersed with brownstone town houses that had long been carved up into apartments. Like the rest of the streets, avenues, and byways of the Village it really came alive on springtime evenings, and on Friday nights it sometimes took an act of God to find a place to park. Forget the parking lot—it was always full. Savage knew just where to go.

He dropped the Ford right below the No Parking Anytime sign in front of St. Anthony's School on Mac-Dougal Street. He knew that Father Vinny would give his blessing, but someplace down the road it would eventually cost him a couple of top-shelf brandies. Savage didn't mind. Father Vinny, a half-Scottish, half-Italian Jesuit, was a regular guy and great company. They often got together at Arturo's for pasta, drinks, and philosophical discussion, if not heavy debate. The more brandies, the heavier the debate. Savage knew that the priest would like nothing better than to bring him back into the church flock. But after the faith-blunting loss of his wife and daughter, and decades of up close observation of the cruelties that men inflict on one another, he had no time for the gobbledygook of organized religion. He got all the creed, doctrine, and canon law he needed from his own church—The Job, the NYPD. Father Vinny knew and respected that, and never pushed. Thorn dropped the PD parking pass on the Crown Vic's dashboard. Like a garlic-encrusted crucifix, the pass would ward off the early-morning vampires from Parking Enforcement, and the car would still be there when he returned tomorrow.

The immature sycamores that lined the sidewalks near the church were beginning to bud for spring. Struggling to survive in their hostile environment of concrete, asphalt, diesel soot and carbon monoxide, they managed to grow within their cramped four-by-four allotments of less-than-fertile earth. Hell, the only attention they ever got was from sniffing, leg-lifting, or squatting dogs. Like most other forms of life in the unforgiving city they had to have character if they were to survive.

It was light-sweater weather. A gentle breeze warmed the night air, bringing a hint of approaching rain. As he walked toward home, Savage realized how much he liked the Village. He liked its urbane feel, he liked the artistic bent, and he liked the genuine sense of community. It had its share of weirdos, no question, but was still the most vibrant neighborhood in Manhattan. It was convenient to his job, to headquarters, and the courts, and when it had mattered, was close to Maureen's place in Soho.

Expert at the risky city game of dodge the Dodge, he crossed Houston against heavy, fast-moving two-way traffic. He was now only a block from home.

Clustered at the edge of the Houston Street park, dozens of evening strollers smiled appreciatively and swayed with the bouncing rhythm of street-corner reggae. A beanpole-slim island black, whose gnarled dreadlocks probably hadn't seen a lick of shampoo

in twenty years, was searching out the tinny notes of
"Jamaica Farewell" on a red, black and green enam-
eled steel drum. His partner, an equally hungry-
looking Bob Marley clone, wailed the familiar words
from a cavernous mouth filled with an incredible set
of perfect white teeth, while thumping bottom on a
beat-up Fender bass minus its fourth string. It was
amazing how these guys could tap into an electrical
supply in the middle of nowhere—a knotted extension
cord ran to a street-lamp base—plug in an amp, and
start making beer money. These two were definitely
fugitives from the mayor's Quality of Life Task Force.

In the constant ebb and flow typical of these street-
corner scenes, onlookers would watch and listen for a
few minutes until their interest waned. Then they'd
drop a spare buck or some pocket change into big-
mouth's velvet-lined instrument case, and move off.
By some as-yet-unknown law of physics, their numbers
were then immediately replaced by others out for dinner and a stroll, and the process would repeat. Truth
be known, the two Muppets probably only knew the
one damn song.

Culture in the streets. Tonight, reggae; tomorrow,
who the hell knew. Gershwin? Dylan? Mozart? Jug-
glers? Mimes? All of the above? Would there be a
quartet in tuxedos dragging catgut across the strings
of somber cellos? Or a pair of teenage wanna-be hip-
pies with an acoustic guitar, a tambourine, and com-
plexions that screamed for Stridex? Savage folded a
single, dropped it into bigmouth's case, and moved on,
his spot quickly filled by another.

Unconsciously cognizant of those things that only a
cop sees, or even bothers to look at, for that matter,
he noted the great variety of license plates on the cars
parked along the curb. For every New York plate,
there was a Jersey, Connecticut, Pennsylvania, or
Maryland. As he neared his building, he spotted a
Colorado on the back of a turbo Saab. The car was
idling through the block, its aging yuppie male driver

and his blond lady companion craning their necks, searching for the unattainable—a free spot.

Lots o' luck!

His policeman's eye was then taken by a new GMC van parked right outside his building. A temporary, magnetic sign on its front door advertised "residential painting contractor," but its New York license plate was not commercial. In fact, the plate bore a letter sequence typically reserved for rental vehicles. Maybe the bald guy sitting behind the wheel painted part-time and was saving himself the full-time expense of owning his own truck. But why a pricey daily rental, he thought? A guy would have to paint an awful lot of wall each day just to cover the cost of the ride.

Dismissing the who-gives-a-fuck-anyway question, Savage reached into his jacket pocket for his keys, trotted up the steps to the front door and let himself into the unlocked outer vestibule. His mailbox was jammed with the current issue of *Hemming's Motor News,* a letter from the AARP, and a statement from First USA Visa that he immediately opened. The charges on this month's bill were for a shirt and a pair of Austin Reed slacks from Barneys, a steak at Gallagher's, and three high-altitude free falls he'd taken two Sundays ago at Felicity Parachuting down in Lakewood. He reminded himself of the upcoming JumpFest to be held there next Sunday. Parachute freaks from all over the country would be there. So would he.

He slipped his key into the lock of the inner foyer door, turned it, and let himself into the main hallway. It seemed darker than usual. Strange, Johanssen's dog didn't bark at the creak of the noisy hinge.

Resting his hand atop the newel post at the base of the long stairs, he paused and looked around. The light at the second-floor landing was dark. The decorative glass globe was gone from the fixture, and all that remained was an unlit bare bulb. Had it burned out? Had one of the other tenants undertaken to fix it?

Unlikely. Mrs. Potamkin from apartment 3 was down in Miami—not due back till late tonight. And forget Johanssen, he'd never bother fixing a light on the second floor—he couldn't care less.

Had someone taken a couple of turns on the bulb to intentionally darken the hall? He knew his suspicious nature. He knew it sometimes overreacted. He also knew he'd have been killed a dozen times in the last thirty years if he'd ignored it. He began to move tentatively up the flight of stairs. Halfway between floors, he looked down over the spindled railing. His eyes now fully adjusted to the dim light, he saw a collection of cloth-draped items stacked along the hallway leading from Tor Johanssen's first-floor apartment door. Though each thing was separately wrapped, the square edges of what could only be portrait frames within gave away their valuable contents. Instantly, the who-gives-a-fuck question of the rental van parked outside and its bald-headed driver made sense.

Fuck me!

Clenching his jaw, Savage slowly set his mail on the next stair tread and unbuttoned his jacket. He reached into his belt line and undid the snap on his belly holster. Below him, at the rear of the long first-floor hall, a man suddenly appeared in Johanssen's apartment doorway. Wearing painter's coveralls, he was tall and had long hair pulled back into a ponytail. He cradled a very ugly machine pistol. At the same instant, Savage heard the squeaking hinge below and behind him. The bald guy from the van—a silenced automatic pistol in his right hand—was slithering his skinny ass past the front vestibule door at the foot of the stairs. Just when he decided that the only way to go was up, and fast, a third man made his presence known at the darkened second-floor landing above him. Even in the dim light, Savage made out the menacing snout of the MAC-10 the stairway guy held, and his cocksure I'm-going-to-enjoy-killing-you expression. From both above and below, Savage had been triangulated into a no-win cross fire.

Great! he thought. His anemic, five-shot Smith against a trio of friggin' automatics with bottomless magazines. *Great! Just fuckin' great!* Then all holy hell broke loose.

A misaimed burst of fire from Stairway Man above tore into the wall at Savage's left shoulder. He recoiled at the bloodletting stings of a thousand hornets as rock-hard fragments of plaster and jagged splinters of shredded wood lath stung and tore at his face and neck. *Time to bail!*

Thirty-eight clenched in his right hand, Thorn vaulted the spindled handrailing with his left, and descended to the lower hallway within a powdery shower of pulverized plaster. He did a PLF—a parachute landing fall—legs locked and slightly bent at the knees as his full weight landed on the hardwood floor below. Strong thighs, like Monroe-Matic shocks, allowed him to collapse, controlled, into a smoothly moving gymnastic ball.

Although a dead-duck target for either guy on the lower floor—one ahead of him, one behind—his sudden presence in the middle put them both at risk of each other's fire. Their resulting momentary delay allowed him to roll once and come up into a combat crouch facing the ponytailed guy in Johanssen's doorway. Ponytail let loose with a quick burst that stitched the floorboards right between Savage's legs. Behind him, Savage heard Baldy making a dash for the cover of the staircase. Pushing the .38 straight out before him in his right hand, and instinctively drawing his left arm across his middle-chest vitals, Savage fired one time. Ponytail's wide shoulders hunched forward, his mouth expelled a coughing gasp, and he reeled backwards, slamming heavily into the apartment's interior-hall wall. The ammo-saving single shot had found its mark, dead center in Ponytail's chest. Unbelievably, the hulk immediately bulled his way right back into Johanssen's open doorway, again raising the muzzle of his machine pistol. The son of a bitch was wearing body armor beneath the coveralls, and aside from a possible slight case of blunt trauma, was still very much alive and very deadly. Making matters worse, Stairway Man was tromping down the steps to get into a better firing position near Baldy. Savage knew he had only seconds to find himself some cover, or become the target of a merciless air strike. Instantly, he raised his aim on Ponytail and fired again. This one dotted Ponytail's left eye, and again slammed him backward against the inner wall. He then crashed face first onto the floor, his huge body twitching like a poleaxed cow in an Omaha slaughter stall.

Like a sinking boat in a violent squall trying to outrun a swamping, life-taking following sea, Savage clawed and scrambled for forward movement as automatic fire from the staircase chased him down the remainder of the hallway. Clambering across Ponytail's still-twitching form, he took cover just inside Johanssen's apartment. Over his own gasping breaths he heard the unmistakable, unnerving metallic clack of spent ammo clips being ejected, and new ones being popped in.

Definitely not a good sign.

If only he could shut and lock Johanssen's door, he could buy some time. Maybe he could even get to a phone, and, if they hadn't cut the lines—which he was sure they'd done—he'd dial 911 and put over a 10-13. But there was a bleeding, two-hundred-pound-plus doorstop preventing that; he needed a different plan, *fast*.

With only three rounds remaining in his five-shot revolver, Savage made a tentative reach for the machine pistol that lay partially hidden beneath Ponytail's facedown body. Apparently reading Thorn's mind, Stairway Man quickly fired a burst into the doorway's opening, putting another half-dozen hits into his fallen compadre's head and back. Ponytail was now very, *very* dead.

Thorn's mind raced. Quickly assessing the grim logistics of his shit situation, Savage realized that in order to get him now, one or both of the bozos would have to make a charge down the hallway. The smartest thing they could do would be for the cocky Stairway Man, overhead and armed with the MAC-10, to cover Baldy. Thorn hoped they weren't that smart. He didn't have to wait. Suddenly Johanssen's doorway lit up like Chinese fucking New Year with full metal jackets ricocheting off the steel door slab and frame like skyrockets flying in every goddamned direction. The beachhead had been established. The invasion assault was on.

Aside from the powdery glow that oozed in from the hallway, Johanssen's place was dark—black—like the inside of a coal miner's mitt. He was sure the circuit breakers had all been tripped. Although he'd only been in Johanssen's place one other time, two years ago, when Maureen had been invited to view the art collection, he was able to recall the flat's layout. If he could grope his way to one of the back rooms, he might be able to get out through a rear window. Scratch that idea, he thought, remembering that all of Johanssen's windows were security-barred. And, what of Johanssen? Alive? Dead? Tied up in a back room? Have to worry about that later; got other things to worry about right now. Concentrate. Concentrate. He'd have to make his stand right there.

Scrambling to his feet, Savage hugged Johanssen's wall, and backed himself deeper into the dark apartment. He found some cover kneeling behind a fluted, stone pedestal that supported an alabaster bust of somebody, Mozart maybe. No good. The column didn't offer enough protection—not against that kind of artillery. Arms locked at the elbows and shoulders, he pushed the two-inch-barreled Chief straight out at eye level. Focusing intently on the opened doorway, he quickly sidestepped and took cover behind the corner of a near wall. He saw that anybody trying to enter would be momentarily backlit, albeit just barely. That was when he'd have to do it—go for a head shot. At best he'd only have time for one.

He caught a break. For a split second he discerned

a shimmering shadow, hovering like a wraith, creating a momentary spot of darkness within the gun smoke and plaster-powder haze that was eerily wafting into the apartment. Seconds dragged like a man attempting to run in waist-high water. It was like waiting for fucking Elvis to appear out of a staged fog. But, it was near time—he felt it. The sense of skulking movement came again, picked up by his acute secondary vision. He could tell someone was nearing the body-blocked threshold. Savage concentrated on a slow and smooth single-action squeeze of the old Smith's trigger.

Suddenly, in one motion, the figure crashed in. Planting his back firmly against the door slab for support, MAC-10 at hip level, the man fired wildly on full automatic into the darkness—anything in his path was coming down. The rounds peppered a plate-glass-mirrored far wall, destroying a priceless display of crystal figurines, porcelain vases, and cloisonné urns. The fragile items were bursting like rotgut liquor bottles stacked behind the bar in a B western saloon shoot-'em-up. The alabaster bust also took a few hits, exploding from its place atop the fluted pedestal into a thousand worthless pieces.

The muffled reports spewing from the MAC-10 were punctuated by a single, loud *blap*. It was the rude return bark from Savage's unsilenced .38.

It was Stairway Man who took the perfectly aimed round between the eyes. Propped by the bullet-peppered door behind him, he slid in stages to a sitting position on the apartment floor. His finger frozen on the trigger, he fired the remaining rounds in his automatic weapon, blasting huge holes into the torso, backside, and outstretched legs of the ponytailed doorstop lying motionless at his feet. Finally, all ammo expended, the cocky bastard's head flopped forward in death. His sneering grin morphed into a stunned and disbelieving gape.

After seconds of an incredible, surreal silence, Savage heard the unmistakable creak of the hallway foyer door hinge. Baldy was bolting. Savage quickly moved from the cover of the apartment's interior corner wall to the body-filled threshold that led to the hallway. Fighting for traction as his leather-soled Florsheims slipped and slid on the blood-puddled hardwood, Savage kicked and rolled Ponytail's draining bulk out of the way. With the adrenaline-generated strength of ten he yanked the still-potent machine pistol from the man's petrified death grip. Now, evenly armed, he charged through the hallway and slipped cautiously through the outer vestibule. He stepped out onto the street.

Baldy had apparently decided he'd had enough. Savage caught the van's entire plate number as the GMC, peeling rubber, pulled from the curb, and raced up Sullivan Street. Rounding the corner at Bleecker, it disappeared.

Quickly returning to Johanssen's devastated apartment, Savage found a phone. The line *was* dead. Groping his way down a darkened long hall, and into the kitchen, he found the electric box and started flipping breakers. He heard the compressor on Johanssen's refrigerator kick in. Flipping light switches and turning on lamps as he moved, he began his search. At the end of a bloody dragline he found Tor Johanssen's body dumped in the bathtub. He found Jo-Jo, the Dalmatian, in a back bedroom closet with half its head blown away.

Concealed within the small crowd of sidewalk concertgoers, his jaw clenched in anger, the field marshal glared into Sullivan Street. It was over. His partisans had been defeated—two-thirds of them, no doubt, slaughtered. The greatly outnumbered enemy, scarred and bloodied from the give-no-quarter battle, but victorious, had just routed the only apparent survivor of the debacle into disorderly flight.

Since their first encounter, the field marshal knew

not to underestimate this foe. He'd known, innately, they were cut from the same warrior cloth. Like Montgomery and Rommel. Two implacable forces, each with no fear of death, only contempt for an inglorious one. The field marshal recalled his failed attempts to convey that all-important factor to his leaders.

As in many instances throughout history, the piddling politics of unworthy leaders had again brought about the unnecessary defeat of soldiers on the battlefield. The defeated general felt no disdain toward the foe. If anything, he had a grudging admiration for a kindred spirit, who probably had his own hierarchical bullshit to contend with. Soldiers like them, he decided, shouldn't have to function under such drivel. They should be allowed to fight their wars unencumbered by unsure and hedging interference.

Siren wailing, a police car turned off Houston and raced past him into Sullivan Street. It slid to a stop in front of the narrow brownstone. In seconds, the short block was congested with an onslaught of the red-light-domed white-and-blue sedans.

The reggae players pulled the plug, packed their shit, and vaporized. The concealing crowd faded.

It started to rain. The field marshal pulled up his collar. Then, with an overlong fingernail, he reset the safety on his automatic. He slipped away into the night.

Richie Marcus checked the time, readjusted the seat back to its full upright position, and raised the binoculars to his eyes. It had been an hour and a half since Hard Guy had been welcomed into the Tudor. Now, carrying a small bundle he held clamped under his left arm, the man suddenly reappeared in the cobbled roadway and was unlocking the front door of his Lincoln.

"Dammit," Marcus uttered, annoyed. He figured the son of a bitch'd be there for at least a few hundred simoleons on the OT clock.

The Lincoln, driven as soberly as it had been earlier, retraced its path right back to the same area of Brighton Beach in Brooklyn. Hard Guy parked the shiny Town Car beneath the dirty el that ran above Brighton Beach Avenue. The small bundle he'd picked up in Forest Hills nowhere in sight, he disappeared inside the Little Odessa Restaurant on the corner. It must be dinnertime.

Marcus took up a position beneath the elevated train tracks a block and a half away. Parked diagonally opposite, and facing the restaurant's entrance so as not to miss the man's eventual exit, he scratched the time onto his Daily Activity Report and wondered what Russian pit bulls ate for supper. He also wondered if the Little Odessa had stroganoff on the menu. Since his stomach had begun growling hours ago, Marcus decided to find out the answer to both questions. He slid the portable radio and binoculars under the front seat, disabled the Toyota's interior courtesy lights, locked the doors, and trotted across Brighton Avenue. Looking casually around the restaurant as he entered, he didn't see Strelnikov. He bypassed the tables and booths, opting instead for a stool at the far end of the half-filled counter.

Thirty minutes later he pushed back his empty plate. The beef, sautéed in sour cream, had just the right blend of onions and mushrooms, Marcus thought. He'd never had better. The only place that even came close was the Uki joint on Avenue B down in the Ninth Precinct. Marcus hadn't gotten his forty-four-inch waist from being unacquainted with foods of all nations, and he considered the Little Odessa his culinary find of the year. There was no question that he'd be back. The only real question was where the hell was Strelnikov?

The place was busy but the man wasn't at any of the tables or booths within the dining area, nor was he at the counter. While wolfing the stroganoff, Marcus had seen several other men enter the place. They didn't eat. They'd each nodded to the cashier by the door when they came in, breezed through the joint, and disappeared somewhere in the back as if headed toward the rest rooms. But they never reappeared. Then, while finishing a second cup of coffee, Marcus watched as a new face emerged from the back, one that he hadn't seen enter. It was too early yet for it to be an after-hours club, he thought.

Noting that the Lincoln was still parked out front, Marcus left the counter and visited the men's room. No Strelnikov, no two other guys. The only other places the men could possibly be were the kitchen, the ladies' room, or behind the steel door just beyond the men's room that was marked *Employees Only*. Marcus spotted a security camera tucked high in a corner of the passageway. Its lens was focused directly on the Employees Only door.

Peekaboo. I got you, motherfucker!

Somewhere behind the Employees Only door had to be a Friday night poker game in progress, maybe even craps and twenty-one. He'd bet on it.

The warthog of a cashier was pulling double duty. From her corner perch, the Foo dog look-alike in the amber necklace had an unobstructed view the length of Brighton Beach Avenue and could also see down most of the intersecting side street. Whatever was going on in that back room—gambling, Mickey Mouse movies, Communist Party meetings—was private, and nobody was getting anywhere near the joint without passing her muster. Marcus was also willing to bet that she had some means of signaling the boys in the back at the first sign of a police raid or the approach of any unwanted visitors. Unsmiling and deliberate, the brutish woman returned to examining the purple polish on her nails after making Marcus's change. He walked back to the counter, belched twice, put down a two-dollar tip for the counterman and left the Little Odessa. Marcus sensed the cashier's following eyes as he stepped out into a clammy beachside drizzle, and took a circuitous route back to the Toyota, arriving there with the first few heavy drops of rain.

Soon, as the low-pressure front coming in off the Atlantic began unloading a torrential downpour on southern Brooklyn, Marcus allowed his thoughts to drift to his second favorite topic. He wondered about Miss Sass, the excellent mudder who was going off in the fourth at Aqueduct tomorrow. Last he'd checked, the filly was eight to one. He'd call his book first thing in the morning and go five times to win. If it kept raining like this, it was a fuckin' lock.

Thirty minutes later, now chewing a toothpick, the silver-haired hard guy who was probably Georgei Strelnikov reemerged from the Little Odessa. He got into his Detroit iron and drove off. Marcus followed through the heavy rain to an austere-looking dark-brick apartment building at 1620 Ocean Avenue—the Ocean Castles. There, the man parked his car and, toting plastic-draped dry cleaning over his shoulder, dashed through the downpour into the building. Pit Bull was home—he was going beddy-bye for the night.

Sweet dreams, motherfucker, Richie thought as he noted the time—2315—onto his DAR. And thanks for the OT. Quickly figuring that six hours and fifteen minutes of overtime came out to $239.25, he decided he'd boost his bet and go ten times on Miss Sass in the morning. He pushed in the cigarette lighter, peeled the cellophane from a fresh pack of Winston, and made a U-turn on Ocean. The cassette tape was now beginning its umpteenth cycle. It was back to "Ain't Too Proud to Beg."

He switched off the department portable, turned up the cassette player's volume, and headed the Toyota toward home. The baby shower would be well over by now, and all the hens would be gone. Energized by his filling dinner and the two cups of strong Russian coffee, his mind then shifted to his third favorite topic.

He'd give Diane a shake when he got home. Hell, she wouldn't mind.

He reached in the glove compartment for his Tums. The onions were beginning to talk back.

SIXTEEN

The second half of Savage's night turned out to be only slightly better than the earlier part. Now, at least, nobody was shooting at him—not bullets, anyway. The lacerations at the side of his face and neck were mostly superficial and didn't require any stitches. After slowly picking away a tenacious fragment of wrapper from a lone Wint-O-Green that must have been hiding in his jacket pocket for months, he slipped the mint onto his tongue.

Who knew? he pondered briefly. If he'd have stayed for one more cocktail up at P.J.'s, he might just be off contorting with gorgeous Jasmine from Yakima right now instead of twisting in a second-floor detective squad room, being made to justify how and why he saved his own life. Next time maybe he'd listen to Frankie McBride and stick around for one more drink. Maybe next time he'd listen to the call of the wild, and wind up writhing under hotel sheets with a foxy mama, instead of writhing under investigation at the Sixth Precinct.

He knew the game. When a New York City policeman fires his weapon, the department immediately conducts a preliminary investigation that is a lengthy ritual. When somebody, no matter how justifiably, gets injured or killed by a cop's bullet, the investigation becomes a torturous all-nighter. Savage was only two days removed from the debriefing rigors of his last shooting incident, and here he was, at it again. He was answering the same stock questions repeatedly. Relating the step-by-step sequence of events as they happened, over and over, to the duty captain, the borough commander, squad detectives from the Sixth Precinct, Crime Scene personnel, and Lieutenant Pete Pezzano, his own boss from Homicide who'd responded from home. Further complicating matters, recently appointed First Deputy Police Commissioner Fiona Rice-Jenkins had arrived at the Sixth two hours ago and declared herself in charge of the "internal investigation." The former department advocate and trial commissioner, she was outranked in the job only by the police commissioner—who happened to be out of town at a law-enforcement convention in Baltimore.

In cop parlance Rice-Jenkins was a headhunter, notorious for eating cops for breakfast at the trial room, then spitting them out—usually right out of The Job. Jesus, Savage thought, didn't she have anything better to do with herself on a Friday night? Why hadn't *Mr.* Rice-Jenkins, or Mr. Rice, or Mr. Jenkins, or whoever the hell he was, taken her out dancing, or to a damned movie or something? Why wasn't she home in bed where she belonged at this hour, instead of here, breaking his balls?

Up until the first dep's unexpected arrival, the shooting investigation had been moving nicely along its well-choreographed path. Although Crime Scene would put together precisely detailed blueprints of his apartment building's entranceway, hallway, and staircase—complete with vivid photos from every possible angle—Savage had earlier drawn a preliminary, rudimentary sketch of the place. It was used to facilitate understanding of his statements as to who fired what and when, where they were standing when they did, and how they got to where they fell with a bunch of holes in them. Commissioner Rice-Jenkins seemed to be having problems understanding how Ponytail wound up with one extra eye in his head, and thirty-

some extra holes in his ass—besides the one presumed
to belong there. Almost immediately upon arrival,
she'd closeted herself, along with the Manhattan South
borough commander, ACI Patrick Feeney, and Petey
Pezzano, in the squad commander's office. Savage
sensed something was wrong. He felt it in his gut.

Jimmy Scacia, the Manhattan South delegate from
the Sergeant's Benevolent Association, had shown up
hours ago advising him not to give a statement until
consulting with the SBA lawyer. The rep stressed how
careful cops needed to be in what they said during
these investigations. Grand juries eventually review all
these matters. Savage hadn't been told anything he
didn't already know, and had gone ahead and made
his statements without benefit of the union council. It
didn't make any difference, he'd thought. The truth
was the truth.

It was 0410 hours, and Savage was sitting at a desk
in the far corner of the squad room. With the preliminary investigation of the shooting virtually completed,
save for the summit conference still going on in the
next room, he was sipping cold coffee and bullshitting
with Ollie Beyeler from Crime Scene. The same shooting team that'd handled the hospital fiasco on Tuesday
had responded on this one, too. It was like old-home
week. As Yogi Berra would say, it was déjà vu all
over again.

"Big deal," Beyeler whispered derisively, seated
half-assed on the edge of the desk. "Rice-Jenkins was
once a fucking lieutenant in The Job. So what. She
may know The Job by the book okay, but I betcha
she never did a damn day on the street. From what
I've heard, she bounced from CCRB to Internal Affairs her whole time on The Job—always looking to
fuck somebody over. She's put more guys outta this
job than bad knees."

The mug of cold coffee encircled in his hands, a
weary Savage leaned forward in his chair and replied
in carefully muted tones, "Tell you what worries me.

She knows as much about actual police work as *I* know about elephant hunting with a longbow and a quiver full of rubber arrows. I don't have a lotta faith in her ability to come up with the right conclusions. Shit, even if she does, it'll be by mistake. You know the old saying: A little knowledge can be dangerous."

"Yeah. And she's got some monstrous axe to grind too," Beyeler said. "You do know that one of her sons got his ass blown away by a Narcotics cop up in the Two-eight, back in the late seventies."

"I remember that," Savage said. "Kid was half a junkie, and in the wrong place at the wrong time. Way I remember it, the shooting was a little hairy. Cop testified he thought he saw a gun in the kid's hand, but one was never recovered."

"Right." Beyeler nodded. "And the cop skated. Ever since, Rice-Jenkins became notorious for a barely hidden anti-cop agenda, and having a *huge* minority-group chip on her shoulder."

Savage shrugged and exhaled hard. Terrific, he thought. Just what I need here tonight. A crusading mother who thinks cops are trigger-happy.

"You know," he whispered to Beyeler. "At first I couldn't imagine what the hell she was doin' here. I can't ever recall seeing a first dep insinuate themselves so early into this kind of investigation. Not unless it smelled bad, or somebody'd made a beef. First dep or not, Rice-Jenkins don't know shit."

Words trickled in a guarded monotone from the side of Beyeler's mouth. "You know, even though she got named to that lofty position by the PC, she really got the job from the mayor just so he could say he'd put liberals, blacks, and women in sensitive positions of real authority within his administration. In Rice-Jenkins he got all three for the price of one, plus a real fucking ball breaker."

"Who made this coffee?" Savage muttered, wanting to change the subject. "It's terrible." Uncomfortable inside his gut, but trying not to show it, he knew that in the next room his professional actions were being scrutinized by a virtual novice with an angry vendetta who could destroy his ass, and with the stroke of a Paper Mate have him squeezing doorknobs on steady midnights in the far reaches of Staten Island. Or worse, if such a thing were possible.

"Just be thanking God the two mopes you dispatched were white guys with long rap sheets and not black, hispanic, gay, from fuckin' Mars, or some other minority or special-interest group," Beyeler whispered wrathfully. Looking cautiously over both shoulders before continuing, he leaned close to Savage and added, "If they had been, she'd have you bent over a fucking desk right now, doing one of her civil-rights colonoscopies with a ten-cell flashlight."

"Ouch!" was all Savage managed to say. It was clear that his old friend was big-time pissed. Savage knew the shootings were good—completely justifiable—but, like Ollie Beyeler, he also knew the system. Sometimes good people got screwed.

Promising himself to never again complain about Brodigan's coffee up at Manhattan South, Savage made a face as he took another bitter-tasting gulp of the Sixth Squad's overbrewed muck.

"Why're you drinkin' that shit?" Ollie asked.

Savage shot Ollie a you-should-know-better glance. "To help me stay with-it, stay sharp, and try not to step on my own prick. I am in my twenty-first hour today."

"Yeah," Ollie acknowledged, "especially with this dildo of a commissioner sniffing around. By the way, you decided where you're gonna crash later? Your building is gonna be a friggin' madhouse for at least another few hours."

"Hadn't thought of it," Savage said.

"My cousin's head of security for Marriott. I can get you a comp room for the night. It'd be quiet there—you'd get some decent sleep."

Savage shook his head. "Thanks. But I'm going back to my own place, and sleeping in my own damn bed."

The military-time clock on the squad-room wall read 0415 when a ruffled Pete Pezzano finally emerged from the closed-door powwow with Rice-Jenkins and Chief Feeney. Pezzano walked directly to where Savage was chatting with Ollie Beyeler. Pezzano didn't look good. He was upset, Thorn could tell.

"We're just about wrapped up here," Pezzano started. "But there's a problem, Thorn. I don't know how to tell you this, but," he leaned past Beyeler and whispered ruefully, "they're gonna put you on Modified."

"What?!" Savage's hooded eyes gaped wide. He exploded from the chair and corkscrewed up to his full six-foot extension. "You gotta be fuckin' kiddin' me! Whose idea is that, *Fiona Rice-Jenkins*?" The tired-looking Pezzano didn't answer but his shrug and raised eyebrows said it all. Ollie Beyeler remained seated at the desk's edge and shook his head.

Savage couldn't believe his ears. "Modified's only used when a cop's actions are questionable, or if he'd fucked up, or if what he did created 'neighborhood unrest.' There's none of that here," he protested. "I got news for ya, Petey. If I *didn't* shoot those sons of bitches, *then* you would have seen some fucking neighborhood unrest. Tor Johanssen was a fucking icon in the Village."

"I know," Pezzano agreed, sighing deeply and shaking his head apologetically. "Chief Feeney and I have gone round and round with her for the last hour, but she's adamant. The chief really went to bat for you, but—"

"This is *bullshit*!" Savage ranted. "Who the fuck is she to take away my gun and shield and destroy my reputation? I haven't done anything wrong, Petey," Savage snarled, outraged. "What's the deal here? I'm guilty till proven innocent?"

"It's wrong," Pezzano mumbled ruefully. "Chief knows it too. But she's the goddamned first deputy commissioner." The lieutenant shrugged, powerless.

"You know, I never liked her because of her politics, but now I got a personal fuckin' reason. I want to talk to her."

"Not a good idea, Thorn," Pezzano cautioned. "Not in this state of mind, anyway. If I know you, you'll blow like Krakatoa in there and wind up gettin' your ass suspended."

"No, Petey," Savage indignantly hissed. "I'm the one being disgraced. Now *I'm* adamant. I'm talkin' to that bitch."

Pezzano puffed his cheeks and gave his sergeant a long, deep stare. "I know better than to waste my time, or breath, when you get like this," Pezzano said dolefully. "I'll tell her you want to see her." He turned and walked back through the busy squad room to the CO's office where Rice-Jenkins had set up shop. Five minutes later, an even more ruffled Pezzano reappeared and motioned for the smoldering Savage to enter.

First Deputy Commissioner Fiona Rice-Jenkins looked every bit as presumptuous and overbearing in person as she'd always come across on the boob tube and, judging by the creases and frown ruts chiseled deeply into her mocha granite countenance, it was clear to Savage that she'd undergone several double-charisma bypasses. The broad-shouldered woman's hair was woven into intricate braids that framed and enlarged her already big head and face.

Pezzano had been right on, Savage realized. He *was* about to go ballistic. He mustered all the deference he could. "There's not one thing wrong with these shootings, Commissioner. I had total justification. I'm well acquainted with both the New York State Penal Law standards, *and* departmental guidelines for the use of deadly physical force."

"If you're going to quote department guidelines, Sergeant," Rice-Jenkins responded, "then I suggest that you take a look at *Patrol Guide* procedure one-eighteen-ten." By no coincidence, she just happened to have that procedural page in front of her. She read a portion of it aloud:

> "A ranking officer in charge or in command may recommend that a member be placed on modified assignment when there is no apparent misconduct and no disciplinary action is contemplated, if facts or circumstances indicate that such an assignment would be in the best interests of the department. The ranking officer may recommend such action to the first deputy commissioner through the department advocate's office."

Laying the dog-eared page flat on the desk, the woman tilted her head back and looked officiously down her broad nose at him. Standing slightly behind her, Chief Feeney self-consciously cleared his throat as Petey Pezzano stood in silence to Savage's right. This was clearly her show.

It mattered little that he'd done nothing to deserve this fate, but, like a cornered rabbit in the sights of a hungry timber wolf, Savage knew he was about to be swallowed up. Outstretching fingertips against the desk edge, he leaned forward for emphasis.

"Those sons a bitches were trying to kill me, Commissioner. They'd already killed my neighbor."

"I never said that you *didn't* have justification, Sergeant," she responded coolly. "I just said that we're putting you on Modified Assignment until we know that for absolute certain."

"Know what for certain? That three assholes killed a man, then tried to kill me? Trust me on this, Commissioner, the investigation's already proved that. Any rookie on his first day at the academy would have the right answer to this one."

"Yes, what you say may be very true, Sergeant."
She further narrowed her lobolike, penetrating gaze,
while her voice took on all the jagged edges of a
smashed tall neck clutched for a street fight. "But *I*
don't know that, okay? And if *I'm* going to err, then
I'm going to damn well err in the department's
favor."

Nodding in the direction of ACI Feeney, Savage
asked, "Haven't you sought any input from the chief
here?" Never relinquishing his intense eye contact
with her, he then jerked a thumb toward his own boss.
"Or Lieutenant Pezzano? These are experienced
street cops who've worked hundreds of shootings. I
know they had to tell you this one is clean as a whistle.
Why are you doing this?"

"You were involved in a shooting incident only two
days ago, were you not? And as a result an innocent
bystander, a nurse, wound up dead. That did not reflect well on this department."

"I held my fire in that incident, Commissioner. I'd
never risk an innocent getting hurt."

"But one did nonetheless. And this is the *third* time
you've discharged your weapon during your storied
career, Sergeant," she shot back.

"So what? They were all good shootings. All justified. First guy was a stickup man—backin' out of a
liquor store with a sawed-off he'd just used to blow
away the old man who owned the place. He turned
the sawed-off on me—had no choice. The second guy
had just shot down two uniform cops on Forty-second
Street—I would have been number three. It was him
or me."

"*Shit!*" Rice-Jenkins scoffed as she flipped closed
the pages of Savage's personnel folder that she also
just happened to have before her. "You've now blown
away four people in your career, Sergeant. It seems
that every time you take your gun out of its holster,
whether you fire it or not, somebody—like an innocent
nurse—dies."

Convinced of the absolute futility in making any further attempts to persuade the unpersuadable, Savage snarled, "That's the general idea, isn't it?"

"In tonight's episode," she responded sharply, "we're left with three dead."

"Yeah." Savage bristled. "But I'm only responsible for two." He looked over at Feeney for support. The athletic-built man folded his arms across his chest and avoided Thorn's stare. Chiefs rarely go to war against first dep's—not on a lowly sergeant's behalf. If they did, they usually found themselves shopping for a condo near a golf course in Fort Lauderdale.

"Do you know what the actuarials are for a cop to be involved in *one* shooting during his career?" Rice-Jenkins asked, then supplied her own answer. "They're about one in a hundred, Sergeant Savage. Three shootings? The odds go up exponentially, to about one in a million."

"I guess I'm one in a million," Savage commented bitterly, unable to conceal his seething anger. "Is that what you're saying, Commissioner?"

"Savage!" Chief Feeney broke in, looking across the top of his thickly framed glasses. "The commissioner's decided that it's in the best interests of the department that we place you on Modified. But she's going to permit a rare exception in your case and allow you to remain assigned to Homicide."

"Ain't that nice," Savage muttered. "With no goddamned gun, shield, or arrest powers."

"You can still administrate your team," the chief continued. "But you'll just have to stay inside for a while till we can restore you. Think of it as desk duty. A week, ten days maybe. It's not the worst thing in the world for crissakes. I think your attitude's a little out of order."

Savage stood mute, containing Krakatoa.

"Art thieves," Rice-Jenkins said, clucking her tongue. "You wound up in a shoot-out with a couple of bullshit art thieves, Sergeant."

"They were no more art thieves than you are a cop, Commissioner," he shot back. Petey Pezzano gasped for air. Chief Feeney shifted his stance and nervously cleared his throat. "Art thieves don't dress up in body armor, tote silenced machine pistols, and carry enough extra ammo to mount an insurrection. They don't go around offing people just for drill. These were not goddamned art thieves."

"If they weren't art thieves, Sergeant, why did they have every damn one of Mr. Johanssen's valuable paintings wrapped and stacked in that hallway? I'll tell you why. They were just about to start loading them all into that van, when you come bustin' in, guns ablazin', instead of calling for backup as you should have. Isn't that right, Sergeant?" she said with a snotty scowl.

He tried to recall the last time he wanted to punch a woman's face. "That *ain't* right. And, although I don't know what their game was, *yet,* I do know they weren't stealing fucking pictures. Let's get real here."

"Oh, I'm getting real, Sergeant. Very real. It seems your attitude is just what I expected it would be—explosive. Is that why you've built up such a high body count down through the years?"

"With all due respect, Commissioner *Rice-Jenkins,*" Savage said, growling the hyphenated surnames. "You don't know what the fuck you're doing."

"I know this, mister," Rice-Jenkins said coolly. "We're sitting your ass down for a while. And we're taking your guns and your department car. And if you don't check that shit attitude at the door, you just might find yourself up on charges of insubordination." Rice-Jenkins turned her well-fed face toward the silent Chief Feeney and Pete Pezzano, as if to say that they'd have no choice but to be witnesses.

Causing the woman to flinch defensively at the suddenness of his move, Savage jerked the off-duty .38 Chief from his waistband. Glaring into her dark eyes, he set the still-holstered weapon firmly on the desk blotter before her as she nervously cleared her throat and shifted her huge form back to some level of poise. He dug his shield case from his pants pocket, opened it, and removed the one-hundred-dollar-bill emergency money he kept folded behind his ID card. He flipped the case containing the card and the gold sergeant's shield onto the desk beside the gun. Turning to Pete Pezzano, he said, "My service revolver's in my locker up at the office. I'll give you the combination." Without another word, he turned and let himself out.

Twenty minutes later, the preliminary investigation was completed and Rice-Jenkins had gone off in her chauffeured Chrysler. Savage left the station house via the door to the side parking lot. Declining Pezzano's offer of a ride home, and Ollie Beyeler's offer of a freebie hotel room, he stepped, uncaring, into the steadily falling rain on West Tenth, and began the twelve-block walk. He wanted to be alone.

Inward, contemplative, and oblivious to the weather, he moved stoically through the soaking downpour. He neither quickened his step nor sought shelter beneath any of the dozens of shop-front awnings along the way. He moved steadily, in zombied thought. By the time he reached Sixth Avenue at Bleecker Street, his wet clothing matched his sodden spirit. His Florsheims squooshed, and thick droplets of water gathered and fell from his knitted brow. A lone pedestrian in the city's predawn world of rushing delivery trucks, bearing their fresh cargos of today's *Daily News* and still-warm loaves of white and rye, he realized it had been thirty-plus years since he'd walked these streets without a police shield in his pocket, or pinned to the breast of the blue uniform he'd always been so proud to wear.

Savage remembered when his younger brother, Brian, was forced into ignominious retirement after a twenty-two-year career in the PD. Caught up in a scandal that he'd had nothing to do with, Brian had simply been hit by the shrapnel. Turning off Bleecker into Sullivan, he recalled Brian's philosophical words at the time.

"Nobody ever said it was going to be fair."

SEVENTEEN

Harry Moon awoke with a start.

He heard the eccentric whir of the out-of-balance ceiling fan directly above his bed. Its warped blades, their leading edges caked with dust, whirled through the heavy and offensive air of the stifling furnished room. The noisy relic managed to blow a cooling breeze against his damp brow. A frightening pulse beat beneath his heaving chest. He lay there, exhausted, shaking, and hung over like a son of a bitch.

It had been a hellish dream, but he would live another day.

Declining to raise his pounding head from the caseless, sweat-stained pancake of a pillow, Harry Moon cracked one bloodshot eye and tried to read the clock on the nightstand. His view was obstructed by the Seagram's label on a nearly empty pint that he now recalled setting there hours earlier. Groaning, he shifted over onto one hip. With his head propped against one hand, he extended a veiny broomstick of a tattooed forearm from beneath the tired sheet, clutched the uncapped bottle, brought it to his lips, and drained the last few drops of rye. A little hair of the dog. It was 9 A.M.

Feeling as if the top of his head could burst, Moon sat up and slid from beneath the covers on the cot. He'd stayed out too late, shot too much smack, and consumed too much whiskey. Last night's job had been a fucking disaster, a catastrophe. Thank God he'd been paid in advance. Hell, they couldn't blame him. He'd done everything he'd been told to do. He had followed the instructions to the letter.

He'd hired two very qualified helpers. On such short notice he was lucky to get anybody at all. He'd glommed a van from the Avis lot out at LaGuardia. The vehicle could never be traced back to him. He'd stage-managed the bogus art theft precisely the way the Russian had ·ordered, and quieted down any source of alarm—the fag and the dog. He felt bad about the dog. Fuck the fag.

He'd perfectly positioned his crew inside the apartment house, then waited outside for the mark to arrive. The trap was set. From there it should have been easy. There was no question that the guy he followed into the building was the same one whose picture was plastered all over Thursday's front page. The guy was a cop, but so what? He was a dead man, or at least he should have been. Moon still couldn't believe it— he'd done everything according to Hoyle. What the fuck had gone wrong? God, his head hurt.

Puny, skag-junkie thighs swam in worn-out Jockeys whose leg elastics had long ago quit. The sagging seat of the graying shorts hung from his bony butt as he moped barefoot to the rust-stained, wall-mounted sink. Hocking a phlegmy glob into its drain, he ran the tap until the water began to run cold, and gulped four aspirins. Without benefit of dish soap he attempted to clean away the tarry gunk from the bottom of the four-cup pot. Failing, he filled it with water anyway and set it on the hot plate. After rinsing the brewer basket, he suddenly realized he'd used the last of the coffee days ago. "Shit," he grumbled under his breath.

Moon plodded the few steps back to the bed and reached for the clothing that lay in jumbled lumps on shag carpet that had once been burnt orange. He dressed slowly, careful of his every move, doing everything not to aggravate his murderous headache. Nervously, praying to God that he hadn't blown it somewhere, he slipped his hand into the pocket of his rumpled slacks. He breathed a sigh of relief when he felt the rubber-band-wrapped wad. He was still in the bucks and, he smiled, as a bonus no longer had to worry about paying the help. He would treat himself to some eggs-over, bacon and home fries at the greasy spoon across from the Navy Yard, then go to the tranny shop and finally get the fuckin' Caddy out of hock. Then he would check himself into much nicer digs.

Last night's rain had stopped, and the sun outside the dingy window was warm. He left the furnished room, double-locking the door behind him. It was gonna be a good day, he thought.

Diane DeGennaro steered the unmarked up the East River Drive in the spotty but light Saturday-morning traffic. Driving aggressively, left foot brake, right foot gas, she crossed into the Bronx via the Willis Avenue Bridge and headed the silver Malibu east on Bruckner Boulevard. Slouched beside her, legs crossed, Richie Marcus drew circles around horse numbers in *The Racing Form*. Last night's heavy rain had stopped and the sun was out in force.

"So much for a muddy field at Aqueduct," Marcus said aloud to himself, x-ing out *Miss Sass* in the fourth, and circling *Bimmie's Pride* instead.

Diane ignored him. Her thoughts alternated between the department's shabby treatment of their boss, and the tangled murder investigation at hand.

"You know," Marcus blurted, suddenly looking up from his bible, "if I was Savage, I'd get all the line organizations together and put on a push to force that bitch out. The fuckin' guy's a hero, and they're treatin' him like a piece a shit."

"It'll never happen," Diane said, steering off the busy Bruckner onto Hoe Avenue in a dreary industrial and warehouse section of the South Bronx. "He didn't do a damned thing wrong. Fact is, he must have done everything exactly right, or he wouldn't still be around. They're gonna have to reinstate him, and then the whole thing'll blow over. But, I'll tell you this, it'll take a new mayor to dump her."

"Yeah, you're prob'ly right, but you watch. They're gonna drag this thing out. If they reinstated him right away it'd make Rice-Jenkins look bad. No way they'll do that. They're just gonna let him hang in the breeze. Hooray for the bullshit commissioner, and *fuck* the hardworking cop."

"Lousy politics rearing its ugly head," Diane muttered. She shrugged and exhaled hard in exaggerated frustration. "It's times like this when you gotta wonder . . ." She slowed the sedan and steered through the open gate of a cyclone-fenced compound at the end of the street. The only structure on the acre-size property was a one-and-a-half-story concrete block building with three overhead garage doors. A sign above the middle door read ART-LEN MANAGEMENT CORPORATION. A pair of no-brand gas pumps stood on a small island just outside. The remainder of the acre was an outdoor storage area filled with hulks of wrecked and worn-out taxicabs waiting to be cannibalized for parts.

"Who we gotta see here?" Marcus asked with his usual acerbic tone, putting down *The Racing Form*. "Art or Len?"

"Stan," Diane replied. "Stanley Fishkorn. He's the dispatcher I just got off the phone with. He's holding Tuesday's trip sheet for hack number 2G44."

"Did you tell him to have a copy ready for us?"

"We ain't accepting no damn copy," Diane corrected. "Stanley-boy can make himself a copy. We're taking the original."

"Well . . ." Marcus offered, snorted, then nodded in afterthought. "That's, uhh, what I meant."

Diane pulled the Malibu to a stop just outside the

center bay door, threw the shift lever into park, and shut off the engine.

Greeted by the ratchet and zing of a high-torque, air-driven impact wrench, they entered the combination office/garage. A mechanic in greasy coveralls was pulling the front wheels off a beat-up Crown Vic taxi. The dented and scarred veteran of many a Gotham Grand Prix was suspended waist high before him on an old dual-post lift. The usual shop smells of grease, oil, and gasoline competed with the butyl aroma of dozens of new tires stored in overhead racks hanging from the building's high ceiling. Against a far wall, a brake rotor spun slowly in a resurfacing lathe. Following a sign to the dispatcher's cage, they were met there by a husky, dark-haired man in his mid-thirties who looked up from the pages of his *Wall Street Journal*.

"You two must be the detectives," he said, carefully refolding the paper and running pinched fingertips along its crease.

"You Stanley Fishkorn?" Marcus asked.

"That's me," the man replied, sliding a sheet of paper through the tellerlike opening of his cashier's cage. "Here. I made a copy of that trip sheet you wanted."

"We're gonna need the original trip sheet, Mr. Fishkorn," Diane spoke up.

"No way!" Fishkorn said, dismissing her. "That original stays right here." He pointed to a door just beyond the brake lathes they'd passed on the way in, as his tone became even more surly. "The driver you wanna talk to is sitting in the break room. Name's Willie Hampton. Oh, and, uh, if you don't mind, I'd appreciate if you'd finish up with him and let him get back on the road. In *this* racket," he drawled sarcastically, "time is money."

Diane turned coolly to Marcus and said, "I'm getting the distinct feeling that perhaps we should have Mr. Hampton accompany us back downtown for a few hours. We could interview him there in the comfort of our office. What are your thoughts on that, Detective Marcus?"

"Yeah! I think you're right," Marcus agreed strongly, then upped the ball-breaking ante. "I think maybe we also should have taxicab 2G44 impounded as evidence. Of course, if we do take it in, we'd have to keep it till the trial's over—which could take a year or more. Whaddaya think, Detective DeGennaro?"

"I think that could all be headed off with a little cooperation, don't you?" Diane said. Both detectives turned a waiting glance back to Fishkorn.

The surly dispatcher smirked and shook his head at the obvious extortion. The exchange for the original trip sheet was made, and the detectives headed to the employee's break room.

"Willie Hampton?" Diane asked. The big black man in his sixties, seated at a banquet-size folding table set in the middle of the room, was the only person there.

"Willie *Randolph* Hampton, to be exact," the man replied, standing to reveal that he was taller, and wider, than the eclipsed Coke machine directly behind him. Wide suspenders that only appeared narrow in contrast to the man's extraordinary size dug deeply into shoulders thick with excess flesh, and traced down across a very stout, flannel-shirt-covered barrel chest. The suspenders were attached to loose-fitting, gray cotton work pants.

"Ever play second base for the Yankees?" Richie asked with his disarming smile.

"Yeah, I wish," the man replied through a life-weary grimace. Then, allowing a toothy grin, he added, "Did have Willie Randolph in my cab one time though. Picked him up in midtown and brought him up to the stadium. Good tipper."

"Mr. Hampton," Diane said, unwinding the string latch of a nine-by-fourteen manila envelope. "We'd like to show you some photographs. But first we'd like to ask just a few questions."

"Fire away," he said, gesturing to the abundance of mismatched metal folding chairs scattered in disarray around the table. Diane sat at the head. The men sat opposite each other.

"Do you remember picking up a fare at Three thirty-three East Seventy-third at about ten forty-five last Tuesday night?" Diane asked.

"Can't say as I do. But y'all got my trip sheet for that night. If it says I was there, then I was there."

Diane slid the photographs from the folder, and laid them before Hampton. "You recognize this scene?"

Staring down at the pictures for a long thirty seconds before speaking, the man finally nodded. "Yeah, I remember. Blond woman. Pretty. In her early forties I'd guess. Smelled good." Looking up at both detectives through murky eyeballs, he raised his brow and added, "She smelled *real good.*"

"Do you remember where you took her?" Diane asked.

"Short haul. Somewhere down in the Forties."

"Do you remember exactly?"

"Forty-ninth and Third," he responded after a moment's deliberation.

"How did she seem to you?" Marcus asked.

Hampton appeared puzzled by the vagueness of the question. He shrugged and shook his head. "How do you mean?"

"How did her voice sound?" Marcus followed up. "Calm? Excited? Nervous? What did she talk about?"

"Never heard her voice."

"Didn't you talk to her?" Diane asked.

"I tried, but she didn't say a word."

"Not at all?" Marcus asked, incredulous.

"Not at all. The woman never done said a damn word. When I mentioned it was a nice night, she just grunted."

"She would have had to tell you where she was going, wouldn't she?" Diane queried with a palm-out gesture.

"She didn't tell me where she was going. He did."

"He?" Diane asked. "What he? She wasn't with a man."

"This guy," Hampton said. The cabdriver tapped a leathery, sausagelike index finger at the picture of the uniformed doorman in the photograph before him.

"You sure?" Marcus asked.

"I'm sure."

Diane and Richie exchanged questioning glances.

"Think back, Mr. Hampton," Diane said. "There's four corners at the intersection of Forty-ninth and Third. How did you know to pull up to La Florentine on the northeast corner, instead of one of the other three? Didn't she say, 'Pull up by La Florentine?'"

"Already done told you, she never opened her mouth," Hampton drawled.

"So it was the doorman who told you she was going to La Florentine." Diane wanted to hear it one more time.

"Yep, it were the doorman. While the lady's gettin' into the back of my cab, he pipes up all official-like and says, 'Mrs. So-and-so will be going to the La Florentine Restaurant at Forty-ninth Street and Third Avenue.'"

Diane and Richie again turned and faced each other. They shared a long, contemplative stare. Then they both smiled.

Diane murmured, "Roger—the *W's* for wise ass . . ."

Richie nodded. "Told ya he was a lyin' sack o' shit."

With only a few hours of almost-sleep separating Savage from the mind-boggling self-esteem broadside he'd received at the hands of the deputy commissioner, he pulled himself together and decided to report for his "modified assignment" duty when he awoke unusually late on Saturday morning. Besides, he thought, he'd promised Petey Pezzano he'd deliver his department car back to the office this morning and turn in the keys. He wasn't going to let the actions of a fucking moron put him into a tailspin. With thirty years in The Job, he'd seen too many of these political appointees come and go. Some, he had to admit, were good. Others, like Rice-Jenkins, had to be tolerated. The PC was due back in town Sunday, and this bullshit *"would,"* the SBA rep had assured him, "be cleared up."

Since Sunday and Monday would be his regular days off anyway, he considered using some lost time and not going into the office at all, thereby giving himself a three-day weekend to work on clearing the accumulated crap out of his head. He decided against it. Clean shaven and dapper in a charcoal pinstripe with a burgundy- and pearl-gray-striped tie, he put down fresh food and water for Ray and left his apartment at 9:45.

Passing the bullet-riddled plaster wall on his way down the stairs, he calculated he'd be over an hour late getting into the office. Sue me, he thought. Tor Johanssen's first-floor apartment, and most of the main-floor hallway that led to it, were still sealed-off with the yellow POLICE LINE—DO NOT CROSS tape. Thank God someone, probably Mrs. Potamkin on the third floor, had arranged for a cleanup crew to come in and clear away the battle debris. Otherwise, the puddled blood would be stinking to high heaven by now.

After reclaiming his car from in front of St. Anthony's, Thorn drove up Sixth Avenue. At West Third he pulled into a bus stop, left the motor running, and walked to Curley's corner kiosk for his morning paper.

His head bandanaed in pirate style, Curley leaned his weather-beaten, unshaven face out over the candy counter. "Can't keep yer ass outta trouble, can ya?" his harsh voice boomed.

An omnipresent, seemingly never lit cigar stub protruded beneath the paraplegic's poorly tended graying red mustache. "You made page three today, handsome," he added, flashing his eyes for emphasis.

Savage turned out his palms and shrugged modestly. "Morning, Curley," he said evenly, then teased, "heard Pittsburgh's lookin' for a new mascot? You might have a future there."

"Actually, my agent did have speaks with Pittsburgh. But I found out they only wanted to use me as third base."

"How about posin' for Toby Jugs? Hell, if I could find one that had *your* face on it I'd buy it."

"Yeah!" Curley chuckled from the non-stogie side of his 'stache-hidden mouth. "And prob'ly use it as a fuckin' chamber pot."

The man's eyes suddenly grew bright. "Hey!" he blurted, tossing a cellophane bag of Wint-O-Greens at Savage. "I almost forgot. They're makin' them available in this six-and-a-half-ounce size now. I got this one on the arm, compliments of my candy vendor."

"Chee, tanks!" Savage said, pocketing the Life Savers. His attention, however, shifted to the variety of glossy covers displayed along every inch of the kiosk's inner walls.

"Crissakes," he uttered to Curley. "You always carry this many different magazines?"

"Tell me 'bout it," the 'Nam vet and one-time cop wanna-be growled. "When my old man ran this place, all he hadda worry about were *Life, Look,* and *Official Detective.* Today I'm carrying over a hundred different titles. Got no choice—people expect it." Curley turned away and spit into a bucket he kept alongside his wheelchair.

Savage slid the topmost *Post* from beneath the iron brick that kept the whole stack from being blown by wind gusts up Sixth Avenue, folded it, and tucked it under his left arm. As Curley made change for his fiver, Thorn continued perusing the dozens of magazine titles.

"Does that say *Tattoo Revue*?" Savage asked, amused.

"Oh, yeah," Curley replied, adroitly spinning his chair and waving to the back wall. "We got magazines for every damn thing. Besides *Mandate* for the fruits, we got *Cigar Aficionado, Shutterbug, Stamp Monthly, Inline Skater, Guitar Player, Cat Fancy, Horse Breeder, Reptiles, Fish, Wine.* Shit, I've even got this month's editions of *Cross-Dresser* and *Model Railroader.*"

"You sell all these?"

"What I don't sell, they take back," Curley replied, turning to make change for two *Times* customers. After another spit in the bucket, he asked, seriously, "So tell me, big guy, how come you keep poppin' up in the headlines all the time? How come you're always around when the shit hits the fan?"

"Never looked for it, Curley," Savage responded with a wan smile, modesty intact. "Trouble just seems to somehow find me."

"Don't gimme that shit," Curley jibed. "I know you too long. You're out there lookin' when you don't even know you're lookin'. Hell, you're prob'ly lookin' right now. But," the man continued with a shrug of wasted shoulders, "at least you keep comin' up heads."

"Tell me something, Curley," Savage said seriously, the seed of an idea taking hold. "Do you carry a magazine devoted to collectors of toy soldiers?"

"I got *Toy Car Collector, Toy Shop,* and *Action Figure News & Toy Review.* I ain't got nothin' devoted just to toy soldiers. But I'd be willin' t'betcha anything you want, there prob'ly *is* such a damn magazine."

Out of the corner of his eye, Savage saw the M-6 bus lumbering up Sixth Avenue. It would soon need to occupy the space his department car was blocking. He gave Curley a wink and trotted back to the Ford. Curley apparently didn't know the name of a magazine for toy-soldier collectors, but Savage knew who might.

There was little activity in the Homicide office when Savage arrived at 1020 hours. The place was unusually quiet. No one from his team was present, and Billy

Lakis and his crew were on their regular day off. Herbie Shaw and Carmen Delgado from Sergeant Unger's team were the only investigators there. Busy at their desks when he entered, they nodded with strained smiles in his direction. He could tell they had heard. Word of suspensions and disciplinary action travels like wildfire. Though they no doubt empathized, the pair didn't quite know what to say to him. They played it safe, and went about their business, opting to say nothing. Just as well, he didn't feel up to a rehash.

He knew that the other cops didn't know how he might be coping with the royal screwing he'd gotten, and they'd try to act as if nothing had happened. He would do his best to put them all at ease, try to play down his problems, and he too would try to act as if nothing had happened.

"Lindstrom's down at the big building, Sarge. And Marcus and DeGennaro have gone up to some cab company in the Bronx," Eddie Brodigan said, sliding his chair aside, allowing Savage access to the command log. "Marcus left a five on your desk in case you came in. It's about the surveillance he did last night out in Brooklyn."

"Thanks, Ed."

Speaking in hushed tones, in an apparent effort to prevent Delgado and Shaw from overhearing, Brodigan said, "Tell you the truth, boss, nobody here expected to see you until at least Tuesday. We all figured you'd wanna take a little bit of a time-out."

Savage shrugged, wondering why in hell he *was* there. Anybody with any goddamned sense at all surely wouldn't be. "What's doing, Eddie?" he asked. "Anything?"

"All in all, it's starting out as a pretty shit day for MSH," Brodigan began. "First thing we hear this morning is how they're fuckin' with you. Then we find out that Sergeant Unger's wife is back in LIJ—doesn't look good. Word is, she might not make the weekend."

"God almighty," Thorn muttered, shaking his head and grimacing. "And I thought *I* had troubles."

"You also got a call a little while ago," Brodigan added, handing him a Post-it with a phone number and a message to call Gina McCormick at home.

Savage turned and walked to Petey Pezzano's office, dropped the keys to car 7146 on the lieutenant's desk, and went next door to the sergeants' room, wishing there was something he could do for his friend Jules. Everyone has problems over which they have no fucking control, he thought. Why should Thornton MacLanahan Savage be exempt from the bullshit of life?

Opening his locker, he saw the empty holster on his uniform gun belt. Lieutenant Pezzano had been there earlier and, in accordance with the rules of Modified Assignment, had relieved him of his only other weapon—his service revolver. Expelling a deep sigh, Savage reached for his empty coffee mug on the locker's top shelf. This whole thing sucked.

After a trip to the coffeepot, he returned to his desk and dialed Gina's number.

"It usually takes a bit of caffeine to get me going on a Saturday," she said, the sound of alarm echoing in her voice. "This morning all it took was your picture on page three of my newspaper to jolt me wide awake. Are you okay?" she asked. He assured her he was.

"When I read the story 'Greenwich Village Art Theft Turns Deadly' I just couldn't believe it. Are you *sure* you're okay?" she asked again. Again he assured her he was.

"You must be exhausted, both physically and mentally," Gina went on, her voice still tinged with great concern. "Under the circumstances, I certainly understand your need to get some rest," she said, as she graciously offered him an out for their date tonight.

He would have none of it. As far as he was concerned, their date was the only thing he'd had to look forward to in weeks. The date was still on. He needed it to be. He'd see her at Palermo's at eight.

He hung up, sipped at his coffee, and turned his attention to Marcus's lengthy surveillance report. He saw that Richie had actually been able to pick up on one of the subjects from Majestic Funding, Georgei Strelnikov, and follow him on a grand tour of Brooklyn and Queens. Savage's eyes were drawn to the references made to the Little Odessa Restaurant in Brighton Beach, where Strelnikov had gone to ground while Richie fed his face. Savage had seen that restaurant's name before. *Of course!* He'd seen it on one of the business cards he recovered from Harmon Mayhew's desk—The Little Odessa. *Jeezus!* A circle was forming. Mayhew's coded calendar notation for last November 16th, *GS-LOR 7:30,* now had potential meaning. It might suggest that Harmon Mayhew had an appointment with Georgei Strelnikov at the Little Odessa Restaurant at 7:30. He signed off on Marcus's DAR and approved the detective's overtime-payment request. It was money well spent.

Another issue of last night's surveillance lay in who lived at the Forest Hills Gardens mansion visited by Georgei Strelnikov. Savage knew that Marcus would begin to pull on that string as soon as he and Diane returned from their interview at the cab company. Setting the report aside, he decided to begin that inquiry himself, but first he looked up Dawson's number and dialed. Trooper Dawson answered on the second ring.

"Old Toy Soldier," Dawson quickly responded to Savage's question. "It's a *bi*monthly." Accent on *bi.* "That's the only magazine specifically devoted to the hobby that this trooper's aware of."

"You subscribe to it?" Savage asked.

"Natch. Got the latest issue laying right in front of me. Want me to run it over, Sarge?" Dawson offered with a helpful tone.

"No, no, you don't need to do that," Savage said. "Just let me have the publisher's information."

"Flournoy Publications. Says here their offices are on North Lombard, in Oak Park, Illinois."

"Ten-four, over and out," Savage signed off.

"Over and out," Dawson responded.

Thorn left the sergeant's room, went to the wheel desk, and commandeered Eddie Brodigan's Manhattan telephone directory. In the customer-guide section at the front of the tome he found the "Area Codes by State" page. Illinois had nine area codes. Oak Park was a suburb of Chicago; that whittled the choices down to two—it would have to be either 312 or 773. He returned to his office and dialed 312 information. Bingo, they were listed.

Expecting no answer on a Saturday, Savage called the number anyhow, just to see if the listing was active. He was surprised when the phone was answered by Carlton Flournoy.

"We're small," Flournoy said. "I'm managing editor, publisher, and chief janitor. That North Lombard address is just a mail drop. I operate out of an office in my basement. But, as far as I know, my *Toy Soldier* is the only thing out there that's dedicated to that hobby."

"What's the circulation?" Savage asked.

" 'Bout three thousand. Twenty-five hundred subscribers nationally. Figure another five hundred to libraries and newsstands."

"How many of those twenty-five hundred subscribers would you say live in the New York City metropolitan area?" Savage asked.

"That's our zone fourteen," Flourney replied. "Not exactly sure. I'd have to check that. Probably a hundred or so."

"Ever profile your readership?" Savage asked. "You know, by sex, age, income—that sort of thing?"

"About three years ago. Like most interest-specific publishers we need to do that from time to time."

"You still have those records?"

"Yes, we do."

"Was that a blind survey?" Savage asked. "Or were the respondents asked to identify themselves by name and address?"

"Our questionnaire got an eighty-seven percent response overall from our subscribers, which is good. And only a few of those who responded didn't supply their names and addresses."

"You mean your records will provide not only their sex and age, but names and addresses as well?"

"Uh-huh! On most of them. They'll also tell you income bracket, married, single, kids, other hobbies, specific areas of interest, et cetera."

"Specific areas of interest . . . you mean like Napoleonic?"

"Un-huh. Napoleonic, American Civil War, British, French. Whatever."

"Mr. Flournoy, I'd like you to send us a list of all your subscribers within zone fourteen. But would you be good enough to highlight the males between say . . . forty-five and fifty-five?"

"I can do that, Sergeant," the man responded promptly. "As soon as we receive an official request on your police department's letterhead."

"How about a fax," Savage said. "I'll get one out to you right now. Then you could be a real good guy and get that list to us today."

After a long pause, Flournoy replied, "Let me have your fax information, Sergeant. It's a Saturday, you know," the man said teasingly. "And given my tough commute, you're lucky I even showed up today."

"I know the feeling, Mr. Flournoy."

Moon thought the eggs were perfect. They were large and fresh, cooked overeasy in bacon drippings just the way he liked them, but the strips of bacon themselves had been a real disappointment. Back when he was doing short orders, he'd lay his rashers on a much hotter griddle. The bacon cooked faster and, as long as he kept rendering the fatty grease, came out dryer and crisper, the way bacon oughtta be. The griddle man in this place was either too lazy to cook it properly, or simply didn't know how. At any rate, for the first time in weeks, Moon's belly was comfortably full.

Glomming a healthy supply of free toothpicks from the jar next to the register, he waited for the septuagenarian bimbo of a waitress, who also doubled as cashier in Louie's Navy Yard Breakfast Galley, to make change of his new fifty. The weird-looking crone appeared wired, as if keeping a finger permanently poked into five hundred volts. The startled expression forever frozen across her shriveled face was no doubt the end product of deep-discounted cosmetic butchery performed on upper eyelids and lower satchels. Her receding, sparse hair was dyed a clownish jet black and drawn into a ratty French twist held in place by a teenybopper's blue velvet bow. And three gallons of five-and-dime Autumn Crimson lipstick bled like flood waters past their dikes, filling the myriad age ruts that fed out like tributaries from her two-gallon lips. Never say die, mama, he thought, dropping a deuce on the counter and pocketing the balance of his change.

What a dump, Moon thought, swaggering from Louie's ten-stool ptomaine palace. He'd never eat there again. If he could parlay his current holdings, he wouldn't have to. Out on the sidewalk he took a deep breath, peeled the paper wrapping from a minted toothpick, and began the five-block trek to Zip Transmissions on Flushing Avenue. Patting the thick wad of cash that still bulged in his pants pocket, he smiled. There'd be no more of this walking bullshit either.

Hiking up the moderate incline of the deserted side street, he was halfway to Kent Avenue when he felt an eerie gust, a strange breeze that flipped up the collar of his jacket. He also felt a sudden, somehow familiar sensation in the pit of his stomach—a rumbling, a signal, a premonition. He shivered at the first indication of a stealthy approach. Footsteps, moving at a tempo greater than his, were closing behind him. Paranoia draped him like watery, cheap syrup on a hot waffle, filling every pore. He fought the urge to look behind, but knew he must. He did.

It was the Russian.

Harry Moon turned and ran.

The footfalls behind him seemed effortless. They were measured, smooth, and graceful. And they were getting closer.

The first silent shot entered through Moon's spinal cord and exited from his throat, tearing away a large chunk of larynx. Pitched forward by the bullet's impact, he slammed nose-down on the sidewalk amidst a pile of garbage-filled Hefty Bags, long overdue for collection. His cheek quivered against the cool concrete as a resigned whimper gurgled up from the freshly made hole in his windpipe. He opened his eyes to find himself face-to-face with a startled mangy stray feeding on a pork-chop bone. As the shadow of his human pursuer fell across him, Moon stared blinking into the dog's curious eyes. The animal stared back and lifted its leg. Moon never felt the next silenced shot that crashed into the back of his bald head.

The gravity-driven stream of dog pee traced along the cracks and hollows of the sidewalk incline. The warm liquid dammed up and collected around Harry Moon's surprised face.

EIGHTEEN

Aside from the mysterious disappearance of Georgei Strelnikov inside the Little Odessa Restaurant last night, and what, if any, significance that disappearing act had, Savage saw that the only other loose end of Marcus's five was the unknown identity of the blonde Strelnikov had visited in Queens. Realizing it had been a Friday night, Thorn had to consider the possibility that Strelnikov had gone to a house party or some other kind of gathering at the Forest Hills mansion. Unlikely. According to the report, no other cars were observed parked on or near the grounds, and no one else came or went while Marcus had the swanky place under observation. Maybe the woman who greeted the subject at the door was his honey, welcoming him in for a little Friday-evening poon-tang. Maybe she was his guru. Maybe the guy sold Tupperware on the side. Maybe. Maybe. It had to be followed up. He knew Richie would've already begun to do just that except he and Diane were already on this morning's out-of-borough jaunt to the taxi company.

The normally hectic Homicide office, which he'd earlier found unusually quiet, was now almost silent. The phones weren't ringing, Diane and Richie were up in the Bronx, Jack Lindstrom was still downtown pulling records, and Shaw and Delgado from Julie Unger's squad had signed out on one of their cases. It was just him and Eddie Brodigan holding down the fort. Glancing out from his desk, he saw the wheelman collating a backlog of Personnel and Special Orders that'd collected in his In basket. Even Eddie seemed desperate for something to do. The clock on the wall said ten after eleven. Seemed to Savage it should be much later. Time was dragging, and he was getting antsy.

Wired by half a pot of Brodigan's invigorating joe, Savage killed another five minutes breezing through the morning crossword. He figured out the jumble. Still antsy. The librarylike silence of the office was a breeding ground for introspection. Negatives began to bubble up from his subconscious. Would the shitty treatment he'd been dealt at the hands of department administrators leave him, like etched glass, permanently marked? Would he lose his edge? Would his zeal and dedication to the job he'd always loved be permanently diminished? Would he stop being a worker, and become a drone? If that happened, he knew he'd have to quit.

Attempting to escape the quickly forming shroud of negative thoughts, Savage steered his mind elsewhere. It was just under nine hours until his dinner date with Gina McCormick. He wondered what that might bring. The start of something? Of nothing? Who the hell knew? Introspective again, he fought off thoughts of Maureen.

Self-pity was not one of his character flaws, but he allowed a moment's indulgence. He realized that his sometimes less-than-idyllic, often-in-limbo private life had always been buoyed and counterbalanced by the positive flow from his always faithful mistress—The Job, the yin to match his yang. But now, even his professional life was in disarray. Last night's fucked-up chain of events had left him empty and morose. He was a man jilted, cuckolded by his longtime mistress. A mistress with a very short memory.

He had to get busy. He had to squelch the negative energy that was trying to consume him.

He reread Marcus's surveillance report, and decided to follow up on loose end number two—identifying who Strelnikov had visited in Forest Hills. Thorn dialed the 112th Precinct in Queens and, as good fortune sometimes has it, the call was answered by an old friend, just the guy he wanted.

"Detective Stewart, One-twelve Squad."

"Donny. Thorn Savage. What's happening, guy?" Unlike the quiet of his office, the 112 squad room was filled with noise.

"Well . . ." Stewart replied, with a breezy now-I-think-I've-seen-it-all laugh. "Except for some jerkoff in a clown suit who just went postal with an AR-16 over at a burger joint here, I guess you could say things are pretty quiet."

"Jeez," Savage said. "Sounds like you got a real mess over there. DOAs?"

"Nah. No one really hurt, thank God. Just a lotta property damage. He shot the place up pretty good."

"Disgruntled employee?"

"Oh, yeah!" Stewart snickered cheerily. *"Real* disgruntled. I don't think the poor bastard really wanted to hurt anybody. With about twenty people in the joint at the time he only winged one guy, and that was a minor flesh wound from a ricochet. But the burger place is definitely gonna need estimates on a ceiling, some illuminated menu signs, and a new fryer."

"Just another average day at the office, eh, Donny?"

"Hey, Thorn!" Stewart suddenly blurted. "I'm the one should be askin' *you* what the hell's goin' on, man. You're the one that's the talk of The Job."

"Boy, word spreads fast," Savage muttered, not wanting to go down that road.

"The jungle drums've been beatin' all night."

"Oh, yeah?" Savage said unenthusiastically, not really caring to know the answer. "What've they been saying?"

"The drums say that if you'da gotten your fuckin'

ass blown away, The Job would've given you an Inspector's Funeral and you'da been a big fuckin' hero."

"But . . . ?" Thorn asked.

"But, since you turned out to be the blow*er*, instead of the blow*ee*, they're gonna fuckwicha and make your life miserable."

"What do you think they're tryin' to tell me, Don?"

"Next time, let yourself get blown away." Stewart's sarcasm seemed a mile deep. "You could avoid all this bullshit, and at the same time become a front-page hero."

Savage knew there was a lot of truth to Stewart's rant. But vivid images of the legless Curley toiling fifteen hours a day inside that claustrophobic kiosk, and the malignant wasting of Becky Unger out at Long Island Jewish Hospital came to his mind. For the moment, at least, they helped keep him squarely centered. "E. coli happens, man. What can I tell ya?"

"Word goin' around is, you were two hundred percent right, Thorn. They oughta be given ya' the Combat Cross *and* the fuckin' Medal of Honor. Lotta people in this job are big-time pissed and bent over what went down."

"They need to tell that to the PC," Thorn muttered.

"Oh, ho," Stewart groaned wrathfully. "He'll find out the minute he's back in town. I heard the SBA's up in arms about this one. I just hope the PC's got the balls to make the right call when he does find out."

Savage let that pearl of political reality marinate awhile. "Listen, Don," he said. "I really don't wanna talk about that bullshit. I called you because I need some help on something else."

"Go."

"I've got a five in front of me on an open homicide we're carrying. One of my guys tailed a possible suspect out to your neck of Queens last night."

"Okay."

"The subject paid a visit to a real swell place in the

Gardens. Need to know who lives there. Can you swing that for me sometime today?"

"Can do. Soon as we get the Burger Boy photoed, printed, and arraigned. Gimme the street address."

"Ten Underwood."

"Ten *Underwood?*" Stewart repeated, then cleared his throat. "You gotta be fuckin' kiddin' me, man."

"Why? You recognize that address?"

"Fuckin'-A," Stewart snickered. "Maloney lives there."

"Gerard Maloney? The senator?"

"You bet. Him and his charming dyke wife."

"Ouch!" Savage said in mock shock. "Doesn't sound as if you're very enamored of our good legislator and his lovely better half." Then, turning serious, he asked, "You absolutely sure of that, Don?"

"Sure I'm sure. Everybody in this command knows that fuckin' address. They know him, and they know his tart old lady. Tell me, in his report did your guy describe the house?"

"Called it a brick and stone, Tudor. Huge. Wide, brick-paved driveway . . ."

"That's it," Stewart assured, cutting Savage off. "It's the only one like it in the whole area. That son of a bitch's gonna be the next fuckin' president. You know that, right?"

"I read just yesterday he's decided not to run. Some kinda health problem."

"Forget that shit. That was yesterday. Today his people are all over the TV denying any such thing. They're sayin' those reports were 'scurrilous' rumors started by Maloney's detractors, and sayin' their man's definitely gonna run. The precinct CO here is wishin' to Christ they'd make up their fuckin' minds."

"What difference does it make to him?"

"He's already gotten the word from the borough. The minute Maloney announces himself as a candidate for president, he's gotta start providing a twenty-four-hour uniformed squat on that place, whether the charming couple's in residence or not. The way he sees it, it's just another drain on his manpower."

Savage offered a lifeless uh-huh to the One-twelve's manpower problem, then continued. "My guy's report also describes a female who greeted our subject at the door. White, fifties, slender, short blond hair . . ."

"Sure sounds like the lady of the house to me. Christine Maloney."

"What's her story, Don?"

"Just like her ol' man. Two peas in a pod. They've got this public persona, game faces that they're always wearing, that'd make you think they're Ozzie and Harriet. I got it on good authority, though, that aside from their selfish ambitions of power they ain't got no real fuckin' use for one another. In public she comes across being warm and concerned like Mother Teresa, but I wanna tell ya, that is one treacherous bitch. She pisses ice water."

"How do you know so much about these people?" Savage asked.

"I've been assigned to this borough a long time, Thorn. The Maloneys are powerhouses out here. They've been the dominant force in Queens politics since you and I were doing push-ups in the academy. Maloney started his illustrious career as a bagman for Ron Mankiewitz back in the late sixties. Mankiewitz eventually became the borough president, back before city hall ripped the balls out of the position. It was the ideal entry-level position for Maloney. He learned how to pull strings, who holds the strings, and how to string others along."

"Maloney's got skeletons?"

"Does Saddam Hussein?"

"How come he's survived without being investigated?"

"It's amazing. The guy's led a charmed life. Prob'ly the most important reason that he ain't got a B-Number's because Ron Mankiewitz was an honorable enough scumbag to blow his own brains out when he knew the jig was up on a boroughwide scandal. Once Mankiewitz was dead, Maloney and a bunch of others skated. Mankiewitz took all the weight with him to the grave. Some of the others, like Maloney, went on to much bigger and better things."

"I remember that bit," Thorn said. "Had something to do with parking meters, didn't it?" Thorn's subconscious had already begun processing and correlating as he spoke. The clappers in those little alarm bells were beginning to stir.

"That was part of it," Stewart replied. "The word at the time was, Mankiewitz and the others had some sort of scheme worked out where they were able to skim the take from thousands of parking meters out here. But it was a lot bigger than that."

"Like what else?"

"Like tow trucks."

"Why *tow* trucks?" Savage asked.

"Back in those days, if a body shop wanted to operate a tow truck, get onto the authorized rotation-tow list, and be permitted to remove vehicles from accidents that occurred on Queens thoroughfares, they needed to have a license, a medallion. Like a taxicab."

"What was the scam?"

"Nobody, and I mean nobody, got a fuckin' medallion without payin' some healthy vig to Big Ron M. Of course, the bagman was rumored to be Mankiewitz's right-hand boy, none other than our esteemed senator, Gerard Maloney."

Thorn's mind raced. He recalled the offhanded reference made by Joe Ballantine of a Queens politico who years ago had been nailing his now-dead sweetie—Candace Mayhew. But the even more disturbing thought revolved around Harmon Mayhew's mysterious notations. The subconscious was hitting on all eight cylinders. Savage turned to his locked case file, spun the combination, and dragged out Mayhew's coded notes.

"You could be opening a major can of worms for me here, Donny," Savage confessed.

"How's that?"

"What year did Mankiewitz kill himself?"

"Nineteen eighty-five."

Running his finger along Mayhew's list, Savage mumbled the coded notations aloud, while drawing his conclusions in silence. "RM Suicide '85" = *Ron Mankiewitz*. "TT Licenses" = *Tow truck licenses.* "QPC" = *Queens Political Club.*

"What're you talkin' about?" Stewart asked, puzzled.

"Tryin' to figure out someone's shorthand—sort of a code," Savage said in explanation. Then, reading from Mayhew's notes, he asked, "What do you think this could mean? 'Q Blvd recon—JCD concrete contractor—82-84.' " Thorn didn't mention the rest of the notation that read, "150K to M . . . Extended to Albany."

"You mean within the context of what we've been discussing?" Stewart asked. "The borough of Queens?"

"Yeah. In that context."

" 'JCD' definitely stands for 'John C. Desmond.' They're the biggest road-construction outfit on Long Island. There isn't an orange traffic cone within fifty miles of here that doesn't have 'JCD' stenciled on it. I've had nightmares about them fuckin' things."

"And 'Q Blvd recon'?"

"Prob'ly refers to the reconstruction of Queens Boulevard. That was a major highway improvement that took freakin' years, and *lots* of J.C. Desmond concrete to complete. I'm sure that project was underway back around eighty-two. I remember that 'cause I'd just gotten assigned to Queens Robbery. I'll never forget the bullshit traffic jams trying to get to work around the construction."

Savage was on a roll. "Since we're playing association involving Queens County, try *this* riddle on for size, Don: '80-84 Land Condemn, FM/near Shea.' Can you interpret that?"

"As I recall, in the early eighties the county got

behind a wholesale condemnation of huge tracts of land near Shea Stadium, some of it made up of has-been automobile wrecking yards—real eyesores—mostly owned by you know who."

"The bent noses?"

"You got it," Stewart said. Then he added sarcastically, "Far be it from me to say that Mankiewitz and Maloney engaged in any collusion with the boys, or that they arranged to have the value of those lands overappraised, but a lot of those junk men walked away with big smiles on their faces and bulging pockets."

"Kickbacks?"

"No question! Wasn't long thereafter that Maloney bought himself the spread in Forest Hills."

"And what of the initials 'FM'?" Savage asked.

"Flushing Meadows. That's the area that surrounds Shea Stadium."

A stimulating rush, the kind that always accompanied an investigative epiphany, coursed through Savage's system. Excited, he moved on, looking down at Mayhew's final entry:

"As per M to C: CM goes both ways. Likes big ladies."

"You did say that Maloney's wife's name was Christine. And, you did call her a dyke, did you not, Don?"

"I did."

"Is that for real?"

"No question."

His steady voice not betraying the look-what-I've-found elation that he was feeling, Savage asked, "I wonder if there's any way to know if the good senator was present last night during our subject's hour and a half visit to his palatial pad?"

"Not possible," Stewart advised. "I know for a fact that he flew outta LaGuardia yesterday afternoon. Back to D.C. A sector team I know escorted him out to a private rent-a-jet. They stuck around drinking coffee and watched the plane take off."

"One more thing, Don," Thorn asked. "Gerard Maloney have a reputation as a swordsman?"

Stewart's reply came through a howl of laughter. "Are you kidding? The bastard's notorious!"

There was still plenty of fog on the horizon, Savage thought as he hung up the phone. But he was beginning to see a dim outline, an outline with vague shape if not substance. Could it be that Gerard Maloney was the Queens politician Joe Ballantine had alluded to? The one who had years ago stolen away Candace Mayhew's affections from him? It would seem far-fetched, but . . .

Thorn was getting that warm-all-over feeling.

He dialed the *Post,* and was told by the reporter manning the city desk that Joe Ballantine wasn't due in for work until tomorrow afternoon at four. He recalled Orel Hersheiser's uniform number 55, and Don Drysdale's uniform number 53, then dialed 555-3555, Ballantine's cell phone. No answer. He'd reach him at work tomorrow.

Briefly taking her eyes from the road, Diane De-Gennaro glanced down at the speedo—she was doing eighty. She loved to drive fast. Heading back downtown from the Bronx, she took full advantage of the sparse, late-Saturday-morning traffic along the FDR Drive. Had it been a weekday, they'd have been mired in bumper-to-bumper traffic. As they neared the Sixty-third Street exit, Richie Marcus looked up from the confiscated taxi trip sheet he'd been quietly studying. He put the form back into the folder on the front seat and turned to her.

"Head over to the Mayhew apartment house," he said suddenly.

"Why?"

"Got an idea."

"Like what?" Diane asked guardedly. "I don't want any pressure applied on Roger *'Dubya'* Hogan yet."

"Just do it," Marcus told her. "I wanna see some-thin'."

Knowing Richie was prone to these kind of sudden brainstorms, and knowing the evasive "I wanna see somethin' " was about all she was going to get in the way of explanation, she flipped the turn signal for a lane change. As four stressed Goodyears squealed a mighty objection, Diane took the exit ramp ten miles an hour faster that she should have, made a right on York Avenue, and headed back north. At East Seventy-third she made a left. A minute later the Mal-ibu pulled in front of the Clarendon.

Diane was relieved to see that they were greeted by a doorman other than Roger Hogan. Hogan must've had the day off. This guy had the name Warren em-broidered on his jacket, and he had the timid I-ain't-terribly-bright demeanor of Stan Laurel. She heard Marcus whisper sotto voce to her, "Just play along, and keep this mope busy outside."

"Hey, Warren!" Marcus chimed genially, flashing his gold shield and reaching out to shake the puzzled man's hand as if he were greeting a long-lost buddy. "Detective Dick Fleugelman, Special Ops. How are you?" Without giving the man a chance to catch his breath, Marcus snapped his thumb toward Diane and continued with his audacious bullshit. "That's Detec-tive Goodleigh."

Warren gave Diane an appreciative, baffled nod.

"Gotta use your phone," Marcus told him. "I'll only be a minute."

Warren opened his mouth and raised a pointed index finger in thought, attempting to get a word in edgewise. Marcus didn't allow it.

"Emergency," Marcus assured. "Just got a message on our radio to call headquarters right away." Without giving the man a fraction of a second to respond, he added firmly, "Relax, enjoy the fresh air. Keep Detec-tive Goodleigh company. I know where the phone is. And don't worry, I'll make it a 'police call'—it won't show on your bill." Heading straight for the doorman's tiny lobby office, Marcus charged into the building, leaving a mystified Warren blinking in confusion beneath the sidewalk awning. He turned to Diane and shrugged.

"*So,*" she said.

"*So,*" Warren meekly responded.

"Nice day, hah?"

"Yeah," he uttered. "Real nice."

Diane kept friendly eye contact with the jittery little man whose small head was all but lost beneath the large uniform hat. But the more she tried to think of something appropriate to say to make the guy relax, the less seemed to come to mind. She hated whenever that happened. After an eon of awkward staring silence, Warren self-consciously turned his head and cast a curious glance into the lobby across a gold-fringed epaulet. He was getting edgy.

"Where's Roger today?" she name-dropped. "I usually see him when I go by."

"Huh?" he snapped his head around to answer. "Oh, Roger? He went to Atlantic City." Then, while checking back over his skinny shoulder once again, he continued, "He'll be back tomorrow, eight to four."

Diane hated when Richie pulled this kind of double-talk shit, always leaving her to be the straight man. Suddenly, she found words. Flashing her beautiful blues, she decided to go fishing with what she hoped would sound like an innocent query. "Oh, yeah. Atlantic City. He goes there a lot, don't he?"

"Every weekend," Warren responded, managing a wan, uncertain smile. "Gets a bus outta the Port Authority on Saturday and gambles all night. Takes a bus back on Sunday morning—gets here just in time for work."

"Yeah!" Diane breezed in her most charming purr. "Old Roger's a real high roller, isn't he?"

"You mean a real high loser," Warren said. "Had to sell his damn car. And haven't you noticed how worn his heels are getting lately?"

"Yeah!" Diane said, acting puzzled and sympathetic. "You wonder sometimes how he affords it."

Probably by doing *anything* for a buck, she thought.

Just then, Marcus came charging out of the lobby. Nodding a hurried thanks to Warren as he headed for the Malibu, he blurted to Diane, "Let's go, Goodleigh. We got a Ten-eighty-five with the rest of the squad down at the Slovenian Mission to the United Nations."

As the puny figure of Warren the doorman, mouth still agape, eyes batting in nervous confusion, faded in the rearview mirror, Diane accelerated the Malibu up the block. Crossing Third, and turning left onto Lexington, she finally scowled and said, "Detective Dick Fleugelman? Detective Good*leigh*? Slovenian Mission? This had better be real good, Richie. Let's hear it."

"Remember the doorman's telephone log?" Marcus asked smugly, his eyebrows in full arch. "The composition book we saw Roger Hogan making notations in?"

"Yeah," Diane replied. "The one he told us that the doormen were required to record all their calls in, or else they might lose their jobs?"

"Yeah. That's the one," Marcus affirmed. "While our hero—Detective Dick Fleugelman—was making his phony phone call a moment ago, he peeked into that little logbook and eyeballed the entries for last Tuesday night."

"And?" Diane asked, her eyes now wide in anticipation.

"Accordin' to the cabbie, it was the doorman— Roger—who told him the destination of the fare would be the La Florentine. Right?"

"Right," she seconded.

"And, according to the cabbie's trip sheet, he picked up Candace Mayhew in front of 333 East Seventy-third at ten fifty-five. Right?"

"Right!" she agreed.

"At ten fifty-six, our boy Roger 'Dubya' Hogan

made an outgoing call to the 917 area code, and recorded same in the phone log. I jotted down the number."

"That's a New York City cell phone prefix."

"Right," he said. "Could be registered to someone in the Bronx, Manhattan . . . Queens. But I'd be willing to bet next week's pay it's registered to someone in Brooklyn." Turning to face Diane, he added, "Maybe even Brighton Beach, Brooklyn."

Looking down her nose at him, she said, "You already bet next week's pay, *last week,* on that arthritic oat burner who's probably still tryin' to find the finish line out at Aqueduct. Have you forgotten?"

Marcus shrugged innocently, and flashed a toothy, disarming grin. "*If* Candace Mayhew *was* the target of the hit, how the hell would the shooter know where to find her in this great big city? How the hell would he know she'd be at the La Florentine on a quiet Tuesday night?"

Scrunching up her face, Diane finally got it. "Unless he was tipped to where she was going."

Marcus was still wearing his impish grin.

"But," she asked, "why'd we have to go through all this theatrical business? We could've had telephone security get us a printout of all their outgoing calls."

"Didn't have the number of the phone in the doorman's office, but now we do!" Marcus responded, doing a Groucho with his eyebrows. "And what's more, for the moment, doorman Roger remains none the wiser. Let's trace this number and see who he called. Then we'll corner the son of a bitch, and he won't have no wiggle room."

"Can't corner him till tomorrow." Diane sighed. "He's off rollin' the dice somewhere down in Atlantic City."

"Ah, shit!" Marcus moaned. "Too bad I didn't know he was goin', I coulda gone with him. I feel lucky this weekend."

"Yeah!" Diane said with a smirk. "Hell, you'd

buddy up with the damned devil if he played black-jack." She paused. "By the way, Richie. Could I not have been someone other than Detective Good-*leigh?*"

"Don't worry, sweetie," Marcus looked across with a playful grin. "To Detectives Dick Fleugelman, *and* Dick Marcus, you'll always be a good lay."

"And to Detectives Goodleigh, *and* DeGennaro, you'll always be a Dick *Head,*" Diane said, flooring the gas to slip through the amber at Fifty-ninth. She smiled. "Where to now?"

"Photo Unit." Revealing a roll of 35mm Kodak in the palm of his left hand, he added, "See if you can work some of your magic with that"—*snort*—"boyfriend of yours down there. I wanna get these surveillance pictures developed right away."

At 1225 hours, Eddie Brodigan dropped three fax sheets on Savage's desk. Carlton Flournoy, Thorn decided, was a man of his word.

Ten minutes later, Marcus and DeGennaro appeared back in the office carrying sandwiches they'd picked up at Carl's Deli across the street. They came right into the sergeant's room.

"Get a load of these shots," Marcus crowed, handing Savage an envelope containing eight freshly developed pictures. "Am I a great fucking photographer, or what?" Diane, standing next to Marcus, batted her eyes innocently and grinned.

"Are we absolutely sure this is Strelnikov?" Savage asked, studying the shots. The silver-haired guy in the pictures did, as Marcus had described, have the no-nonsense air of a pit bull.

"That's the guy who was behind the desk at Majestic Funding," Marcus replied. "And it's the same guy who drove Strelnikov's Lincoln out to Queens, and the same guy who went home to Strelnikov's apartment. I know that's still not positive identification," Marcus added. "So I'm gonna try to get a DMV photo to make sure."

Savage nodded.

Diane and Richie then went into detail about the information they'd gotten that morning from Candace Mayhew's last cabdriver. They also detailed Richie's ballsy flimflam at the Clarendon, and the curious information he'd uncovered in the telephone log there.

Savage, though elated with the investigative nuggets they'd turned up, reminded Marcus to get a court order for the doorman's phone log.

"I'm gonna knock out the fives at my desk," Diane said. "Meanwhile, Richie's going to get with Telephone Security and see who Hogan called that night."

"Suppose Telephone Security tells us the call went to Hogan's own home?" Marcus asked. "Still want me gettin' a court order?"

"I don't care if the call went to his goddamned mother-in-law, or to freakin' Dial-A-Joke," Savage responded. "I consider the timing of the call significant, and I want it scrutinized. If it turns out that Hogan had called someone to tip off Candace Mayhew's destination, this little nugget becomes a big gold bar. We gotta cover ourselves in court. Just get the order."

Normally, at this point, Roger Hogan would've been hauled in for questioning. But he was MIA somewhere in Atlantic City. Marcus and DeGenarro would have to come in through the back door. In the meantime, they'd put everything on paper, enjoy their hero sandwiches, and await word from Telephone Security as to just who Hogan had called.

Jack Lindstrom got back to MSH at 1300. He stepped into Thorn Savage's office just as Marcus and DeGennaro were leaving.

"Georgei Strelnikov," Lindstrom announced, opening a manila folder and dealing a mug shot of the man onto Savage's desk.

"Hey, Richie," Savage called out into the squad room. "Forget the DMV photo on Strelnikov, we don't need it anymore."

Lindstrom continued. "Georgei Strelnikov, aka

George Standish, George Stephans, Gregor Stevens, has racked up two pages of yellow sheets down at BCI."

"I'm impressed," Savage said. "What's he like to do?"

"He's got a consistent history of arrests going back to 1985. His specialties seem to lie in the areas of felonious assaults and extortions, but he also shows a manslaughter in '92, and an arson dating back to '89."

"Convictions?" Savage asked.

"None," Lindstrom said, sighing. "In every case, the records show eventual dismissals by the Kings County Courts."

"Do we know why he has no convictions?" Savage asked.

"Seeing the odd pattern," Lindstrom said, "I reached out to a connection in the Brooklyn DA's office, who happens to be very well versed on Georgei Strelnikov, Majestic Funding, and the difficulty in successfully prosecuting them."

"And?"

"And, as we suspected," Lindstrom said, "Russian mob. Every time the Brooklyn DA went to bat against Strelnikov, or Majestic Funding, witnesses disappeared, developed amnesia, or turned up DOA."

"Brooklyn's their playground," Savage said, thinking aloud. "We haven't had that much experience with the Russians here in Manhattan."

"We're gonna," Lindstrom countered. "My source tells me that their operation's growing by leaps and bounds. In years past they were content to limit most of their activities to Brooklyn. But now, especially with loan-sharking, they're expanding to the other boroughs as well. Manhattan, of course, is the plum. In fact, I'm told they're getting so strong that they're networking nationally. Stolen cars for export, that sort of thing."

"Anything on the other corporate officers?" Savage asked.

"There's no record at all on the president, Nikita Relska, who, my Brooklyn source tells me, happens to be a real tough broad and is the unquestioned brains of the outfit. They've had her in a few times for questioning. She sometimes uses the name Nikki. The secretary, Dmitri Nakovics, and the treasurer, Peter Kozyukova, both have some minor bullshit—harassments, possession of stolen property. Misdemeanors."

"Take a look at this," Savage said, handing Lindstrom the freshly faxed subscriber list to *Old Toy Soldier*.

"*Hmmm,*" Lindstrom began. "Interesting approach to . . ."

Beaming, Richie Marcus stuck his head into the sergeant's room. "Just heard back from Patti Capwell over at Telephone Security," he said.

"And?" Lindstrom said coldly, clearly irritated by the rude interruption.

"*And!*" Marcus replied, looking straight-faced at Lindstrom. "She told me the secret of keeping an asshole in suspense."

"Oh, yeah?" Lindstrom fell. "How?"

"Tell you, Tuesday." Marcus snorted.

"You remember going to school as a kid, Marcus?" Lindstrom immediately parried.

"Yeah! I went to school. What about it?"

"Was it a *big* yellow bus that picked you and the other kids up on the corner . . . or was it one of those *little* yellow buses that came and picked you up right at your house?"

"Up yours, Jack," Marcus said, and turned toward Savage. "Patti claims the number that Hogan the doorman entered into the log belongs to a cell phone registered to a Nikita Relska at, get this, 1620 Ocean Avenue, Brooklyn."

Shooting a how-do-you-do glance at Lindstrom, Savage then turned back to Marcus. "According to your five from last night, that's Strelnikov's crib."

"Right on," Marcus agreed. "Want we should go talk to this Relska broad?"

After some contemplation, Savage replied, "Nah. We'd better do this by the numbers. Let's talk to the doorman first. He's gotta be the weak link. According to Diane, he's MIA till tomorrow morning. If he caves, we'll be dealing from a much better position of strength when we talk with Strelnikov or Relska."

Marcus nodded his agreement.

Lindstrom piped in. "We've also gotta consider the problem of disappearing witnesses when it comes to these people. If we talk to the Russians first, and rattle their cage, we might never get a chance to talk to Hogan. The boss is right, we better just sit tight."

The fog was continuing to lift, and the shape of the investigation was coming more into focus, but Savage still wasn't sure what it was he was beginning to see. He looked up at Marcus. "Afraid we're gonna have to cancel that little get-together you and Diane had planned for tomorrow. You're all gonna be on overtime."

Marcus's beam became even brighter.

"I want you and Diane waiting for Hogan when he arrives for work tomorrow morning," Savage said to Marcus. Then he turned to Lindstrom. "I want you to start running down the names of those magazine subscribers that just got faxed in."

"There's a lot of names on that list," Lindstrom said, grimacing at the thought of the daunting task. "And the addresses are all over the five boroughs, Westchester, Nassau, and Suffolk. I guess I'll start by checking all the forty-five to fifty-five males for wants, warrants, and priors." He shrugged.

"Forget that for now," Savage said. "You gotta remember, I saw this guy up close. I want you to start by running the name of every male on that list through Motor Vehicle. DMV now has a digital photo database. Have them e-mail us the photos of any who are licensed drivers. I'll go through those right away. That should shorten the list substantially."

Scanning the faxed pages, Lindstrom added, "Some of these subscribers are unnamed persons at post office boxes. You know, *Boxholder,* PO Box so-and-so," he advised.

"Contact Rudy Caparo over at Postal Inspections," Savage said. "He'll get us the names and addresses attached to those post office boxes when that survey was done. Run those names through DMV also. Then, if we still come up dry with the photos, the legwork that'll be left won't be so bad."

"Sarge!" Eddie Brodigan called out from the wheel desk. "Pick up line two. Brooklyn North Homicide's on the line. They got a DOA gunshot victim on a sidewalk out there who fits your description of the bald guy from last night. And, get this, he had almost ten Gs in his pocket."

Slouched in an old swivel chair, the snow-tire tread of his rubber-soled military low-cut shoe crunched against a file drawer pull, the uniformed security guard in the small anteroom seemed annoyed at having to take his attention from the dog-eared Ninja Turtle comic book. He offered Savage and Lindstrom an indifferent nod. When Lindstrom flashed his gold detective's shield, the put-upon guard pressed a button on his desk that released the electronic lock on the swinging doors that led into the basement morgue of the Kings County Medical Examiner's Office. Savage and Lindstrom pushed through them. Savage caught his first whiff of that butcher-shop aroma. He quickly reached for a Wint-O-Green.

"Think he was actually reading?" Lindstrom said, as they headed down the tiled corridor.

"Nah," Savage replied, wishing he were somewhere else. "Just looking at the picures. Prob'ly studying for the security guard sergeant's exam."

"Unh," Lindstrom grunted. "Nothing like being well read."

The profound unease he always felt when entering such places began to gnaw at him. Savage hated morgues even more than hospitals. In particular, he very much disliked the Kings County Morgue. As a longtime boss in Homicide he understood death, but didn't much like being totally surrounded by it. Aside from the forensic value that autopsies could provide in determining cause, or establishing or recovering evidence in an investigation of unexplained death, morgues were nothing more than overbooked DOA storage units. They overflowed with the unidentified, the unwanted, and the unclaimed. Men and women, young and old, black and white and all shades in between. Corpses, stacked like cordwood till planted in potter's field, or shipped off to some science lab or anatomy class.

"Is it dark in here, or is it me?" Lindstrom asked, squinting his eyes.

"You expected maybe a tanning salon?" Savage quipped.

Weary fluorescent tubes, prematurely dimmed by the no-time-out demands of 24/7 institutional service, provided less-than-adequate light to the glazed concrete block walls and linoleum tile floor of the lengthy, windowless passageway. The space had an overall pallor akin to the shroud of darkness that usually precedes a late-afternoon summer storm. The forbidding atmosphere rocketed to surreal at the sight of the charred remains of a dozen children scattered about a storage room they passed. No litters, no gurneys, their bodies tossed randomly about on the concrete floor like twisted wrecks in a junkyard. The blackened forms of two infants, their tiny barbecued arms frozen grotesquely as if reaching out for help, were cast haphazardly across the top of an old desk. Probably the victims of that big fire in Bed-Stuy he'd read about. He and Lindstrom exchanged horrified glances and continued down the hall past a caravan of cadavered gurneys lined up outside the glassed-in autopsy room with its dozen workstations. Everything in this place was cold. Everything was constructed of glass, concrete, ceramic, or stainless steel—everything except the clients. But again, they too were cold.

Inside the production-line autopsy room, pathologists, inured to gore, casually sliced into scalps, sawed into skulls, and cracked open sternums with wooden-handled Craftsman pruning shears from Sears. Laughing, jiving assistants wheeled out the old, and wheeled in the new. Joking with one another, they lackadaisically chucked human bodies back and forth from gurneys to procedure tables as though they were silent bundles of rags or soulless sides of beef. Apathy reigned supreme here in the city's biggest human meat locker.

Catching the attention of one of the pathologists, Savage entered the shambles and identified himself.

"Brooklyn North called and said to expect you," Dr. Hermanski said, using the back side of both wrists to raise a clear plastic visor from his face.

As Dr. Hermanski led him and Lindstrom through the autopsy room to a sheet-covered cadaver on table six, Savage noticed several lengthy mustard drips and the residue of cigarette ash comingling with the bloody stains on the surgical drape that covered the man from neck to ankles.

"He came in with a priority about an hour ago," Hermanski said, yanking back the sheet.

"Baldy?" Lindstrom asked, staring at Savage.

"That's Baldy," Savage replied.

"He was shot twice," Hermanski said. "One entered the back of the neck, and came out the throat. But because the other wound in the back of his head showed no exit, Brooklyn North asked us to do him right away to recover the round. We just finished up."

"Brooklyn North Homicide will be taking charge of any evidence, Doc," Savage said. "But I'd like to see the bullet."

"Nine millimeter," the doctor squawked through a hacking episode of smoker's cough, while handing over a small plastic envelope containing the copper projectile.

Savage bit contemplatively at the inside of his cheek. "I was somehow sure it would be." Turning to Jack Lindstrom, he added, "How much you wanna bet it came from a Glock?"

NINETEEN

Savage pit-stopped at home for a shower, shave, and change of clothes. The charcoal pinstripe he'd worn to the office didn't seem appropriate for tonight—too dressy. Also, it may have picked up that morgue stench from his late-afternoon visit with Baldy in Brooklyn. He went with a Bill Blass blue linen blazer and gray slacks, a button-down black watch Van Heusen, and his favorite burgundy loafers. He double-spritzed Obsession and brushed his teeth, then put away the dishes that'd been draining in the sink, put out the garbage, and changed the sheets on the bed—just in case. At five minutes to eight he arrived at Palermo's on Hester and waited outside beneath their red, white, and green striped awning. Gina McCormick hadn't gotten there yet.

The last time he'd dined at Palermo's was ten years ago, Christmas. It had been a cop thing, a squad Christmas party. He was then in the Street Crime Unit. A dozen of them had gone to Palermo's after the completion of their last day tour, pushed three or four tables together in the back room, and broken bread. He couldn't remember if the food was good, but he certainly didn't recall it being bad. Italian restaurants usually didn't survive long in Little Italy serving anything less than decent chow. He did, however, remember the house red. They must have consumed gallons of it that night. The wine—made right on the premises—was definitely good, and paralyzingly potent. Everybody had gotten happily blitzed.

At precisely eight o'clock Gina McCormick came into view, entering Hester Street from Centre. She, too, was punctual. He liked that. And alluring, even more so than he remembered, alluring in that simmering-beneath-the-surface way known only to Mediterranean females and long-dormant volcanoes about to let go. Wearing a champagne-hued tailored suit over a high-necked bronze silk blouse, she was proper enough for an audience with the pope. Fortunately, the garment did nothing to conceal the wonderful curves that filled it, or the fine calves its knee-length skirt revealed. As he watched her stride up the gentle slope from Centre Street, he resolved to bulldoze the bullshit of the past few days into some remote corner of his mind, and enjoy the evening and the beautiful woman who'd invited him here.

"Waiting long?" she asked, a fetching smile on perfecto lips.

"Just got here," he replied with a welcoming grin. He twisted the knob on the glass-paned door that opened into the smaller of the restaurant's two dining rooms, and again caught a whiff of her as she breezed closely past. The perfume was the same she had been wearing at the hospital a few days ago. It was still sultry and intensely provocative, but he was no closer to identifying it.

Inside Palermo's they were greeted by a swarthy young man in his twenties whose face and neck were full of cuts and nicks. He looked as though he'd shaved using the jagged edges of a broken beer bottle as a razor, and probably without benefit of a mirror. He had patent-leather hair and a De Niro mole on his right cheek, and looked like an unmade bed in scruffy double-pleated high-waters and a dingy white shirt beneath a snug-fitting black vest. He clutched an armful of menus, their once clear vinyl jackets stained with tomato sauce and yellowed by age. In broken

English, he introduced himself as Claudio and led them through the bustling room to a round table for two in a far corner.

Though cramped for maximum seating capacity with an eclectic assortment of chairs and tables set with unmatching plates and silver, the room had an earthy sort of charm. Latticework, laced with runners of silk English ivy that had missed their last six scheduled dustings, bordered their table and offered some sense of intimacy. Palermo's was hardly Peacock Alley at the Waldorf, but it did have . . . *something*. In its own unrefined way it had a comfortable atmosphere. And it was crowded, which Savage took as a definite plus.

Setting the menus on the table before them, Claudio whipped a small pad and pencil stub from his vest pocket. After a lengthy but uninspired recitation of the day's specials, which included stromboli, fettucini Palermo, and something "Ahvongoolah," Claudio finally asked, "Dr*eeenks*?"

"I'd like a glass of your house red," Gina said softly, looking directly at the waiter. Then, facing Savage, she said, "I've had it before. It's really good."

"Taking the local, eh?" Thorn kidded her, then said to Claudio, "I'd like an extra-dry Bombay martini, straight up, with a twist. Make it a double." Turning back to face Gina, he said, "I'm taking the express."

"Can't say that I blame you," she said with a sympathetic chuckle. "After last night . . ."

The waiter shuffled away while barking something in Italian to a busboy resetting a booth in the corner.

"He told him to finish up there and give Nunzio a hand in the kitchen," Gina interpreted.

"You speak the lingo?" Savage asked.

"Oh, yes. I picked it up from my grandmother when I was a child. She was from the old country—Sicily. Came here as a young married woman, but never quite mastered the new language."

"How's your pop?" Thorn inquired, thinking the question to be his proper opener.

"Doing fine." Gina nodded, shyly flashing her dark, almost mahogany eyes. He swore he felt a breeze from her long lashes. "Thanks again to you," she said.

"Does he know who his beautiful daughter's having dinner with tonight?"

"No!" she responded coyly, unfolding her napkin. "But," she quickly added with an even coyer grin, "my mother does." She draped the napkin across her lap.

Claudio was back—the service bartender must have been a magician. The waiter placed the martini with a twist in front of Thorn, a goblet of red before Gina, and a woven basket piled high with warm bread and sesame-seed-encrusted garlic sticks between them.

"How did it come to pass that a nice Italian girl like you wound up with a last name like McCormick?" Savage asked. There seemed no time like the present to get right down to it.

"I was married to one," she said, fondling the wine goblet with elegantly manicured fingers. The polish on her nails was a deep magenta, fastidiously layered on—one of the best fingernail paint jobs he'd ever seen.

"I took the liberty of assuming as much," he said. "What became of Mr. McCormick?"

"Buddy McCormick loved me," she said, gazing contemplatively at her wine. Then, looking up into Thorn's eyes, she said, "Trouble was he loved women, period. He was a rascal, that Bud McCormick was." She half-grinned. "We've been divorced about ten years. You?"

"My wife died a long time ago."

"Sorry."

"I play house with a cat," he said with a tight grin that pulled at the old scar on his lip.

"That can have its benefits," she said.

"Yeah!" Thorn replied. "He sometimes lets me eat in front of the television."

Gina chuckled. "Who gets to handle the remote in a two-male house?"

"Me, mostly," he responded, smiling at the way Gina could banter. "He's always complaining he doesn't have a thumb." Savage raised his chilled glass. "Cheers," he said softly, mesmerized by Gina's *It*, whatever the hell *It* was.

"Cheers," she said, as their glasses clicked. "Here's to a wonderful night."

He wondered what she meant by that as he took his first sip of the chilled gin. When Savage finished the martini, he joined her by switching to the house wine. Claudio served it to them in a tall carafe.

Dinner was frutta d' mare for two, one of Palermo's seafood extravaganzas. Thick chunks of lobster and crab meat, colossal shrimp, sweet-tasting mussels and baby clams—still in their shells—calamari, and a wide variety of other delicious, unidentifiable marine creatures, all draped with a spicy fra diavalo tomato sauce over a bottomless bed of al dente linguini. They augmented the unblushing feast with dessert of amaretto-flavored napoleons and rich cannoli. They also shared a pot of steaming espresso, softening its tart flavor with peel of lemon and splashes of Sambuca.

Conversation was fluid and easy, and revealed much that they shared in common. In minutes he'd begun to feel as if he'd known her a long time. She was an expert downhill skier—he, almost. They agreed that Gray Rocks in the Canadian Laurentians had the best slopes in the east. They also agreed that Stratton and Killington in the Green Mountains of Vermont were tied for a close second. Unlike Thorn, Gina had never thrown herself out of a perfectly good aircraft at ten thousand feet, but confessed that she'd "always wanted to parachute." Savage, on the other hand, had never visited Italy and toured Rome, but had always wanted to.

Their shared meal was a sensual experience; it was an orgy of food. It took on an intensity suggestive of an alternative form of foreplay. They lost all connection with the noisy, crowded room in which they dined. He could tell by the way her glances met his that she was feeling what he felt. Was it the house red? Was it only the wine fueling the seductive flames he was feeling?

It was her eyes.

The cares that had plagued these past days all seemed distant, muted in his mind by the numbing effect of Palermo's house red, but mostly by the comfort zone he found in Gina's incredible warmth. Gina was the thing. Gina was the focus.

After dinner she invited him back to her place in Brooklyn Heights. He discovered that Gina McCormick needed him every bit as much as he needed her. They made love for hours. When they'd finally exhausted themselves they slept away what was left of the night coiled in one another's arms.

TWENTY

The five a.m. Tan and Orange out of Atlantic City would arrive at the Port Authority Bus Terminal at Fortieth Street and Eighth Avenue at 7:30, leaving him adequate time to taxi over to East Seventy-third, get into his hateful monkey suit, and be on the door by eight. Roger Hogan knew every step of the trip's two-and-a-half-hour schedule because it had been his regular weekend junket for years. From his window seat at the rear of the bus, he pressed his nose against the cold glass and gazed out at the rural New Jersey scenery rushing by. He could set his watch by where the bus was on the Garden State Parkway, on either the outgoing southbound or the Sunday run back.

Hogan couldn't believe the success he'd had on this trip. He'd arrived at Harrah's just before noon yesterday with the thousand he'd scored for making one lousy phone call, and here he was returning less than a day later with sixty-two hundred. When you're hot, you're hot, no two ways about it.

Removed now from the casino's compelling atmosphere of garish carnival lighting and sound effects, designed to ward off player boredom and keep losers losing, he heard only the monotonous drone of scenic-cruiser rubber greeting macadam. The gambler's high he'd been riding had begun to wane. As those happy thoughts diminished, dark musings of Mrs. Mayhew from 21-G began spilling into, filling, and ultimately overflowing the banks of those introspective voids. The haunting was back, *damn it all*. Her murder *had not* been his fault, he was certain. His actions had played no role in her death, he tried to assure himself. The thousand-dollar stake he'd parlayed into big bucks this weekend *was not* blood money.

He knew he was lying.

It had all seemed so innocent. Five hundred to pump the Mayhew broad for her destination whenever hailing her a cab. If it turned out to be Forty-ninth and Third, or, more specifically, the La Florentine Restaurant, there would be another five for immediately making one telephone call. That big-chested broad who'd made the proposition, and who'd fronted the first five hundred, hadn't said why, or why she was willing to pay so much to have it done. He hadn't bothered to ask. In his heart he'd known right along there was something evil about it all, but, nefarious or not, a thousand bucks was a thousand bucks. *One lousy phone call.* Maybe this week he'd go to confession, he thought. It would help cleanse his mortal soul. Maybe this week he'd go to the police and fess up. Hell, he'd even turn over the thousand. It might help clear his conscience, and besides, he'd still be fifty-two hundred to the better. He just needed a little more time to build up the courage. Maybe a day, maybe two. Maybe he wouldn't even have to turn over the thousand. He sighed deeply, and tried to clear his mind of the nagging guilt.

He periscoped his head above the seat backs fore and aft and saw the usual near-capacity load of spent weekend gamblers making their way back to the Apple. A few, like him, wore smiles. Most, however, did not. Most were lucky they'd paid for a round-tripper on the front end or they'd be hoofing it back to New York this morning. He knew the feeling. Sprinkled among the smilers and frowners were the snoozers and snorers, sleeping off Harrah's comp booze, exhausted by the dice-rolling, slot-feeding marathon they'd just completed. Hogan realized he hadn't slept a wink since the two hours he'd grabbed on yesterday's bus ride down, but any fatigue he should have felt had probably been assuaged by the inner elation and adrenaline kick of being, at long last, a winner.

Still, it was going to be a long day, he realized. He'd be on his feet till at least four this afternoon. Careful not to disturb the weird-looking guy with the goofy fingernails who was sawing wood in the aisle seat beside him—*the things you see when you ain't got a gun*—Roger shifted his weight and leaned his shoulder against the upholstered panel to his right. He allowed his head to come to rest against the coolness of the window, its wind-driven chill fed by the steady sixty-five-mile-an-hour pace.

As the bus roared north past the exit for South Tom's River, Roger closed his eyes; at best he could get an hour.

Despite the dearth of actual sleep, when Savage emerged from beneath the warmth of Gina's down-filled comforter, and swung his naked feet to the polished hardwood floor, he felt like a million. Considering his double-martini-prefaced consumption of vast quantities of guinea red, followed by an entire night spent loving Gina, he should have felt like he'd been in a train wreck. Instead, he wanted to take on the world. Gina, it appeared, was an elixir.

After showering together at her place, they shared a pot of hazelnut coffee and picked apart an Entenmann's cheese Danish she'd pulled from her freezer and nuked into palatable submission. Their kiss goodbye was long and hot, and seemed so . . . natural. This, he was sure, was the start of something big.

The taxi ride back to his place in Manhattan from Gina's digs in Brooklyn Heights took all of ten minutes; Sunday morning, no traffic. He left the taxi waiting and ran upstairs for a quick change. Figuring he'd be landlocked in the office because of the bullshit

Modified Assignment, he dressed down in a pair of
khaki Dockers, tassled Easy Spirit loafers—no socks—
and a sharply creased, hunter green cotton long-
sleeve. Running late, he didn't bother to shave, and
never thought to check his answering machine for
messages. He topped off Ray's chow and water bowls,
double-dosed on the ginko biloba, and reboarded
the cab.

Short of time, he skipped his usual Sunday-morning
paper routine. He'd pick one up at Curley's on the
way home and read it tonight in his own living room,
in the casual comfort of an old pair of boxers and his
favorite cut-down Yankee sweatshirt; his only company would be a few cold Buds and the Sunday *Times*
crossword. The mostly fucked-up week he'd just lived
through was catching up—he looked forward to the
oasis of solitude. Although, the thought occurred, another night at Gina's wouldn't be too hard to take.
They'd tentatively set another date for next Friday;
Jesus, was he already counting the hours?

At 8:30 the cab dropped him in front of the Thirteenth Precinct.

As Savage signed himself into the command log,
Eddie Brodigan opened the Telephone Message book
and pointed out the entry of the notification he'd
taken earlier.

0700:   Notify Lt. Peter Pezzano, Commanding
          Officer, MSHTF, and Sgt. Thornton Sav-
          age, MSHTF, to report to the office of the
          Police Commissioner at 1100 hours, this
          date. RDOs cancelled.

"Tried to call you at home with the forthwith,
boss," Brodigan said. "Did'ja get the message I left
on your machine?"

"No," Savage answered tersely, feeling no need to
explain further. "Did you notify Lt. P? He's on his
regular day off."

"Oh, yeah, I got him at home at oh-seven-oh-five. He said he'll meet you downtown at eleven hundred. I was starting to get worried about reaching you, though. I kept getting no answer."

"Well," Savage said, "consider me reached."

"Figure this has to do with the shooting from the other night?" Brodigan asked, a sincerely concerned and hopeful look painted across his ruddy Irish face.

"No doubt," Savage replied, while turning in the direction of his office. "I'm sure he's not calling us down there for Sunday brunch and Bloody Marys."

Savage couldn't help thinking how pissed the PC would probably be about having to come in on a Sunday morning, as soon as he'd gotten back in town, to deal with some SBA beef. *Shit! And me with no fuckin' socks.*

Savage exchanged glances with Jack Lindstrom and nodded good morning. Lindstrom was busy taking notes over the phone at his desk. Savage could tell by the man's intensity that he had something to report. It was no surprise that Lindstrom came directly into the sergeants' room after hanging up.

"Just got with Rudy Caparo over at Postal," Lindstrom began. "Gave him those ten PO box numbers. Says he'll get right on 'em."

"I thought only cops and firemen worked Sundays," Savage said, reaching onto the top shelf of his locker for his old Norelco.

"Cops and firemen, always. Postal Inspectors, sometimes."

"What about DMV? They gonna accomodate us, or make us wait till tomorrow? You know—Monday to Friday, nine to five and all that bullshit." Clicking the ON-OFF switch back and forth, Thorn got no response from the shaver. He looked to Lindstrom. "Battery's dead." Then, getting right back to business, he said, "I hate having to deal with those bastards at Motor Vehicle."

"Got that ball rolling too," Lindstrom reported.

"Believe it or not, DMV's gonna try to take care of business. I think we got lucky. The guy I talked to up in Albany was glad to help, says Sundays usually drag. Told me their computers have been up and down all morning, but if they stay up he figures he can get those photos e-mailed to us by noon."

Savage gave a look of exaggerated disbelief. "Jesus!" he said sarcastically. "Motor Vehicle's gonna do something without our having to kiss their ass. Will wonders never cease."

Thorn pulled a charger base from his locker, plugged it in at his desk, and set the shaver into the receptacle. He checked his watch. The recharge would take half an hour.

"What else we got on the agenda for the day, boss?" Lindstrom asked.

"I figured we'd go through channels to advise the powers that be that we intend to speak with Senator Maloney's wife, Christine, about her Friday-evening visitor. But since I'm meeting with the PC in a few hours, I'll run it all by him first."

"Why do we need to do that?" Lindstrom asked. "She's just like everybody else, ain't she?"

"Protocol!" Savage announced. "It's all political bullshit. Maloney's all but announced his candidacy to run in the presidential primaries. With him being in the opposition party from the mayor, it might give the impression that our actions are politically motivated and designed to embarrass Maloney. The powers might not think we've got enough to go on yet before we go knocking on her door. If there's any problem, the PC can at least cover his own ass by getting with the mayor, and forewarning him of our intentions."

"That's a bitch," Lindstrom said, shaking his head indignantly. "If she were the wife of some poor Joe Dokes, or the wife of *Jack Lindstrom*, for that matter, we'd just go and knock on her damn door. *Right?*"

"Right," Savage agreed. He turned and began to rummage through the top shelf of his locker. "Let's

wait and see what DeGennaro and Marcus get out of
that doorman Hogan. Then I want you and Marcus to
get out to Brooklyn and visit Nikita Relska."

Lindstrom nodded, then asked, "And DeGennaro?"

"Once I clear it with the PC, Diane and I are gonna
pay a visit to the senator's wife out in Forest Hills."
Shaking his head in frustration, Savage mumbled,
"Shit! The only pair of socks I've got in here are
black."

It was now ten after nine, and Roger Hogan still
wasn't on the door at 333 East Seventy-third. When
DeGennaro and Marcus arrived there shortly after
eight, some midget named Hector was there. Hector
had worked the midnight-to-eight shift and was still
waiting for his relief.

"Try him at home again," Diane said, checking
her watch.

Hector rolled his eyes and hit redial. There was no
answer. "I tol jou, he not hone," Hector said in his
South Bronx Puerto Rican English. "Every Sunday he
coming in by bus from Ellanic City. Maybe de bus
is late?"

"This ever happen before?" Marcus asked.

"Never," Hector replied. "Roger is always on tine,
man."

Diane took the phone receiver from Hector's hand
and dialed Manhattan South.

"Calling the boss?" Marcus asked.

"Yes," she replied. "I'll see if he wants us to continue to hang around, or what."

Sitting contemplatively at the oak table beside the
window in her breakfast nook, Nikita Relska took a
long, slow drag on what was left of her second Virginia
Slims of the new day, and looked out at the parklike
rear yard of the apartment building at 1620 Ocean
Avenue.

Children were playing, laughing loudly, swinging, and climbing for all they were worth. Gone were the heavy coats, scarves, and gloves they'd been wrapped in all winter; now they romped freely in the lighter clothing of spring while their parents and sitters watched, content to bathe in the gentle sun and look on from the cast-iron-framed benches that rimmed the private playground. Nikki's attention shifted to a bushy-tailed squirrel racing like a four-legged Wallenda along the telephone wire that ran high above the property edge. The surefooted creature then took a daring leap into the flimsy branches of an old weeping willow and disappeared from her sight. She thought about how hard it was to make it in this world, and how the animal was doing whatever it had to do to survive. Nikki took one more deep drag and crushed the cigarette in the ashtray.

She took a sip of her black coffee—three sugars—that had gone cold in the cup. Then, after inhaling a chunk of marmalade-slathered melba toast, slowly turned the pages of Sunday's *Parade* Magazine. Nikki really wasn't interested in the paper—there were far more critical issues to be dealt with and decided this day. Georgei was in the bathroom. She would finish eating the toast before he got out and clear all evidence of that course away. After he left, out would come the pastries, bakery rolls, and butter. She was hungry this morning—even more than usual. It must be her anger, or her apprehension, or her woman's intuition. Dammit, she thought, every time she got that way she really overate.

She and Georgei had important things to discuss this morning—she would put him to the test and find out the truth.

After carefully working the last gooey bits of marmalade from the glass jar, she licked the sticky spoon and hoped Georgei had the right answers. When she heard the bathroom sink water stop running she ditched the empty jar beneath some papers in the kitchen trash can. At the sound of the bathroom door opening, she lit another cigarette.

"You were out late last night, Georgei," she said flatly as Strelnikov strode into the narrow kitchen. "I did not even hear you come in," she lied.

"You were sleeping. I tried not to wake you," he soothed. "Was Nakovics able to get any information on that reporter, Ballantine?"

Nikki handed him a piece of notepaper as he passed. "He called early this morning," she replied. "I have written it all down." She watched as Strelnikov laid the note on the table and read it while squaring the knot of his silk de la Renta tie.

He poured himself a cup of coffee.

"He drives a beat-up 1993 Mercury Cougar," she said. "White. Dmitri also got the license-plate number. Ballantine is going to be at an alcoholic's meeting at two o'clock this afternoon. That is where I want him hit."

"Where is alcoholic's meeting taking place?" Strelnikov asked curiously.

"St. Agnes Church on East Forty-third Street," she said, taking a pen and adding that information to the note. "Like clockwork, he attends an Alcoholics Anonymous meeting every Sunday afternoon in the basement."

Strelnikov nodded.

"But," Nikki said, "the question is, do we *need* to kill this man? He is many years removed from the Mayhew woman and Gerard Maloney."

Strelnikov leaned back against the counter and took a first tentative sip of his black coffee. "He is link that someday could break."

The words hit Nikita Relska like a brick through plate glass. *Where have I heard that expression before?* she mused, fighting to cloak her festering anger. "And say what?" she asked smoothly. "That Gerard Maloney once had an affair with Candace Mayhew?"

"Yes! That, and possibly many other things."

"So what if he once had an affair?" She shrugged. "Many American presidents have had many affairs in their lives. People are used to that sort of thing now."

"True enough," Strelnikov said, nonchalantly returning the shrug. "But the women they had affairs with did not wind up getting murdered shortly before those men announced as presidential candidates. And," he went on, "we do not know what the Mayhew woman may have revealed to this man Ballantine years ago. After all, they were living together at same time she was working closely with Maloney."

"My guess is she did not tell him anything," Nikki lied, only for the sake of argument.

"She was known to have big mouth," Strelnikov shot back, sipping again at the hot coffee. "And phenomenal memory. Look at every minute detail she told her husband years later about the senator's crimes."

"Yes," Nikki acknowledged. "But her husband is now dead."

"I know that. But now that Candace Mayhew has been killed, this Ballantine may feel need to come forward and stir up some questions."

"Without Candace Mayhew around to substantiate anything he might say, it would all be considered hearsay, secondhand nonsense," she said, still playing devil's advocate.

"That may be true," Strelnikov agreed, "but is possible he could cause enough waves to get police to look at Maloneys—maybe even talk to them—about Candace Mayhew murder."

"The blame for her death will fall on her jilted, jealous husband, or her lover's connection to the Italian mob. And both those avenues are dead ends. I planned it that way," Nikki said assuredly, "and that is the way it will work out."

"The man is investigative reporter," Strelnikov pressed, "who still may be passionately angry that Gerard Maloney stole away best screw of his life. He doesn't even have to prove anything, he merely has to print connection, imply something, and let it hang there. Public opinion may finish Maloney as candidate and everything we have worked for will be finished."

We? Nikita thought, still controlling her anger. "Yes, I see." She nodded with a faint, sarcastic laugh. "I do have far too much invested in this coup to have it spoiled by some horny man." Bitterly, she added, "Is that not so, Georgei?"

Strelnikov didn't reply. Instead, he picked up the note, reread it, and asked, "Have you contacted 'your friend' and made arrangements for Ballantine?"

Now, stewing, Nikita remained silent.

He took a final gulp of coffee and laid the note back on the table. "I must leave now, I have matters to tend to."

Barely able to control her fury, she said, "Tell me again of your visit with Christine Maloney the other night."

"Tell you what?" Strelnikov said, his tone dismissive. "I have already told you everything."

"Tell me again," she blurted harshly, then, inhaling a deep drag of smoke, recovered her poise. "Do the Maloneys still think it was actually the Mayhew woman and her Italian boyfriend who were shaking them down?"

"I am quite sure they do, Nikki," Georgei assured, now shuffling aimlessly through sections of the morning paper. "There is no way the Maloneys, or anyone else for that matter, could ever find out that it was us from very start, and that Candace Mayhew and her greaseball friend were merely masks."

"Us?!" Relska raged, finally losing it. "It was me, Georgei! All me! I was the one who saw the value of Harmon Mayhew's information. I was the one who wormed into Christine Maloney's life. I was the one who thought of the blackmail ploy. I was the one who gained her total confidence. Have you forgotten that, Georgei?"

"You are right," he soothingly acknowledged. "It was all you, Nikki. You were the one who allowed Mayhew to trade his information about Maloney against his debts. It was you who saw ingenius way to set Maloneys up. And, I must say, your plan to use Mayhew's stupid bigmouthed wife and boyfriend as dupes was sheer brilliance."

"You're damn right it was brilliance. And it was me who got Christine to say the right words on tape. Let me remind you, Georgei," she said, bristling, "without those tapes that I worked damned hard to get, we would have had nothing for leverage."

"Tapes can be damning," he affirmed with a shrug.

"Yes," Nikki icily replied. "Tapes can be most damning, Georgei." There was a brief and uncomfortable silence.

Trying, but unable to control the angry rant, Nikita Relska raved on. "And, in case you have forgotten, it was also *my* scheme to have the Mayhew woman and her boyfriend killed. And by so doing, I disposed of the two dupes who could prove they never bothered the Maloneys. And, at the same time, forever cemented the Maloneys into our grasp."

Strelnikov listened in respectful silence, giving continual nods of acknowledgement.

Snuffing out her half-finished cigarette and regaining composure, Nikki shifted to her next query. "Was she grateful when you told her we would forego the twenty-five thousand she owed if we came to terms?"

"Very," Strelnikov replied casually. "She said something about returning it right away to safe-deposit box."

"Did you bed the skinny bitch?" Nikki blurted pointedly.

"Of course not." He dismissed the question with an assuring grin and wink. "We both know she would much prefer you in that department."

"Christine Maloney is a size triple-X ego, in an

eight-petite dress," Nikki growled. "The whole time I had to endure her, it was all I could do not to vomit."

"Do you think she will live up to word?" Strelnikov asked.

"Her word?" Nikki shot back. "The only thing we can rely on her to do is whatever is best for her. For now she has no recourse. She is scared to death of being revealed in a murder conspiracy."

"And what of Mayhew Fashions? With Majestic Funding as partner, with rights of survivorship, we now own it outright."

"We leave the cousin in charge," Nikki muttered, unable to hide her lack of interest with the new topic. "He can run it, till we can peddle it off."

Strelnikov stood. "So, I go," he said. "And again, I think it's time to contact 'dear friend' and have Ballantine matter resolved."

"No," Nikita replied, again reaching for the pack of Slims. "My *friend* is much too hot right now, with that policeman business and all. I want *you* to take care of Mr. Ballantine. I want you to be at that AA meeting, today."

"As you wish." Strelnikov shrugged, and headed for the door.

"Take the information with you," she urged, pointing to the slip of paper he'd left behind on the table.

"Don't need it," he said. "Have it memorized."

Nikita Relska saw her longtime lover, companion, and business partner to the door, set the dead bolt and chain behind him, and stormed back through the apartment to the small den off the living room. She dug beneath the cushion of the Victorian settee for the mini cassette player and tape that had been delivered yesterday while Georgei was out. She listened stolidly, fast-forwarding and reversing, over and over. It was not just the groans of the recorded sex that was upsetting her. Georgei, after all, was only a stupid man, doing what men always do—going for slim thighs. No, what really bothered her was the bold lie he had just told about the twenty-five thousand he had pocketed. And it was the private, inside track that *he* was now *laying* into the Oval Office.

Her jaw tight in anger, Nikki left the apartment and walked to the telephone booth at the corner of Avenue J and Ocean. She dialed the number she'd dialed many times before. After two rings, she heard the receiver pick up.

"Hello, Mr. K," she said. "This is a dear friend."

"Hello, dear friend," came the reply. "What can I do for you?"

"Port Authority Police. Lieutenant Benderoth speaking. How can I help you?" Although the man was saying the right words, his monotone of a voice wasn't exactly full of enthusiasm.

"Loo. This is Sergeant Thorn Savage over at Manhattan South Homicide. How you doin' this morning?"

"Not bad," the monotone replied. What can I do for ya, Sarge?"

"We're tryin' to track somebody who should have been at his job over an hour ago. It's believed he should've bussed into the Port sometime earlier this morning, coming in from Atlantic City."

"A weekend roller?"

"Yeah."

"What do you want us to do?" Benderoth asked, his blasé attitude mixed with befuddlement. "None of these bus lines manifest their passengers."

"Can you find out if any bus, from any line, scheduled to arrive from AC this morning is overdue? Broke down on the road possibly?"

"I guess I could. I'd have to get back to you though. Probably take me awhile."

"That'd be fine, Loo. I'd really appreciate your help on this. It *is* important."

"Hold on a second, Sarge," the Port Authority police lieutenant suddenly said. "Did you say this party was due in on a bus from Atlantic City?"

"Right."

"Could it be you're looking for a white male, late fifties, red hair?"

"Uh-huh."

"Could his name be Roger W. Hogan?"

"Yep."

"Got the aided card right in front of me. Tan and Orange bus driver found him DOA in his seat. Bus arrived on time at seven-thirty, everybody except this guy got off. Driver thought the guy was sleeping. Probable heart attack; possible stroke. ME's already picked up the body."

"Why do you say possible heart attack or stroke? No signs of foul play?"

"That. And the fact that he had sixty-two hundred bucks stuffed in the pockets of his Levi's. Shit," Benderoth laughed, his gruffness suddenly gone. "If I ever returned from AC with over six grand in my kick, I'd probably take a fuckin' stroke too."

TWENTY-ONE

When the elevator door slid open and Thorn Savage stepped onto the fourteenth floor of One Police Plaza, an unsmiling Lieutenant Peter Pezzano was waiting for him. Pezzano was pacing like a caged cat in the short hallway that serviced the opposing elevator banks. The hall was the crosspiece of the H-shaped layout of all the floors at NYPD headquarters.

"Where you been?" Pezzano asked, anxious.

Savage checked his watch against the hall clock that also read five to eleven. "I'm five minutes early."

"The PC's a punctuality freak," Pezzano grumbled. "The only reason he's here on a Sunday is because of us. We're supposed to go right in." He turned and led the way to the long south corridor, then hung a left.

Savage couldn't help thinking that Pezzano might need a Valium or two. "Relax, Pete. This is the police commissioner we're here to see, not the friggin' Wizard of Oz. Neither of us is made of tin or straw."

Pezzano's response was a forced, halfhearted laugh. He kept moving.

"Got a new wrinkle in the La Florentine case, boss." Savage's words matched the harried tempo of his lieutenant's rapid steps. "The doorman up at the Mayhew apartments . . ."

"Hogan!" Pezzano tersely blurted, pushing open the doors to the PC's general offices. Pezzano had a phenomenal memory for names. Savage, on the other hand, always had a tough time with names but never forgot a face.

"Found DOA on a bus this morning," Savage said.

"Was he killed?" the lieutenant asked, jerking his head around to momentarily face his sergeant.

"Don't know yet."

"When will we know?" Pezzano said, still maintaining the awkwardly quick pace as they wound their way through a maze of royal blue carpeted inner hallways.

"It's being carried as a possible heart attack or stroke," Savage replied. "But I've contacted the ME and told them to check for needle marks."

"What're you thinking?" Pezzano asked. "Pentobarbital, and that other sodium—what was it?"

"Phenytoin," Savage said. "When the mixture was almost used on Tony DiLeo, the ME told me that if they weren't looking for it at autopsy, it would've taken Toxicology days to find it."

"That's gonna be interesting to see," Pezzano muttered contemplatively, slowing, seemingly calming down. "What've you got your team doing today?"

"Got Marcus and Lindstrom heading over to Brooklyn this morning to interview the Russian that Hogan made the phone call to."

"What about DeGennaro?" Pezzano inquired.

"She had to drive me down here," Savage shrugged, displaying an ironic grin. "They took my wheels away, remember? Maybe Rice-Jenkins would've liked me to use the Lex IRT or the Third Avenue bus. In which event, on a Sunday morning I'd have gotten here about an hour from now."

Entering a plainly decorated anteroom, they were greeted by the PC's looker of a receptionist, a lean straw-blonde who introduced herself as Detective Janet Andersen. She asked them to stand by, and, after tapping lightly on the commissioner's door, let herself into the private inner office.

"Something else to tell you before we go in," Savage said, turning to Pezzano. "As soon as we're done here, DeGennaro and I are gonna take a run out to Forest Hills."

"I've been reading your reports." Pezzano nodded. "Figure it's about time to talk to the Maloneys, eh?"

"With Hogan dead, and the toy-soldier trail growing cold, it's the only thing we got goin' right now."

"Of course, you know, that per the restrictions of Modified Assignment, you ain't supposed to be out on the fucking street," Pezzano reminded.

"If you don't tell, I won't tell."

"Jesus, Thorn. Not only are you devoid of any police identification, but you aren't even armed for crissakes. And if Rice-Jenkins gets wind of it, it'll be both our asses."

Savage shrugged. "Hey, I'm shorthanded. What the fuck am I supposed to do? Slow down the investigation, and give these bastards time to get their fuckin' ducks all in a row?"

Pezzano's Sicilian dark-browns widened in emphasis. "Courtesy demands that we tell the PC that Manhattan South Homicide intends to interview the wife of a United States senator in connection with a murder investigation," he drawled.

"Yup."

"But if it's your intention to be the interviewer, and it explodes in your face, then you're on your own."

The door to the inner office opened. "Sergeant, Lieutenant," the leggy detective said, "come in. The commissioner will see you now."

Neither standing nor offering his hand, the fit and slightly balding police commissioner, Thomas C. Johnson III, abruptly motioned them to two chairs that faced Teddy Roosevelt's mahogany desk where he was sitting. As Detective Andersen excused herself from the room, Savage caught the gimme-a-call-sometime twinkle in her eyes.

"Let's make this fast," the notoriously tart commissioner began, obviously pissed. "The SBA's been hounding me about this matter since I got back in town last night. To say the least, I don't appreciate that. In my absence, Deputy Commissioner Rice-Jenkins made an executive decision. I stand by her, and by her decision. What makes you think that I would countermand her?"

Petey Pezzano spoke up. "We're not asking for you to countermand the first deputy commissioner, sir."

"Well, just what the hell *are* you asking for, then?" Johnson shot back, doing nothing to hide his annoyance.

"Anybody who was involved in that shooting investigation, Chief Feeney included, will tell you that Sergeant Savage acted properly. There was nothing, not a shred of evidence, uncovered to indicate otherwise," Pezzano said, the tenor of his voice becoming more confident, if not aggressive. "I need this man restored to full duty and put back on the street as soon as possible."

Savage was impressed by his boss's sudden rising to the occasion, and his strong, albeit respectful, display of balls. Pezzano, he decided, wasn't the Cowardly Lion either.

Johnson shifted gears. "Lieutenant," he said patronizingly, "I think it's safe to say that everybody in this forty-thousand-man department now knows of Thorn Savage. And I'm also well acquainted with your manpower problems. However, I just got off the phone with the mayor. Off the record, although he feels it's unfortunate that the provisions of Patrol Guide 118-10 were exercised in this matter, he wishes the process to proceed *by the book*."

"What you're saying, Commissioner," Savage broke in, "is that the mayor's playing politics. He doesn't want his questionable appointee to the heavy position of first deputy police commissioner to be countermanded, thereby possibly embarrassing her and, indirectly, him. Despite there being no evidence to support her."

"As the mayor pointed out, there was also no evidence to suggest that her actions were spurred by anything other than the department's best interests," Johnson curtly replied. "But if you have something tangible to indicate otherwise, Sergeant, please speak up. Absent that, I fully intend to preserve the sanctity of chain of command."

"Commissioner Rice-Jenkins has no experience at all in these matters," Savage protested patiently, as if walking on eggs, knowing that any display of temper at this point would only be counterproductive. "It was she who disregarded the chain of command, sir. She ignored the findings of all the experience available to her, and embarrassed everybody from Chief Feeney down. That's hardly in the best interests of the department, Commissioner. That's just sheer arrogance."

Johnson glared. "The mayor wishes no action be taken that could be perceived as diminishing the stature and reputation of any of the deputy commissioners. Therefore . . ."

Shaking his head in disgust, Pezzano spoke up. "Therefore, he's opted to preserve the reputation of a politically appointed empty suit, at the cost of the spotless reputation of a thirty-year-plus good soldier. With all due respect, Commissioner, that just don't seem like any way to run an airline."

Glaring now at the Homicide lieutenant, who'd had the temerity to interrupt and admonish him, Johnson leaned his big frame across the ancient desk. "Neither me, or the mayor, want bosses in this department who can't make decisions, or can't take fucking orders," Johnson declared, raising his voice. "We want proactive bosses who can take the heat, bosses able to make hard decisions on their own without constantly running to the top for approval of their actions. Rice-Jenkins made such a decision. Bosses, especially squad commanders, who can't live up to that, and who feel they can do an end around the chain of command, will find themselves out of their tit job, back in the bag, supervising barrier details on rainy Thanksgivings." Johnson narrowed his frosty gaze on Pezzano. "You get the picture, Lieutenant?"

"Wide-screen, Commissioner," Pezzano said evenly. Unless Savage missed his guess, his smarting lieutenant was right now wondering about the size, shape, and possibly even the location of his new asshole.

"And you, Sergeant?" Johnson asked.

"You're coming in loud and clear, sir." Savage couldn't wait for the sham of a meeting to end.

"You know," Johnson said, leaning smugly back into his chair, "the whole department's waiting to see if I'll overrule Rice-Jenkins, and reinstate you to full duty. That *ain't* gonna happen. However, in order to placate the Sergeants Benevolent Association, and, as a concession to you, Savage—because of your otherwise sterling record—I've notified the CO Firearms Unit, and the Firearms Review Board, to place this matter at the top of their agenda and come up with a finding at their very next meeting. Which, I'm told, will be this coming Wednesday."

"In the meanwhile, Commissioner," Petey Pezzano pressed, his words sounding more like advice than protest, "the department's best investigator remains hamstrung."

Johnson said nothing. He didn't have to. His stone-faced glare and silence said it all. The meeting was over. Pezzano and Savage let themselves out of the office, closing the door behind them.

"Sergeant," Detective Andersen said, handing Savage a scrap of paper. "Your office called while you were inside. I took this message."

Savage quickly read it, folded it in half, and slipped it into his pocket. Then, remembering his intended call on Senator Maloney's wife, and its possible political fallout, he turned to Pezzano and muttered, "What about that other piece of business, Pete?"

"Later!" came the terse reply.

Their departure from the PC's corner of the building, back down the long corridors, was accomplished at a much slower, less frantic pace than their arrival.

"Sorry I fucked up your RDO, Pete," Savage said, pressing the subbasement call button as they boarded the elevator. "You needed this like a fucking hole in the head."

"Not your fault," Pezzano assured genially. "Anyway, my wife and I are going to her sister's for dinner this afternoon. Too bad this meeting didn't last all day." Then, with a sly grin and a glint in his eye, he added, "Can't stand my fuckin' brother-in-law." After a brief silence, both men broke into a hearty laugh.

"That phone message anything heavy, Thorn?" Pezzano asked, as the elevator opened onto the building's bunkerlike garage.

"Gotta run right back to the office and eyeball a stack of photos that just came in from DMV," Savage replied, his baritone echoing in the all-concrete, low-ceilinged vastness. "One of them just might be the shooter."

On Sunday morning, the headquarters garage was nearly empty. Pezzano's dark blue Impala sat in a spot only steps from the elevator.

Savage's boss opened the door of his car and slid behind the wheel. "You wanna know why I didn't bring up the Maloney thing with the PC, don't you?"

Thorn nodded.

"Courtesy might dictate that I go right back up to the valley of the shadow, and personally notify the PC of what's coming down," Pezzano said. "Then he in turn can look great by alerting the mayor."

"If you don't, he might just take your head," Savage reminded. "And, your squad commander's money."

"I'm going by the book," Pezzano replied coolly. Then, apparently getting his guinea up, his voice turned surly. "I'm sure the PC wouldn't want me violating the chain of command. I'll notify him, but I'll do it through channels. He'll find out about it sometime tomorrow . . . maybe." Pezzano winked and turned the ignition. "Don't worry about it, Thorn. I've been giving some thought to putting my papers in anyhow. Maybe the PC just helped me make my decision. If this whole mess don't come out the way it's supposed to, come Thanksgiving, I might just be carving my turkey in the mountains of North Carolina." Tires squealing against the sealed floor surface, Pezzano's Chevy peeled off.

As Richie Marcus shamelessly tailgated a dirty and dented Dodge van—way overloaded with bearded and yarmulked Hasidim—across the Brooklyn Bridge, Jack Lindstrom rechecked his seat belt connection and rolled his eyes. He'd forgotten that nobody—except maybe Diane—ever, *ever,* let Marcus drive. Richie had the aggressive drafting inclinations of a NASCAR wannabe. He seemed also to have the depth perception of Mr. Magoo, and the *oops—sorry* reflexes of a Valiumed spaz.

Averting his eyes from impending disaster, Lindstrom gazed out instead at Lower Manhattan's redesigned skyline with its painful in-your-face absence of the Twin Towers. He recalled that September morning and the thousands—including his fraternal twin, Cheryl, and two very close friends—so barbarously snuffed by a handful of scumbag religious psychos. *Damn!* he thought, how he hated those towelhead cocksuckers. Suddenly, he realized Marcus had taken his eyes from the road while lighting a butt.

"You know, Marcus," Lindstrom said, scowling and thinking what it would be like to have shattered windshield fragments surgically plucked from his eyes. "You oughta open a driving school for the blind."

"The blind?" Marcus echoed, incredulous.

"Yeah!" Lindstrom went on, feeling the muscles of his face tense. "You could teach driving by braille. Lesson number one—*Don't stop until you feel something.*"

Marcus snorted.

"I could really see you operating such a school. I've never seen *anyone* drive like you do."

"I ain't hit nothin' yet," Marcus growled, his voice sounding like a box of quarry slag. Taking his eyes from the road again, he turned and faced Lindstrom. "So you just sit that skinny Swedish ass of yours back and relax. All right?"

"You ain't hit nothin' yet *today,* you mean," Lindstrom countered. *"Watch ittt!"* he suddenly blurted, pushing both hands to the dash, bracing himself for impact as the van full of Hasidim inexplicably slowed, and what little gap had existed between it and the Malibu's nose was reduced to centimeters. Marcus locked up the four wheels, and somehow—miraculously—avoided the need for a wrecker with a hook. Lindstrom shook his head and blew a hard exhale of fear and frustration. This, he knew, was gonna be a long ride.

Twenty minutes and two close calls later, the Chevy pulled in front of an apartment complex on Ocean Avenue. Stepping from the passenger side of the car, Lindstrom considered falling to his knees and kissing the ground. Instead, he motioned for Marcus to hand over the keys. "I'm not going through that again on the way back," he said with a shiver. After a few nasal snorts, Marcus chucked the ring of keys across.

The dark and looming Ocean Castles were probably from the twenties or thirties, Lindstrom figured. The complex was a square of four large and stately turreted ten-story buildings that faced one another, each accessed from a central courtyard that rarely saw the sun. Good place to grow mushrooms, he thought, taking in the brooding structures faced in a dreary, no, somber deep red clinker brick. He saw that the one-time whiteness of stone lintels that capped each of its many windows, ornate cornices that rimmed the roofs, and ogee arches at each building's entryway were stained black by time and its destructive partners— unkind elements and poor upkeep. Large, wildly spiked, hand-peened black iron lanterns hung above the entrance to each building. The entry doors themselves were of plank. They were thick and swung on massive strap hinges, giving the place the ambiance of the fortified residence of Vlad the Impaler.

The northernmost building was 1620. "Not much of a crib for people who're supposed to be mob bosses," Marcus observed, as they read mailboxes and the tenant roster in the entry vestibule. "This place just barely makes lower-middle class."

"I'm told these Russians love to flaunt their money," Lindstrom murmured, pointing to box 1-F that bore the name RELSKA. "But, aside from clothes and cars, they stash it. Anyway, this is a damn sight better than winter in Petrograd."

Marcus snorted.

Not wishing to make premature announcement of their arrival—by ringing Relska's intercom button—they instead let themselves into the locked building on the heels of an elderly couple who'd probably just returned from church.

Marcus rapped loudly on 1-F's metal door.

"Nikita Relska?" Lindstrom asked of the robed blonde whose meaty fingers held the door open to the limits of the security chain.

The woman's eyes focused tightly on the gold detective shield he held up to the opening. He could tell her tapes were running, analyzing the moment, and making instant decisions. Lindstrom exchanged a quick glance with his partner. Marcus apparently was getting the same read. Her cool-greens clicking once, the woman looked up into Lindstrom's face.

"I am Nikita Relska," she said calmly.

"I'm Detective Lindstrom, and this is Detective Marcus. May we come in?" The door closed, the chain slid, and the door reopened wide.

Generally speaking, the Ocean Castles complex itself was certainly nobody's Dakota, Lindstrom thought—he'd had no fear of running into Yoko Ono in these austere hallways. The interior of Relska's apartment was no departure. The quarters were long, narrow, and, with the shades drawn, intentionally dark. Seemingly reading his mind, the wide-hipped barefoot woman moved silently across the carpeted floor and opened the shades at the far end of the living room, then did the same in the adjoining breakfast nook.

The place was garishly decorated with a middle-European flavor, lots of red and gold velvet. Budapest and earringed gypsies came to Lindstrom's mind. Somebody, he also concluded, was into art. At least a dozen oils hung on the long wall separating the living room from the equally long kitchen it paralleled. The paintings were Picasso-like in their abstraction, but the dominating theme of the artist's subject matter appeared to be life in Russia.

"I see you appreciate art collection," Nikita Relska said genially to Lindstrom, rejoining both detectives in the center of the living room.

How coolly observant of you, Lindstrom thought. "Chagalls?" he asked.

The woman nodded. "Knockoffs, of course," she said. "But very well done, do you not think?"

"Extremely well done!" Lindstrom replied with knowledgeable approval, now knowing where she was spending her clothing money.

Marcus snorted.

Her unbrushed hair backlit by the light that now poured in from unobstructed windows, she sank heavily into a sofa of bright yellow velvet. She reached down and pulled her thick ankles and pedicured feet beneath her expansive robe. "What is it that you officers want from me?" Nikita Relska asked in a controlled, tranquil tone. "Are neighbors complaining about noise perhaps?" she asked, eyebrows high.

"No noise complaints," Lindstrom said. "We'd like to ask the nature of a phone call you received late last Tuesday night."

"Tuesday night? Late?" The woman squinted in thought. "I do not remember receiving any late calls last week."

"It came in on your cell phone," Lindstrom said. "At exactly ten fifty-six."

"I remember no such call," she repeated firmly. "How do you know I even got such a call . . . and what is this all about, anyway? Have I done something wrong?"

"Do you know a man by the name of Roger Hogan?" Lindstrom asked.

"Hogan? I know nobody by that name," she said with certainty. Avoiding eye contact, she reached to the lamp table beside the dazzling sofa for a near-empty pack of Virginia Slims. Sticking one into her mouth, she asked, "You officers mind if I smoke?"

Oh, this broad's too cool, Lindstrom thought. This is gonna be like throwin' spitballs at a battleship. "He's a doorman," Lindstrom said. "He works at 333 East Seventy-third in Manhattan, the Clarendon. He made a connection with your number at ten fifty-six Tuesday evening." The information impacted her, Lindstrom saw—she'd forgotten, if only for a fraction of a moment, to light her cigarette.

"I know no such person. And I received no such phone call on Tuesday night," she said adamantly. "How can you be so certain that I did?" She finally struck a match and lit the extralong, slender butt.

"Telephone-company records," Marcus said.

"Huh!" she grunted, then exhaled a long, steady stream of smoke. "Probably wrong number. I get a lot of those."

"No wrong number, lady." Lindstrom came on. "We believe that you were expecting that call."

"And just how would you know that?" She smirked with a sly grin. "You men got crystal balls, maybe?"

"No crystal *balls,* ma'am." Marcus smirked back. "Just a matter of permanent record. Verizon printouts show that he called you from his job."

"He also handwrote your number in a company telephone log," Lindstrom added.

"Have you asked this Mr. Hogan why he called this number?" she asked, shrugging. "Perhaps he has explanation. Because I certainly do not."

"Mr. Hogan was found dead this morning," Lindstrom said calmly. "We believe he was murdered. And we think that you and Georgei Strelnikov may know something about that."

"Are you men accusing me?" she said angrily, flashing her eyes back and forth between the two detectives. "Or Georgei? Of some kind of crime? Are you saying that we could have had something to do with death of a perfect stranger?"

"Where were you and Mr. Strelnikov early this morning?" Marcus asked. "Say, between five o'clock and eight-thirty?"

"Right here in this apartment!" Her response was unequivocal and curt. It was as if she was daring them to make a case. "Here together—sleeping in bed."

Boy, you're good, lady! Lindstrom thought.

"I bet I know what happened," she suddenly blurted, taking another quick drag on the smoke, then casually tapping the gathered ash into the brass tray she held on her lap.

Lindstrom and Marcus stood silent and expressionless, allowing her to continue.

"Georgei must have taken that call last Tuesday night," she said faintly, as if speaking to herself. Then, looking up at the cops, she said, "I am still willing to bet it was wrong number, but it must have been Georgei who answered call. I was probably in the tub. I take long hot baths in the evening."

"Georgei's your roommate, right?" Marcus asked. "Georgei Strelnikov?"

"He is more than my roommate, Detective," she corrected sternly. "He is love of my life."

"Yeah," Lindstrom sneered, deciding it was time to let her know they'd done some homework. "He's also the vice president of Majestic Funding. That bullshit loan-sharking operation that you happen to be president of."

She blew smoke.

"Where is he?" Marcus asked flatly.

"Out," she coolly replied. "Out for the day. He will be home in time for dinner, though. Say . . . five-thirty. We are having Chicken Kiev, his favorite."

"Mine too," Marcus faintly muttered.

With newfound serious eye contact, she looked back and forth at both men. "You'll have to speak with him, I'm afraid. Maybe he can tell you something about that call. I certainly cannot."

"Does the name Christine Maloney ring any bells?" Marcus asked, pulling a pack of Winstons and a BIC lighter from his jacket. "Mind if *I* smoke, ma'am?"

"Not at all, Officer. Go right ahead," she said, beginning to rise. "Let me get you ashtray."

Nodding toward the table in the breakfast nook over her shoulder, Marcus casually motioned her to stay seated. Moving quickly, he said, "Never mind, there's one. I'll get it."

Lindstrom could barely conceal his frustrated anger as Marcus stepped away, pissed at the man's damnable need for a coffin nail. The impromptu intermission, no matter how brief, would break the tempo of the questioning they'd built up. He watched Marcus reach for the ashtray, hesitate, then pick up a scrap of notepaper that'd been lying on the table beside it. After quickly reading whatever was written on the scrap, Marcus placed it back on the table where he'd found it. Winking now at Lindstrom, the burly detective reentered the living room carrying only the ashtray.

"Of course I have heard of Christine Maloney," Nikita Relska then announced. "Has not everybody? She is wife of the big-time senator. Right?"

"Do you know anything else about her?" Marcus asked.

"No," she said promptly. "Should I?"

"Can you think of any reason that your friend Georgei may have had for visiting her at her home on Thursday night?" Lindstrom pressed.

"None at all, gentlemen," she said breezily. "Georgei is businessman. He has many contacts that I am unaware of. Like I said, you are just going to have to speak with him."

"I cannot stay long," Strelnikov announced as Christine let him into the sumptuous suite at the posh Sherry-Netherland.

"What about brunch?" she asked, her tone one of coy disappointment. "We're sure to have ravenous appetites when we leave here."

"No time!"

"Why is that?" Christine pressed, closing and relocking the heavy door behind him. "What've you got," she pried jokingly, "another date?"

"Da. I have other date all right," he responded sarcastically. He withdrew a Camel from a crush-proof pack and set the filter end between his lips. Slapping at his pockets, he realized he was out of matches. "I got a two o'clock with *New York Post* reporter Mr. Joseph Ballantine." Coolly surveying the staid grandeur of the high-ceilinged suite and its rich decor, he asked, "How you manage to get in here without identifying yourself, and having only small tote? This is very prestigious hotel."

Christine walked to a marble-topped credenza, reached into a crystal bowl, and withdrew a fresh book of matches. She handed them to him. "I gave them an assumed name, Georgei. And told the desk my other bags were being delivered later."

"Yes. But with no identification?"

"I only booked it for one day. I paid cash. There's an old American saying. Money talks—bullshit walks. They didn't care who the hell I was."

As he lit the cigarette and pocketed the matches, he felt her firm body press against him from behind.

Her small but strong hands reached up and massaged the back of his bull neck, then kneaded the tops of his bulging shoulders.

"Today?" she whispered into his ear, talented hands moving to more sensitive areas of his anatomy. "It's going to happen today, Georgei?" she asked.

"Yes!"

Preoccupied, he stepped from her seductive grasp and moved to the chintz-draped window that looked down at the southeast corner of Central Park. Across Fifth Avenue on Central Park South, opposite the Plaza, he saw a queue of horse-drawn hansoms at the curb. All the carriages, except one, were open topped and painted white with red upholstered seating. The lone exception was a highly polished black two-place. It had an oval window cut into the back of its canvas top that was pulled snug against a series of graduating bows. He could not see the upholstery in that one. Clustered on the sidewalk nearby, colorfully scarved and top-hatted chauffeurs passed the time gabbing with one another while awaiting their high-dollar fares.

Only in America, he thought, undoing the knot of his silk tie, would people pay unconscionable amounts to be ridden around in fucking horse carts. He'd fought his way to the U.S., leaving the primitive horse carts of Mother Russia behind, determined to never again strap a feed bag to his mode of transportation. In the intervening years, he'd become used to lounging on the leather of Lincoln land yachts, or cruising comfortably in overpriced Cadillacs. He would never give that up.

"*You're* going to do it?" she asked, breaking into his momentary trance. Her brows were low, and she wore a look of surprise. "I thought such nasty business would be delegated to lesser-ranking people within your organization."

"Normally, it would be so," Strelnikov huffed, removing his jacket, and draping it across the back of

one of two club chairs that stood catty-corner on the
Aubusson before the window. "But *she* wants *me* to
do this one." He looked at Christine and shrugged,
discerning the look of consternation reflected in her
intelligent eyes.

"Why is that, Georgei?" Christine probed, peeling
a shoulder-length, poufed blond wig from her head.
She carefully set the tangle of cotton candy on the
room's long, low dresser, and laid it beside an oversized pair of dark-lensed Saint Laurents.

"Our usual . . . *technician* . . . ?" Strelnikov said,
self-conscious and unsure of his less-than-perfect English, yet striving to select a good euphemism for assassin, "is unavailable right now." Sighing, he added,
"I am sure that Nikki is testing me—my loyalty." He
took a deep drag, and exhaled hard.

"Does she suspect anything?" Christine murmured,
turning to face him as he slid the holstered SIG Sauer
from his belt, and stepped from a pair of soft kid
loafers. "About us, I mean," she added, as he set the
pistol atop the nightstand.

"I do not know," he answered truthfully, removing
a pair of pleated-front Hickey-Freeman slacks, and
same-brand matching tan socks. "I don't know how
she could." Down to briefs, he jerked back the brocaded spread and top sheet, propped the pillows upright against the inlaid headboard, then stretched out
on the king-size bed. Pensively, he said, "You never
know with her." He turned and squashed the cigarette
into the nightstand ashtray.

"She's a liability now, Georgei," Christine uttered
singsong.

"How you mean?" he demanded, gnarled-knuckled
fingers of lumpy hands entwined at his hair-matted
chest, and tree-stump legs slowly crossing at the
ankles.

"What I mean is, you no longer need her. *We* no
longer need her, for that matter. The deal has been
struck, Georgei. We have an agreement. *You* and *I*."

She removed her bra, slipped from lace panties, and crept in from the foot of the bed, her head coming to rest atop his firm abdomen. Her hand slipped beneath his shorts. She clutched him, and added, "What do you need her for any longer? Now you've got me."

Christine went to work.

He lay there wanting ecstacy, but feeling only the pause that her last remarks had given him. Christine was correct. What the hell did he need Nikki for any longer? With each passing day the sow was demanding more, and appreciating him less. Slowly, down through the years, he'd watched her autocratic grip on the organization expand—like her dress size—turning her into a fucking *tsaritsa*. She had forgotten where she had come from, and had begun treating him as a subject, rather than a peer. Nikki was brilliant and had set up this whole thing, but nobody needed Edison anymore to turn on a fucking light.

With Nikki out of the way he could take over the entire operation. It was time he moved up anyway. Dmitri Nakovics would go along with the coup—he had never trusted Nikki. And if Nakovics went along, so would Kozyukova.

All right then.

He reached down to Christine. He pulled her up till they were face-to-face. Eyeball to eyeball.

He realized his power.

Supercharged, he rolled her over on her back, and took what was now his.

TWENTY-TWO

The lavish brick-and-stone Tudor had been well described in Marcus's report, Savage thought, looking out onto its winding slate pathways and ornamental landscaping.

Diane shifted the car into park and switched off the ignition. "Some place, Kemosabe," she said, awed, gazing at the impressive Casa Maloney. "Next time me be law*maker,* to hell with this law*man* stuff."

"No shit, Tonto," Savage mumbled, equally taken by the manicured majesty of the place. His cell phone went off just as they reached for their door handles. The call was from Richie out in Brooklyn.

"How'd it go downtown with the big guy?" Marcus began.

"Nexxxxt question!"

"That bad, huh?" Marcus growled, and changed the subject. "Talked to the office, heard the MV photos came in. Any hits?"

"Nope. Not in that first batch," Savage replied. "Maybe he'll be one of the PO Box names we're still waiting on. That's assuming he even subscribes to that magazine . . ."

"Or that he even has a fuckin' driver's license," Marcus noted.

"Right," Savage agreed. "You get with Relska and her friend?"

"Jack's inside with her now," Marcus said. "Strelnikov ain't here. I stepped outside for a little privacy."

"Is she the female you photographed with Strelnikov outside Majestic Funding the other night?"

"Definitely," Marcus affirmed. "But this broad's one fuckin' iceberg, Sarge. She's as cool as they come, but she's fulla shit. She's layin' the phone-call business off on Strelnikov, sayin' he musta taken the call, and that it was prob'ly a wrong number anyhow."

"Jeez," Savage said. "With friends like her, sounds like Strelnikov don't need no enemies."

"Yeah," Marcus interjected. "It must be Fuck Your Buddy Week out here in Brooklyn."

"With that call lasting only thirty-two seconds," Savage said, thinking out loud, "and without Hogan around to give it up, it's unlikely we'd ever be able to prove it wasn't a wrongo, and *who* actually took the call . . . unless we can get one of them to turn."

"Her wrong-number jive sounds like reasonable doubt to me though," Marcus offered ruefully.

Biting at his lip, Savage dug a Wint-O-Green from his pocket. "We know Hogan dialed Relska's cell phone at least once."

"Right," Marcus said.

"Let's get back to Patti Capwell at Telephone Security," Savage continued. "Ask her to go back ninety days to see if any of Relska's phones—home number, cell phone, Majestic Funding—ever dialed Hogan's number, either at his home or at the Clarendon. If it turns out to be so, that would negate her suggestion that Hogan's call was merely a chance wrong number."

"Not for nuthin', boss," Marcus reminded, "but today's Sunday. I can almost guarantee you that Patti's off. And I can also guarantee you that nobody else down there is gonna hop right to."

"Shit, I forgot," Thorn mumbled. "What's Relska saying about Strelnikov's visit to Forest Hills the other night?"

"She don't know nuthin'."

"She say where Strelnikov is now?"

"Out for the day. Tells us he's due back by five-thirty for din-din. Whaddaya want us to do, boss? Wait here, or come back later?"

Savage checked the time. It was only minutes after one o'clock. "Milk it awhile, and don't let her outta your sight," Thorn said. "Give it an hour. If Strelnikov don't show by then, I want you to bring her in for investigation."

"We got enough to do that?" Marcus asked.

"Oh, yeah. We got tons of questions we can ask her. Besides, if we leave her home alone, I guarantee you she'll somehow contact Strelnikov and let him know what's coming down. If they haven't already done so, I don't want those two getting a script together before we get a whack at him. Let's see what he says about that phone call. Maybe we'll catch him flat-footed and get some inconsistencies we can work. Besides," Savage added dryly, "Madame's played this game before. We're not sullying anybody's virgin here."

"Anything else, boss?" Marcus asked.

"I'd like to get a look at the Maloneys' telephone records," Savage mused. "See who they've been calling. See if they know Relska, Strelnikov, or Majestic Funding. But, we don't have near enough cause yet to officially make that request."

"Patti's a good friend of mine," Marcus said with a snort. "Want I should make an unofficial request tomorrow?"

"You can try. But since Maloney's on the Armed Services Committee, I'd be willing to bet his telephone records are security blocked well beyond her reach."

"I hear ya," Marcus said. "But I'll ask her anyhow." Then as an afterthought he added, "By the way, I saw some very interesting notations on a slip of paper inside Relska's apartment. It was lying right on top of the kitchen table."

"Let's have it," Savage said.

"Cougar, white '93," Marcus began. "Left front fender banged in. RRH-683, AA/STAGS basement,

Forty-third Street. Two o'clock on Sunday." Savage echoed the message as Diane scribbled the information onto a clipboard.

"That's it?" Savage asked. Diane's palms-out shrug told him she was equally baffled.

"That's it!" Marcus said. "Prob'ly nuthin', but I'm gonna give it to Central to run the RRH-683. It's probably a plate."

"Good," Savage agreed. "But while you're at it, ask them to have Operations check with Central Records. If RRH-683 does come back as a plate, see if they've got anything on the registered owner."

Marcus closed the phone conversation with a "Ten-four."

"RRH-683 is undoubtedly a plate number," Diane observed. "But what do you make of AA/STAGS, Forty-third Street? A restaurant?"

Savage shook his head, made a funny face and shrugged. "Been in every saloon in Midtown; never heard of an AA/STAGS," he said, pulling on the door handle. "Could be Forty-third Street in Brooklyn."

They both stepped from the car and began the slow trek up to the showplace home of Gerard and Christine Maloney. The volume was turned low on the portable radio Diane carried in her purse, but they could still hear Marcus's dulcet tones breaking through to Central.

"Manhattan South Homicide 909 to Central K."

"Go ahead, 909."

"Nice-sounding chimes, huh?" Diane noted, after twice pressing the bell.

Savage nodded, his own attention diverted by the richness and beauty of the hand-rubbed finish of the door itself. The grain of the dark wood—mahogany, he thought—was set off by the gleaming brass hardware. He'd always been partial to brass. The kick plate appeared never to have been kicked, the thumb latch never thumbed. His glance wandered to the eleven-section Palladian window above the door and the matching leaded cut-glass panels that ran alongside it. When the chimes stopped, the door was answered by a very large black woman dressed in a maid's uniform. Diane handed her a PD business card.

"I'm Detective DeGennaro, Manhattan South," Diane said. Then, omitting Savage's name, she said, "My partner and I wish to speak with Mrs. Maloney please."

"I'm sorry, officers," the maid apologized. "But, Mizz Maloney's not at home. Afraid you've missed her. She's gone off to have brunch."

"Did she say where she was having brunch, or what time she'd be back?" Diane asked.

"No, Mizz M didn't say."

"What's your name?" Diane inquired.

"Twyla. Twyla Poussaint."

"Are you the Maloney's regular housekeeper?" Savage asked.

"For many years," the woman said with a wide, friendly grin.

"Were you here last Friday evening?" he asked.

"No," Twyla replied. "I was off."

"Are you generally off on Friday night?" Savage gently pressed.

"Usually, no," Twyla said, then added guardedly, "Mizz M gave me that night off." Her brown eyes clicked back and forth between the two investigators. She didn't appear nervous, just defensive.

Firing for effect, Savage inquired, "Is Senator Maloney available?"

"The senator's down in Washington, sir. He went back Friday afternoon." The woman's response jibed with Don Stewart's information.

Savage gave Diane his "let's go" glance.

"You have my card," Diane said to the maid. "Please give it to the senator's wife when she returns, and ask if she'd be kind enough to call me at that number at her earliest convenience."

"I'll do that," Twyla assured, stepping back to close

the heavy door. "But my guess is, she's gonna be gone most of the day."

As he and Diane wended their way down the slightly inclined path of gray and red flagstones, Savage was struck with a hunger pang that immediately triggered a terrific idea.

"Wanna grab some lunch?" he said as Diane twisted the key in the driver's door of the Ford. "I know this terrific German deli over on Metropolitan Avenue," he urged persuasively. "It's only five minutes from here."

"Great!" Diane replied, with enviable, ever-present enthusiasm flashing from her bright eyes. "I'm starved."

As they drove off, Savage wondered if Palladian windows were in keeping with authentic Tudor style architecture. He'd look it up.

Georgei Strelnikov ambled up to the Church of Saint Agnes twenty-five minutes before the AA meeting was scheduled to begin. Joe Ballantine's white Mercury Cougar was nowhere in sight.

The bronze plaque secured to the front of the structure that stood in the midafternoon shadows of the Chrysler Building stated:

A parish for the Catholic people of Turtle Bay, founded in 1873. Rebuilt after a fire in 1992.

The off-white limestone ediface was clearly neo-Italian Renaissance. If he didn't know better, he would have thought he was in Rome.

As Manhattan churches go, he thought, this one seemed small—there were no massive stairs leading to its entry. Heavy wooden center doors, accented with ornate bronze castings, were set at sidewalk level. Interior steps, behind those doors, probably accessed the nave. One could also enter the building through less-ornate portals set at either side of the main entry. A temporary sign, created from a sheet of lined, three-ring loose-leaf paper, and inadequately Scotch-taped to the door on the left, whipped and blew in the mild spring breeze. It read:

Friends of Bill—2:00—Church undercroft.

Undercroft? Shit! he thought. Just fancy name for fucking basement.

He'd left the silver Town Car parked on Vanderbilt Avenue, a few blocks away, safely out of sight on the other side of Grand Central. He would take care of business here on Forty-third, then walk, as if nothing had happened, across Lexington Avenue and disappear into the vast terminal. When he exited on the Vanderbilt Avenue side, he'd get back in the Lincoln, go east on Forty-second Street to the FDR Drive, then head downtown and return to Brooklyn through the Battery Tunnel. Good plan, he thought. Foolproof. And the best part was that this would be the last order he'd ever have to carry out for Nikki.

Looking up and down the length of the block, he saw that it was typical for midtown. Aside from the church, he counted three shoe stores, a luggage shop, two jewelry stores, and some sort of odd-lot outlet. Also, there were at least three coffee shops. It was quiet, and because it was Sunday and parking regulations were relaxed, parking was plentiful. Aside from the No Parking Anytime zone directly in front of the church, there were any number of open spots for Mr. Ballantine to drop his beat-up car when he arrived.

Deciding on a position opposite the church, Strelnikov crossed Forty-third to the south side, and stepped into a doorway next to an Andrew's Coffee Shop. From there he had a straight-on view of the church's entrances, and also a complete view of the entire block, from Third Avenue on the east to Lexington Avenue on the west.

By the time fifteen minutes had elapsed, a dozen

men and five women had entered through the church's door that bore the flapping paper sign. Some had arrived on foot, some in taxis; most, however, had arrived in personal cars and taken up most of the available parking spots on the block. But the white Cougar, and Joe Ballantine, had yet to make an appearance. The meeting was scheduled to begin in less than ten minutes.

Shit! he thought, unconsciously tapping the holstered weapon strapped beneath his camel jacket. Let's get this party over with.

The boiled ham had been sliced so perfectly thin that Savage could have read the *Times* classifieds through it, and it was piled on. The Swiss was imported and equally delicious. And forget about the mustard—hot and spicy like he'd never been able to find anywhere else. And where did the guy get fresh rye like this on a Sunday? Cut into thick, soft-centered, hand-sliced slabs with a crunchy hard crust, the bread was still warm. Ignoring the dill-pickle slice that came with it, he washed the sandwich down with a frost-covered bottle of Heineken. Diane had opted for the lean roast beef, lots of salt and pepper, lettuce, tomato, and a dollop of horseradish, all packed on a poppy-seed hard roll. She knocked off both their pickle slices, and drank a hot tea with lemon.

The only disappointment was the coffee afterward—a little on the timid side. Then again, he reminded himself, after years of squad-room java, any normal coffee was likely to come off as weak.

At 1:35 they heaved their sated bellies back into the unmarked sedan, and Diane headed west on Queens Boulevard toward Manhattan. They would return to the office, and hope to hear something from Rudy Caparo over at Postal Inspections. Savage wanted to rule out the few remaining holders of the blind post office boxes. At the same time, they'd await a call from Christine Maloney, which, of course, would probably never come. If it did come, they'd set up an appointment to interview her. If it didn't come, he'd be knocking on her castle door at sunup tomorrow morning.

Savage calculated that Marcus and Lindstrom would probably arrive back at the office with Nikita Relska—and maybe Georgei Strelnikov—in tow at about 2:30. Whatever, he thought, he and his crew of detectives would all manage to stay busy for the rest of the day. The city was paying them handsomely for their overtime, but they'd be earning it.

As Diane steered the Crown Vic into Queens Plaza, at the approach to the Queensborough Bridge, their portable radio scratched to life. They overheard an exchange between the Citywide dispatcher and Richie Marcus out in Brooklyn.

DISPATCH: *"Citywide to Manhattan South unit 909. K!"*

MARCUS: *"909, standing by. Go, Central!"*

DISPATCH: *"Operations advises that New York plate number RRH-683 is registered to a 1993 Mercury, two-door, white in color. Vehicle is registered to a Joseph Ballantine of 229 East Twenty-ninth Street, New York City. Operations also advises: No record, wants, or warrants outstanding on auto or owner at this time. K."*

MARCUS: *"Ten-four, Central, 909 copies. Try to raise the Manhattan South Homicide supervisor in auto 7146. Supervisor needs to be apprised of that information, K."*

Clenching the Motorola portable tightly in his left fist, Savage broke in before dispatch could speak. "7146 to Central. Be advised, this unit read your message five by five." He looked over at Diane. She was looking back at him with a startled grimace and raised eyebrows. They both now understood the significance of the note Marcus had found, and the meaning behind the letters *AA/STAGS* it contained. He reached for the emergency red light on the tranny hump, switched it on, and set it on the dash as Diane put her foot in the tank. "Central," he added, "also be advised that this unit is responding forthwith to the Church of Saint Agnes, Forty-third, Lex to Third."

"When we get there," he hollered to Diane over the wail of the siren, "maybe we oughtta circle the block real quick, see if we can find that white Cougar. See if anybody's staking it out. If it's there, then we gotta find Joe in that church before one of those Russian vultures does."

Without taking her eyes from the bridge roadway, Diane nodded complete understanding. It was five minutes of two. Time, they both knew, was now critical. Bearing down quickly on a clutch of slow-moving traffic ahead, she gave two short yelps on the siren, broke briefly into the bridge's Queens-bound lanes, and roared past them doing eighty-five. At the bridge's Manhattan end she slowed for traffic, then ran the light, taking a hard left southbound on Second Avenue. Savage fished for a Wint-O-Green. He was fresh out.

It was a long shot to be sure, but Thorn clicked on his cell phone and started dialing: *Orel Hershiser, Don Drysdale, Orel Hershiser, Don . . .*

TWENTY-THREE

No wonder this asshole was late, Strelnikov mused, as he watched the white Cougar make the turn off of Third Avenue into Forty-third Street. The car was a piece of shit. From his doorway recess, Strelnikov could see that the left front fender had the appearance of a soup can that had been crushed by Godzilla, then half-assed straightened by an amateur body man with a sick sense of humor. The car's left-side headlamp and turn-signal assembly was duct-taped into place, and a section of grille was missing, as was the left-front wheelcover. The wheel's camber setting looked to be about twenty degrees out.

Loping slowly to the middle of the block, steadily dripping antifreeze or power-steering fluid, the shitbox stopped and backed into a spot east of the church on the north side of the street. A graying, fiftyish, stoop-shouldered six-footer emerged. With hair that needed brushing, and wearing a well-worn tweed herringbone that was too short in the arms, the guy looked as much of a schlump as his car did. Reaching back onto the front seat, he picked up a large bag of groceries—it must have been his turn to pick up the bagels and donuts for the boozer meeting. Locking the doors, as if anybody'd even think of stealing the piece of shit, he began walking toward the church, slowly yet steadily, struggling with the bundle he cradled in his left arm and supported with his right. No free hands, Strelnikov thought. *Good!* A lamb to slaughter.

Again Strelnikov patted the blue steel bulge at his waist, then undid the button of his jacket. Ballantine was getting closer, it was almost time to move. Senses heightened, Strelnikov looked up and down the block. There were no other pedestrians. He listened intently. A siren he'd heard wailing nearby minutes ago had dwindled to nothing. A fire truck probably, he reasoned, or maybe an ambulance. Ballantine was now almost directly opposite.

Strelnikov stepped from the doorway, charting his course for the deadly intercept.

Crossing the street diagonally from the south sidewalk to the north, he began to time and gauge the length of his strides. He calculated that when their paths converged, he would fall in right behind Ballantine. Just for a moment, just as Strelnikov neared the north side of the street, they made eye contact. The man toting the bundle looked directly at him, smiled warmly, and nodded. Stupid fuck, Strelnikov thought, returning the nod and painting on a friendly grin. Then, stepping from the roadway onto the sidewalk that fronted the church, he again adjusted his pace, ensuring that his prey would have the lead.

It was time. Reaching beneath his jacket, Strelnikov undid the holster snap. Clutching the SIG's grips, he pulled the weapon free from its leather sheath, sliding his index finger into position on the trigger as he did so. Now, moving in cadence two steps behind the reporter, he pulled out the pistol and began leveling it at the back of Ballantine's head.

Suddenly, Ballantine had become Baryshnikov. Pivoting on the ball of his left foot, he'd whirled in a complete one-eighty. In that one fluid motion, he'd jettisoned the grocery bag and assumed a combat crouch, a three-inch-barreled revolver clutched tightly in both hands and aimed directly at Strelnikov's chest. Bagels rolled in crazy circles around their feet.

"Give it up, Georgei!" the hauntingly familiar man in the Harris Tweed snarled.

Completely stunned, Strelnikov hesitated long enough to think, *How does this fuck know my name?*

He'd heard no equivocation in Ballantine's command. There was not the slightest hint of fear augmenting the voice, nor showing in the face. The one thing truly clear in the man's attitude and incredibly intense eyes was a decidedly cold indifference as to which way Strelnikov opted to go.

Reflexively, going for it all, Strelnikov committed. Neck muscles and veins popping, he swept the muzzle of his SIG Sauer toward the reporter's face. Jaw tensed, eyes bugging, Strelnikov began his trigger squeeze. In that slow-mo millisecond, he realized that the familiar-looking man, who'd somehow known his name, had already read his go-for-broke intention.

The three shots were fired in such rapid succession that only a singular echo bounced around the concrete canyons of midtown. But there had been three. Strelnikov felt every one of them impact.

Feeling as if molten pokers had been plunged into his chest, and gasping for needed breath but inhaling only blood that rapidly filled his airways, Strelnikov stumbled backwards. He tripped awkwardly over his own feet at the curb's edge and fell heavily into the street. He was amazed that he felt not the slightest sensation of pain.

Strelnikov lay on his back, one leg still draped over the curb. His other leg, torso, head, and arms twisted crazily on the pavement. His eyes stared up at the No Parking Anytime sign that was framed by a cloudless blue sky, and he still clutched the SIG Sauer in his right hand, a right hand he was unable to move. He heard the approaching roar of a car engine as someone kicked the gun from his grasp. The car slid to a stop only feet from where he lay—he could see part of a green fender. The doors swung open, then slammed shut. He heard a woman's voice, then a man's, and then another man's. Sirens wailed in the distance, and then nearer.

He heard the woman ask, "Are you all right, Sarge?"

Then he remembered the face: Front page . . . newspaper . . . cop! *Savage!*

For a moment he saw the docks of Murmansk. Then everything faded to darkness.

TWENTY-FOUR

The lipstick was hideous. Bright, *bright*, red—certainly not her. Christine leaned closer to the mirror and began laying it on, reapplying all she'd worn off when performing prolonged fellatio on Georgei's knob. She'd succeeded in leaving plenty of evidence on him, evidence that would transfer to his shorts. He'd had no time to shower after their steamy matinee, no time to scrub himself clean, she'd made sure of that. He'd left hours ago, gone off to his two o'clock appointment, but he'd been branded, and Nikki would know the color.

Finding front and center of the mesh crown of the shoulder-length wig, she set it on her head and pulled it firmly down into place, careful to tuck in and completely conceal any strands of her own hair beneath the wildly flowing tresses. She turned left, then right, checking her profile in the mirror, deciding with a snicker as she brushed a few unrulies into place that she was ready for an appearance at the Grand Ole Opry.

"Why, Scarlett!" she said breathily, batting heavily mascaraed lashes and emoting into the mirror with a plantation drawl. "You look like a real southern belle, girl."

She slid the oversized sunglasses in place, careful not to disturb the tendrils at her ears. Her own mother wouldn't recognize her in this getup. For that matter, no one would. The only other person, besides Georgei Strelnikov, to have ever knowingly seen her in this particular incognita was Nikki—that rotten bitch.

She stuffed the lipstick and hairbrush into the cosmetics compartment of a soft-sided overnighter and zipped it shut. She checked the suite to make sure she had everything, then, remembering, hurried back into the bathroom for her travel bottle of Listerine. While there, she gargled and rinsed for the third time since Georgei had left. Carefully running through her mental checklist, she surveyed the suite one more time. Satisfied, she slid the long straps of the nylon bag over her right shoulder and left a ten on the dresser for the housekeeper.

Casual, in an A-line jumper of soft blue denim complemented by a bright yellow kerchief tied smartly about her slender neck, and wearing a pair of cork-soled flats that looked good for walking, she rode the elevator to the lobby and strode past the front desk where, earlier, she'd forked over four hundred dollars in cash. Suite charge, room tax, sales tax, the fees had gone on and on. Expensive for the use of a bed for a few hours, but a good investment to be sure—one that was going to pay off in spades. She was positive that if she played her cards and Strelnikov correctly, she would eventually gain possession of all the copies of those incriminating videotapes.

She spun through the revolving front door of the Sherry-Netherland, mimed a silent no to the doorman who asked if she needed a cab, and quickly crossed Fifth Avenue. From there, she walked west along the perimeter wall of the park until she was directly opposite the Plaza. When the crosstown traffic subsided she hurried across the wide thoroughfare, strutted boldly into the hotel's Central Park South entrance, and headed directly for the ladies' powder room off the lobby. Relieved to see that she was alone, she let herself into the largest of the four stalls, the one marked with the handicapped symbol. Hanging the bag from the clothing hook on the back of the stall door, she opened one of its side compartments and withdrew a five-times makeup mirror. She hung the mirror from a side hook.

Twenty minutes later, sans Saint Laurents, sans wig, and sans the overdone makeup, Mrs. Gerard Maloney emerged from the Grand Army Plaza side of the hotel. She had unclipped the detachable shoulder straps and packed them away—she now carried a soft-sided satchel in her right hand. Dressed in a tomato-red two-piece buttoned demurely at the collar, and charcoal Gucci pumps, she waited regally as Jorge, the Plaza doorman, whistled the senator's wife a cab.

Every one of Savage's senses told him he might have really done it this time. He might have really iced the freakin' cake. In his heart, he knew he'd done the right thing, but sometimes doing the right thing didn't count for squat in the NYPD. The road to police-department oblivion was littered with right things that crashed and burned.

He could've played along. He could have played the game. He could have sat it out, as he'd been ordered to by no less than the goddamned police commissioner, until the Firearms Review Board met Wednesday and exonerated him on the last fiasco—which they surely would have. He could have easily sat around the office, feet up on his desk for three more lousy, stinking days, keeping up with the funny pages, or sharpening pencils, or honing his crossword skills. But he hadn't. He couldn't. And, he reasoned, because he hadn't and couldn't, Joseph Ballantine was still alive and well, with some Russian-mob mutt DOA in his place. Nonetheless, as a result of his spur-of-the-moment actions a half hour ago, all sorts of departmental holy hell had broken loose. Thorn was back in the hot seat, and they had him strapped in tight.

Throughout the station house, words like *suspension* and *termination* were being whispered. He'd heard the

words; he'd read the lips. As to his own fate, Savage
was stoic and unruffled. He was determined, this time,
to let the chips fall wherever. As far as he was concerned, he'd do it all over again in a minute if he had
to. He was, however, brooding about Diane DeGennaro and how the fallout of his actions and decisions
could adversely affect her. He worried about what the
powers might do to her, when the only part she'd
played in this latest megillah was simply being there
and taking his orders.

The second-floor squad room at the Seventeenth
Precinct looked like a convention of blue-serged brass
manufacturers displaying their polished wares. Every
chief and subchief in The Job seemed to be there.
Chief of Inspectional Services—IAB—Roland Hetzel
and two of his crack IAB headhunters were about to
interrogate Diane in a room down the hall. Chief of
Detectives Raphael Wilson was in another room taking a statement from Joe Ballantine. Savage knew he
was being saved for last.

Lieutenant Pete Pezzano had been called away from
homemade lasagna, chilled Bardolino, and fresh can-
nolis at his sister's in Malverne to coordinate the investigation. At least it had gotten him away from his
aggravating brother-in-law. Isolated in the corner office of the squad room, Pezzano walked Savage
through the statement he'd ultimately have to make.

"All right," Pezzano said, recapping. "I'm with you
so far. You're out in Forest Hills to interview the wife
of Senator Gerard Maloney—Christine Maloney—
who you figure is *somehow* tied in with a cell of Russian mobsters who operate out of Brooklyn." Rolling
his eyes, Pezzano added as an aside, "PC and the
mayor are gonna love that shit." Savage shrugged.
"Anyway, turns out she's not home. So you and De-
Gennaro decide to come back to the office, but you
stop along the way for a sandwich. Right?"

"Right."

"Then, just as you're crossing the bridge, at about

five minutes to two, you overhear a radio transmission that causes both you and DeGennaro to believe that Joe Ballantine might, at any minute, be the target of an assassination attempt. Right?"

"Right."

"And you believed that to be true," Pezzano emphasized, "based on information provided to you sometime earlier by Detective Marcus. Information uncovered by him, in the form of a handwritten note, at the Brooklyn apartment shared by Nikita Relska—the head of this Russian mob cell—and one of her henchmen, the late Georgei Strelnikov. Right?"

"Right."

"Information that was ambiguous until the blanks were filled in by that radio message. Right?"

"Right."

"Okay. I'm still with you," Pezzano said, nodding understandingly. "Let's take it from there."

"Believing," Savage began, "based on the information found by Detective Marcus, that the AA meeting was due to start in five minutes, Detective DeGennaro put her foot to the floor, taking the shortest possible route toward East Forty-third Street."

"Then?" Pezzano asked.

"Then I tried raising Ballantine at his cell-phone number . . ."

"You just *happened* to have Ballantine's fucking cell-phone number with you?" Pezzano broke in, playing disbelieving devil's advocate. "That's a point that's gonna be a little hard for them to swallow, don't you think?"

"I had the number memorized," Thorn assured with an I-don't-give-a-fuck look.

"All right," Pezzano nodded, knowing the look and seemingly convinced. "Then what?"

"Ballantine answered. He was down at the Murray Hill Bakery, Thirty-sixth and Third. It was his turn to pick up the bagels for the AA meeting. I told him not to move, to stay there till I got there."

"Did he wait?"

"He waited. Hell, Diane got us there in under two minutes."

"From here on in I'm sure it gets very interesting, Thorn," Pezzano said, hands in front of his chest, palms out, in a "stop" motion. "So I want you to take it real slow for me, okay?"

Savage nodded and picked up the story. "Outside the bakery we told Ballantine briefly what we had, and what we believed was about to happen. He claimed he wasn't at all surprised that he'd become a target. Said he 'knew too much' about Gerard Maloney. Also told me that he'd just completed a scathing exposé on the senator's venal past. Said it's due to hit the streets in tomorrow's edition. He claims it's gonna derail any of Maloney's presidential hopes, if not send him to the slammer."

"Then what?"

"I knew that if an assassin was waiting for Ballantine to arrive at that AA meeting, the only way to flush him out would be to have Ballantine arrive there on schedule, and let the guy make his move. And we were running out of time—it had to be done right then."

"So?"

"So I had Ballantine go with DeGennaro. I put on Ballantine's raggedy sport coat, mussed my hair a little, and took his car keys. I ordered DeGennaro to give me her piece, and told her to put our car in position on East Forty-third, between Second and Third. Once she was in position, I drove Ballantine's car into Forty-third between Third and Lex, and parked in a spot that gave me plenty of hang time. I had Diane's gun in my right hand, tucked behind the bag of bagels that I was cradling in my left arm. I began walking toward St. Agnes' Church."

"Besides having a complete description of the car," Pezzano interrupted quizzically, "one would have to think that the assassin would know what Ballantine looked like. No?"

"That's what made my doing this even more compelling," Savage said. "Joe and I sort of look alike. Years ago, people mistook us for brothers."

Pezzano nodded. "So, using your training from all the years you spent as a cop in Street Crime Unit, you decide to do a fucking decoy. Big balls, Savage!"

"The rest happened real quick," Thorn went on. "Just as I'm nearing the church, a guy I know to be Georgei Strelnikov steps from the shadows and crosses the street in my direction. Without it looking obvious, I try to pace my steps so he can't get behind me, but he does a clever stutter step, and next thing I know, he is."

"Then?"

"Without moving my head, I do a hard eyeballs right. I see our shadows against the front of the church. His has got the outline of a gun in its out-stretched hand. He was gonna waste me from behind."

"*Whew!*" Pezzano gasped, wide-eyed, obviously putting himself in the life-or-death spot. "How'd you get the drop on him?"

"I don't know," Thorn said reflectively. "It happened too fast. I spun, drew down on him, and told him to give it up. He decided to roll the dice. He got snake eyes."

"*Jesus!*" Pezzano said, sighing. "You never cease to fuckin' amaze me, Savage."

When the taxi driver pulled to a stop in front of Target on Queens Boulevard, the meter read $25.50. Unzipping a small side compartment of her tote, Christine Maloney withdrew three crisp tens and told the driver to keep the change. It was, she concluded, a perfectly unmemorable tip.

Dragging the bag with her, she slid from the cab's backseat. After it had driven off, she turned and walked half a block back to the sidewalk entrance of the department store's self-contained, multilevel parking facility. She took the stairway to level two, and headed to section E. Her black BMW 328i convertible was parked in the last spot at the very end of that aisle. She'd always made it a habit to look for end parking spots. That way, at least, she thought, one side of her car couldn't be dinged by the swinging doors of careless, insensitive assholes.

It had been a tough day, she felt. Mentally tough. She was tired by it all and longed for the comfort of her recliner. There would be time to relax when she got home, maybe watch TV or read a good book. These past days had been so hectic and nerve-wracking, she hadn't even cracked that new novel by Grisham. She'd also call Gerard, in Washington, and continue to put his mind at ease. For dinner, Twyla could fix a nice salad.

Always aware that, to a great extent, she was a public figure and, therefore, subject to unwanted recognition, she looked around and was relieved that no one was in sight near her car. She popped the BMW's trunk, set the bag containing her alter ego inside, and tapped the keyless remote to unlock the car doors. Slipping in behind the wheel, she stuck the key into the ignition switch, and after quickly checking her face and hair in the rearview, cranked the engine.

The explosion came up through the floor and blew off both doors and the trunk lid. It lifted the car four feet off the ground. When the remainder of the Beemmer flopped back down on its broken axles, it was consumed in a bright orange fireball.

"Will that be all, sir?" the clerk asked, counting back the change from a fifty. She placed a 24 pack of X-ACTO blades, a 300 pack of Q-tip safety swabs, and a plastic spray mist bottle into a Target bag along with the sales receipt, and handed it to the customer.

Suddenly, the store—if not most of Elmhurst—was rocked. Tremors from the rumbling jolt shook the checkout counter.

"That's all for today, I think," Andy Karis replied with a satisfied smile. He turned with his purchase and headed for the escalator.

*   *   *

"There's no point in trying to delude ourselves otherwise," Pezzano said. "The PC wants to crucify you, Thorn. He's downstairs waiting for the statements from DeGennaro and Ballantine. Then he intends to look on, like fuckin' Caesar in his box at the Coliseum, while Wilson and Hetzel take your statement, so he can go thumbs-down and have them feed your ass to the lions."

"Well, that's poetic," Savage replied sarcastically, grimacing. "Thanks for sharing that with me, Pete."

"I know that Chief Wilson's on your side," Pezzano whispered, leaning close. "But, under the circumstances, I don't think there's a whole lot he's gonna be able to do for you. PC's hot as hell."

"I could tell by the look on Wilson's face when he got here that he was feeling Johnson's intimidating presence," Savage mumbled, straddling a chair and staring idly out a window that overlooked the intersection of East Fifty-first Street and Third Avenue.

"You guys were cops together in Street Crime years ago, right?"

"Yeah. Back in the real Street Crime Unit, before idiot politicians—like one of our former police commissioners, and his staff of jerk-off deputies—monkeyed with it, overexpanded it, and fucked it all up."

Pezzano had been right about Ray Wilson, Thorn thought. The chief of detectives had been given a mission he didn't really want. He'd been handed the assignment of putting together a case against a man, an old friend, whom he liked and respected—a case that would no doubt cost the man his job. Despite his own problems, Savage couldn't help but empathize with Wilson's unhappy plight. It was all political bullshit, but once you rise above the rank of captain in this job, you'd damn well better become a political animal, or you're toast.

"I'm urging you to get some union representation before you go in," Pezzano said, breaking into Savage's reverie. "They're gonna try to tear you apart. If

I were you, I wouldn't say a fucking word till I talked to a lawyer."

Thorn nodded, only half hearing. It was times like this, he thought, allowing his mind to wander off to Maureen Gallo, when a man needs to know that he's not alone in the world. He could have thought of Gina, but sweet Gina was too new—she really didn't *know* Thorn Savage, didn't know how much The Job meant to him.

Looking down from the second-floor window, Savage watched the flow of weekend traffic as it moved unhurried along Third Avenue. He wondered what Maureen was doing this fine Sunday afternoon.

"By the way"—Pezzano spoke through gritted teeth, seemingly aware that Savage had been elsewhere and trying to bring him back—"Rice-Jenkins is here too."

"Terrific."

"She's hovering, outwardly projecting professional indifference, but I know that inwardly she's salivating about her coming victory and vindication." Shaking his head in frustration, Pezzano summed up, "Sergeant Thorn Savage is once again in her crosshairs. He shot and killed a man a couple of hours ago in front of a Catholic church—after she'd taken away his fucking guns."

Squinting up at Petey Pezzano through his heavily hooded, always sad eyes, Thorn finally muttered, "Fuck her, and the horse she rode in on. And screw the lawyers. The only one I'm worried about here is First Grade Detective Diane DeGennaro. It was her goddamned gun I used. And I *ordered* her to give it to me. Is The Job—Rice-Jenkins and the PC—gonna try to skewer her for that?"

"You betcha," Pezzano regretfully intoned. "If they gotta do it to get to you, they will. I don't have to tell you how the game is played. Everybody goes when the whistle blows!"

Savage knew his boss wasn't overstating the fucked-up dilemma. Ironic, he thought. The powers were looking to take his head for disregarding the orders of a superior, and Diane DeGennaro's for obeying them. He hoped Diane would cover her ass. But in his heart, he knew she would stand up.

The small interrogation room on the second floor of the Seventeenth was bare-bones and windowless. In the center was a large table surrounded by five uncomfortable-looking chairs. On the table was a Panasonic reel-to-reel tape recorder and a microphone. Diane DeGennaro was sitting alone there when Herb Tobias let himself in. "The IAB team is ready to interview you," he said. "They're waiting outside the door. As soon as we're ready, I'll call them in."

Diane DeGennaro liked Herbie Tobias a lot. She thought the Detective Endowment Association attorney was a real nice guy. They'd met several times before, most recently at a Saint Patrick's Day racket up in the Two-O. Richie, she recalled, also liked him. Today, however, there was no racket, no fun and games. Herbie Tobias had been sent over by the DEA to represent Detective Diane DeGennaro's legal interests in a departmental shooting investigation.

Tobias, clipboard and notes in hand, sat opposite her in the room to which she had been banished a full hour ago by Internal Affairs.

"The headhunters have ordered me to remain in here," she said, flipping her hands up nervously from her lap. "They want to keep me isolated, unable to communicate in any way with my boss, Thorn Savage."

"Where is he?" Tobias asked.

"Isolated in some other part of the building, I suppose. IAB doesn't want us comparing notes, or formulating any kind of strategy."

"God forbid," Tobias intoned sarcastically. "You know what they want, right?" he asked.

"I'm not sure what they want," she replied.

"Your supervisor, Sergeant Savage, has got some

major problems," Tobias began. "Based on a discussion I just had with First Deputy Commissioner Rice-Jenkins, I can assure you—with a great degree of certainty—that he's already lost his job. The only question that seems to remain here is whether or not you take any kind of fall. That, I'm informed, will all be dependent upon your cooperation. The first dep strongly 'suggested' my client—you—fully understand that which is at stake here."

"Savage was doing his job," Diane said, bristling.

"It's the first dep's argument that technically Savage had no job." Tobias shrugged sympathetically. "Officially, he was on the payroll, yes. But also officially he was on Modified Assignment. No gun—no shield—no police powers."

"He did the right thing," Diane blurted.

"Right thing, wrong thing," Tobias countered. "It ain't gonna make any difference. Either way, he's a goner. My job is to keep you from getting scorched."

"What *do* they want?"

"It's the department's position that this whole matter could have been handled much differently," Tobias said with a somber grimace. "They feel Savage should have called for assistance on the radio. The whole area could have been flooded with uniforms, and a shooting—that resulted in a death—might, therefore, have been prevented."

"There was *no fucking time*!" Diane lashed out, her patience all but gone. "And the whole damn thing was handled in precisely the right way. If a whole bunch of uniforms had shown up, the shooter would have simply split, and gotten to Ballantine tomorrow . . . next week. Who the hell knows."

"Relax," Tobias said calmingly. "Whole thing boils down to this. When it comes to the question of whether or not Sergeant Savage *had* adequate time to call for assistance before this event unfolded—"

"They want me to state that I felt there *was* enough time?" Diane broke in, infuriated.

"It doesn't even have to be that strong," Tobias said. "All you need to say is there could have been adequate time to call for backup. That statement isn't going to hurt Savage any more than he already is. But, I'm telling you, it'll surely save your butt."

"And if I don't go along, what can they do to me, Herbie?" Diane asked, knowing full well the answer.

"For starters," Tobias said, rolling his eyes, "you could get flopped from your prestigious command and bounced back in grade, which would cost you thousands in annual income, not to mention tens of thousands in retirement money someday. Also, an administrative blemish like that on your record would effectively finish you in The Job. With the stroke of a pen, the first dep could have you banished to one of the many obscure and undesirable assignments the department has an abundance of. Places where people mark time, praying for their twenty."

Diane puffed up her cheeks in deliberation, slowly exhaled, then took a deep breath. "Call them in," she said. "Let's get this interview started."

"Detective," Tobias said, rising from his seat and moving for the door, "once that interview team comes in here and turns on that tape recorder, we will be on the record. Any answers you give will be *carved in stone*. You'll have to live with them."

This whole thing was shaping up like a departmental lynching party, she thought. Herb Tobias—a nice enough guy—was doing what he had to do: protecting her. But the other bastards, all of them, were sharks circling for the kill. On the record, or off the record, it would make no difference. She would say nothing that could be construed—or misconstrued—by anybody that could have any negative connotations at all for her boss. If Thorn Savage was about to fall prey to these man-eaters, it would be without her help. *That,* she knew, was the only goddamned thing around this room that *was* carved in stone.

*   *   *

"You couldn't be in a worse position, Thorn," Pezzano warned. "The Charges and Specs they can bring you up on'll be as long as the Declaration of Independence. Violation of the provisions of Modified Assignment. Disregarding the direct order of a superior. Unauthorized possession and use of a weapon not listed on your ten card. And, let's not forget the ever popular catchall, Engaging in conduct prejudicial to good order, efficiency, or discipline of the department. Want me to go on?"

Thorn nibbled his lower lip, then exhaled hard through partly pursed lips. He wished he had some Life Savers.

"All right then, Thorn," Pezzano finally said, his voice doleful. "They've finished taking their statements from DeGennaro and the reporter. They're ready for you. You ready for them?"

"Ready as I'll ever be," Savage answered surely. "Let's do it."

Waiting in the interrogation room when Savage entered were Police Commissioner Thomas Johnson and, seated beside him like a vulture waiting for roadkill, First Deputy Commissioner Fiona Rice-Jenkins. Also present, to do the actual interrogation, were Chief of Detectives Wilson and the IAB boss, Chief Roland Hetzel. Everything said from here on in was on the record. When all nodded ready, Chief Hetzel pressed RECORD on a Sony reel-to-reel. Then he curtly read Savage the provisions of Department General Order 15.

"I wish to advise you that you are being questioned as part of an official investigation by the police department. You will be asked questions specifically directed and narrowly related to the performance of your duties. You are entitled to all the rights and privileges guaranteed by the laws of the state of New York, the constitution of this state and the constitution of the United States, including the right not to be compelled to incriminate yourself, and the right to have legal counsel present at each and every stage of this investigation. Do you understand?"

"Yes," Savage said firmly. "I understand."

Hetzel went on. "I further wish to advise you that if you refuse to testify, or to answer questions relating to the performance of your official duties, you will be subject to departmental charges which could result in your dismissal from the police department. If you do answer, neither your statements nor any information or evidence which is gained by reason of such statements can be used against you in any subsequent criminal proceedings, should there be any. However, these statements may be used against you in relation to subsequent departmental charges."

TWENTY-FIVE

Chief of Detectives Raphael "Ray" Wilson was born and raised on 118th Street just off Lenox Avenue. Growing up in Harlem in the sixties, he'd seen a lot of life's underbelly, and gotten more of an education in man's inhumanity to man than he could have ever learned in any sociology classroom.

Wilson understood the rules of the street. He knew all about survival of the fittest. Throughout his life he'd seen just how the strong preyed on the weak, and how evil preyed on good. Raised in a three-room tenement apartment by a tiny, raw-boned, no-nonsense grandmother, Ray never missed a day of school as a child. He was made to do chores, go to church on Sundays, and say yes, no, please, and thank you. When he was nineteen, a strung out junkie trapped his Grammy in a stairwell. The lowlife took the few dollars she had and then proceeded to beat her brains in. After a week on life support, the doctors pulled the plug and Ray Wilson was alone in the world. Two years later, he joined the New York City Police Department.

Now, nearing his thirty-fifth year in The Job, and being the first black man to ever attain the sublime position of chief of detectives, Ray Wilson figured he'd seen just about all the bullshit and misery there was to see in life, humanly or otherwise possible—terrorist attacks, suicides, mass homicides, plane crashes, train

wrecks, rapes, robberies, civil disorders, and pure
fucking mayhem. He could, and had—thanks to the
backbone and character instilled in him by his
Grammy—handled most all of it at one time or another during his years as a cop.

But if Grammy had left him with anything, it was
his intolerance of injustice. He could never idly stand
by and watch a flawed system destroy a good cop. He
wasn't about to start today.

Savage had fully answered every question hit to him
by everyone in the room. Like a slick-fielding short-
stop covering his position, he'd allowed nothing to get
by. Not the tepid ground balls from Wilson himself,
or Hetzel, or the red-hot line drives from the PC or
Fiona Rice-Jenkins, who clearly had her own agenda
and a massive axe to grind. When the inquisition was
finally over and Savage had been excused from the
room, Chief Wilson knew where he came down on
this one. Exonerated. He could also tell that Chief
Hetzel was sympathetic to Savage's plight, though trying to conceal it behind his pasty face. But Hetzel
would go whichever way the fucking wind was blowing. There was no question where Rice-Jenkins stood,
and the PC was privately conferring by phone with
the mayor to see how he should go. As soon as that
call was over, Savage's fate would be sealed. Wilson
hated to admit it, but it wasn't looking good. Five
minutes later, when the PC finished his call, the
tribunal-plus-one was reconvened.

"Okay," Johnson announced, as the three filed back
into the room and found their seats. "I've just gotten
off the phone with the mayor. Does anybody have any
final thoughts?"

"Commissioner, sir," Wilson began. "We've now
completed exhaustive interrogations of the first-
grader, Diane DeGennaro, and the reporter from the
Post, Joe Ballantine. And, we've just completed the
questioning of Sergeant Savage. Beyond that, we've
also contacted Citywide radio and confirmed times

and gotten transcripts of radio messages that jibe with what they're all saying."

"And?" Johnson said, sighing impatiently.

"And," Wilson continued patiently, "we also have in our possession the handwritten note found in the apartment in Brooklyn that helped trigger today's events."

"So, from your point of view, what do we have, Chief?" Johnson said tartly.

Glancing briefly at Rice-Jenkins and the hawk-nosed IAB boss, Hetzel, then turning back to face the PC, Wilson firmly answered, "What we have is this, Commissioner. If Thorn Savage had lived up to the provisions of the Modified Assignment—that he'd been improperly placed on—and hadn't been where he was, when he was today, we'd all be up to our fucking eyeballs investigating the assassination of a newspaper reporter instead of the justifiable homicide of a known leader of the Russian Mafia. If that'd happened, I can just see tomorrow's headlines—TOP INVESTIGATIVE REPORTER MURDERED ON MIDTOWN STREET."

"Are you defending Savage's actions, Chief?" Johnson asked coldly.

"What I'm saying," Wilson replied, "is that Sergeant Thornton Savage unquestionably saved the life of Joseph Ballantine this afternoon." Peripherally, he saw Rice-Jenkins's eyes roll in her head.

"Am I reading you correctly, Chief?" Rice-Jenkins said sharply. "Are you defending the fact that this . . . *Savage,* with his notorious hair-trigger temper, disregarded my direct orders to remain unarmed and stay off the streets in the capacity of a police officer?"

"What temper?" Wilson said. "I never met a man with a stronger sense of control, or one less capable of just 'going along' with bullshit nonsense. Which may explain why he's such a goddamned good cop."

"Chief," the PC explained, "I personally backed up Commissioner Rice-Jenkins this morning. I personally told this guy that he was to remain on Modified until Wednesday. Once the Firearms Review Board gave a green light on his actions—and you and I both agree that they would have—he'd have been reinstated, no worse for the wear. But he disobeyed me and went right back out on the street. That was insubordination."

"If it *was* insubordination, Commissioner," Wilson promptly responded. "then it was very fortuitous for all of us. Fact is, in actuality all he did was accompany one of his detectives on an interview. He simply took a ride. He had no way of knowing how events were to unfold, or that he'd wind up in a gunfight. But let's look at where we'd be if Savage hadn't used his discretion. And, I might remind everyone," he continued, now glaring at Rice-Jenkins, "put *his* goddamned life on the line."

"That wasn't his decision to make," Rice-Jenkins broke in. "May I remind you again, his discretion in police matters had been removed. Imagine the audacity of this man. Who the hell does he think he is? He was virtually under suspension, and he goes out of borough to interrogate the wife of a United States senator for crissakes. Did you know of, or approve, that action, Chief Wilson?" When Wilson made no attempt to answer, Rice-Jenkins uttered a derisive sneer.

"That's another thing here, Chief," the PC said in an admonishing tone. "Just what the hell was Savage doing out there trying to interview Christine Maloney in the first place? Implying that she's somehow involved with, or has some sort of connection to, a faction of organized crime? Russian organized crime at that. Why, that's just plain fucking preposterous." Johnson's muscles and veins were beginning to pop in his thick neck. "When I told the mayor that, he almost had a damn shit hemorrhage. Even more than this shooting, that move to question the likes of a senator's wife is going to turn out to be very embarrassing to both me and the mayor."

"I've known Thornton Savage for more than thirty years, Commissioner," the chief of detectives replied. "I can't as yet totally explain his actions as they pertain to Senator Maloney and his wife. After all, we didn't go into that aspect of today's events very deeply. But I'm willing to go on record. I have absolute faith in his investigative talent and any method he may employ in working a case." In his fervor to defend, Wilson added, "If Thorn Savage feels there's legitimate and ample reason for us to investigate Jesus Christ, then I'll sign off on it, and have him go knock on heaven's door."

"You just want to give this guy a blank check, don't you?" Rice-Jenkins screeched in outrage.

"Not so! But there's a *New York Post* reporter out there whose life was saved today by the guy you want to hang. A reporter who eyewitnessed today's shooting, and states that Savage had no choice at all. It was kill or be killed. That reporter is gonna tell it just like it was in tomorrow's paper. The way I see it, Commissioner, you're in one of those departmental binds that come along every now and then. Either you go with the flow, smile, and give Savage a fucking medal, or you buck all the media and throw him off The Job. The choice is yours."

Thomas Johnson III's neck veins were really popping and Fiona Rice-Jenkins was about to self-combust when a knock came at the office door. Chief Patrick Feeney stuck his head in.

"Commissioner, sir," Feeney announced respectfully. "Pick up on line seven, sir. It's the mayor."

"Yes, Mr. Mayor," Johnson said cheerfully into the phone. "We're just about wrapped up here, sir." Then the PC's smile immediately faded. Ray Wilson didn't miss the color draining from the man's face. Johnson was listening intently, then began spluttering "Yes, I understand, Mr. Mayor," every few seconds. Finally, brooding, Johnson hung up.

"What's wrong, Commissioner?" Chief Hetzel asked.

"Get that Homicide lieutenant Pezzano in here

right now. On the double.'' In less than a minute, Petey Pezzano had joined the PC, Chiefs Wilson and Hetzel, and Deputy Commissioner Rice-Jenkins behind closed doors. After a prolonged silence, Johnson spoke.

"You and Sergeant Savage were present in my office this morning, Lieutenant. Do you recall the substance of our conversation?"

"Well . . . yes, sir. I do."

"Do you recall it completely?"

Wearing a puzzled look, Pezzano glanced around at the others present, then slowly answered, "Yes, Commissioner. I remember each and every word of it."

Glaring intently into Pezzano's eyes, Johnson leaned forward from behind the desk. "Is it *not* true that this morning I told you that I was *immediately* reinstating Sergeant Savage to full duty?"

"*Re*instating him, sir?" Pezzano asked lamely, cramping his face. "I don't quite understand, sir."

"That's exactly what I said this morning, Lieutenant," Johnson said firmly, keeping up the stony glare. "I told you both, in my office, that I was taking Savage off Modified Assignment, and reinstating him to full duty immediately." Manipulating Pezzano's response with frazzled eyebrows arched high and taut lips, he added, "Is that not so, Lieutenant?"

Chief Wilson saw that Pezzano didn't know whether to shit or go blind, but it appeared that the lieutenant was beginning to get the PC's drift. Wilson, himself as confused as anyone else in the room, observed in silence.

"Y-yes, sir," Pezzano finally said tentatively. "That's what you said, sir. You were reinstating him, sir."

"And did I not also approve the immediate return of his weapons?" Johnson asked sharply.

"Uhh . . . why yes, sir," Pezzano stumbled, but was clearly gaining momentum. "You did say that. Yes, you did."

"Take a seat, Lieutenant," Johnson directed, then

looked slowly around at all present before continuing. "I have determined that this matter is closed. Sergeant Savage was acting in the proper performance of his duties today. Does everybody hear what I'm saying?" His piercing eyes shifted about quickly to everyone in the room.

Chief of Detectives Wilson knew that the cryptic conversation between the PC and the mayor had nothing to do with saving Thorn Savage's ass. What it did have to do with was saving the mayor's and the PC's. But, he reasoned, you take your breaks where you find them. Wilson spoke right up. "Then I will gladly mark this matter closed," he said with an agreeable smile. "And, I might add, you made an excellent decision this morning, sir." He turned to see Chief Hetzel's mouth hanging agape, and Rice-Jenkins's anger about to make her go postal. Pezzano, he saw, was expressionless, thinking.

Johnson cleared his throat and spoke. "Now that we're all singing from the same piece of music," he began, stopping to shoot a get-control-of-yourself glare at the fuming Rice-Jenkins, "I have an announcement to make. As you know, I just received a call from the mayor. He'd just been notified by Operations that Christine Maloney, the wife of Senator Gerard Maloney, has been killed. Her car was bombed, blown to bits out in Queens. The mayor was also advised that it was probably an assassination."

Ray Wilson looked around the room. There was no doubt in his mind that all present now understood the political ramifications to the PD, the commissioner, and the mayor if Savage were not upheld in his actions. Smiling contentedly to himself, Wilson thought, Politics *is* sometimes a double-edged sword.

"Chief Wilson," the PC commanded, "your work is done here. This investigation is through. You need to be on your way out to Queens. There'll be plenty of work for you there."

"Yes, Commissioner," Wilson agreed, but then, to

rub it into Rice-Jenkins, casually added, "First I better huddle with Sergeant Savage to find out what he knows."

"Anybody have any questions?" Johnson asked, a daring tone riding on his words. Unbelievably, Petey Pezzano spoke up.

"Just one, Commissioner," Pezzano said directly, a slightly tart, not-so-fast edge to his voice. "I just wanted to make sure that everybody here understands *everything* that you and I have discussed today."

Wide brow furrowed, eyes narrowed and dancing, the commissioner of the New York City Police Department squirmed anxiously in his chair. "Like . . . what else did we talk about, Lieutenant?" he mumbled, clearing his throat.

"Your desire to see that Savage is awarded the Police Combat Cross for the 'extraordinary heroism' he displayed in the wild shoot-out at his apartment house Friday evening."

Johnson sat, big hands clasped in his lap, defensive eyes measuring the Homicide commander. "Yes," he finally said tentatively, obviously aware that he was being whacked for something by a lieutenant who had his time in, and whose civil service rank he could not tamper with. "I do remember that."

"And surely you recall your promise this afternoon to follow up with the Honor Committee to ensure that Savage is awarded the Department Medal of Honor for his outstanding act of gallantry and valor today. How did you put it? 'At imminent personal hazard to life—with full knowledge of the risk—above and beyond the call of duty.' Isn't that right, Commissioner?"

Long silence.

"*Veni, vidi, vici,* Lieutenant?" the compromised commissioner finally uttered in a sarcastic whisper, glaring daggers at the ballsy Italian who held all the cards.

"Not at all, sir," Pezzano replied, staring intently back. "Let's just call it a quid pro quo."

"Yes," Johnson spluttered finally, in front of all. "Savage will receive those recognitions. On that I give my word."

Good for you, Lieutenant, Chief of Detectives Wilson thought, looking on in amazement. Score one for the good guys.

TWENTY-SIX

Sunday-evening TV was alive with it, breaking into regularly scheduled programming with updated bulletins. It was the only topic of every talking head on every station. Karis flashed back and forth through all the channels but finally settled on CNN.

The heavy news coverage of the car bombing in Queens was far more than he'd expected. But then, he hadn't known the target was to be the wife of a United States senator. Relska had neglected to tell him that. Normally, when contracted, he required considerable background information on the intended: a good, clear, recent photograph; a detailed physical description—height, weight, hair and eye color, marks, scars, tattoos; name and address; place of business; favorite haunts; et cetera. In this case, however, he'd been specifically contracted to kill a car, a black BMW convertible that he'd been assured would be parked somewhere in the Target garage today. He had skillfully defeated the car's alarm by wiring the explosive device directly to its exhaust-system oxygen sensor. He was assured payment regardless of who it was who eventually turned the key and started the motor.

Relska had supplied a description of the car, its license-plate number, and where he would likely find it parked. Relska's information on target location was always impeccable. It often amazed him how accurate she could be in that regard. But it angered him that she'd omitted revealing the identity of the intended target in this one. He'd asked, but she'd demurred. Had he known who it was, it was likely he would have passed or at the very least bargained a much, *much* higher rate. Killing a senator's wife would intensify investigative efforts, not only by the locals, but by the goddamned feds as well.

Though Karis was certain that no clues connecting him to the bombing could possibly have survived one of his custom explosions, what he hadn't expected was the seemingly unrelated item also being broadcast on the evening news:

"Russian mob henchman gunned down by police in midtown."

The two stories would seem unrelated to most, at least for now. A politician's wife getting knocked off out in Queens, and a reputed Russian mob figure being shot down by a cop on Manhattan's East Side. He hoped the stories were still unrelated in the minds of the authorities. He knew that was a false hope. The TV reported that the cop who'd put three into Georgei Strelnikov was Sergeant Thornton Savage, the cop with nine lives. This was no matter of coincidence, he mused. Savage must have been deep into Brooklyn's actions. Karis sucked on his yellowed teeth, then bit down on his upper lip.

He took another sip of the Earl Grey, and flicked the channel over to NBC. Their updated report stated that not only was Georgei Strelnikov dead, but Nikita Relska, "the reputed head of the New York Russian mob," had been taken into custody and charged as an accessory in an attempt to murder Joseph Ballantine, a *New York Post* reporter.

It wouldn't be long now, he thought. Facing big jail time, Relska would never stand up. And, unlike some witnesses against her in the past, the *New York Post* could not be intimidated or disposed of. At this point in time, what better card could Relska play than to cut a deal for herself? It was clear. She'd have no choice but to hand up the contractor in the Maloney matter.

Time was short—he'd have to hurry. He had plenty of bubble wrap and a good supply of sturdy crating boxes. He'd work through the night.

As the TV commentator's voice droned in the background, Karis looked out from his Thirty-fifth floor terrace at the overbuilt expanse of Manhattan Island that lay before him. He eyed the orange brick building just blocks away, beyond the traffic-congested Brooklyn Bridge—One Police Plaza, the headquarters of NYPD.

From out of nowhere, his mother's words from long ago harkened back to him. "It's time, Andric! It is time for you to leave the Steppes." He gulped the last of his tea.

TWENTY-SEVEN

Yesterday had been a long day, one that sapped marrow from bone and squandered zillions of brain cells. But Savage felt good to be back at his desk at Homicide with the pressure off. As per the memo he'd been handed when he'd entered the office, he immediately put through a return call to the chief of detectives.

"Morning, Chief. Thorn Savage here."

"Just wanted to touch base with you this morning," Chief Wilson began, "and bring you up to date on that Christine Maloney fiasco."

"Must have been a mess out there, huh?" Savage asked.

"Wasn't enough of Maloney's old lady left to put in a sandwich bag, never mind a body bag. What wasn't blown to smithereens was reduced to ash."

"How'd you make the positive ID?"

"Couple of partial prints and dental records," Chief Wilson replied. "We found one of her hands about twenty yards away."

"How'd you get a hold of dental records so quickly?"

"It was Senator Gerard Maloney's wife for crissakes—all the stops magically came out. Before you could say 'flossing is fun' Major Case and the FBI had their hands on the dentist who worked on a bridge for her molars. They dragged the poor bastard away from a doubleheader at Shea with his family."

"Any usable evidence recovered?" Savage queried.

"That's what I called to congratulate you on. The only thing that survived the blast was an overnight bag that must have been blown clear. Inside it we found a change of clothes, a wig, and a receipt from the Sherry-Netherland Hotel dated yesterday. We connected that to the Sherry-Netherland matches you recovered from Strelnikov's body."

"And?"

"Crime Scene came up with both their prints in that hotel room. *Touchdown, Savage!*"

"That's good to hear," Savage thankfully acknowledged the Chief's enthusiastic additional vindication. "And based on all Joe Ballantine's now told us, coupled with what we've put together since the La Florentine homicides, there seems to be no question of a Russian mob connection with the Maloneys. I'm also convinced that the same guy who did the La Florentine job was also responsible for the fireworks in Queens yesterday."

"Figure the Russians were shaking them for money?" Wilson asked.

"Either that," Savage verbally shrugged, "or they were shaking them for influence. Can you imagine if those bastards had strings connected to the president of the United States?"

"Why do you figure they killed the Mayhews?"

"According to Ballantine, Candace Mayhew was a warehouse of knowledge about Gerard Maloney's dirty past. Once the Russians gained the same knowledge, they had her and her husband killed to shut down those sources. Yesterday they tried to do Joe Ballantine to close off that possible avenue of knowledge. It appears they wanted to be the only mechanics in town with a monkey wrench on Maloney's nuts."

"Why kill Maloney's wife?"

"Don't know yet," Savage said, puzzled. "Can't say. Something must have gone wrong there."

"I read you," Chief Wilson said thoughtfully. "And

I buy it. I'll pass it along to the PC and mayor. Talk to you later."

As Savage cradled the receiver, Richie Marcus bounced into the office, coffee in hand, and straddled Jules Unger's chair.

"Man, I bet you'd like to nuke old Fiona-baby," Marcus supposed right out with a faint laugh. "She really did her best to try to fuck you."

Savage shrugged noncommittally. "Fact is," he felt strangely obligated to admit, "in this old world there's only three things I truly can't stand. Irish music, Geraldo Rivera, and liver."

"What's wrong with liver?" Marcus asked.

Savage threw his head back and roared. "Richie, you're a pisser." It seemed like the first good laugh he'd had in weeks.

"Gotta bring you up to speed on Nikki Relska," Marcus said. "Jack and I spent hours with her while they were puttin' you and Diane through the wringer up in the Seventeenth yesterday. The broad's tough. We didn't get much."

"It's the note you glommed from her kitchen table that's gonna hang her," Savage explained. "It literally outlined Ballantine's time and place of execution. What'd she say about it?"

"Says we must have planted it," Marcus growled.

"Planted it?" Savage chuckled in disbelief.

"That's what she's sayin'," Marcus growled some more, grinning ironically. "Can you imagine the balls . . . ?"

"What did she have to say about Christine Maloney getting disassembled?"

"Had a quick answer for that too. Said it was probably done by some right-wing extremist group. But that it would surely backfire on them, because Maloney would now get the sympathy vote, and be guaranteed to win."

"She is a cold bitch, ain't she?" Savage mused.

As Marcus lit a Winston, Diane DeGennaro and

Jack Lindstrom ambled in, cramping the small office. Diane was carrying a packet of DMV photographs.

"These just came in from Albany," Diane said. "They're the last of the batch."

Savage quickly shuffled through the dozen pictures, then shook his head. "He's not in this group," he said tersely. He handed the packet back to DeGennaro.

"Well," Jack Lindstrom said, leaning against the doorjamb, "that narrows down the subscriber list to only five possibles, none of whom are licensed to drive, so we were unable to get photos on them."

"Did Rudy over at Postal at least get us their names and addresses?" Savage asked.

"He did," Lindstrom said. "And I've already determined that two of those five are dead. One, Fred De-Vane, lived in a residence hotel down in Chelsea. I called there to see if he was still registered. Manager remembered him, said he was a frustrated writer who'd committed suicide last year by jumping out his tenth-floor window. The other guy, Horace McGrath, got himself axe-murdered in his sleep by his own wife last June. Unger's team handled that case, remember?"

"Maybe McGrath's old lady didn't like his hobbies?" Marcus ventured. "A big man playin' with little toy soldiers. Maybe Mrs. McGrath wanted him to play with her some more?"

Lindstrom "ahemmed" patiently, not cracking a smile. "As to the remaining three, I guess we gotta go knocking on a few doors."

"What're their names?" Savage asked.

"Alphabetically, by last name, we got a Remy Bouchette up in Riverdale, a Yanni Grizopoulos over in Astoria, and an A. Karis," Lindstrom answered, looking up from his notes. "No first name, just an initial."

"Where's he?"

"Downtown. John Street. Who do you want to start with? The Queens Greek, the uptown Frog, or the downtown initial 'A'?"

Savage's phone rang at that instant.

"He was here!" Dawson screeched excitedly into the phone.

"Calm down!" Savage soothed. "When?"

"Five minutes ago. He just left. He's gotta be the *ugliest* man I ever saw in my whole *life. Oh my God!* I just can't imagine *ever* waking up next to that."

Cupping the phone's mouthpiece, Savage quickly told the team what was up and to get ready to leave. "Did you speak to him?" he calmly asked Dawson.

"Of *course* I spoke to him!" Dawson almost choked in his excitement. "I just don't *believe* it. A *killer* here in my store. I thought I was gonna *wet my pants.*"

"Where did he go?"

"Don't know. *Oh my God!* I wasn't about to *follow* him, Sarge. He was *so* mean looking and everything."

Savage was sure the ersatz Green Beret was hyperventilating himself into a panic attack.

"Did he have a car?"

"Don't *know.* I watched him through the window as he walked away. He walked funny, like he had a broomstick up his butt, know what I mean? I lost sight of him when he turned the corner at Greenwich. I just had to *force* myself to look. *My God,* what if he turned around and *saw* me?"

"Take a few deep breaths, Dawson," Savage soothed again. "Then tell me which way he went at Greenwich."

"He went downtown."

"Tell me what he said to you."

"He didn't say very *much,* I'll tell you that. I had just opened the store when he came in. I heard my alarm buzzer, and when I came out from the back he was already standing there at my display cases. I *just* thought I'd *die.*"

"What did he say?"

"He wanted to know if I had any other toy soldiers besides the ones on display."

"And?"

"I asked him what he was looking for. He said he was looking for Heydes."

"What did you tell him?"

"Well, if you can *believe* it, by then I'd begun to collect myself somewhat, know what I mean? So I told him, no, I didn't have anything else here, but that I did have access to a nice collection of random Heydes—I *lied*. They should give me an *Oscar*. I asked if he was looking for anything in particular."

"What'd he say?"

"French," Dawson replied. Then, after gulping several deep breaths, he added, "French *infantry*."

"What'd you tell him?"

"I told him I was sure the collection included French artillery, cavalry, even some infantry. Told him I could make an inquiry, and if the pieces were still available I'd have them on hand for him to view."

"Un-huh," Savage uttered. "Then what?"

"I asked him for a name and phone number where I could reach him. I just don't *know* where in God's name I got the *nerve* from."

"You're doin' terrific, Dawson," Savage buoyed the man. "Did he give you a name?"

"Andy. That's all he said."

"Andy?"

"Yeah. No last name, no phone number. Said he was leaving town for a while. He can't leave *soon* enough for me. Said *he'd* get back to me."

"Then what?"

"He took one of my *business* cards off the counter, and left."

"Great work, Dawson. God bless you." Savage hung up, reached for his sport jacket, and turned to the three members of his team. "Lets go. Forget the Frog and the Greek, we're gonna start with the initial 'A' downtown."

The thirty-five floors of 199 John Street used to be home to countless insurance companies, brokers, and allied insurance fields. Twenty years ago they all moved out, and, after standing vacant for years, the entire building was converted to private residences—condominiums, most of which were owned by Wall Street brokerage houses for use by their executives who'd worked late and were due in early—or who had a tryst to complete. There were very few full-time residents.

The doorman on duty was Alphonso. He took one look at the artist's sketch shown to him by Detective DeGennaro and said, "Thirty-five N. Mr. Andrew Karis."

"Is Mr. Karis at home?" Savage asked, his mind beginning to work out a battle plan.

"Don't know," Alphonso replied. "Just came on duty half hour ago. If you like, I'll ring his apartment and find out."

"I'll want you to do that, Alphonso," Savage said. "But not just yet." Thorn knew full well that what he really wanted was to ride the elevator to the thirty-fifth floor, solo, and personally kick in the door to 35-N, all the while hoping to God that Mr. Karis would opt to violently resist arrest, in which event he might have to put one between Mr. Karis's fucking eyes, just the way Mr. Karis—*Andy*—had put one between Caroline Durante's eyes. Or, Savage thought, he might be forced to chuck Mr. Karis from his fucking terrace. Or he might be forced to do both—shoot *and* toss. He took a deep breath, considered the bullshit of the past few days, and decided to do this one by the book. He turned to Richie Marcus.

"Get on the radio, and request Emergency Service to respond forthwith. No lights or sirens. Also, see if we can raise an Aviation Unit to hover-and-cover the roof. Have Operations notify the PC and Chief Wilson as to what's goin' down." Savage turned his attention back to Alphonso. "Tell me all about the underground parking, other exits to this building, and the emergency stairwells that service the thirty-fifth floor."

Within ten minutes, two Emergency Service teams, each with flack jackets and heavy weapons, had silently stationed themselves in the hallway outside apartment 35-N. They would make the initial entrance into the apartment. Aviation Unit chopper number two hovered discreetly above at about a thousand feet. Radio car teams from the First Precinct covered all the stairwells, the basement garage, and fire exits. It seemed to be going well, falling neatly into place. But Savage was edgy—he had a bad feeling in the pit of his stomach.

From the hallway of the thirty-fifth floor, Savage whispered into the portable, "Have the doorman ring the room."

Jack Lindstrom, posted in the building's lobby, acknowledged, "Ten-four."

With his radio's volume set as low as it could go, Savage barely heard Lindstrom's reply. Savage, De-Gennaro, Marcus, and the four Emergency cops all backed against the near wall and waited. They heard the phone begin to ring inside the apartment.

"I'm not getting any answer," Lindstrom's voice finally came back. "I've let it ring a few dozen times."

"Ten-four," Savage whispered into the handset. He looked across to the Emergency Service sergeant, and nodded. The burly man slipped the house passkey into the door lock and released it. He did the same to the dead-bolt lock above. After getting a ready nod from the detectives and his team of uniforms, he turned the knob and swung the door open. The flack jackets went in first, quickly leapfrogging their way through the entire apartment. Savage, Marcus, and DeGennaro, weapons drawn, cautiously followed. As they made their way into the large, sunlit rooms, they found themselves in a completely different world. Savage heard Richie Marcus mumble in awe under his breath.

"What the fuck?"

The apartment was richly furnished in oriental motif. A lot of black lacquer, and a lot of expensive cloisonné. Wall hangings were still in place. Dishes, glassware, pots, and pans filled the kitchen cabinetry. Clothing filled the closets. But the place was empty—vacated—and Savage knew it. He felt its emptiness.

"Look at this shit," Marcus exclaimed, staring bug-eyed at the miniature world at his feet—a world of tiny pastures and mountains, roadways, bridges, and cities that spread throughout every room of the apartment except the kitchen and both baths. "He's got this entire place set up like dozens of dioramas on every damn square inch of floor. Where the hell does he walk?"

"Unbelievable!" Diane whispered. "Look at the detail on all these bombed-out-looking buildings over here."

"Yeah," Marcus agreed. "And you'd swear that goddamned grass in those fields was real."

"And real snow on the hillsides," Diane noted.

"We got all sorts of Lilliputs here, Sarge," Marcus said. "But no Lilliputians."

"Yeah," Savage muttered, staring down at the empty battlefields. "And no Gulliver either." Those fucked-up computers in Albany had caused this, Savage thought. If they'd had this information yesterday, they'da had this bastard.

"All clear," Sergeant Ramos from Emergency announced as he and his men wandered back into the main room after scouring the entire apartment. "There ain't a living soul in this joint," he said. "But whaddaya make of all this?" he asked, throwing his thick arms around at the floor displays.

Deep inside himself, Savage dolefully shrugged.

"Sarge," Diane said, reinspecting the kitchen. "Come look at this."

Tacked to a cork bulletin board just above the sink was a solitary handwritten note:

'Tis a wise soldier who lives to fight another day.

"What a strange-looking tack," Diane observed.

"It's not a tack," Savage said, bristling, deflated, withdrawing the taunting note from the board. "It's a bayonet. A toy-soldier's bayonet." Savage knew where the tiny bayonet had come from, and he knew the scabbard it would fit back into. He also knew he'd be spending some time with Frankie McBride that afternoon.

TWENTY-EIGHT

Savage was awakened Tuesday morning by the heft of Ray's somnambulant mass curled like an eighteen-pound dumbbell atop his uncovered legs. The scruffy tom seemed to be quite comfortable.

After yesterday's disappointing miss at 199 John, Thorn had finished out the day, and the frustrating week, with a solo visit to Frankie McBride at P.J.'s. He recalled that after adequately dulling his senses there he'd come directly home and crashed on his bed without even pulling back the covers. Apparently he'd had the energy to take off his clothes, but hadn't hung them up; they were draped over the chair next to the bed.

He'd needed some deep z's to combat the internal wringing that had been slowly sapping his energy for weeks—his breakup with Maureen; The Job; Caroline Durante; his harmless, but nevertheless dead art-collecting neighbor, Tor Johanssen; The Job *again*. And now Karis slipping the noose and getting safely into the wind.

Thorn wasn't completely sure that had he decided to become a CPA instead of a COP when he was twenty-one, *his* personal life would have fared any better. But he was sure that a certain nurse would still be rushing around Four-West taking temps, and a harmless man would still be searching out Goyas and Picassos and rationalizing the annoying actions of his idiot dog.

He did a slow leg lift, dislodging the snoring cat. Ray stirred, stretched elaborately, and with a don't-talk-to-me-yet glaze on sleep-squinted golden eyes, lay right back down on the bedspread only inches away. He was bye-bye again in seconds.

Thorn rolled and sat at the edge of the bed. His Smith & Wesson Chief and the ring of keys for department auto 7146 sat atop the nightstand. Next to them, the Westclox read 7:20. He stood, stretched, and plodded into the kitchen, downed two gingko biloba with eight ounces of OJ, then went into the bathroom and brushed his teeth.

The game of life never seemed to change.

* * *

The headlines of every morning newspaper stacked outside Curley's kiosk centered around the Maloney story.

MALONEY TO QUIT RACE AMID
ALLEGATIONS OF CORRUPTION. *Daily News.*

EVIDENCE MOUNTS IN MALONEY PROBE!
HE TOOK ME TO THE CLEANERS! *New York Post.*

With no time to chat with his handicapped friend this morning, Savage paid Curley for a *Post* and a *Times,* then drove directly to the office. As he walked through the door he was greeted with a grim announcement posted on the bulletin board behind the wheel desk.

Sergeant Unger's wife, Rebekah Lynn, passed away.
Funeral Service: Wednesday, 9 A.M.
Five-Towns Memorial Chapel, Woodmere.
Interment: Beth Israel Cemetery, Pinelawn L.I.

He signed in, fixed a quick coffee, and called his team into the sergeants' room. Jack Lindstrom and Diane each came in carrying folders from old cases.

Richie Marcus strolled in dunking the edge of a cruller into his maxisize mug of coffee. *The Racing Form* was folded into his back pocket.

"*What?*" Savage managed to tease. "No sugar-raised this morning, Richie?"

"I'm on a diet," Marcus grumbled, completely earnest. Jack Lindstrom gagged.

"First off," Savage inquired, "how much is the flower fund for Becky Unger?"

"Pound a head," Marcus choked, his maw half-full of cruller. "That'll cover the hundred-dollar piece from the office."

Thorn dug out a fiver and handed it over. He'd call a florist later and send his own piece. Then, he decided, as long as he was calling a florist, he'd just go ahead and send a dozen long reds to Gina McCormick at her office. He'd also call her today and set up another date ASAP. Maybe for tomorrow night—maybe for *tonight*. It was time to change at least one thing about his life.

"We get anything back from Interpol on Karis?" Savage asked, facing Diane.

"They've sent through some preliminary info on him," she replied. "But it's gonna take a few more days to get the complete dossier. Andric Karazov, aka Andy Karis, has been quite the busy guy these past few decades. They've flagged him for killings in France, Belgium, Monte Carlo, and Hungary."

"We've gotta stay on this son of a bitch or he's gonna slip away from us forever," Savage said.

They all nodded solemnly.

Eddie Brodigan's voice broke the momentary silence.

"Sergeant Savage, Operations is on the line. Midtown South has got a badly decomposed torso and legs of a child at the bottom of an elevator shaft over on West Thirty-fifth. They need us to respond."

Savage and his three team members glanced back and forth at one another for a long second.

"Let the games begin," Richie Marcus declared, quickly downing the rest of his coffee.

Savage opened his desk drawer and reached for a fresh roll of Wint-O-Greens. "Let the games begin," he murmured to himself.

Lowen Clausen

FIRST AVENUE

Written with compelling authenticity by a former Seattle police officer, this debut novel is the passionate and powerful story of a Seattle cop who can't shake the image of the abandoned, dead baby he finds in a seedy hotel—and who can't give up on finding the truth until those responsible are brought to justice...

"*First Avenue* is as moody as Seattle in the rain, and just as alluring. A skillful, memorable first novel."
—Stephen White, *New York Times* bestselling author

"I loved this book...[it] has an authenticity only a real cop could convey."
—Ann Rule, *New York Times* bestselling author of *The Stranger Beside Me* and *And Never Let Her Go*, and a former Seattle cop herself

0-451-40948-5

To order call: 1-800-788-6262